THE LUCKY
PENNY

THE LUCKY PENNY

STEPHANIE VACCARO
& LOUISE ALLEN

ISBN eBook 979-8-9902396-2-3
ISBN Paperback 979-8-9902396-3-0

Some characters and events in this book are fictitious. Any similarity to real persons, living or dead, is coincidental and not intended by the authors.

Edited by Kate Allyson
Formatting by Tamara Cribley, The Deliberate Page
Front cover and maps by Louise Allen

Printed in United States of America

Contact: asgantiscreations@gmail.com

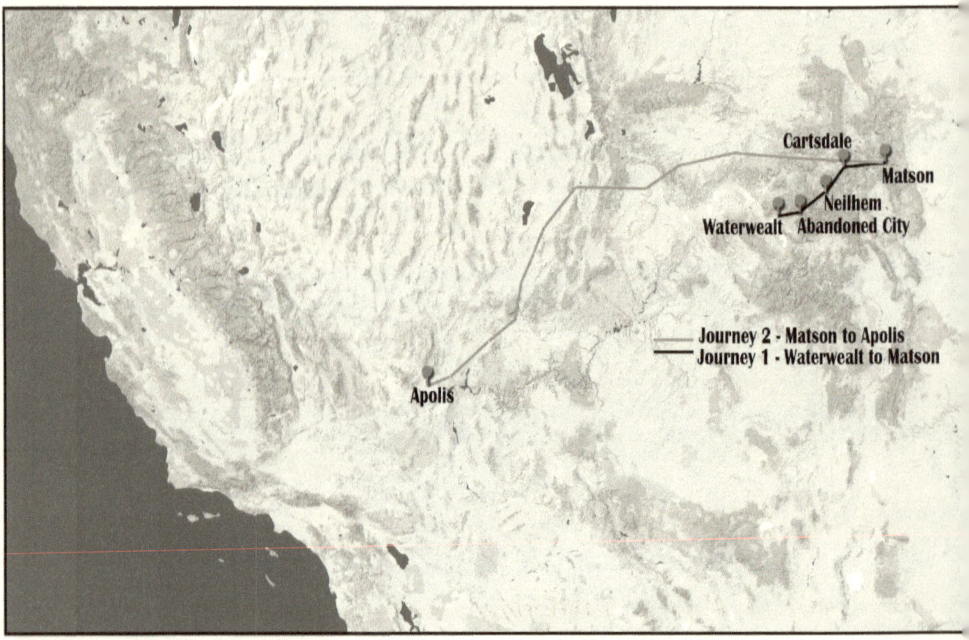

Cartsdale
Matson
Neilhem
Waterwealt Abandoned City

Apolis

Journey 2 - Matson to Apolis
Journey 1 - Waterwealt to Matson

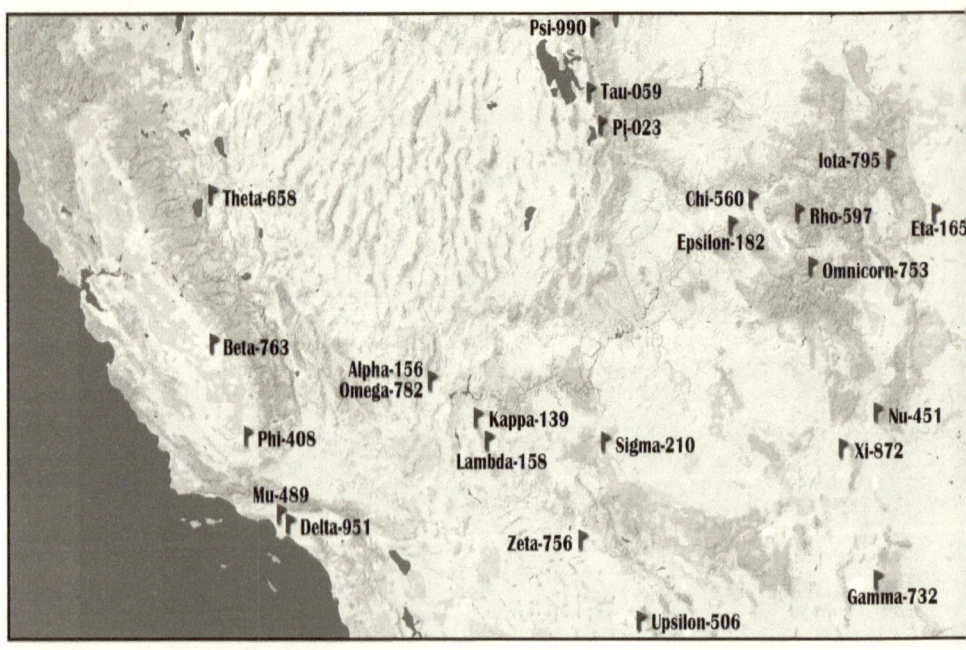

Psi-990
Tau-059
Pi-023
Iota-795
Theta-658
Chi-560
Rho-597
Eta-165
Epsilon-182
Omnicorn-753
Beta-763
Alpha-156
Omega-782
Nu-451
Phi-408
Kappa-139
Sigma-210
Xi-872
Lambda-158
Mu-489
Delta-951
Zeta-756
Gamma-732
Upsilon-506

PREFACE

I t started with a picture and a Discord call.

How this book came into being is far from the ordinary process. I, Stephanie, was looking for backgrounds for my work computer when I came across an interesting image that made me go "I want to write a story for that." Problem was, I couldn't think of anything. So I did what I usually do in these situations, called my best friend from across the pond, Louise. After explaining to her my initial thoughts, she told me to give her a couple days.

She got back to me with three images: pictures of the people who would become the main characters of this story. She then prompted me to give them names and some background. We figured we could use this as a way to get me to learn to write better. A writing session later and boom we had three characters. Next she gave me what I lovingly describe as "the vaguest writing prompt in history."

Theme/Style: Post-Apocalyptic Dystopia

Greater Conflict: Great Ruler in Place, Bad person attempting to take over

The 'Arcane': Magic Extremely Rare, Usually only one type (bottleneck)

Main Characters Initial Relationship:
Charles & Julietta are not married
Penny is neither of their kid.
Penny only talks when something is important to say

"Build me a world," she said. So I did.

Joking aside it was a loose prompt that I ran wild with and in many cases twisted beyond recognition. So this process continued. I wrote a section, Louise reviewed and suggested edits, edits were made, then another prompt was given. By the time we got half way through this process it became more of a discussion of direction rather than me being blindly led into a writing abyss. And thus The Lucky Penny was born!

We hope you enjoy reading this as much as we enjoyed writing it.

Special thanks to the friends and family who supported us, especially my family who had to listen to me read this book aloud probably upwards of thirty times. Also, thank you to the friends who became unwilling listeners to our very obscure conversations on Discord while trying to figure out just where this story was going.

CHAPTER 1

"Penny?" Julietta called, not looking up from her work. "Penny? Oh, where has that girl wandered off to again?"

A small giggle was heard from within the workshop space.

"I heard something." Julietta smiled, setting down her tools and removing her goggles. "Oh, where is my Penny?"

Another giggle was heard coming from one of the storage closets.

"Hmmm, is my Penny here?" Julietta pretended to be annoyed as she lifted the curtain on one of the workshop tables.

"No? Then how about here?" She lifted a dust sheet from a nearby chair, once more feigning ignorance of the laughter coming from the cabinet.

After a few minutes of this charade, much to the enjoyment of little hidden Penny, Julietta finally stood directly in front of the giggling cabinet. "I just can't seem to find her. Where, oh, where can my Penny be? How about in HERE!"

She grabbed the cabinet doors and flung them open, to find the cabinet empty. "Huh." Julietta was genuinely confused. She had been sure that Penny was hiding there.

Another giggle came from the cabinet. Looking down, Julietta smiled. Opening the large drawer at the bottom she found two bright blue eyes staring back up at her. "There's my Penny!"

Up until Julietta found little Penny over a cycle ago after a horrible dust storm, her life revolved around her work. Now, although her work was important, a good portion of her time was spent taking care of Penny, who was now nine Dust-seasons old.

It wasn't easy raising a child in the wastes, certainly not easy when you yourself were only 24 Damp. Growing up, Julietta had rarely seen

3

other children. As only one of five in her entire settlement of about 230 people, opportunities to interact with one another were rare. Such was the way the world had been since the Great War over a hundred cycles ago.

"Well, Miss Penny, you got me."

Penny just laughed in response.

"Quite the little ninja you are. Though I'd dare say you'll have to find a new hiding spot soon. You are getting taller by the minute, I swear!" Julietta shook her head, helping Penny sit up.

Penny shook her head, sticking her tongue out slightly.

"I saw that, little miss," Julietta chastised. "Now, I have some errands to run in town this afternoon, want to come with me?"

Penny nodded her head furiously, her black ponytail nearly hitting Julietta in the face as she climbed out of the drawer and ran straight for her backpack. Putting it on she pointed at the shelf above.

"Yes, you can bring Nelson too. So long as you promise to keep hold of him, okay?"

Penny jumped up and down excitedly. Nelson was a small metal robot toy that Julietta had given her from the museum's collection not long after she'd found her. It quickly became her favorite thing to play with.

Packing up her backpack with the pump for the baker and a few other gadgets she had repaired for the townsfolk, Julietta went to fill her canteen. "Water pressure's low. I'll have to ask Harrison what's up."

She barely managed to put on her backpack, attaching the canteen to it, before Penny grabbed her hand, pulling her to the ladder that led down to their loft and the museum proper.

Locking the museum door with her makeshift mechanism, Julietta took Penny's hand as they began the 10 minute walk toward the town of Waterwealt. It had been about four cycles since Julietta had settled here. At the time, she had planned to stop in town to resupply before heading to one of the bigger cities that were looking for restorers. Instead, she found herself falling in love with the abandoned Science and Natural History Museum.

It took little effort to convince the mayor, Maxwell Harrison, to let her stay to restore the museum. Her engineering ability would allow for the advancement of the town. Over the past few cycles, she helped Waterwealt not only find a more efficient method to purify their stream, but also automated a few of the more mundane tasks about the town.

It was rare for many towns to have a convenient water source. The Great War had all but turned the world into a dust bowl. Many waterways had dried up or become contaminated by the horrible chemical fallout that had destroyed a majority of the world's population. Even over a hundred cycles later, not much of the land had recovered. There were only small patches like Waterwealt slowly restoring it.

As they approached the town, Penny let go of Julietta's hand and ran for the bakery. Exchanging pleasantries with Marius, one of the town's farmers, as he was leaving the shop, she entered. As expected, the baker, Marisa Healey, was already offering Penny a cookie, the young girl jumping with joy.

Marisa was about 40, with dark hair and eyes. Other than her leather boots and the knife at her hip, she was the spitting image of a mother from the times before, wearing a light tan dress and brown apron. Despite the rough and tumble life, Julietta found her to be cheery; she always seemed to have a smile on her face.

"Penny, what do we say?" Julietta nudged.

Penny smiled brightly at Marisa, giving her a nod of thanks.

"For you, my little button, two cookies." Marisa smiled, handing the girl two peanut butter delights.

While Penny took a seat on the ground, eating her treat, Julietta approached. "You know, you spoil her."

"Oh hush, it's nothing," Marisa chuckled. "There aren't many children here in Waterwealt, or anywhere for that matter. What little joy I can bring the ones we have is worth it. How are you, Jul?"

"Doing all right, just working on that old water drilling device. Promised Harrison I'd get it working as soon as possible."

"A good thing too." Marisa frowned. "Been having issues with the water pressure even before my pump broke. Husband's getting more frustrated by the day with waterin' his crops."

"Speaking of your pump…" Julietta reached into her bag, pulling out the small device. "Should work now. Just needed some gear realignment, cleaned up the tubing as well and replaced a leaky one."

"You do too much." Marisa took it, reaching for the coins in her pocket. "Five pieces?"

"Should cover it."

"Then here's seven," Marisa chuckled, handing over the money.

"Cheeky."

"Hey, you have a little one to look after. And from what I've been hearing from the travelin' news the capital is having some problems. Rumors of an uprisin' or something. Money gonna get scarce if another war breaks out."

"You listen too much to the rabble. Best to just keep looking to tomorrow, or in my case, the past to fix tomorrow."

"Well, it's just as well. We are so far removed from any of 'em big cities. Not much to worry 'bout in little ol' Waterwealt. By the way, been meanin' to ask. Has she said anything?"

Julietta shook her head. "Not a word. She is starting to write basic things but… that's it. I'm trying my best but—"

Marisa put a comforting hand on Julietta's shoulder. "You are doing great, deary. That little girl is happy and healthy, which is more than what she was 'bout a cycle ago when you found her."

A flash of memory from that night sent a chill down Julietta's spine, the image of poor little Penny cold, dusty, and hurt, stumbling up to her museum at its forefront. The only identifying thing on her was a necklace with an old penny engraved with strange markings.

Penny stood up, taking Julietta's hand and shaking her from her memory. Looking down at the little girl's smiling face, she couldn't help but smile herself. "Yes, I think she is doing much better, wouldn't you say so, Penny?"

Penny answered her with a hug.

"We really should be going. I have a few more things to deliver before heading back to the museum and continuing on the drill. Thanks again, Marisa."

"Stop by anytime. Oh, and be careful around town. There's been a strange man walkin' around askin' about arc something or another. No clue what it's 'bout but it seems odd."

"Noted."

Penny waved goodbye as they left to continue their errands.

Penny's silence had been a point of concern for Julietta for a long time. At first, she wondered if the girl was just mute, but she had heard her, occasionally, whispering to herself while she played quietly. Why Penny would not speak aloud to anyone, she did not know. From what she could gather, the poor child had been through something traumatic, if her minimal research had any merit.

Penny was also highly intelligent, taking a particular interest in the historical electronics section of the museum. Julietta would often find her tinkering with various machines called 'computation' machines and mechanical men. Though her tinkering had not yielded any usable results, taking them apart and putting them back together seemed to amuse her.

Too bad I can't find any books on electronics for her. Maybe someday when we go to a big city some copy will have turned up, though I don't know if I'd have the funds to even check the book out for an hour.

Books, scrolls, and most manner of paper-based knowledge had been destroyed in the later cycles of the Great War, the rest used as kindling while the world struggled to rebuild. Without electricity, the 'computation' machines and other 'digital' knowledge holders were useless. At least the administration that took hold of the world a few cycles ago seemed to turn its attention to the recovery and restoration of knowledge. It was slow progress, but it was progress.

The next few stops were quick and easy, earning Julietta a bit more coin, enough, she hoped, to get some extra materials from her last stop, the purifier.

Byron Galigar was the lead chemist in charge of the purifier. An older gentleman, with gray hair and green eyes that spoke volumes of his wisdom, he was very stern but kind. It was his help and Julietta's mechanical know-how that got the stream of Waterwealt clean enough to sustain the town for cycles to come.

Byron also happened to be the town's head scavenger. Any pieces and parts of old found by travelers or townspeople were brought, meticulously cataloged, and then sold. It was this second job that brought Julietta to his shop today.

"Julietta, just the person I wanted to see," came the voice of Mayor Harrison who happened to be in the shop chatting with Byron. "How's the drill pump coming along?"

"That's actually why I'm here. Need a few parts. Hoping Byron has what I am looking for or at least something I can modify."

"Good, with the lack of rain this past Damp, the stream is getting rather thin. Don't know if you noticed but the pressure's getting low."

"I've noticed." Julietta frowned, irritated at Harrison's accusatory tone. Of course she had noticed. Why else would she be fixing the drill pump?

"What are you looking for?" asked Byron, stroking his gray mustache and beard.

Julietta began to rattle off a list of parts and descriptions while Penny perused the shop, Nelson clutched tightly in her hand. Walking down a row of shelves she spotted a tiny brass knob, just about the right size to fit in one of the many holes on Nelson. Reaching up, she frowned, realizing she was not quite tall enough. She was about to turn to go back to Julietta when a voice stopped her.

"Were you trying to reach that?"

"Sorry, I couldn't get all the parts, travelers are getting scarce," Byron looked downcast as he totaled up the items.

"What about that one fella? The one askin' about Arcane shit," Harrison chuckled. "Didn't have any magic wands to sell you?"

Byron rolled his eyes but continued tallying.

"Was there someone really asking about magic?" Julietta quirked an eyebrow. "That's—"

"Does this little one belong to any of you?" came a male voice.

Turning to the voice, Julietta frowned. "Penny, what did I tell you about bothering strangers?"

Penny walked over sheepishly, holding the small brass knob.

"I spotted her trying to reach that. She wouldn't tell me—"

"Sorry, and thank you," Julietta replied curtly, taking the knob from Penny and placing it with her other parts. "Can you add that?"

"For little Penny, free," the old man winked.

"You know it really wasn't any trouble." The man smiled, his gray eyes mirroring the gesture. "Name's Charles, I'm in town right now looking into—"

"This here's the magic man," Harrison butt in, chuckling.

"I see." Julietta's brow furrowed. "Well, it was nice to meet you, Charles, but we really must be going." The sound of the wind picking up outside seemed to echo her sentiment. "Dust storm. How much do I owe you, Byron?"

"Three coin, giving a discount since it's going towards the new pump."

Paying Byron, she quickly gathered her items. "Thanks again, you've been very helpful. Mayor, I'll give you an update by the end of the week on the drill pump." She turned to Charles. "Goodbye, sir." She took Penny's hand and all but dragged her from the shop.

CHAPTER 2

They reached the museum just as the dust storm began kicking up. "I'm sorry for scaring you in the shop, but remember what I told you about strangers."

Penny nodded, a couple of tears sitting in her eyes.

"I know you are curious, but you have to be careful. Okay? Next time, come find me."

Penny nodded again, holding up Nelson.

Julietta smiled, grabbing the knob from her bag. "Why don't you go put this new part on Nelson? I'll be up in a minute to cook dinner, okay?"

Penny smiled, hugging Julietta before taking the knob and racing towards the stairs to the loft.

Alone in the atrium, Julietta sighed, taking in the dusty and damaged museum around her. She wondered to herself what it would have been like in its heyday before the Great War, before all knowledge of the known world had essentially been wiped out. Many nights she'd find herself wandering this great mausoleum of the past, digging through broken glass, trying to decipher all the faded text on displays. So much of history had been lost, so much knowledge. Now everything was a big unknown.

Lost in her thoughts and the sound of the wind whistling through the various small gaps and cracks she almost didn't hear the pounding at the front door. Startled, she reached for one of the knives she kept hidden in her heavy-duty black work boots.

Pulling up the neck duster she wore just for storms such as this, Julietta cautiously opened the door. The wind was brutal, giving her no time to react as someone shoved past her and stumbled into the atrium.

Her heart racing, she managed to slam the door shut quickly. Spinning to face the would-be intruder, she was surprised to find Charles, covered in dust and sand, coughing up a lung.

"Are you insane?" She shouted, returning her knife to her boot.

"I... wasn't... trying..." Charles slid to the floor, leaning against the atrium desk still trying to dispel the storm from his lungs.

Julietta reached for her canteen. "Here, drink this."

After a minute Charles finally was able to catch his breath. "Thank you, um, pardon, but I don't know your name."

"Julietta."

"Well, thank you, Julietta." He breathed heavily, leaning his head against the desk. "That's some brutal weather you got here."

Taking a good look at Charles, Julietta frowned. He was dressed like most wasteland travelers and townsfolk: dark black boots, black jeans, and a light cotton shirt beneath his knee-length dark brown duster jacket. He had a backpack, and she assumed likely had at the very least a knife hidden about his person. The only gear he seemed to be missing was a neck duster or scarf.

"You know you really shouldn't be out in a dust storm and don't come telling me you've never experienced one."

"No, no, you're right." Charles chuckled. "I did try to seek shelter in town, but no one would open their door to me. I got a bit desperate when I spotted this place on the horizon. Lost my scarf on the way over here. Thought this place was abandoned and I could break in. Guess I should be counting my lucky stars someone actually lives here. You do live here, I assume?"

Julietta felt conflicted, this man didn't seem like the crazy stranger people had mentioned. He seemed rather polite and handsome with his dark brown hair and trimmed beard, if she was being honest with herself.

"Yes," she finally answered warily. "I'm the local restorer."

"Figured that, given the laundry list of parts you gave to that shop owner. I'm a doctor, well what passes for one these days. Lived in the city of Matson for a good portion of my life. They had some medical books and I had too much time on my hands."

"I heard you were a researcher."

"More of a pastime, though more of a focus lately. I am in the business of researching the unknown, the Arcane."

"So, you are a doctor with delusions of grandeur?"

"I prefer the term truthseeker." Charles began to sit up, Julietta reaching once more for her knife.

"Woah." Charles held up his hands. "I'm friendly. If you want to know, I have a knife in my right boot and a gun at my waist, but it's holstered. I also suppose the meager medical supplies in my pack could be considered weapons in the wrong context. I mean no harm, honest."

Reaching for his boot, she felt for the knife. Surprisingly, he was telling the truth. "Show me the gun, but don't unholster it."

Keeping his hands visible, Charles undid his jacket, pulling it back so she could see the weapon. "It's not working anyhow, found it about a month ago while scavenging. Haven't come across anyone to fix it, let alone ammo for it."

"Fair enough," Julietta sighed, relaxing a bit. "I suppose I can't exactly in good conscience throw you back out in that storm."

"Take it."

Julietta quirked an eyebrow, Charles holding his hands up. Keeping her knife pointed at him she unholstered the gun. With a brief inspection, Julietta confirmed that the gun was not in working condition.

Handing him the gun back she shook her head. "You'll have to excuse my caution."

"Don't blame you. Young woman in the wasteland, technically anyone in the wasteland needs to be cautious, let alone one with a child."

Putting her knife away, Julietta stood holding out a hand. "Storms around here are pretty fierce. Usually lasts a few hours." Charles allowed her to help him up. "I was about to make dinner. Care to join us?"

"Would be my pleasure." Charles smiled, brushing some sand out of his shaggy brown hair. "You wouldn't happen to also have a place I can dust off?"

Before Julietta could answer a loud boom echoed through the atrium. "What—"

Any words were lost as a moment later the entire museum began to shake violently. Grabbing Charles, Julietta pulled him under the central desk as the sound of old stone, plaster, and glass crashing to the floor filled their ears. Cramped together face to face neither dared to move an inch, hoping nothing dangerous would land on them.

Then it was over, as quickly as it had started the shaking stopped. "Penny!" Julietta screamed. Scrambling out of their tight hiding place, she raced for the stairs.

The loft was in shambles. Dishes and various decorative curios lay broken and smashed on the floor. Unbolted cabinets and furniture had been upturned, their contents now strewn across the room.

"Penny?! Penny, where are you?" Julietta cried, desperately searching the room.

To her relief, she heard a small sob coming from one of the cabinets that happened to be bolted to the wall by the ladder to the workshop. Flinging its doors open she found Penny, curled up with Nelson, unharmed but frightened.

"Oh, Penny come here." Sitting in front of the cabinet she pulled the scared girl into her lap, holding her. "Are you hurt?"

Penny shook her head, burying her face into Julietta's jacket.

"Is she okay?" Charles panted, out of breath.

"She's all right, just frightened. We've not had an earthquake before."

Glancing up at Charles, she became more concerned, seeing his gaze fixed on the far window.

"That was no earthquake." His face fell, as he stepped closer.

Holding Penny in her arms, Julietta stood, following him. Her heart leapt into her throat before reversing its course and sinking into her stomach. Though the storm raged on, it was obvious what had shaken the earth. Far off, maybe hundreds or thousands of miles away, the sky was turning black from a mushroom-shaped cloud that could only be a bomb.

Having cleaned up the loft, eaten dinner, and put Penny to bed in her now rebuilt makeshift fort, Julietta sat down at the table with two cups of coffee.

"How're the lungs?"

"Recovering, most of the dust was in my throat. Thankfully, I didn't lose my scarf until I was much closer. Also helped that you gave me some water. After the delicious dinner you made and the fun of helping Penny rebuild her fort, I should be fine with a night's rest."

13

"I'll have to take your word for it. I've read some basic first aid stuff and perused the medical wing, but that's the extent of my knowledge. Also, thanks for keeping Penny busy and helping clean up."

"My pleasure. And maybe I should visit that wing. See if I learn anything new."

"You are welcome to." Julietta yawned, the adrenaline rush finally wearing off.

"Mushroom cloud, that can't be good." Charles coughed, looking out the window beyond where Julietta sat.

"No, it's not. There is an exhibit that talks of such things. Usually, they are associated with war."

"Rumor has it war is inevitable. In my travels, I've heard that some folks are upset with the new administration and their restorative ventures."

"And you?"

"I'm a doctor and someone who likes to research the Arcane. Restorative ventures are my bread and butter," Charles smirked, taking a sip of the coffee.

"You mean magic? Seeing as you are a doctor, I am shocked you would even entertain the notion."

"What is magic, but what we call the unknown or unexplainable?"

Julietta paused her mug of coffee at her lips contemplating an answer, but none came.

"Before we knew what fire was and how it worked, did we not think lightning setting a tree ablaze was magic? What about medical science or your machines?" Charles smiled, a mischievous twinkle in his eye.

"Just because we can't explain something doesn't mean it is magic. Surely at some point, things become explainable."

"Yes, but not all things. Until then they are labeled as unexplainable or Arcane."

"That's wordsmithing."

"That's the magic of science."

Setting down her mug, Julietta shook her head. "So, you don't actually believe in magic."

"I consider myself a healthy skeptic with an open mind."

"Whatever helps you sleep at night." Julietta chuckled, taking another sip of her coffee.

"Speaking of. I hate to bring up the elephant in the room but—"

"If you are wondering if you can stay the night, yes. That storm is still raging and I am not one to send someone out to their potential death, so you can stay."

"Thank heavens for someone with some hospitality."

"That being said, you can't stay up here with us. You understand, I am sure?"

"Of course. Wouldn't want to make anyone uncomfortable."

"It's not so much comfort as—"

"Protection?"

"Smart one you are, but yes."

"Where shall I stay then?"

"The transportation exhibit, third floor on the right. There are some train cars with sleeping berths. You can use one of those."

"Sounds pleasant. Thank you."

After Charles left for the transportation exhibit, Julietta changed out of her dusty clothes, switching into a clean pair of black jeans, a white cotton long-sleeve shirt, and a brown sweater before turning in. She awoke some hours later surprised to find the sun had not yet risen. Upon closer inspection, however, she realized it had, but was blocked out by swirling black soot and dust.

"Penny..." she called, but there was no answer.

Walking over to the fort that constituted Penny's bed she pulled back the curtain; it was empty. Concerned, she quickly checked the door to the workshop, locked. Penny wasn't allowed in there without her supervision. However, she was allowed to explore the museum.

Reaching the landing that led to the third-floor galleries, she heard Penny's laughter echoing from nearby in the transportation exhibit. Heading over she found Penny seated on the floor with Charles in one of the train cars.

"I was wondering where you wandered off too." Julietta's eyes fell directly on Charles, watching him closely.

Penny turned to Julietta sheepishly, holding her Nelson which now had a makeshift sling on its arm.

"It's all right, Julietta, I was already awake. Penny's friend Nelson seemed to have gotten a bit hurt in the shake yesterday. I patched him up for now, but he'll need some minor surgery by a qualified mechanical doctor." Charles winked.

Seeing Penny was unharmed Julietta shook her head but smiled. "I'll fix him up for you after breakfast, Penny. Why don't you head upstairs and start getting the ingredients out for some pancakes?"

Penny smiled, hugging Charles and then Julietta before racing out of the car.

"I'm sorry. I was about to take her straight back to you when she showed me, Nelson. She looks so upset I—"

"That was very kind of you to do that for her. You'll have to pardon my rudeness."

"No, no, I completely understand. I'm a stranger and Penny is… your child?"

"Not my child, not by blood anyhow. I found Penny, well more like she found me, about a cycle ago. She was sick and injured. I nursed her back to health and acted as her guardian since. I'd protect her with my own life if I had to."

"I suspect she has been through something traumatic. Such a bright child. Was able to explain to me what was wrong without words."

"She does speak, but to no one but herself and Nelson." Julietta sighed. "I've tried, but I don't want to force it."

"You are doing the right thing, medically speaking, at least from what I've read." Charles chuckled, putting away the gauze he had used for Nelson's sling.

"That's all any of us can say nowadays. Based on what I've seen, read, and experienced; it's all we got to understand the world."

Standing, Charles looked Julietta over, taking in her dark brown hair, up in a messy bun, and dark brown eyes full of concern and wonder. "How many seasons?"

A simple question, one with a not-so-simple answer. No one really knew how old they were year-wise, there was no good way to keep track. Instead, people had taken to counting the relatively consistent season cycles that passed since their birth season. There were four of them: Damp, Hot, Dust, and Cold.

"About 24. I'm a Damp season, so just passed despite the fact we got little rain."

"27 Cold. Penny indicated to me she is nine Dust." Charles held up nine fingers and then covered his mouth like a duster as Penny had.

"Yep, my little dust tornado." She chuckled. "Speaking of, we best get upstairs. She's likely caused a dust storm of flour."

"You're letting me stay?"

"You haven't seen outside yet?" Julietta frowned. "The storm's still raging, in fact, it's worse now with black soot. Since you are stuck here, you can explore the museum. Couldn't hurt to have you look at the medical wing. Any knowledge is good knowledge, right?"

"You aren't wrong there. Maybe I can share some of my Arcane theories with you and you can use the items in your museum to prove me wrong?"

Julietta laughed, shaking her head. "Sounds fair to me."

There was a clatter of a bowl falling from above. "Sounds like we better get moving," Charles smirked, grabbing his bag and following Julietta back to the loft.

CHAPTER 3

Julietta and Charles found Penny waiting by the ladder to the workshop, pouting, as she examined Nelson's loose arm.

"All right, Penny, let's go fix up Nelson." She turned to Charles. "Want to come?"

Charles looked surprised. "Sure," he shrugged with a smile.

Climbing up into Julietta's workshop, Charles was shocked. Given the loft seemed to be some sort of office space turned home, he had expected the workshop to be little more than a few tables scattered about. Instead, he found himself in a rectangular room with a domed roof, likely an old storage space, set up to be a proper artisan's workspace.

Gazing around the room, Charles admired Julietta's work. Various cabinets lined the walls, some locked, others with only a curtain covering them each marked with their contents: paint, cleaning chemicals, oil, and the like.

A covered easel pushed up against the wall nearest him stood out amongst the machines, tools, covered furniture, and storage. It wasn't this, however, that drew his attention the most. It was the four large tables that had been pushed together at the center of the room, heavily laden with scattered parts and complex projects he couldn't even attempt to understand at first glance.

"Pardon the mess. I had quite a few fixes to do this week. Haven't had time to clean up. Add in that drill pump engine over there and well…" Julietta sighed, shaking her head. "I really need to organize.

Penny sat Nelson on one of the few clear spots on the table, looking up at Julietta expectantly.

"Right, now let's see what we can do for Mr. Nelson here."

As Julietta began to inspect the toy, Penny walked over to Charles, pulling him closer to them.

"Looks like the joint came loose, needs a new screw. Let me see," Julietta frowned, walking over to one of the unmarked cabinets and sifting through the various containers within. While she did, Penny took Charles's hand leading him over to the covered easel.

"You want me to see this?"

Penny nodded, smiling from ear to ear.

"Are you sure Julietta won't mind?"

"Julietta won't mind what?" Julietta, having found what she was looking for, returned to the table.

Without a word Penny pulled on the dust cover, revealing the painting hidden beneath.

"Penny, what did I tell you about playing with that?"

Charles stood in awe. The painting was that of a night sky filled with stars over a small seaside town. Though the paint seemed worn and faded in many places a good portion of it had started to be restored. "It's beautiful."

"It's a work in progress," Julietta frowned, slipping on her goggles. "I've been meaning to work on it more but, duty calls."

"How are you restoring it? This doesn't look like chemical-based restoration."

"You know about that?" Julietta quirked an eyebrow as she lowered her magnifier on her goggles, setting to work on Nelson's arm.

"Medical books weren't the only thing I read. I'm a researcher, I like to diversify."

"Fair enough. You're right, it's not chemical. The canvas is too delicate on that one for it. I've been…repainting it."

"And here I thought you were only a mechanical wizard." Charles chuckled. "Apparently, you are a painting fairy too."

"Ha ha, very funny, magic man," Julietta teased, tightening the new screw in place. "I used to draw when I was little. Wasn't that good but it helps to be able to sketch what I am building beforehand. That should do it. Nelson's surgery is complete, does the good doctor want to take a look?"

Charles smiled walking over to her as she pulled her goggles off her head. Taking the small toy in his hand, he gently tugged on the repaired arm. "In my humble opinion, I'd say he'll make a full recovery. What do you think, Penny?" Looking around the room, Charles became concerned. "Penny?"

Setting down her goggles Julietta laughed. "Seems like you've been struck by lightning-quick Penny. She's hiding somewhere in here."

Charles looked at her incredulously. "In here…with all this machinery and—"

"Don't worry, I've locked up the dangerous stuff and the machines are manually powered and locked with a key. You don't think I'd let her up here without childproofing?"

"Sorry," Charles frowned. "Just…"

"Just what?" Julietta scowled, crossing her arms. "Just because I am 24 cycles?"

"No, no, no, it's not that. I was just surprised that you'd let—"

"I've told you I'd protect Penny with my life. You really think I'd let her into any danger?"

"No, I don't believe you would." Charles sighed, realizing his mistake. "Honestly, I was just more surprised she'd find anywhere to even hide in here. You seem to have this place on lockdown."

"Oh," Julietta relaxed.

Charles heard a small giggle from beneath one of the counters near the sink.

Julietta leaned in closer to Charles. "If you want to make her happy, pretend you didn't just hear her laugh and search everywhere else for a few minutes."

"Gotcha," he winked, beginning to help her 'search' for little Penny.

After a few more rounds of hide and seek, Julietta showed Charles around the museum. It was a three-story affair with offices and storage above. Each floor was set up to tell the history and science of a particular subject: Ancient Civilizations on the first floor, the Natural World on the second, and "Modern Man" of the before times on the third. There was also a basement, Julietta explained, but the entrance was blocked by large debris that could not be moved.

"We'll start on the third floor and work our way down. You already know the transportation exhibit, so let's start in 'Houses through the Ages,'" Julietta smiled, leading the way.

Entering the exhibit, Charles could tell Julietta had spent a bit of time working here, though quite a few items were missing that he recognized as now being in use in the loft.

"This area of the museum was surprisingly intact when I got here. Guess people forgot about this exhibit or didn't think older furniture and appliances were of much use." Julietta took a seat at an old plastic-covered dining set. "This one was from an era apparently where these 'moving picture boxes' were commonplace in the kitchen. Can you imagine that?"

"Moving picture boxes? That's interesting." Charles raised an eyebrow. "How do you reckon they got the pictures to move?"

"No clue, I haven't messed around much with electronics. My best guess is something to do with electricity and the glass bulbs. There were a few broken ones that had bulbs in them."

"Maybe there was some sort of energy source that made the pictures move? Something exciting the stagnant image to morph and change?"

"The way you describe it makes it sound…" Julietta didn't want to say magical, but no other word was coming to mind.

"Arcane?" Charles smirked.

"It's lost science," Julietta chuckled, sticking out her tongue. "Though from what I've learned from this era, I'd probably hate it. Women wore dresses and cooked dinner while the men dressed in stuffy suits and worked behind desks."

"What a dreadfully boring life." Charles smiled as he explored the diorama.

"Not always, the time before is actually fascinating. Seeing how people like ourselves used to live and how that changed."

"All I know is what happened led to where we are now. Though I do enjoy seeing all this tech, this gives some credence to my theories."

Their conversation came to a halt as the sound of a chair sliding across the floor in another diorama space reached their ears.

"Better go see what Penny found." Julietta rolled her eyes.

Penny was in one of the more 'modern' dioramas, the one showing the 'living room of the future' at the time. She had managed to drag one of the large chairs over to a dust-covered display case.

"What did you find, Penny?" Charles asked as they approached.

Penny pointed to the display case containing a small red car with a button-covered device.

Brushing the dust from the case Charles read the display tag. "Toy remote control car using radio waves."

"Remote control?" Julietta quirked an eyebrow.

Charles shrugged. "Never heard of that."

Penny tapped the display case, looking up pleadingly at Charles.

Charles looked to Julietta, who nodded with approval. Retrieving his knife, he pried the case open. Dusting off the car, he handed it to Penny.

Penny smiled examining the toy, her eyes drifting over to the 'remote' device. Pointing, she gave a look of curiosity.

"You want the remote? It won't work."

Penny continued to point, undeterred.

"Can't hurt." Julietta shrugged, looking around the diorama. "Everything here is benign without power."

The little girl jumped with joy, giving Charles a big hug as he handed her the remote.

"You're welcome," he smiled.

They spent a bit more time in the exhibit, Charles debating back and forth with Julietta on what was Arcane, what was already figured out, and what was simply unknown.

"How about I show you my favorite exhibit on this floor?" Julietta offered.

Exiting the 'Houses Through the Ages,' they passed through the clothing exhibit. Julietta paused briefly at one of the display cases marked "Party Wear—1920s". It was this case that caught her eye time and time again. Inside was a black sequined dress with a feathered headband, said to have been worn by what were known as 'flapping women.' Beside it was a man's suit, tailored with tails.

"Extravagant and impractical," Charles observed.

"Yeah," Julietta frowned.

Seeing her expression, Charles's brow furrowed. "You like it?"

"Yes…I mean no." Julietta's face flushed. "Just…never wore a dress before. Like you said it's…impractical. With the dust and weather, it's always been thick long pants, cotton shirts, sweaters, and duster jackets." She shrugged. "I'll be honest, sometimes I wonder what it would have been like to dress like that."

"I can respect that," Charles sighed, shaking his head. "Growing up in Matson, there were a few folks in the more rebuilt parts of the city who would throw parties and dress up," he smirked. "I was poor, so my family never went to anything like that. Me and some of the other kids would sneak to that part of town on occasion and watch through the windows."

"I thought you said you read medical books? Was there not a fee for checking them out of the archives?"

"Never said I checked them out legitimately." Charles rubbed the back of his head. "I wanted to learn and advance. So, I befriended a historian in the archives and got him to give me books during off hours. Eventually, I was given a basic medical science book and I was hooked."

"Fair and smart," Julietta smiled, taking one last look at the display before heading toward their destination: the Industry Sciences.

'Tools and Industry through the Ages' was Julietta's favorite exhibit in the entire museum. This is what made her decide to stay in the fledgling town of Waterwealt. Here, she could spend hours watching the world progress from basic hand tools, to power tools, to the grand machinery of industry.

"I see why you like this place, considering your workshop," Charles commented, admiring a machine labeled as an 'automated packing machine' for ice cream, a food not seen in centuries.

"I've always loved machines," Julietta sighed, picking up a loose gear that had fallen from somewhere. "Seeing the moving parts, making them come back to life, albeit manually...my mother was a tinker, my father a farmer. I'd help her fix up old farm equipment to make his job easier."

"What made you want to come to Waterwealt? Surely your skills would have been better suited for a city?"

Julietta's face fell. "There was a bad dust storm, a tornado. It...wiped out most of my town. I was one of the few survivors." She gave a knowing look to Charles indicating what happened to her parents. "I don't know what happened to the others, but I set off for the nearest city. Ended up in Waterwealt to resupply and fell in love with the museum. It reminds me of my home."

Charles approached, holding up a hand, debating if he should place it on her shoulder.

"It's all right. I've made my peace with it. Come on, Penny's probably already in her favorite place here."

Weaving their way between the industrial age machines they finally came to the back of the exhibit: The Digital Age. They found the girl exactly where Julietta expected. Little Penny was sitting in front of a display, wires of all lengths and colors, electronic chips, and the like, scattered about.

"She likes to take apart the electronics and put them back together. The heavens know why but it keeps her mind busy."

Charles raised an eyebrow, looking over Penny's work. "Most adults would struggle to do what she is doing."

"She is very intelligent, seems to have a knack for it."

Walking back over to Julietta, he frowned. "Has she ever told you or given you any indication of where she came from?"

"No, why?"

"It's just...I've not seen many children in the wastes. Even in Matson, growing up there were not many of us. I do remember though there were a few of them like Penny, very intelligent. They gave us a test, I remember, when I was about seven Cold. Unfortunately, my parents died in an accident not long after, so I went to work and never got my results."

"What happened to the other children?"

"No clue. Once I started working, I never saw them."

Penny approached Julietta and Charles holding up a small board with wires and bulbs.

"Is that your latest puzzle?" Julietta smiled, her earlier concern washed from her face.

Penny nodded, pressing a button, but nothing happened.

"That's very nice, Penny." Charles nodded.

Penny frowned, looking down at the board.

"It's all right, maybe if you work on it a bit more, we can hook it up to one of the manual cranks and get the bulbs to light. For now, how about we grab some lunch?"

Penny nodded sadly, walking back over to the cabinet she used as her workstation. She returned to them with the remote car in tow.

"After lunch, I'll show you the War exhibit up here and then the medical one on floor two. Penny will probably come back here. Those exhibits make her nervous."

CHAPTER 4

The storm had still not let up. After lunch, Julietta sent Penny off to the electronics exhibit to work while she took Charles to the War section of the third floor.

This part of the museum always gave Julietta an air of foreboding. It seemed colder than the rest of the museum, more dead than alive. From the look on Charles's face, she could tell he felt the same as they strode past the various cases filled with long-forgotten weapons, medals, and the like. Occasionally they would stop to read a not-so-destroyed placard here and there. At some point, while they passed a weapons case, Julietta spotted a gun, not so different from the broken one on Charles's hip. A quick look at Charles indicated he had seen it too, along with the ammo cartridges beside it. He did not say anything about it, instead making his way past her to view something far more dangerous and too close to home.

Following Charles, they both stopped in front of a large, faded picture. A mushroom cloud, not unlike the one from the night before, loomed over them. A chill ran up Julietta's spine, a feeling shared by Charles.

"You...you don't think it was nuclear, do you?" Charles asked, frowning.

"I...I don't know. Nuclear, dirty, does it matter?"

The rain of bombs, nuclear, dirty, or otherwise, nearly did the world in. It was the one subject everyone knew something about.

"No, not in the slightest." Charles sighed, shaking his head. "Let's just hope it was a one-off or a mistake, someone accidentally setting off some old dead piece."

Julietta was about to correct Charles about the impossibility of a centuries-old bomb suddenly going off, but seeing his dark expression she knew he was only trying to fool himself to steal his nerves.

"Come on, let's go to something I know you'll enjoy," Julietta sighed, gently setting a hand on his arm.

Charles gave her a sad smile, letting her lead him away.

The Human Body and Medical wing proved to be fruitful in information. Julietta listened intently as Charles explained the various devices and models they passed. He was indeed telling the truth about his medical prowess. It wasn't that she had disbelieved him, but the fact of what passed for a 'doctor' these days rarely actually merited more than basic first aid.

Stopping in front of an exhibit explaining the complexities of surgeries, Charles's brow furrowed.

"Something wrong?"

"No, just…There is so much knowledge here. Even though the machines would likely never work again, their processes, mechanically speaking, could be used to…save so many people if we could figure them out."

"You really do know your stuff, far more than any doctor I've ever seen."

"I wish I could tell you I am one of many, but even the doctors in the cities…let's just say when I worked there, I was given the hardest cases." He shook his head, frowning.

"Why did you leave? If you were the best doctor—"

"It wasn't willingly."

Julietta froze, her stomach turning. "Can you—"

"If you want to know, it was a failed attempt at surgery. The governor of Matson was shot in the arm and the bullet ended up in his side. When they brought him in it was…bad. I tried my best but with limited supplies as they are and no good way to stop the bleeding…There was so much blood." His voice cracked a bit, his head bowed. "I tried everything, but he didn't make it."

"Charles…"

"They blamed me. Someone caught wind of my extra studies of the Arcane and outed me. Said I was a fraud and chased me out."

"But that makes no sense, why would your extra studies affect the surgery?"

"It didn't, that's what the medical community agreed to as well, but the person who outed me had power, and coin talks. Despite the fact that I am a decent doctor, no one in cities would take me for fear of retribution."

Julietta frowned, taking a step up beside Charles. "So, you wander now?"

"Yes, wander and research. I've stopped here and there helping people medically for a bit, but most small towns don't need another doctor. Big cities are mostly connected so they know my reputation and would love to have me, but my shame follows."

"Not a shame." Julietta placed a comforting hand on his arm hoping he wouldn't pull away. When he didn't, she slid her hand to his squeezing it. "From what I am hearing and what I've just listened to for the past two and a half hours, you know your stuff."

"Thanks."

"Come on, there are a few more exhibits to explore," Julietta smiled, pulling him towards the stairs.

As they were about to reach them, she paused at the last display. Within glass walls were mannequins, dressed in full white suits, their hands gloved, and eyes covered with plastic goggles. "This one scares Penny the most. She seems to panic when she sees it."

"I really wonder what happened to her."

"You and me both."

By the time they finished exploring the first floor, debating all the while about Arcane versus science, it was nearing dinner. Making their way back up to the loft they found Penny already there playing with Nelson.

"Looks like the storm's finally let up," Julietta noted, seeing she could now look out the window.

"Guess that means I'll be leaving."

"I mean, it is late. You could stay, just for the night," Julietta offered.

"You sure?"

Penny jumped to her feet and ran over to Charles to hug him.

"Looks like Penny has something to say about it." Julietta chuckled. "Do you want Charlie to stay?"

"Charles, please if you don't mind."

"Sorry, Charles. Penny, do you want Charles to stay?"

Penny hugged Charles tighter, looking up at him with a pleading smile.

"Survey says, yes," Charles smirked. "All right, I'll stay tonight."

After dinner, Charles played with Penny while Julietta cleaned up the dishes. Though it wasn't long before Penny was falling asleep. Tucking her into bed, Julietta kissed her forehead, and turned her attention back to Charles.

"Coffee or tea?"

"Tea tonight, I think, thank you." Charles smiled, taking a seat at the table. "You know I owe you for your hospitality. How's 10 co—"

"Penny seems to really like you Charli—Charles."

Charles paused, surprised at the change of subject. "I suppose so. She's a bright kid. Both emotionally and electronically intelligent I'd say." Glancing around the room he took in just how much work Julietta had done to make her little loft a home. "You really did turn this place into a home for yourselves."

"Thanks, borrowed stuff mostly from the homes exhibit. Couldn't use the electrical devices, but the wood-burning ones work well enough. When I first got here all I had was a mattress on the floor, a sink, and an oven. Over time I fixed it up and got some crates to make a bed frame, and some cabinets to hold spare clothes and blankets. When Penny came, she wanted a fort, so I built her one."

"You are a really good mother to her."

"I try," Julietta sighed, setting down two mugs of tea on the table before taking a seat. "I hadn't thought about having kids when she turned up at my door. I was only 23 Damp. But having taken care of her for over a cycle, I'm glad to do it."

The two sat in awkward silence, neither sure what to say.

"You know, I've been working on the museum for four cycles now, and barely scratched the surface."

"It's a great deal of work for just one person."

"It would be a benefit, I think, to have someone somehow document all the stuff in the medical wing. I don't know when I'll get to it, and even if I do, I won't understand half of it."

Charles paused with his mug at his lips. "Are you asking me to stay beyond tonight?"

"I'm asking, if you are interested, maybe we can talk about you working here to document the medical wing. You could stay in the transportation exhibit or set up something near the medical wing. Of course, you'd be expected to also contribute to the household."

"So, I would work and live here and contribute to buying groceries and such, how?"

"By acting as Waterwealt's doctor."

Charles nearly choked on his tea. "You're joking."

"Waterwealt doesn't have a doctor. When Penny showed up at my door injured and sick, it was me, myself, and I that had to nurse her back to health. I would have given anything to have a doctor nearby."

Charles frowned. The thought of little Penny hurt and sick turned his stomach.

"Just think about it; wouldn't be all the time either, just when someone needs you. I can talk to Harrison about adding you to my stipend, as he calls it, for restoring the museum. Fixing things for the people in town is my second job."

Charles was deep in thought. After a while, he said, "I'll think about it."

"Anyway, I want to check on the town tomorrow, now that the storm's stopped. Make sure everyone is all right."

"Of course," Charles nodded in agreement. "I wouldn't expect anything less."

It was the middle of the night when Penny awoke. Looking over at Julietta she gave a small smile. She loved Julietta, she was much nicer to her than...She shook her head, not wanting to think about that. She wasn't there anymore. *Julietta keeps Penny safe. Julietta loves Penny.*

Pulling on her boots, Penny grabbed Nelson and the remote car the nice man Charles got her today, before quietly sneaking out of the loft and heading for the stairs.

Stopping on the landing to the third floor, Penny listened closely. From somewhere in the transport exhibit she could hear the soft snoring of Charles, sound asleep. Happy that she wouldn't be discovered, she made her way in the opposite direction toward what she considered her workshop.

Though the room was dark, Penny maneuvered through it easily. Setting Nelson and the car on her makeshift desk, she headed for her hidden stash of supplies that she kept behind one of the mechanical men. Retrieving matches and a candle she placed it in its holder near her workstation before lighting it. Situating herself, she began tinkering with the circuit board she'd shown Julietta and Charles earlier.

Adjusting a few more wires, Penny reached for the car. Using the tiny screwdriver set Julietta had given her to explore the various small electronics, she undid the back, pulling out the batteries. Success one, find actual batteries.

Next, she began attaching the batteries to her board. Using some black tape she found inside some of the dead computation machines, she connected the wires, then pressed the button. Nothing!

She had expected that. The batteries were very old based on what she heard Julietta tell Charles earlier.

Unhooking the batteries, she held them between her fingers. It had been over a cycle since she had tried this; the last time being the way she got out of her horrible situation and into her current much better one. Taking a deep breath, she closed her eyes. As she slowly let it out blue sparks seemed to arc from where she held the battery giving off a dim glow.

Opening her eyes, she smiled. Placing the battery once more in her board she pressed the button. This time the lights flickered to life, one by one.

Julietta awoke covered in sweat. It seemed, overnight, the Hot season had finally decided to reveal itself. Climbing out of bed she peeled off her cotton long-sleeve heading for the cabinet with spare clothes. Fixing her hair back up in her messy bun, she dug out a couple of plain short-sleeve T-shirts for herself and Penny. Changing quickly, she then went to wake the girl.

From the state of Penny's hair, Julietta could tell she was going to be equally miserable with the heat. "Come on, my lucky Penny, time to get up."

Penny grumbled, turning away from her.

Julietta chuckled, shaking her head. Walking over to the sink she wet two towels with cool water, settling one over the back of her neck, before returning to Penny's side. Gently placing it on the back of her neck she asked again, "Penny, can you get up please?"

The cool towel seemed to rouse her as she turned to face Julietta, eyes starting to open. "There is my lucky Penny." Julietta smiled, using the towel to wipe Penny's face. "Are you okay?"

Penny nodded, waving her face with her hand.

"I know, it's really hot today. I have a cooler shirt for you to change into. Why don't you take it and head into the bathroom to comb your hair?"

Penny nodded as she took the shirt and cool cloth from Julietta before groggily stomping for the attached washroom.

Chuckling, Julietta headed for the kitchenette to start breakfast.

She was just about done cooking when there was a knock at the loft door. As she expected, there was Charles, looking very hot and sweaty. He had discarded his duster jacket, and his long sleeve changed into a white short sleeve.

"Need this?" Julietta asked, holding out a wet towel.

Charles nodded, letting her place it over the back of his neck. "Thank you," he panted, taking a seat at the table.

Just as Julietta set breakfast out, Penny came bounding out of the bathroom, taking the chair beside Charles with a bright smile.

"Good morning to you too, Miss Penny." Charles laughed, looking over to Julietta who had just set down three glasses of water. "Children are so resilient."

"You weren't the one to wake her up," teased Julietta, taking a seat and starting to fill her plate.

"Is it usually this hot?"

"I mean, it is the Hot season. Surprised it took this long to become warm, though it has never been this hot before."

Penny shook her head in agreement.

"Strange, at least I know I am not the only one thinking this is a bit absurd."

"Definitely absurd. Good thing we are planning to head to town today. It can get awfully stuffy in here during the Hot season. Usually, I'd leave the windows open while we were gone to try and air it out, but with the dust storms being so unpredictable lately..."

"Probably for the best not to then," Charles agreed. "Speaking of town, I thought about what you offered last night..."

"Oh?"

"I'm interested, let's talk with the Mayor today about it."

Penny looked at the two curiously but said nothing, continuing to eat her breakfast. Once they had finished, Charles washed the dishes while Julietta got Penny ready.

"Here," she handed Charles a duster scarf, the inside of it wet with cool water. "Can't very well go out without one."

"Thank you," Charles smiled, wrapping it around his neck as he grabbed his bag.

After convincing a stubborn Penny to wear her duster, the three were off to Waterwealt.

CHAPTER 5

Waterwealt looked unharmed, save for the black soot that seemed to coat just about everything. Many of the residents were out and about, some trying to clean off the sides of their homes, while others resigned to continue their work regardless.

They had just entered the town limits when Mayor Harrison approached them. "Julietta, Penny, and Charlie, was it?"

"Charles, sir," Charles frowned, looking a tad annoyed.

"Anyhow, are you all right? Storm didn't cause you any trouble?"

"No, Harrison, we were fine. Charles here ended up at the museum and stayed with us."

Harrison eyed Charles suspiciously. "You were a right gentleman I presume."

As if to answer him Penny took Charles's hand with a smile. Seeing this Harrison backed down.

"He was an honorable guest, Mayor. In fact, he and I spent quite a bit of time talking."

"Please don't tell me he's got you believing in fairies now?"

"No, despite what you may have heard, Charles here is actually a doctor."

"Doctor? Of what? Unicorns?"

It took every bit of Charles's patience to not answer back, Penny's hand in his the only thing keeping him from lashing out.

Glancing over to Charles, Julietta gave him a sympathetic look. "He is a very intelligent man, I assure you. He really knows his stuff. I'd like you to consider extending him a stipend like mine to work on cataloging the medical wing of the museum with a side condition of being the on-call doctor for Waterwealt."

"Did you inhale soot?" Mayor Harrison burst out laughing. "You must be joking. You expect me to believe this strange man is a doctor?"

Before Julietta could reply, Oliver Healey ran up looking terrified. "Julie, it's Marisa. She is sick something fierce. I...I can barely get her to stay awake."

Mayor Harrison's face fell. "You really are a doctor, Charlie?"

Ignoring the wrong name, Charles nodded. "Yes."

"Prove it."

Oliver led them to his home. Mayor Harrison stayed with Penny in the living room, while Oliver escorted Charles and Julietta to his wife.

"Please, help her," Oliver begged.

Setting down his pack on the nightstand, Charles pulled out a small cone device. Pressing it to Marisa's chest he listened. "Heart sounds fine but elevated. Her lungs are clogged. She is breathing, but it's not sufficient." Setting the cone beside his bag, he turned the woman's head so he could look at her nose. "Soot, lots of it."

"She went out last night as the storm was settling to grab something. I told her not to."

"I need some clean warm water in this, a towel, and an empty bowl." Reaching into his bag he pulled out what looked to be a small teapot.

Taking it from him, Oliver ran out of the room, returning with the items a moment later.

"Julietta, I'm going to need your help," Charles said, handing her the bowl and setting the teapot on the side table. "I'm going to turn her on her side. I need you to hold the bowl beneath her head."

As Julietta moved into position, Oliver interrupted, "Wait, what are you going to do to her?"

"This device is called a nasal pot. I am going to use it to flush the soot out of her nose. I need to clear her airways before I help her lungs."

Oliver looked to Julietta, who nodded.

Taking a deep breath, Charles grabbed the nasal pot. Gently holding Marisa's head so it would allow the water to drain, he began to pour it into her nose. All was silent for a few seconds, then Marisa began to sputter.

"It's all right, ma'am, I promise," Charles soothed, relieved to see the water was pushing out the soot efficiently.

He continued this process slowly, carefully wiping away soot and water in between pours, while reassuring both Marisa and Oliver. Finally, after two and a half pots the water from Marisa's nose ran clear.

"Good," Charles sighed, giving Julietta a look of relief. He checked her vitals again. "You can go dump that."

"How is she?" Oliver asked.

"Not there yet, she is breathing a bit better. I've cleared her sinuses, but the lungs need some help. I have something that I can do. I'll need a couple of damp towels."

Oliver returned just as Julietta did. Charles had dug another strange object from his bag, a small plastic dome with a tube that had a plastic ball attached to it. Taking the towels from Oliver he placed one beside Marisa and handed the other to Julietta.

"I am going to hand you the mask in between uses. Need you to wipe it, please," he explained, reaching for a bottle in his bag. "I'm going to irritate her nose. See if we can get her coughing a bit."

Twisting it open, he held the bottle under Marisa's nose. To his relief, she coughed a little. Placing the bottle on the table, he then grabbed the mask device. Carefully he positioned it over her mouth and nose before squeezing the ball once, twice...

Marisa began to cough hard, startling Oliver and Julietta.

"It's all right, that's what we want," Charles calmed.

Handing Julietta the mask, he firmly thumped Marisa's back as she continued to cough into the damp towel. Once she subsided, he wiped her mouth. Taking the now-cleaned mask from Julietta he repeated the process for a few minutes until Marisa's eyes fluttered open.

"Wha...what happened?" Marisa coughed as Charles removed the mask once more.

"Marisa!" Oliver cried, tears in his eyes.

"It's all right Marisa. Charles here is a doctor."

Charles nodded, reaching for his cone again. Placing it against her chest he listened. "Much better. Still a bit wheezy but much better. Should clear up itself." Checking her pulse against her wrist he smiled. "Heart rate is back to a normal range. If you rest and drink plenty of water, I'd say you'll soon be back on your feet."

"Thank you, Mr. Charles." Oliver relaxed, moving over to sit on the bed by his wife. "What do I owe you?"

"It was nothing, sir," Charles sighed, cleaning up his supplies. "Here, if she says her throat hurts, make some tea with this." He handed Oliver a small pouch. "That should help it."

"Please take this." Oliver reached into his pocket, pulling out two coins.

"That is plenty, thank you," he replied, taking only one.

"Thank you, Charles," Marisa smiled, her voice already sounding better.

Julietta nodded at Charles as they headed into the living room.

"Well?" Asked Mayor Harrison, looking concerned.

"She'll be all right, just inhaled too much soot. I've suggested bed rest, water, and gave them a natural tea blend that should help her throat."

Oliver appeared a moment later, closing the door behind him. "I can't thank you enough, Mr. Charles. When she would barely wake up I—"

"Just Charles, and it's all right, I'm just glad I could help." Charles shook the man's hand.

"Well then," Mayor Harrison raised an eyebrow, a bit shocked. "I suppose I should consider that stipend and position for you."

"Stipend?" Oliver questioned.

"Charlie here wants to stay in town helping Julietta at the museum and act as our on-call doctor."

"Considerin' what he just did for my Marisa I'd agree to it. I've never seen anyone work so quickly. I've seen folks around here perish for less."

Mayor Harrison frowned. "I…I suppose you are right. Well, Charli—Charles, what do you say?"

Before he could answer, Penny, who had been quietly playing with Nelson, jumped to her feet, ran over to Charles and hugged his legs.

"Well, I think I know Penny's vote," Julietta chuckled.

"You want me to stay, Penny?"

The little girl nodded happily.

"Then I guess it's settled," Mayor Harrison announced. "Let's go to my office and write you up a contract. Maybe, with you helping Julietta, that water pump will get done sooner? With this heat, I am getting more worried 'bout the ol' stream."

"I don't blame you," Oliver frowned.

"I'll get back to work as soon as we head home," Julietta sighed, taking Penny's hand as they wished Oliver well before heading to the Mayor's office.

Julietta lay in bed, exhausted, but too hot to sleep. Opening the windows in the loft and workshop, she had hoped to at least rid the rooms of some heat, but to no avail. She had spent the better half of the afternoon working on the drill pump upstairs in the stifling room, only to come back to the blazing loft. At least she didn't have to cook dinner. Charles had already taken care of it.

Despite resigning herself to sleeping in only her cropped undershirt and shorts, she still felt as though she was melting. Getting up and checking on Penny, she replaced the now warm towel on her neck with a fresh cool one. She shook her head as she adjusted the light nightgown she had given her to wear in the hopes of keeping her cool.

If we are melting, I can only imagine Charles. Heading for the sink, she swapped out her own damp towel, making another one and grabbing a bottle of water. She debated with herself for a moment putting on a shirt, but she thought better of it considering the heat, before silently sneaking out and heading for the transportation exhibit.

Approaching the car she knew Charles was using for a bedroom she knocked. "Charles?"

"Come in." Charles's voice sounded rather faint.

Entering the car, she found him stripped down to his undershorts, sitting on the floor, his medical supplies lying beside him. He was sweating as much as she was and breathing a bit heavily.

"I thought you might be a bit hot. Brought a cool towel and some water," she frowned, kneeling beside him.

"Thank you," he sighed, holding out a rather shaky hand.

"You're trembling."

"I'm all right." He shook his head, taking the water from her, and drinking a bit.

Placing the back of her hand on his forehead, Julietta frowned. "You're burning up." Taking the damp cloth, she gently wiped his face.

Charles closed his eyes, letting her cool him off. "I…that woman…"

"You saved her."

"Yes…It was…it was bad. So much soot. I knew I had to…do something."

"It worked beautifully."

"She was lucky," he sighed. "I've done that same procedure a thousand times, but it doesn't always work. It's all we have."

"It did work, though, and if you hadn't done it?"

"She likely would not have recovered." Charles opened his eyes, his gaze meeting Julietta's, a look of fear in them.

"You were scared." She frowned, wiping his neck gently.

"Beyond. I wanted to save her. I had to save her. Seeing Oliver's face…"

Julietta paused, bringing the towel to rest on his chest, feeling his thundering heartbeat. "It's okay Charles, she is all right. I know how you feel, I've been there."

Charles took a deep breath, willing himself to calm. "Penny?"

"You did a good thing today, despite how Harrison treated you. That shows strength of character."

"You do not know how frustrating that was. Honestly, if it wasn't for Penny taking my hand…I probably still wouldn't have said anything but having her there…It made me want to set a good example."

Julietta chuckled, shaking her head. "I know what you mean. Sometimes I wonder if I am the one teaching her or if she is teaching me."

"Can't it be both?" Charles smiled.

"Yes," Julietta grinned, feeling his heart rate calming. "Feel better?"

"Still melting, but yes, better. Thank you." He chuckled. "You weren't such a bad doctor yourself today. First helping me with Marisa, then just now helping me."

"Thank you," Julietta blushed, hoping that Charles would think it was just the heat.

Before either of them could say anything more there was a crashing sound from the far end of the exhibit hall.

Racing towards the source of the sound, Julietta and Charles were relieved to find it was Penny. She had snuck out of bed to the electronics exhibit. While stumbling around in the dark, she accidentally knocked over one of the smaller mechanical men.

"Penny, you should be asleep," Julietta sighed, shaking her head.

Penny shook her head, holding up the battery from the remote car.

"Yes, that's a battery," Charles frowned, looking confused.

That look of confusion turned to shock as he and Julietta watched blue sparks appear between Penny's fingertips casting an eerie blue glow where she held the battery. Before either could think what to say or do, they watched as she carefully placed the battery in the back of Nelson.

The two bulbs that constituted Nelson's eyes lit up, illuminating the room slightly.

"Penny…" Julietta knelt in front of the girl, her voice barely a whisper. "How?"

"Hello, Miss Penny," came a robotic voice. "Are these the two nice people you were telling me about?" Nelson was talking.

CHAPTER 6

"So…" Charles's brow furrowed.

Julietta and Charles stared at Nelson, perched on the table without a battery. With Penny back to sleep, they could now focus on him.

Julietta grabbed the battery, bringing a finger to her lips. With a nod of her head, she indicated her intention to talk, but not in the room. Moving out to the hallway, she quietly closed the door behind her.

"Well," she sighed, looking at the battery in her hand.

"Well, what?" Charles smirked, a twinkle in his eye.

"Well, you are a doctor, explain what just happened."

"You aren't going to like my answer."

"If you are about to suggest that what just happened with Penny was anything but a scientific fluke…"

"You just saw Penny create power from nothing."

"It's not magic."

"It's Arcane." He held up his hand, shrugging.

"You are delusional."

"Yet that little girl just brought to life a robot with nothing more than her fingers. I never thought—"

"There has to be an explanation." Julietta frowned, crossing her arms. "For you to stand here as a doctor and tell me it's magic is ridiculous."

"I am a doctor, but a healthy skeptic. What happened is unexplainable right now, Arcane in nature."

"Healthy skeptic, pfft. You are fooling yourself, Charlie."

"Charles, please," he replied, sounding rather annoyed. "Look, if you want, I can do some research on—"

"You're not suggesting…"

"No, no. Never that! I wouldn't even think to—"

"All right, all right," Julietta wiped her brow. "I believe you, just… Penny is my world and—I don't know. Sorry, you were saying?"

Charles eyed her warily, then relaxed. "I know, you'd protect her above yourself."

Julietta nodded, leaning back against the door behind her. "So, your plan?"

"While I'm documenting the medical wing, I can keep an extra eye out for anything of interest that may explain what Penny did." He shook his head. "Exciting as it was to see someone actually do what honestly should be impossible, it also worried me."

Julietta took a step toward him. "We live in a dangerous world, Charles. All I know is whatever Penny did, was something she clearly did before. She hasn't told me anything about her past, but she showed me…us…this."

"I know you've only known me a few days, but trust me when I say I don't want anything happening to that little girl. I just want to help you."

"I…well, I need help, with handling this new thing with Penny, and restoring this place. You are a very intelligent man, Charles. You'll be a great asset." She gave him a small smile. "Also, helps that Penny seems to trust you."

"You know, I was surprised you asked me to stay." He chuckled, his shoulders slumping. "This heat is draining. Probably, best to discuss more in the morning. We'll have to keep this a secret, of course."

Julietta raised an eyebrow. "I was about to say the same."

"Most people, from my experience, tend to react poorly to the unknown. It's only logical."

"We'll have to explain that to Penny."

"Something tells me it won't take much given how little she's already given us." Charles wiped the sweat from his brow.

"Right now, I agree, we need sleep to digest this. If we can get any. That stuffy train car can't be comfortable."

"Why do you think I am in my underwear?" Charles gestured to his black undershorts.

"I mean…" She gestured to herself. "Why don't you move up into the workshop? There is a couch up there under one of the dust covers. It's not much better heat wise but at least you won't suffocate with the window open."

"You sure?"

"If we are going to work together, I suppose we'll have to start with building a bit more trust somewhere," Julietta smirked. "That, and I don't exactly want to be held responsible for you boiling to death in that train car."

"Thank you," he smiled. "I promise, I will do everything I can to help you with the museum and Penny so long as you let me. Deal?"

"Deal."

After breakfast the next morning, Charles and Julietta waited for Penny to put the battery in Nelson. They had already talked with her about what she had done last night. Having assured her that she wasn't in trouble, but that she needed to keep this their little secret, the girl had agreed to turn on Nelson for them.

Nelson's eye lights flickered to life. "Hello again, Miss Penny."

Penny smiled at Nelson.

Nelson looked over to Julietta and Charles. "You must be Miss Penny's friends. Miss Penny has told me a bit about you, Julietta and Charles."

"I see," Charles nodded, eyes wide.

"Miss Penny informed me last night she wishes to apologize for scaring you. She wants you to know she didn't expect to have to tell you about what she can do, but that she trusts you to understand why she kept it a secret."

"Of course," Julietta sighed, giving Penny a sad smile. "You know I only want to help you." Looking over to Charles, she gave a small nod. "*We* only want to help you."

"Miss Penny thought you would feel that way. She has also instructed me to tell you that she is not quite ready to explain more, but will in time. Right now, she just wants to live a normal life."

"Of course."

"As she wishes," Julietta agreed.

Penny looked relieved. Pressing a button on the back of Nelson the robot's eyes once more went dark.

"Thank you, for sharing with us." Charles scratched his head, his mind turning.

"Well, we have some work to do. I'll be up in the workshop and Charles in the medical wing. You are welcome to join either of us."

Penny shook her head, pointing to Nelson.

"You want to work on Nelson?" Julietta asked.

Penny nodded, pointing at the door.

"I'll be just one floor below the electronics exhibit. Just a stairway away. I can listen for her." Charles offered.

"All right, but please be careful, Penny?"

Penny smiled brightly, leaping off the chair and disappearing into the museum.

Time passed, nearly three weeks since the soot storm. Despite the insane heat, things were going relatively smooth. Most mornings the three would enjoy some breakfast together before Julietta went about her work in the workshop, focusing on the drill pump and minor fixes she picked up during their various goings to town.

Penny continued to work on Nelson, improving his circuitry and showing him off anytime something new was functional. Though she allowed Nelson to speak with Charles and Julietta on these days of show and tell, she still wouldn't give any additional information about herself, nor did either of them pry.

Charles had started to catalog the knowledge and techniques in the Medical Science wing, keeping notes in various notebooks labeled with the subject of interest.

Lunch was taken whenever they got hungry, though Charles usually had to interrupt Julietta to remind her to eat. Evenings were quiet, with dinner, a round of hide and seek, then chatting about their discoveries and restorations once Penny had gone to sleep.

By the beginning of the fourth week, the heat still had not let up. As such, Julietta was receiving more and more pressure from Mayor Harrison to get the drill pump up and running. It was late, the sun already set and Penny asleep, when Charles appeared in the workshop.

"Sorry, had a medical call in town. Lady named Ira, bit of heat exhaustion, nothing too serious."

"I sure hope not," Julietta sighed. "Let me guess, the call isn't what took you so long to get back?"

"I may have gotten stopped by Mayor Harrison, who talked my ear off." Charles set down his bag, peeling off his sweat-soaked shirt.

"Saved you some dinner." She pointed to a covered plate near the end of the mostly clear table, a glass of water beside it.

"Thank you," Charles smiled, digging into the sandwich before taking a seat on the couch that now constituted his bed. "You are up here late."

"I got the pump working today, in theory. I was able to test the individual components by hand but…I need a way to power it."

"I am guessing the standard manual method of a crank isn't going to fly?"

"Not with the depth this needs to go. I told Harrison when he asked about the pump originally this would become an issue, but he heard the words 'clean water source' and 'pump' and nothing else."

"Sounds about right for him." Charles took a sip of water. "He was hovering around me while I tended to Ira's husband. Kept asking why I was doing what I was doing. At first, I thought he was just curious, but…"

"He still giving you a hard time?"

"Magic man, he keeps calling me. Says I work my magic. Asks if I saw any fairies lately."

Julietta rolled her eyes. In the weeks she had gotten to know Charles she had started to understand a bit better his definition of Arcane. It wasn't magic, not exactly. It was a word to describe the truly unexplainable, like what Penny could do.

Charles had kept his word; he'd been scouring the medical exhibit for anything and everything that could explain Penny's abilities. He'd found something about electricity and the body in a display, explaining how it was used to correct heart rhythms as well as static electricity party tricks. There was nothing, however, to explain a human creating electricity out of thin air. He kept Julietta in the loop on this, much to her appreciation.

"Don't take it personally. He doesn't treat me with much more respect. I am just a tool to be used," she explained. "That little fact has become apparent."

"So, you are looking for a power source? Surely there is something here in the museum you could use? An engine?"

Julietta shook her head. "Most engines require more than just a bit of wood to run."

"Water power?"

"Doesn't that defeat the point? We already have low water pressure."

"True, sorry, my mind is rather tired."

"Don't blame you. You spend all day in that exhibit and then spend most of the evening reteaching it to me. Which I appreciate, I like hearing you talk about your work."

"Hey, you do the same for me. How many nights last week did I talk your ear off with questions about gearboxes?"

Julietta chuckled. "Two knowledge seekers starving for our meal."

"Suppose so," Charles sighed, setting down his now empty dishes on the table in front of him. "What other power sources were there in the past?"

"Aside from electrical, there was coal, but not much of that around here. Nuclear…" Both went silent, a quiet understanding between them about why that was not an option. "Then there was steam, but you need water for that…"

The window of the workshop rattled a bit, the wind outside signaling a dust storm.

"Great, just what we need, another dusting. The town is still covered in soot." Julietta closed the window. "I noticed the wind picking up earlier and closed the loft window. Was hoping to keep this one open a bit longer. It's awfully stuffy lately."

"Wind…wind is a power source, is it not?"

Julietta paused, taking her seat at the table once more. "Wind… that's it! Charles, you are a genius!"

"I have my moments."

"In the industrial exhibit, there was a section on alternative energies. Wind was one of them. People used to build windmills? I think that's what they were called. They used them to turn things. If I could make a windmill…I need to sketch this."

Charles smiled. He loved seeing Julietta light up when she talked about her work.

Grabbing some paper and a pencil Julietta began to draw. She didn't make it very far when she paused.

"Oh, um, sorry, I can go back to the loft and let you get some rest." She was about to pick up her things when Charles approached her, placing a hand on her arm.

"You can stay. I'm rather curious about this windmill of yours. Why don't you explain it while you sketch?"

Julietta spent the next couple of hours sketching her plan for the windmill, explaining the science behind it to Charles. As she was finishing up, Charles excused himself to wash his dishes and use the restroom in the loft. When he returned, he found her sound asleep with her head on the table.

Carefully, he picked her up, laying her on the couch. Removing the dust sheet from another living room chair, he made himself comfortable before drifting off to sleep.

Penny woke in the middle of the night needing to use the restroom. As she was returning to her bed, she glanced over to where Julietta usually slept to find she wasn't there. Concerned, she placed her battery in Nelson, waking him.

"Something wrong, Miss Penny?"

Penny whispered something to him.

"Maybe she is still in the workshop?" Nelson answered.

Carefully climbing the ladder, holding Nelson close to her chest, Penny lifted the unlocked hatch. Peering into the darkened workshop it took her a moment to see anything. When her eyes adjusted, however, she smiled brightly seeing Julietta asleep on a couch, Charles on a chair not far away.

Closing the hatch, she carefully climbed down heading for her bed.

"Everything okay, Miss Penny?"

Penny laid down, whispering once more to Nelson.

"I don't know, Miss Penny, maybe. Goodnight." Nelson answered as Penny removed his battery before turning over and falling back to sleep.

CHAPTER 7

Julietta was startled awake by the sound of a pan hitting the floor. "Ah!" It took her a moment to realize she was asleep on the couch in the workshop. She glanced around, remembering what had happened the night before. It didn't take her long to spot Charles, sound asleep, on the chair towards the back of the room.

Shaking her head, she approached him. "Charles…"

"Five more minutes, Mom," he mumbled.

"Well, I must say even in my time taking care of Penny I've never been called mom," Julietta laughed.

This time Charles heard her, his eyes fluttering open. "Huh? Oh, sorry. Must have been dreaming."

"It's all right. I suppose I should thank you for letting me use the couch last night?"

Charles ran his hand through his already messy hair. "Eh, you can thank me, or you can help me up out of this chair. Between sweating to death and the late night, I need a bit of assistance."

Julietta held out a hand. "Is that proper medical terminology? Sweating to death?"

Taking her hand, Charles stood with a groan. "I suppose not. I am still alive after all, though I feel like a sticky mess."

"Join the club."

There was the sound of another bowl hitting the floor.

"Methinks your lucky Penny is trying her luck at pancakes," Charles teased, putting on a clean shirt.

"Methinks you are right, and we better hurry or we'll have a tornado of flour to clean up." Julietta chuckled heading for the hatch.

After helping Penny clean up the mess, the two were discussing their plans. "I think we should head to town with the drill pump today. We can start setting it up and let Mayor Harrison know about our progress," Charles offered.

"Sure, we need to work off those pancakes anyway," Julietta agreed. "Would you mind taking a break from your work this week to help me?"

"Of course," Charles grinned.

Over the course of the week, the two slowly assembled the drill pump in its predesignated location, as determined by Byron. Then, they erected a windmill beside it, so it was ready to test by the start of the next week.

"Here goes nothing." Julietta bit her lip, letting the windmill lose.

At first, nothing happened. Then the drill spurred to life. Slowly, Mayor Harrison, Julietta, Charles, Byron, and Penny watched the drill begin to sink its teeth into the ground. Lower and lower it tunneled. For a moment everything seemed well, then there was an awful grinding sound as the pump came to a halt.

"What happened?" Mayor Harrison grumbled. "I thought you said it was supposed to work."

"Hang on, let me take a look." Pulling down her goggles, Julietta opened the side panel on the pump. "Darn it."

"What's up?" Charles frowned, wiping sweat from his brow.

"The gears are working right, but there isn't enough power."

"Well, fix it," Mayor Harrison snapped.

"I can't just fix it, Harrison. I'll need to think about it."

"Think about…think about! That's all you seem to do is think about it."

"I'm trying my best." Julietta slammed the door shut on the pump. "I don't see anyone else around here trying to figure this out."

"That's what I pay you to do!" Mayor Harrison spat back.

Penny had moved to hide behind Charles. "Julietta…" Charles cautioned.

"That's enough," Byron spoke up. "Max, Julietta has been working hard all week with Charles and I to get this thing built and even longer still on her own just to get the pump restored. If she needs a bit more time to get the windmill power working, then so be it. Right now, I think we all need a break. I don't believe I speak just for myself when I say the heat and soot are getting to us."

Mayor Harrison frowned but didn't protest. "Figure it out, Julietta," he barked before turning towards the town hall.

"Thank you, Byron." Charles sighed, placing a comforting hand on Penny who was still hidden behind him.

Noticing Penny, Julietta frowned. "I'm sorry. I lost my temper. You're right, it's the heat. I think we all could use some rest."

"Sleep on it. I know you'll come up with something." Byron smiled, patting Penny on the shoulder before heading back towards his home.

Penny tugged on Charles's shirt, looking sad. Kneeling next to her he was surprised as she wrapped herself around him. Understanding he held her, lifting her up. Walking over to Julietta he shook his head. "I think Penny wants to go home."

Julietta nodded, looking defeated.

Adjusting his grip on Penny, he freed one hand, gently placing it against Julietta's forehead. Feeling how warm she was, he frowned. "Let's go."

"I'm fine, honest," Julietta argued, taking a seat on her bed.

Having returned to the loft, Charles first gave Penny some water before sending her off with Nelson to the electronics wing, hoping it would cheer her up, while he took care of Julietta.

"You've been working in the hot sun all day and barely took a break. I know you didn't drink enough water," Charles challenged, handing her a glass of water, his other hand pressed against her forehead. "You are burning up."

Julietta sighed, drinking the cool water slowly. "I have such a headache."

"Heat fatigue, you need to cool down." Walking over to the sink, he rummaged around in a drawer for some towels.

Downing the rest of her water, she set the glass beside the bed before peeling off her sweat-soaked t-shirt.

Turning back to her, Charles didn't say anything but, "Lie down."

"I'm fine."

"Doctor's orders, lie down." He sat down beside her, placing a cool damp towel behind her neck.

She rolled her eyes but, given her pounding head, didn't protest. Shivering slightly, she settled into the coolness. "That…feels good."

"Told you." Charles frowned, taking two more damp towels, and wrapping them around each of her wrists. Julietta closed her eyes.

"Better?"

"Guess you were right."

He shook his head, taking the last towel and gently pressing it against her face and neck. "I know you wanted it to work."

"Yeah…I was hoping it would work first try but…when does anything?"

"From my experience, only in ideal scenarios."

"That we can agree on," Julietta frowned. "Poor Penny, I didn't exactly set a good example today."

"You are human, we all slip up sometimes. Like Byron said, the heat and soot sure don't help."

"No, no they don't."

"Too bad you can't run an engine on residual heat. We seem to have plenty of that lately."

Julietta's eyes shot open. "Wait…" She tried to sit up, but Charles stopped her.

"You need to rest."

"You said heat, we can't use residual heat but, we can use what generates it."

"The sun?"

"Solar power, Charles," she exclaimed, grabbing him by the shoulders. "In the electronics exhibit, there are solar panels. I don't know much about them but from what I've read when combined with an engine and some energy storage device…" Her head spun.

"Easy, you are still unwell," Charles chastised, continuing to press the cool towel to her neck.

Taking a few deep breaths, Julietta stabilized herself. "Sorry, you're right. But maybe…maybe that's the key. Solar power and a…battery."

"Penny knows about batteries. Maybe she can try to explain to us how they work, and we can…"

"But her secret…"

"We don't have to reveal that. Penny is a smart kid. People in town know she carries around Nelson, right? That she tinkers with him?"

"Yes…"

"So, it wouldn't be too strange for her to have found some dioramas that she understood enough to show us how it works?"

Julietta thought for a moment, a smile crossing her face. "Did anyone ever tell you, you are a genius?"

Charles chuckled, shaking his head. "If you hadn't told me that at least once this past week, I'd say the heat has gone to your head."

"Maybe it has, but the sentiment stands."

Placing his hand against her forehead again, he breathed a sigh of relief. "Your temp's coming back down. How's this? When Penny comes back up, we ask her? Then tomorrow we start working again. I want you to rest tonight and sleep on it. Doctor's orders."

"All right, Dr. Charles...um...I actually don't know your last name."

"Hawthorne."

"Milard."

"Well, Ms. Milard, if you follow my instructions, I dare say you'll make a full recovery to tinker another day."

"Thank you, Dr. Hawthorne." Julietta laughed. "The heat really must be getting to me."

Charles smirked, resting the cool towel on her forehead. "I'm going to get you some more water. Rest."

They asked Penny about the panels at dinner. To their surprise she turned on Nelson, having him explain what she knew. Julietta listened to Charles and rested for the evening. However, the next morning she was up and at it, beginning to work on the panels with Penny.

It took about another two weeks to get the panels, battery, and windmill system up and running. Julietta once more stood beside the drill pump, nervous. She had let the solar panels start to collect energy the morning before, hoping it would be enough stored, along with the windmill, to get the drill moving.

Flipping the switch on the drill, she took a step back and waited. Slowly it groaned to life. Once more, it began to bore into the earth. Several minutes passed, the drill continuing unabated. Then, the first sign of success—mud.

"Yes!" Julietta cheered, Penny jumping up and down beside her.

"It's mud." Mayor Harrison rolled his eyes.

"Yes, it is, you know how mud is made right?" Charles chuckled, relieved and happy to see the machine working.

"Water, Harrison." Byron smiled, pleased. "If the drill keeps going…"

As if to prove his point muddy water began pouring from the hole.

"Water!" Mayor Harrison cheered. "Well, guess I shouldn't have doubted you."

"I'll have to get a hose out here to hook up to it so I can start filtering," Byron explained.

"You'll also have to keep the panels clean as best you can," Julietta noted. "The less dust on them the better."

"That is a you problem," Mayor Harrison chided.

"Uh, what do you mean?"

"Your next assignment, my dear. Dealing with dust, well soot really."

"You're serious?" Julietta looked exasperated. She had hoped to get a bit of a break to work on more of her restoration ventures.

"Over a quarter of a season since the soot storm and we are still trying to clean it out of everything. Our homes, our water, even our bodies, you need to figure out a way to get rid of it."

Julietta sighed, shaking her head. "I suppose that is important. It's not healthy to be breathing it in all the time." Glancing at Charles, he nodded in agreement.

"So, when can I expect a solution?" Mayor Harrison asked, sounding impatient.

"Well, I'll need some time to analyze the soot. Maybe, Byron, you can help me with that? I'm no chemist but knowing its makeup could help. Once we get that, then, Charles, maybe you can come up with a way to help us counter any issues that may arise medically while I figure out a safe way to dispose of it?"

"Works for me," Byron shrugged. "Aside from monitoring this new drill pump, I'll have time. I already started analysis when it first happened to pull it out of the water. More than happy to continue."

"Of course, I'll help," Charles agreed. "Medicine is my bread and butter."

"You mean you don't dust your toast with sunshine and rainbows?" Mayor Harrison chuckled, ignoring the glaring looks from Julietta and Charles. "So when can I expect the solution?"

"To be honest, with how much information I need, at least another quarter season, if not more."

"I'm giving you 'til the end of the week."

"Excuse me?" Julietta looked stunned. Mayor Harrison had never given her a hard deadline.

"I'm tired of the soot, Jul, it needs to go. You want your funding to work on your little restorative bull, I need a solution quick."

Charles stepped forward, annoyed. "Julietta has given you a clear plan and what I think is a reasonable timeframe. Surely, you don't need to resort to threats."

"The boy is right, Harrison. It will take me at least a week to get some basic analysis done," Byron frowned.

Ignoring Byron, Mayor Harrison stepped up to Charles, closing the gap to mere inches. "Listen, Charlie, I'm the mayor of this town. It's my job to ensure the people 'round here get what they need when they need it. That means I need a soot fix in a week. Now if you think Julietta can't do that and you can't help her then maybe I should reconsider my previous offer of letting your magic ass stay here."

"Don't call me Charlie."

"Or what are you going to do, Charlie?"

During this exchange, Penny ran over to Julietta, hiding behind her. Glancing down at her, Julietta noticed a blue glow coming from her hands. Pushing her further behind her, she began to panic.

"Charles…"

Charles turned to look at Julietta, seeing the fear in her eyes and little Penny cowering behind her brought him back to himself.

"Look, Mayor Harrison," Charles continued calmly. "Science and medicine take time. Now you want a solution in a week. That can happen, but the solution you get will not be ideal, let alone efficient or long-term. If you want this done right so you never have to worry again you got to give us at least a quarter season."

"He's right." Byron stepped forward, placing himself between the two men. "I need a week, Maxwell. I can work directly with Charles here so we can expedite and maybe get the medical solution moving sooner, but to really be honest a quarter season is the bare minimum. You saw what that last dust storm did. We need time to do this right, or you're putting a bandage on a gushing wound. Remember the first well?"

Mayor Harrison backed down, his face growing pale. "Fine, a quarter season. By then I expect results." He spat, storming off.

"Sorry again." Byron grimaced. "I honestly don't know what's gotten into him. First arguing with you last week, now this?"

Penny moved out from behind Julietta, her hands no longer glowing.

"It's all right, Miss Penny," Byron smiled. "I won't let mean ol' Harrison hurt your family."

Penny ran up to Byron, hugging him.

"No problem, now, why don't you run along to Marisa's? I heard she has some new cookies that she's been wanting you to try."

Penny's face lit up looking over at Charles and Julietta.

Julietta nodded. "Go on."

With Penny off and running, Byron turned back to the two. "Poor girl, Harrison seems to scare her something fierce lately. Don't quite blame her. I remember my son when he was her age."

"You have a son?" Julietta asked.

"Had. Used to live in Kentburg, over by the former coast. Worked as a chemist, while raising my son, Francis, on my own. My missus passed from illness when he was a baby. They gave my son a test when he was around nine or 10 Damp. Said he was smart enough to go to some fancy school in the capital. They promised me they'd make sure he kept in touch but…that's how I ended up here. When I didn't hear from him after a season, I made the trip to the capital. They wouldn't let me see him, said they never heard of him. I was so lost I…wandered until I wound up here just as the town was settling and decided to stay. Julietta came around about a cycle later and we fixed up the water system."

Charles shook his head. "I'm so sorry."

"Ah, here I am rambling, an old man in his memories." Byron shrugged. "Long story short, Penny is a good kid. I am happy she has you, Julietta and it seems now, Charles, to look after her. Guess I best be heading back to the purifier. Need to get the hoses to hook up to the pump. Charles, if you could give me a hand?"

"Of course."

"By the way, I lied to Harrison. I already have the chemical makeup of the soot. How else was I able to get it out of the water? I have my notes for both of you. That should get you a head start."

"Thank you, Byron." Julietta breathed a sigh of relief, shaking her head. "You've saved me a headache."

"No, Julietta, thank you."

CHAPTER 8

New orders in hand, Charles and Julietta set to work on the soot issue. Thanks to Byron's notes, this was made slightly easier, giving them some context at the very least.

Having read them over, Charles started looking into all possible medical repercussions.

"Magnetic powder, iron-like in nature, inactive charcoal powder…" He had read and re-read the ingredients for days. Other than making it hard to breathe due to its rather sticky nature, thankfully nothing else seemed to have a long-term effect.

"That's a relief," Charles sighed, having finally confirmed his findings against the knowledge gathered in both the medical and chemistry wings of the museum. Something still bothered him, however. This soot was from a bomb, a mushroom cloud-generating bomb. Surely, he was missing something. Not wanting to leave any stone unturned, he resigned himself to head to his least favorite location, the War Exhibit.

Entering, Charles hesitated. Seeing the machines and tools made just for the purpose of killing shook him. For all the good people could do with their inventive minds, they could equally do the opposite.

Arriving at the Modern Warfare section, Charles made straight for the early bombs. Spending an hour or two perusing the tattered and torn papers, smashed cases, and daunting models, he became more uneasy. The soot ingredient list matched closely enough to basic components. That, however, wasn't surprising. What made him uncomfortable was as he looked into the dirty and nuclear ones, there was nothing that matched. His research seemed to indicate that it had come from a test explosive with no payload. Who would be dropping a bomb, let alone a test one, he didn't know. All he knew was if someone was testing this, they were likely planning to make more, probably deadly ones.

Having had enough of dark thoughts, Charles decided to call it quits on research for the day. As he turned to leave, his eye caught a title on a plaque nearby that gave him pause: 'The…School for the Gifted,' part of the name scratched out.

Byron's story fresh in his mind, his stomach dropped as he read the description of the display. From what he could glean from the deteriorating information cards, at some point during one of the worldwide wars, a school for 'gifted' children had opened. These children were said to have 'special' insights and high intelligence. Something about the faded pictures and glowing reviews attached to them sat wrong with Charles. Prying the case open with his knife he removed a few of the more intact papers. Part of him wondered why he bothered; the school was long gone. Yet, something about it seemed all too familiar, too close to home.

Shoving the papers into his back pocket, now truly exhausted and getting rather overheated, he headed for the main staircase and the respite of the slightly more comfortable loft.

Charles found Penny sitting at the kitchen table, a glass of water beside her, and Nelson standing in front of her.

"Hello, Mr. Charles." Nelson turned, taking a shaky step towards him.

In the passing weeks, Penny had gotten Nelson stable enough to start walking.

"Hello, Nelson, Penny." Charles smiled, heading for the sink to get a drink. "How have you been today?"

Charles waited a moment for Penny to whisper to Nelson her answer. "Miss Penny has had a wonderful day, aside from melting. She wishes it wasn't so hot."

"You and me both." Charles chuckled, drinking some water.

"Miss Penny would also like me to tell you she is happy you have stayed with her and Miss Julietta. She likes to play hide and seek with you both."

"I am guessing Miss Penny wants to play hide and seek tonight after dinner?"

"Miss Penny says yes."

"Okay, we can play."

Penny smiled brightly.

"Shit!" Charles heard Julietta's voice from the workshop above.

"Um, I am going to check on her." Charles quirked an eyebrow, making for the ladder. Before he climbed up, however, he stopped, turning back to Penny. "Don't repeat that word by the way. That's a grown-up word."

Penny nodded, giving him an innocent smile, her eyes looking a bit mischievous.

"Penny…"

Penny laughed, nodding again, indicating she knew she shouldn't use it.

"Good, I'll be back in a minute to make dinner."

Entering the workshop, Charles spotted Julietta at her workbench, her latest attempt at a soot fix strewn about the table.

"You okay? Penny and I heard you downstairs."

"Yeah, I'm fine," Julietta frowned, licking a bit of blood off her finger. "Caught my finger in between the magnets. I am trying to modify this vacuum too—wait, Penny heard me?"

"I already told her not to repeat," Charles chuckled, approaching. "Let me see."

"It's just a bite," Julietta chided, turning back to her work.

"I know you; you could be missing a limb and still say it's just a scratch. Let me see."

"No."

"Julietta…" Charles moved closer.

"What are you going to do about it?" She teased, backing away from him.

"That depends on what you let me do."

"Nothing, absolutely—Ah!" In her attempt to jokingly run away, she had misjudged where the living room chair was, falling into it.

"Julietta!" For a moment, Charles was actually concerned. It was short-lived, however, when she began to laugh.

"Serves me right for teasing you," she grinned, "though I suppose it's your fault for starting it.

"Hey, I just asked to see your cut."

"You are a mother hen, I swear."

"Need a hand?" Charles held out a hand, Julietta taking it.

"How's the research coming?"

"Good and bad."

She raised an eyebrow. "Care to elaborate?"

He went on to explain what he had discovered about the bomb. "It all seems wrong."

"I mean, at least it was just a test bomb. No radiation or chemical contamination, right?"

"Yeah, but it worries me what the person has in mind."

"That I can understand," Julietta sighed, shaking her head. "At least one of us is making progress. I've taken apart and put this vacuum back together about a hundred times today and still don't think I've gotten anywhere."

"It's not a problem so easily solved. This soot just clings to everything, it's annoying."

"You are telling me." Again, she wiped her finger off.

"You gonna let me see it or not?"

"Fine…" Rolling her eyes, she held out her hand. "Mother hen."

Walking her over to the sink, Charles took a quick look at the cut. "Not bad, definitely broke some skin." Turning on the water, he pulled her hand under it. Julietta winced.

"Sorry, don't want it infected." Blood cleaned off, he took another look. "Looks like it's sealing already but probably just want a little bandage on it if you are going to keep working to keep the dirt off."

Julietta bent down, retrieving the first aid kit from beneath the sink. Charles smiled, grabbing a small bandage and applying it to her finger. "I think you'll make a full recovery."

"You are so dramatic," She laughed. "How did I end up with you as a roommate again?"

"You only have yourself to blame."

"Clearly I'm insane."

"You said it, not me," Charles winked, closing up the kit and putting it away. "Not that I am not enjoying our banter, but I do have something I want to show you. I found this in the war exhibit." Pulling out the papers from his back pocket, he laid them out on the table.

"School for 'Gifted' children…special insights…what…what is this?" Julietta questioned.

"Byron's son was taken after a test. I was tested as a child but wasn't taken. Some of my friends at the time were. Much like Byron, I haven't seen heads or tails of them since."

"You don't think they are doing this again?"

"It does seem to line up. Has Penny ever said—"

Before Charles could finish his question, the hatch to the workshop opened, little Penny's bright blue eyes peering inside.

"Hungry, Penny?" Julietta gave Charles a worried look, shaking her head.

Penny nodded, smiling sheepishly.

"Why don't you finish what you were doing? I'll get dinner started." Charles glanced at the papers knowingly.

"Sure," Julietta smiled, giving him a terse nod as he ushered Penny down the ladder, leaving her with a great deal to think about.

Wanting to update Byron, they headed to Waterwealt the next morning. When they arrived, Charles headed off towards Byron, while Julietta and Penny made a detour towards Marisa's to pick up some sweet bread.

Entering the bakery, Penny immediately ran up to Marisa who was just restocking some bread rolls on the counter.

"Why, if it isn't my favorite little customer? How are you doing, Miss Penny?"

Penny smiled, giving Marisa a hug.

"I'll take that as good," Marisa chuckled, looking up at Julietta. "And how are you, Jul? Having fun with that handsome man you now live with?" She raised her eyebrows suggestively.

"It's not like that." Julietta laughed, hoping she didn't notice her blush. "We are good friends and technically co-workers."

"Doesn't mean you can't be more…I mean he is a wonderful doctor. Look what he did for me," she teased.

"I am just happy you are back to your usual cheery self."

"That I am, which means…" Marisa winked at Penny. Turning around, she grabbed two sugar cookies from a basket. "Fresh from the oven, my dear."

STEPHANIE VACCARO & LOUISE ALLEN

Penny smiled brightly, giving a nod of thanks as Marisa handed her the treat. "I'm guessing you are here for something?"

"Got any more of that sweet bread? Charles made this delicious dish with it for breakfast last week with eggs and sugar. I thought Penny would never want to eat anything else ever again with her reaction."

"A doctor and a cook? Tell me you aren't the least bit interested."

"Marisa..."

She shrugged, a twinkle in her eye. "You're in luck. I made a fresh batch this morning. One sec." Turning towards the back room she shouted for Oliver to bring some sweet bread up front. He appeared not a minute later.

"Ah, Julie and Miss Penny. A pleasure to see you. Where's Charles?"

"Went to talk to Byron about our latest project."

"Heard about that. You three did a mighty fine job on that pump. Not a pressure issue since. Glad you convinced ol' Harrison to let Charles stay. I'm forever grateful for what he did for my Marisa."

"I'll be sure to tell him," Julietta smiled. "How much Marisa?"

"Two coin."

Julietta handed her three. "Don't even think about it."

Bagging up the sweet bread, Marisa threw in a few cookies, sticking out her tongue. "Got to treat the little one, don't we?"

"You spoil her."

"Her and little Ken and Leah. Children are so rare, Julietta. Gotta spoil them when I can."

"Speaking of children, did you tell her about the strange man?" Oliver frowned, giving a sad look towards Penny.

"Strange man?"

Marisa's usual cheerful demeanor fell. "There's a stranger in town, he claims to be from the capital. He wants to test the children to bring them to some fancy school if they pass."

Julietta's heart dropped, glancing over to Penny she could see a flash of fear in the girl's eyes. A deep frown formed on her face as she stood, hugging Julietta tightly.

"It's all right Penny, I won't let anyone take you away."

"None of us will," Oliver sighed. "Has Byron told you?"

"Yes, about..."

"Francis." Marisa shook her head. "The man is talking with Harrison now. News travels fast around here. Everyone agrees that this all seems too strange for our liking. Michael and Sarah already agreed to refuse to get Ken tested, same with Ryan and Victoria. As far as that man knows, there are no children in Waterwealt for testing."

"Thank you." Julietta could feel Penny still trembling. "I should get going. We're supposed to meet Charles at Byron's."

"Be safe, Jul. You too, Miss Penny," Marisa smiled sadly, as Julietta took Penny's hand, holding it tightly as they walked back out into the streets of Waterwealt.

"Byron?" Charles called. "Byron?"

"Charles! Where's Jul? Where's Penny?" Byron looked terrified.

"At Marisa's. What's—"

"You need to get Penny home, now."

"What do you mean? She's with Julietta she's fi—"

"It's not safe for her. It's not safe in Waterwealt! They've come... they've come for the children."

Charles's heart sank into his stomach. "Who?"

"The capital, they've sent an agent, same as the one that took my Francis. I've already warned everyone and told them to send him away. Tell him there are no children here."

"Surely no one is going to think sending them away—"

"I...I don't know." Byron was shaking now, his eyes manic. "You can't let them take her. You can't let them take little Penny. The poor girl...the poor girl..."

"Easy, Byron, why don't you sit down a minute." Charles frowned, his own heart threatening to leap out his throat. "I won't let anything happen to Penny, I can assure you."

"I can't...I have a lot of work to do. I need your help. I need something from the museum."

"What?"

"I need a transmission device. Something from the old war days. I can't remember the before term for it, but it was a device that sent...signals to similar devices. I need you to look in the museum for one for me."

"I'll try." Charles brow furrowed in confusion. "I'll ask Julietta about it."

"Good…good. You should go. Go get them, and get Penny home safely. I'll come to check on you when the man is gone. Promise me you won't bring Penny back here 'til I give the okay."

"I'll tell Julietta."

"Please do. Now go. Go!"

CHAPTER 9

Julietta's heart sank seeing Charles running toward them. "What's wrong? What happened at Byron's?"

"He was in a panic. Something about a strange man…"

As if on cue, down the block, they spotted the Mayor exiting town hall, a man, dressed in unusual clothes beside him. Before they could react, Penny began to panic.

"Penny, what's wrong?" Julietta frowned, struggling to keep Penny from running away.

"Penny?"

Penny paused, tears streaming down her face. Shaking her head, she tried again to pull Julietta away.

"We should go." Charles scooped up Penny in his arms and made for the museum.

Julietta didn't argue. Following quickly behind, her heart skipped a beat as she spotted the Mayor heading off with the strange man toward the main housing area of town.

"It's all right, Penny, we won't let anyone take you," Julietta comforted, holding the crying girl in her arms.

They returned to the loft, Charles carrying Penny, trembling, the whole way. Taking a seat at the kitchen table with Penny, Julietta listened while Charles made some tea and explained what Byron had told him.

"Marisa said something similar. No one in town likes what's going on." Julietta sighed, gently untangling Penny's hair. "Why come to a little hole in the ground like Waterwealt?"

"I don't like the sound of it. Byron's son, my childhood, Penny's reaction…this screams bad news."

Penny shifted in Julietta's lap holding her tighter.

"It's all right. I'm here; Charles is here. We won't let that man take you."

"Here, I made you your favorite tea," Charles offered, setting Penny's special mug on the table beside them.

Slowly Penny uncurled herself from Julietta, sitting up. He carefully handed her the mug, making sure she had a grip on it before letting go. "So, what's the plan?"

"Well, first off we can't go to town anytime soon, at least not together." Julietta looked deep in thought. "Guess we wait until Byron gives the all clear?"

The wind outside began to rattle, a sign of a dust storm approaching.

"Guess Mother Nature wants to help that," Charles chuckled nervously, trying to lighten the mood as he closed the window.

Though Penny had calmed, the three spent the rest of the day in the loft, not feeling like being apart. As evening drew near, she climbed into Julietta's bed.

"You want to stay with me tonight?"

Penny nodded, clutching Nelson tightly.

"Okay, Penny," Julietta smiled sadly, kissing her forehead. "I'll be right here."

The child nodded, her eyelids drooping. It wasn't long before she was sound asleep. Taking Nelson from her and setting him on the bedside table, Julietta shook her head.

Charles, having finished washing up the dinner dishes, pulled up a chair from the dining table. "You all right?"

"Would you believe me if I said yes?"

"And you call me delusional."

Julietta shook her head. "At this point, I don't even know anymore."

The two sat in silence, wanting to say something, but at a loss for words.

"Charles…this may be a bit of an ask but…I don't feel comfortable sleeping right now. Storm or not, I—"

"You want to take watches?"

"It's…I sound crazy, don't I."

"No, not in the slightest. Not to me anyway. Not after hearing Byron."

"You'll stay?"

"I'll take first watch."

Julietta relaxed, feeling a weight lifted from her shoulders. "Thank you. I…owe you one."

"You owe me nothing. You gave me a chance here. If anyone owes anyone—"

"How about we call it even?"

"Who said I was keeping score?" Charles smirked, mischievously.

Julietta stifled a laugh, aware of Penny sound asleep behind her. "I guess I better get some sleep. Sooner I do, the sooner you get some too."

Charles moved his chair back to the dining table, facing the door. Reaching in his boot he pulled out his knife, laying it on the table in front of him. "I'll wake you around sunrise. I can sleep in the morning in the workshop."

Julietta walked over to him. She paused a moment before giving him a hug. "Thank you, Charles, it…means a lot."

He reached up a hand, resting it on hers, a silent understanding passing between them. "Get some sleep." He smiled as she let go.

Tired, but determined, Charles sat at the table, his mind thinking back over everything he had learned. He would protect Penny, just as she did. And so he sat, waiting, watching until the sun rose and Julietta came to relieve him.

The storm outside still raged the next morning. As the three were eating breakfast, Charles remembered something else he had planned to tell Julietta.

"I almost forgot. Byron, he wanted me to look for something in the museum."

"Oh?" Julietta looked confused. "What exactly?"

He tried to explain what Byron had described to him. "He said it was something used before, but he couldn't remember the name."

"Communication device? Signals? That…doesn't ring a bell."

Suddenly, Penny was on her feet, her eyes wide.

"Penny, what's wrong?" Julietta stood, concerned.

Penny grabbed Nelson. Turning him on she whispered something to him before setting him on the table.

"Miss Penny has asked me to remind you of the toy car you gave her."

"Toy car?" Charles leaned back in his chair, thinking. "It was... remote-controlled? Said something about..."

"Radio waves!" Julietta's eyes lit up. "Radios! He wants a radio?"

Penny whispered once more to Nelson. "Miss Penny thinks so. She said that she read about radios in the Electronics Exhibit, but there wasn't one there."

"I've seen some, but you aren't going to like where they are, Penny."

"War Exhibit..." Julietta frowned. "I can go get one after breakfast."

"Miss Penny wants to come too," Nelson said.

"You sure?" Charles looked at her curiously.

"Miss Penny is brave. Miss Penny wants to see the radios."

Heading down, it didn't take long to find the radios. Unfortunately, they were in pieces. "I'm going to have to rebuild it for him." Julietta's shoulders slumped.

Penny, who up to this point was clinging to Charles, stepped forward, pulling on Julietta's shirt.

"Yes?"

Penny pointed to herself, then the radio.

"You want to help me with the radio?"

Penny nodded, pantomiming taking apart something.

"She's been playing with electronics for a while, right?" Charles smiled, realizing what Penny was suggesting. "She probably could figure it out quicker than either of us."

"I mean...I still have Harrison's soot problem to deal with. The deadline is coming up quick," Julietta frowned, thinking.

Penny pointed again to herself, then the radios.

"I think what she's trying to say is she wants to rebuild the radio herself," Charles offered.

Penny nodded, a smile on her face.

"All right, Penny," she smiled. "We will bring the parts up to my workshop. That way I can help you if need be...and maybe you can teach me a thing or two. What do you say?"

Penny answered by hugging her.

Charles laughed, moving to grab some parts. "Welcome to the restoration team, Penny."

The storm let up after three days. By this time, Penny was already well on her way to cobbling together a working radio. Charles and Julietta were quite impressed seeing how hard the girl worked, and how knowledgeable she seemed for someone her age. She had even taken to keeping Nelson on longer and longer, using him to explain to them what she was doing.

Julietta stood just inside the atrium, her bag at her feet. "Penny, I'm sorry but you can't come to town with me."

Penny pouted, pantomiming using a radio.

"I know you want to show Byron what you are working on, but it is just not safe. I promise I'll let him know what you are doing."

Penny still pouted, pantomiming again using a radio.

"Penny…"

Their argument was interrupted by the sound of someone pounding on the door. It was as if the air had been sucked out of the room; a sudden feeling of deep dread passing over the two of them.

"Julietta, it's me, Mayor Harrison. I have something to talk to you about."

Penny immediately backed away, her eyes filling with tears.

"Go upstairs and find Charles," Julietta whispered. "Let him know what is happening, okay?"

Penny nodded, immediately bolting for the central staircase.

Julietta waited until she was out of sight, ignoring the Mayor's increasingly agitated pounding. Palming her knife, she approached the door.

"I know you are in there, Julie—"

"Mayor Harrison," she greeted sweetly, opening the door only just enough to seem friendly, but not inviting. "Sorry, didn't hear you at first. Museum is awfully big after all. You are lucky I happened to be coming down the stairs."

"Well, now that I have you here, I'd like you to meet Mr. Turner. He is from the capital. It seems they have taken an interest in some of the more advanced little towns. They want to test the children to see if they are gifted and send them to school in the city so they can help better the world."

"That's nice." She shrugged, feigning disinterest as she glanced over at the visitor.

Mr. Turner was a tall, lanky man, with a pale face. He was dressed very strangely, in what looked to be a business suit like the ones she saw in the 1950s Clothes Exhibit. It seemed very out of place in the wastes.

"Don't know why you are telling me this, Harrison. Now if you'll excuse me, I have a soot problem to deal with."

Julietta attempted to close the door, but Mayor Harrison, unfortunately, was stronger, shoving it open and storming in. "You know very damn well why I'm telling you this. Where is she?"

"Where is who?" She asked, still feigning ignorance as she moved to place herself between the men and the stairs.

"Your lucky little Penny," Mayor Harrison sneered. "I already told Mr. Turner about her. He wants to speak with her."

"No." Julietta dropped her pretense, stepping firmly between the men and the stairs. "As her guardian, I have a say who speaks to her."

"You aren't her guardian, nor her mother. You were just the person who found her."

"Leave, now," she growled, her hand ready to flick the knife.

"Julietta, you are being unreasonable." Mayor Harrison stepped forward, closing the gap between them.

"Leave! Now!"

"Not a chance, sweetheart," Mayor Harrison chuckled as he dove for her.

Charles was in the far back of the Medical Wing, taking notes on a detailed, though rather faded display of the human nervous system. He was so lost in his work he almost didn't hear Penny approaching.

"Penny? What's—" He stopped, seeing the tears in her eyes.

Penny pointed at the stairs, gesturing scared.

"Scared? Why are you scared? Where is Julietta?" He walked towards the main staircase, but Penny stopped him, pulling on his shirt and shaking her head.

"What is it? Please, tell me."

Penny held up a finger to her mouth, pulling on her ear.

Charles stopped and listened closely. He could hear heavy footsteps coming up the stairs, two male voices, one he recognized and one he didn't, echoing off the museum walls. His heart sank realizing what was happening.

Grabbing Penny's hand, he pulled her into the back staircase that was attached to the digital exhibit. Closing the door, he jammed the lock, assuring it couldn't be used without great effort before scooping the girl into his arms. As they quietly made their way up, the voices on the main stairwell became clearer.

"She has to be around here somewhere."

Hearts racing, they dashed for the loft. He needed to buy them time. Setting Penny down he pointed to the workshop. "Hide up there and don't come out until I or Julietta tell you, okay?"

Making sure Penny locked the hatch, Charles grabbed a few items, attempting to hide the ladder before racing towards the main stairwell. Reaching the landing, his heart leaped. Lying at the bottom was a still figure, Julietta.

Checking briefly for the two men, he ran to her. "Julietta..." He panted sitting beside her, carefully turning her onto her back.

To his relief, she was alive, though dazed, with a nasty gash above her right eye.

Grabbing the towel he had on the back of his neck for cooling, he pressed it to the wound. "Julietta..."

Her eyes fluttered open. "Charles...Penny..."

"She's hidden, but we don't have much time."

She tried to sit up, but her head spun.

"Easy..."

"We need to get Penny out of here," she spat, her head settling.

"I need to at least stop the bleeding. Your duster!"

Thinking fast, he pulled up the neck duster Julietta wore, using it to hold the towel over the wound.

"It will have to do." She staggered to her feet. "Where is she?"

"Workshop. Go get her. I'll meet you at the top of the stairs."

STEPHANIE VACCARO & LOUISE ALLEN

Hearing the two men somewhere on the second floor, the two ran faster, Julietta vanishing into the loft, while Charles made for the War Exhibit.

Running straight for the firearms display, he smashed the case labeled 'Sig Sauer' containing a gun similar to his broken one. Loading it, he removed the safety before heading back to the stairwell. He was greeted by Julietta looking distraught.

Seeing the weapon in his hand, she took a step back. "She's not up there."

"Then there is only one place she can be."

Rushing into the Electronics Exhibit, they began to search. "Penny…" Julietta whispered, hoping she was loud enough to be heard by a hiding Penny, but not by the searching men.

"Penny…" Charles repeated, searching behind a mechanical man.

They were getting desperate when Julietta heard soft crying coming from a cabinet against the back wall. Opening it she was relieved to find little Penny, crying but seemingly unharmed.

"It's all right, Charles and I are here."

"Come on, let's—"

Charles stopped as Mayor Harrison and the man from the capital entered.

"Well, well, looks like we finally found you. You sure gave us quite a chase." The capital man grinned, his voice like oil. "You were right, Mayor, this one is special."

Julietta closed the door to the cabinet, shielding it with her body. "You can't have her."

"Oh, come now Jul, you are being unreasonable." Mayor Harrison started to step forward but stopped as Charles raised the gun.

"Stay back," he spat.

"Charlie…"

"Leave, both of you."

"Charli- Charles, I just want what's best for little Penny. Mr. Turner here says they have a lovely school for smart kids like her in the capital. Don't you want what's best for her?"

"I said, leave," he repeated, eerily calm, keeping himself firmly between the men and the girls.

"Charles, I know you believe in all that Arcane bull, but even you should know guns don't work. Why do you think no one carries one?

They are an old war piece, a long-lost remnant that is little more than a toy. You know as well as I do that little thing won't—"

There was a loud bang, the sound of glass shattering, and a pained grunt. The Mayor looked wide-eyed at Charles, holding his right arm where the bullet had grazed him.

"Leave, or next time I won't miss," Charles stated bluntly, his eyes locked on the men.

Mayor Harrison began to back away, but Mr. Turner stood firm.

"I don't believe you understand, Charlie, was it? I am not leaving without…'Penny'."

Charles pointed the gun at him, his eyes still watching the Mayor. "You have five seconds," Charles glared.

Mr. Turner took a step forward.

BANG

Charles watched as the body of Mr. Turner hit the floor, dead. The bullet, however, had not been from his gun. Standing behind the fallen body, their gun now pointed at the Mayor, was Byron.

CHAPTER 10

I t took Charles a moment to register what was happening.

"I suggest you leave, Harrison. Some of the boys in town are waiting for you downstairs," Byron growled. "You'll be happy to know I told them not to kill you. Not just yet anyway."

Eyes wide, Mayor Harrison booked it for the stairwell. Ensuring he was gone, Byron turned his attention back to Charles, who still held his gun pointed ahead.

"It's all right, Charles, I'm here to help."

Charles did not take his eyes off of him as Byron put the safety on and holstered his gun.

Raising his hands, he didn't move further. "I wasn't about to let anyone take Penny or any of the children. Not again."

Charles hesitantly lowered the gun, still unsure of the situation. It was Julietta's hand on the back of his leg and a nod of confirmation that finally brought his guard down.

Taking a deep breath, he put the safety on before slipping the gun under his belt. Kneeling beside Julietta, they opened the cabinet once more.

"It's okay, Penny, the bad man is gone," Julietta smiled, her voice gentle and calm.

Penny slowly crawled out of the cabinet, almost immediately placing herself into Charles's open arms.

"I'll take care of the body. You get these two ladies fixed up." Byron sighed, stepping out of their way. "I'll be up when I am done."

Penny kept her face buried in Charles's chest as he lifted her. Holding out his other hand to Julietta, he helped her to her feet, letting her lean on him. With a brief nod to Byron, they made for the stairwell.

Julietta sat on her bed, Charles setting Penny down beside her. Unholstering his gun and placing it on the table, he grabbed his medical bag. Pulling up a chair, he gave Penny a quick check-over knowing Julietta wouldn't let him touch her until she was deemed unharmed.

Satisfied the girl was all right, he turned his attention to Julietta. Removing the makeshift bandage, he kept a neutral expression as he began to clean the wound in silence.

Penny snuggled up on Julietta's good side, her head resting on her shoulder. Julietta took her hand, giving it a squeeze.

"It's not as bad as it seems," Charles sighed, cleaning off the little remaining blood. "Doesn't need stitches. Head wounds seem to just bleed like no one's business." Taking a small container from his bag he paused a moment. "Antiseptic. This is going to sting, bad."

Julietta closed her eyes, bracing herself, as Charles applied the cream. She could feel Penny's hand grip hers tighter as she winced.

"Sorry," he whispered, his voice shaking slightly.

Taking a deep breath, Julietta opened her eyes. "Thank you."

Charles shook his head as he properly bandaged the wound. "You're getting a black eye."

"He hit me pretty hard. I tried to fight him off, but he was too strong. Stunned me."

Cleaning up his supplies, Charles returned with a lit candle. "Look at the light for me?"

She did as instructed, her gaze easily following. A look of relief washed over Charles's face. "No headache?"

"Surprisingly, no."

"Nausea?"

"No."

He reached up, gently pressing on her forehead feeling for anything unusual. "No concussion. Your reflexes are good, and everything physically feels normal." Blowing out the candle he tossed it into the sink. "Does anything else hurt?"

She shook her head. "Just tired from all the running."

Charles relaxed back in his chair, nodding in understanding. "So long as we keep that gash clean you should be fine. A good night's rest would help too."

They sat a moment in silence, the adrenaline from earlier finally fading.

"You protected us." Julietta placed a hand on his knee, giving it a knowing squeeze.

"Yes," he replied, his voice a bit shaky.

Penny moved from the bed, taking a seat in Charles's lap. On instinct his arms wrapped around her, as she settled herself against him.

"You—you didn't know if the gun would fire, did you?"

Charles glanced over to the weapon, safety on still, lying on the table. "No."

"You would have fired it again?"

He closed his eyes, holding Penny a bit tighter. "Yes."

"Thank you." Julietta swallowed, tears in her eyes.

"I would protect Penny with my life."

"You did, Charles. She is safe. I am safe…We are safe, because of you."

They sat in silence, a mutual understanding passing between them. It was broken a moment later as the door to the loft creaked open.

Charles and Julietta both jumped slightly but relaxed seeing it was Byron.

Hands up, he waited at the entrance. "I am going to set my gun beside yours, if you don't mind."

Pausing for confirmation it was all right to do so, he set his weapon beside Charles's, ensuring they could see the safety was still on.

Stepping back, he took a deep breath. "I suppose I have a great deal of explaining to do."

Byron remained silent for a moment, waiting for any sign that he should continue. "I've taken care of Mr. Turner. There is still some blood though."

Julietta moved to take one of the empty chairs beside Charles. "We'll deal with that later. Please sit."

As he took a seat across from them, Penny climbed off of Charles's lap. Grabbing Nelson, she sat in Byron's lap, to Charles and Julietta's surprise.

"Hello, Miss Penny." He sighed as she situated herself. "It's been a long time."

Penny nodded, turning on Nelson.

"Hello, Miss Penny. Hello, Sir Byron. Penny has told me a good deal about you. She asked me if I ever got the chance to ask you why you have avoided talking to her?"

"I'm so sorry, Penny. I…I didn't know how to bring it up and was worried if anyone found out…You understand that, don't you?"

Penny nodded, sadly.

"You…you knew about Penny…and her—" Julietta was at a loss for words.

"Explain," Charles stated bluntly, eyeing the man warily.

"Yes, there is much to explain, but I do not have the time, given the situation with the Mayor. Therefore, I'll be brief, then return tomorrow to tell the rest."

"Go on." Julietta urged.

"The school Mr. Turner was talking about in the capital…isn't real. It's a farce. A means of luring people into sending their gifted children to the government."

Penny flinched at the mention of this, a reaction not unnoticed by Charles and Julietta.

"It was about 15 or 16 cycles ago when my son, Francis, was taken from me under the guise of attending the Apolis Academy for the Future. As I mentioned before, I went to Apolis after receiving little to no updates for a season. He wasn't there and they claimed he never was. Distraught, I begged them to help me find him, but my pleas fell on deaf ears…or so I thought."

He paused, unable to read Julietta's or Charles's expressions.

"A professor named Ola Hampton agreed to help me. She had her own suspicions of the school. She took a great risk and acquired my son's file from the records, along with the records of many other children who had mysteriously vanished. They had all been transferred to various 'alternative facilities.' Francis was sent to Rho-597."

Penny shifted uncomfortably, tears in her eyes.

"Penny?" Charles frowned.

"I'm sorry," Byron apologized. "But they should know."

Her shoulders slumped, but she nodded in agreement.

"Rho-597 is just outside Johani, a few days' journey from here. They frame it as a branch of the Apolis Academy. What it actually is, is a facility for intelligent children who are, let's say, adept in the unexplainable." Byron glanced over to Nelson who was watching Penny attentively. "They call them the 'Curied.' What that means, I honestly do not know."

"Penny was…was Rho—" Julietta stopped, seeing Penny refusing to meet her gaze. Instead, the girl reached for Nelson.

"I am permitted to tell you this. Miss Penny was a Curied at Rho-597, transferred from Kappa-139. Sir Byron was one of her assigned attendants. She is not ready to say more."

"Just as well." Byron sighed, shaking his head. "I should be getting back to Waterwealt and you all could use some rest after your day." He grimaced, noting the bandage and black eye Julietta now sported.

Penny climbed off him, standing beside the table.

"Thank you, Byron." Julietta's brow furrowed in thought as he stood, holstering his gun.

Charles gave him a nod of thanks.

"I'll return tomorrow. I'm sorry."

With Byron gone, an uneasy silence fell over the space.

"Miss Penny is sorry she didn't tell you about Rho. Miss Penny was scared," Nelson explained.

"Penny," Julietta knelt beside her, wiping the girl's tears. "I can't imagine what you've been through. You were very brave today."

Penny wrapped her arms around Julietta in a tight hug.

"You are safe now. Charles and I will keep you safe."

"Always," Charles echoed, running a hand through his hair. "We got you."

Charles sat at the kitchen table, his mind reeling. Julietta had asked him to move into the loft, a set of blankets and pillows on the floor in front of the table as his bed until they could get a mattress.

His eyes wandered to the gun still resting on the table beside him. He could have lost Penny today. He could have lost Julietta. The memory of her lying at the bottom of the stairs flashed through his mind, his heart once more in his throat.

Shaking his head, he glanced over to the bed where the girls slept. They were sound asleep, Julietta a protective arm resting on little Penny beside her. He bowed his head. Things could have gone so wrong.

Resting his arms on the table he took his head in his hands, running them down his face. He would have done it, killed Mr. Turner. His hand was on the trigger, ready. The five seconds, that wasn't to give Turner the chance to run; it was only to steady his nerves for the inevitable. He could see it in the man's eyes. Turner wasn't taking no for an answer, and neither was he.

He had suspected Penny had been through something horrible. Julietta had told him enough about the condition she was in when she first arrived. Hearing Byron's story, as vague as it was, shook him further. Who in their right mind would do this to children, to families, to people? It made him feel sick.

The hold he had kept on himself finally broke, tears falling.

What if Byron hadn't shown up? If the gun hadn't fired? Penny could have been caught. The Mayor could have more seriously injured Julietta. Turner could have spotted us in town. What if Byron and Marisa didn't get the chance to warn us? Could Byron have stopped this if he hadn't panicked? Could I have done something different to change this? What if—

His thoughts were interrupted by a small hand coming to rest on his arm. He jumped slightly, only to relax, finding it to be Penny staring up at him.

"Penny," Charles sighed, his exhaustion sinking deeper into him. "You should be asleep. You've had a long day."

Penny climbed into his lap.

"Did you have a nightmare?"

The little girl shook her head.

"Worried about Julietta?"

She shook her head again.

"What woke you?"

She reached up, wiping away a few tears from his face.

"I'm sorry. I didn't mean—"

He stopped, Penny, shaking her head. Wrapping her arms around him she gave him a tight hug. Charles closed his eyes, hugging her back and letting his tears fall.

"I'm all right, Penny. We are going to be all right," he whispered, his heart feeling lighter. After a few moments, he opened his eyes, tears subsiding.

Penny shifted in his arms, resting her head against his chest. It wasn't long before she was sound asleep. Leaning back in the chair, Charles smiled sadly. He sat there for a moment, letting his mind finally rest before carefully rising. Laying Penny beside Julietta, he sighed. "Thank you."

Moving the gun closer to the front of the table, he retrieved his knife, setting it beside the weapon. He glanced once more at the door, before lying down facing it. They were safe. His girls were safe. Closing his eyes, he took a deep breath before slowly falling into a dreamless sleep.

Julietta lay awake. She had awoken when Penny had but had remained silent, watching. She looked on as Penny climbed into Charles's lap, witnessing his silent tears, his facade of strength broken when he thought no one would see. Her heart broke, then mended, as Penny, wise beyond her cycles, wiped them away and hugged him while he cried, eventually falling asleep in his arms.

Charles was a good man. She hadn't realized how much she had come to trust him, to care about him, during the past couple of months. As Charles rose to put Penny back to sleep, she closed her eyes so as not to be discovered.

When she opened them again, he was preparing for bed, assuring the gun and his knife were in arms reach. They were safe. Mr. Turner was dead, and Mayor Harrison soon to be punished. Yet here was Charles, their friend, and guard. She debated for a moment calling to him, but as she saw him fall into sleep, she thought better of it. He needed rest as much as she did. Closing her eyes, she hugged her Penny beside her. *I—We got you, Penny. We won't let anyone take you away again. Promise.* It was those words she let sit in her mind as she too drifted off into a dreamless sleep.

CHAPTER 11

Julietta was sitting on the bed, braiding Penny's hair, while Charles was drinking coffee at the kitchen table, when Byron arrived.

"I'm sorry to keep you waiting. Harrison has been detained and in the interim, the town has agreed for me to act as de facto mayor. I spent the better half of the morning answering questions about what happened."

Penny frowned hearing this.

Byron shook his head. "I only told them Harrison was trying to get you sent to the capital school, Miss Penny. I didn't tell them the whole truth, not yet anyway."

Penny nodded, still looking upset.

"Penny, why don't you head up to the workshop and continue on the radio," Julietta suggested.

She thought about it for a moment before nodding and heading for the ladder. Once they were sure she was out of earshot, they began discussing.

"I know it upsets her," Julietta started. "As much as I'd like to know her story, I don't—"

"I understand," Byron sighed.

"I am guessing it was nothing like these photos?" Charles set down his mug, pushing the papers he was reading toward Byron.

Picking them up, the older man's eyes narrowed. "Where did you get these?"

"War Exhibit. I came across them on accident while researching the soot components. Turns out those are from a test bomb."

"Is there more?" he asked, sounding curious.

"It's better if I show you."

"Lead the way."

Charles led Byron and Julietta straight to the display case. Byron stood silently for a few minutes, scouring the faded text. "So, it's been done before." He turned to face Julietta and Charles. "Rho-597, Kappa-139, Psi-990…they are all part of this…system of facilities."

"What exactly do they do at these places?" Julietta questioned, crossing her arms.

Byron's eyes echoed the emotion in his voice. "Three cycles after Francis was taken, I learned the truth. Ola did her best to help me. I stayed in the capital while she worked her magic, figuratively speaking, to get herself moved to Rho-597. By the time she got there, however, my son had already been transferred to a new facility: Psi-990."

He paused, letting the memory fade. "She did her best to find the location, but higher security protocols had been put into place. With no leads, I was a mess, helpless. Ola knew about my chemistry background and decided it would be better and more efficient if I worked with her at the Institute. My eyes were opened that day, and my heart broken."

Charles felt Julietta brush against him, nervous on her feet as he continued.

"The children in Rho-597 were indeed highly gifted intellectually, many wise beyond their cycles. They were also, for lack of a better word, Arcane, as you call it, Charles. Every child had an…ability. Some could manipulate water, others earth. Some could levitate small objects with their minds. It was astonishing and terrifying."

The memory of little Penny generating electricity to bring Nelson to life flashed through Charles's mind. The feelings of excitement and fear from that night rushed through him once more.

"I was first assigned as a general chemist. My job was to develop and stabilize some rather unusual concoctions for some unknown purpose. I later learned they were used in…testing the children," Byron's voice faded, his head bowing.

"When I realized what my work was being used for, I vowed to find a way to help these kids, even as I couldn't help my own. Working with Ola we started to formulate a plan to help make the children's lives a bit more comfortable, and less frightening. I wanted to break them out, but we didn't have the resources."

Julietta's gaze fell, finding herself unable to look at Byron. "It took seven cycles for us to earn enough trust, enough allies to plan and stage an escape. It...it was around this time I met Miss Penny."

Charles and Julietta both stood up a bit straighter.

"She was only about four or five Dust then, one of the youngest I'd seen brought in. I was assigned to her as one of her attendants. Basically, a scientist meant to monitor her progress with her powers and learning. She was so frightened when I first met her. I don't know exactly what her circumstances were, they never gave us the children's history. They didn't want us to get attached."

A few tears escaped Byron's eyes. "We staged the escape to happen overnight about five cycles ago. We thought we had everything in place, but some failed to appear when they said they would. Our allies betrayed us, and Ola was caught while I made my escape. Injured and weak I wandered the wastes until I came to Waterwealt, barely settling. I set myself up here, healed, and plotted ways to get back to Rho-597. Then, about a cycle later, you showed up, Julietta. When you started working in the museum, I had hoped you would eventually come across a radio so I could try to contact some of our external allies, but then the Mayor kept you so busy and I didn't know how to start explaining."

"That's...that's why you made sure I helped with the water? You wanted me to stay to help get you a radio?" Julietta frowned.

"Yes, initially. Then I came to know you and realized you may actually be an ally if I could ever get the courage to explain. In fact, I was about to seek you out when Penny appeared. I almost didn't recognize her for how much she grew in three cycles, but I could never forget the necklace she wore."

"Necklace?" Charles quirked an eyebrow.

"Her penny?" Julietta queried.

"Each child in the facility was given a medallion with a symbol related to their power. It's sort of a catalog system they used. Metal being a precious commodity, they used old coins. Penny being electrically inclined—"

"Is Penny her real name?" Julietta asked.

"It is the name she responds to," Byron replied, solemnly. "When Penny came to Waterwealt, I knew I needed to keep her safe, but I couldn't be the one to do it. If anyone recognized me, she would be at risk. So, I brought her to the museum—"

"You…you were the one who left her at my door?" Julietta looked shocked.

"It was the hardest thing I've ever had to do." His voice cracked. "I knew she needed someone to take care of her and you were the only one I trusted."

Julietta fell silent, unsure what to make of this information.

"She needed someone kind and caring, but someone who also wasn't tied up in Waterwealt or close to me." Byron's shoulders slumped. "I don't regret my decision for a minute. Every time I see her with you, Julietta, and now you, Charles, I know she is safe."

"I am…honored you chose me." Julietta finally said, her voice barely above a whisper.

"I could think of no better people," Byron smiled sadly. "I'm sorry for having kept this secret so long, but after losing my Francis, and witnessing what I have…"

"Trust is hard to come by." Charles sighed, shaking his head.

"That it is," Julietta agreed. "So, now that we know all this, what do we do?"

"Well, I need that radio working for a start. Also given your museum seems to have knowledge about past schools like this—"

"What is Penny's symbol?" Charles asked, curiously.

"If I remember correctly, it's something with circles and arrows?" Byron's brow furrowed, thinking hard. "Sorry, it's been cycles. The symbols were something I didn't get a chance to research."

"It's two circles with arrows coming off of them," Julietta confirmed.

"That…sounds familiar." Charles's eyes wandered, his mind turning. "Do…do you think she'd let me see it?"

"Maybe?" Julietta shrugged. "Would it help us?"

"Any information is useful information," Byron added.

"Then let's find out."

Penny was sitting at one of the workshop tables, tinkering away at the radio. She was nearly ready to test it when Charles, Julietta, and Byron appeared.

"How's the radio coming, Penny?" Charles asked, cheerily.

Penny smiled, reaching for a battery.

"Before you do that, could I ask you something?" Charles crouched beside her so he was at eye level with her. "Could I see your necklace?"

Penny froze, thinking for a moment.

"It's all right if you don't—"

She shook her head. Slowly she removed the penny from beneath her shirt and held it out to Charles.

His eyes immediately lit up with recognition. "Fire?"

Penny frowned, a look of concern crossing her face.

"Thank you. I appreciate you showing me." Charles patted her shoulder as he stood. "Did you know, Penny, that is an alchemy symbol?"

Penny looked down at the coin, curiously, shaking her head.

"Alchemy is a very old form of chemistry. It was how we explained chemicals and the like before we knew what chemistry was. It was an early form of Arcane study."

She quirked an eyebrow.

"Fire? She is marked with the alchemy symbol for fire?" Julietta scratched her head, clearly confused.

"Fire is closely linked with electricity," Byron replied. "I'd be curious if there would be something more."

"Another thing to research," Charles shrugged. "But first I believe Penny wanted to show us her work?"

Penny was smiling once more, nodding happily as she charged the battery between her fingers. After a minute of this, it was ready. Placing it in the slot on the side of the repaired radio she flipped the on switch. Static. Adjusting a few knobs, the static grew louder then softer until a mumbled voice began to fade through. Curious, Penny kept adjusting until finally a low female voice was heard.

"The second bomb test should be ready within the next cycle. If it is as successful as the first, then we will be discussing phase two of the plan and the next-gen payloads we've been working on."

Everyone was silent; the only sound in the room was the static from the radio. Byron moved first. Reaching for a scrap piece of paper and a pencil lying on the table he scribbled down the dial numbers Penny had tuned to.

"What...why?" Charles shook his head, dumfounded.

"It wasn't a fluke." Julietta bit her lip. "There was a part of me that hoped..."

"No, it wasn't," Byron sighed.

Penny looked scared. Jumping off the chair she ran for the ladder, disappearing into the loft before anyone could move.

"Penny..." Julietta made to follow only to be stopped by Byron.

"Let her. It's probably best she doesn't hear what we discuss now."

"As in, what do we do now?" Charles crossed his arms, leaning against the table. "Is there anything we can do?"

"No, there isn't. Not until I can reach my contacts, at least." Byron switched off the radio. "I need time with this to try and find their stations. It's been cycles, there is no way they are using the same frequencies as before."

"There has to be something we can do," Julietta huffed, sounding annoyed.

"We could research," Charles suggested.

"Research what? How to stop a bomb?"

"No, but if we look into what they could be creating maybe we can figure out at least what we are potentially up against. I already know some basics from researching the soot problem."

"That and what the schools of the past were looking into." Byron shrugged. "Any information is good information. At this point, we are between a rock and a hard place."

Their conversation was interrupted as Penny returned to the workshop, Nelson in hand.

"Miss Penny has something important to tell you. Miss Penny knows something about the bombs." The three adults froze in place as Nelson continued. "Miss Penny, though small, remembers overhearing some of the attendants in Rho-597 talking about bombs. They used to mention something called Iso-210 with HL-138. They would say it was dangerous and highly unstable. They also would mention the word genome and some strange-sounding long words that made no sense to her."

"That doesn't sound good," Charles frowned. "No idea what Iso or HL could be, but genome...that's genetics."

"Genetics? I mean they were studying—" Julietta stopped, her eyes glancing over to Penny who somehow seemed so small at that moment.

"More to research." Byron interrupted, heading for the hatch. "I need to get back to Waterwealt and question Harrison about what Turner told him. In the meantime, if you and Charles can do some digging on what we know and see if we can puzzle this out, that would be great. I'll be back to try the radio during the week."

He paused at the ladder. "For now, this will be our secret. No one needs to know about the pending bomb, and no one should know about Penny's ability."

"Agreed." Charles ran a hand through his hair, nervously.

Julietta frowned but nodded in agreement.

"Good. I'll be by later this week to test the radio. Here's hoping it won't be long before we have some answers."

Byron was worried. First the schools, now this? When the bomb had gone off at the start of the Hot season he had been deeply concerned, but when nothing came of it, it became background noise to his more pressing matters.

He hadn't remembered seeing much of anything regarding bombs in Rho-597, but then again, Penny had been there for three cycles after him. The chemical concoctions he used to make for the machines, were they related? What did the machines do? He never saw anyone physically hurt by the machines, at least not when he was present. Was this all connected?

His mind was still quite distracted when he arrived in Waterwealt and was almost immediately accosted by several citizens asking him questions about Mr. Turner, Harrison, Julietta's museum, Penny, and the like. He assured them he was looking into it, that there was nothing wrong with the museum, and that he was planning to talk to Harrison about what exactly happened.

The only people who knew the truth about what had happened to Mr. Turner were Julietta, Charles, Penny, himself, and Oliver Healey who had helped get rid of the body. As far as anyone else knew, after Harrison was caught trying to forcibly take Penny, Mr. Turner ran off.

Heading straight for what was considered the town jail, Byron finally shook his trailers. He needed to talk to Harrison, and it needed to be done alone.

Entering the room where Harrison was being held, he closed the door behind him with an audible click.

"So, you've decided I'm worth talking to now, huh?" Harrison scowled. He was sitting on a chair beside a small desk, holding his bandaged arm. It wasn't just the bullet wound he was sporting, however, as it seemed the men of the town hadn't been so gentle bringing him in, his left eye black and visible bruises on his arms.

"You are in deep trouble, Max. I suggest you be compliant."

"And why should I? What are you going to do?"

Byron shifted his duster, revealing the gun at his waist.

Harrison shrunk. "What do you want to know?"

"What did Mr. Turner tell you?"

"What do you mean?"

"What did he tell you to get you to be so hell-bent on sending away our poor children?"

"You know as well as I do, Byron, Waterwealt is nothing. I simply thought I'd be doing the children a favor. The capital, after all—"

It took every ounce of Byron's patience not to smack the man. "Harrison, do you honestly believe I think that was your motive?"

"You give me no credit, Byron."

"I give you as much as you deserve, now tell the truth. What did Turner offer you?"

Harrison paused, shaking his head. "Should have just asked that question first."

"Well?"

"He offered me the chance to put Waterwealt on the map. To be honest, I didn't very much pay attention to what he was talking about. Something about a fancy school for smart kiddos in Apolis. I couldn't care less 'til he offered me some money and a promise to send engineers."

Byron's blood boiled. "You were willing to give up our town's kids for some lousy money and a promise?"

"Waterwealt is slow in progress. Little Miss History-Junk over there is far too concerned with that little girl to be of much use, and don't get me started on the magic man. Come to think of it, you haven't helped much being a scientist either."

Byron stepped closer, causing Harrison to sink back further into his chair.

"Julietta and Charles are fine people, better than most and certainly better than you. What have you done for this town, Maxwell? Forced people to do work? Scared poor little Ken and Leah into thinking they'd be taken away? And don't get me started on that stunt you pulled with Penny."

"Mr. Turner was most curious about Penny. I told him she wasn't worth his time, little thing doesn't even speak. What good—"

The leash on Byron's anger snapped as he smacked Harrison across the face. "Don't you EVER talk about Penny like that!"

Harrison was stunned. "You—you must care about that girl. Why?"

Byron took a deep breath, steeling his nerves back into submission. "I had a child, Harrison. I wasn't about to let anyone else lose theirs."

Harrison's gaze dropped, finding a spot on the floor interesting. "I just…I wanted Waterwealt to thrive."

"But not at the cost of others. Have you forgotten the well?"

Harrison went silent.

"How many people died because you didn't listen? Because you were so worried about progress?"

The man refused to meet Byron's gaze, tears now in his eyes.

"Think about what you've done, Harrison. And be grateful I don't just throw your ass out to the wastes to see what it's really like to survive."

With that, Byron made for the door, leaving Harrison alone in his room, a broken man.

CHAPTER 12

Time passed, but the trouble didn't. Over the next few weeks, Charles and Julietta scoured the museum for anything and everything related to bombs, gifted schools, Iso, HL, and the like, but little to nothing could be found.

Byron, despite his now seemingly endless duties as mayor, found time each week to visit. He would get an update on any research, then spend time fiddling with the radio that now sat at a small desk in the loft. During many of these visits, Penny would join him, sitting on his lap while he adjusted the dials. She had taken it upon herself to write down the various channels he tried so he wouldn't try them again. Occasionally, he would tune into the channel that Penny had found originally, but there were no further transmissions.

In the course of one of their dial testing sessions, Byron mentioned the range seemed too short to fully check the frequencies, so Penny took that as a personal challenge to solve.

It was mid-afternoon, the Hot season, which should have ended a few days ago, decided to have one last push as a massive heat wave hit. This wouldn't have been so bad if not for the fact that the season had already been on the extreme end of hot, but was now made unbearable.

Julietta had kept Penny in the loft the majority of the day, ensuring the girl was drinking plenty of water and had a cool towel on her neck at all times. Meanwhile, Charles had made a trip into town to talk to Byron and pick up a few groceries.

In the weeks since the incident with Harrison, Julietta and Charles had taken to visiting the town separately, keeping Penny at the museum out of caution, something the young girl didn't protest.

The concern, they quickly realized, was not unwarranted. Where once they could find themselves exchanging pleasantries with most anyone, they now found themselves treated rather coldly. It was as if someone flipped a switch. Though most seemed to outright ignore them, those who did dare acknowledge them often asked about Penny, very prying questions, that left Charles and Julietta fumbling for a non-answer that would satisfy them.

Leaving Penny in the loft, Julietta spent some time in the workshop, melting as usual, working on a small restoration project for Charles. He had mentioned to her not long ago about some medical equipment: a device called a stethoscope, some scalpels, and a few other small handheld devices that he wished could be restored to replace his rather old medical set. Over the last couple weeks, she had snuck down to the Medical Wing to retrieve them and began working on restoring them.

She had just finished sharpening a scalpel and placing it in her hiding spot when she heard Charles climbing the ladder.

"Hey, you okay up here?" Charles panted, hot and sweaty.

"I should be asking you the same thing," Julietta chuckled. "I'm all right."

"Been drinking enough water? Cold towel?"

"Yes, and yes, Dr. Hawthorne," she teased, reaching for a spare clean towel and wetting it. "From the looks of you, you could use one."

Charles gave her a grateful smile as she placed the towel on the back of his neck. "I put the groceries away downstairs. Penny is busy with her radio. Figured I would get some water and come check on you." He handed her one of the bottles of water he was holding before taking a drink from the other. "Anything new?"

"Nothing new, and thanks." Julietta wiped the sweat from her brow, taking a sip. "Ended up just fiddling with a few small things today up here rather than continuing to search given this place feels like an oven."

"Town was no better."

"People still being nosy?"

"Too nosy. It took me nearly 10 minutes to shake Marius off. He wouldn't stop asking about Penny."

"Had the same problem with Ira the other day. Marisa told me some people started harassing her and Oliver too. They refused to say anything about Turner and obviously, they don't know anything about Penny."

"Just as well. Don't want to drag anyone else into this." Charles flopped down on the couch. "However, we do need to talk."

"What's up?" Julietta leaned on the table in front of him.

"Has Penny said anything to you?"

"About?"

"About Rho-597?"

Julietta shook her head. "No, why?"

Charles shrugged. "Would be easier to find information if she'd just tell us what—"

"I am not asking her, Charles. That is non-negotiable," Julietta spat.

"Easy, I wasn't saying you should. I was just saying if we had some more information, it would be easier…"

"It would be but it's not happening."

"I know," Charles frowned, brushing some sweaty hair from his forehead. "Sorry, I'm just on edge. We are in Dust now, well supposed to be, and the radio transmission said within the next cycle the next bomb test will be ready. And don't get me started with this heat."

"I get it." Julietta deflated. "But what can we really do? We don't even know where they plan on dropping this next test bomb. Heck, we don't know where the first was dropped."

"Exactly. That's part of the problem. We are hitting a dead end with the limited information here. Maybe—maybe we should consider leaving."

Julietta's eyes went wide. "Leave Waterwealt? And go where?"

"Not sure, maybe another settlement or a city?"

"I don't think that's a good idea. Byron wants us to research here in the museum."

"We have, from top to bottom. Honestly, I don't think we are going to find anything else here. Plus, how much longer do we have until someone comes looking for Turner?"

"You realize what you are suggesting is insane, right? It's crazy to want to leave."

"Is it, though?" Charles stood, looking a bit flustered. "Turner was supposedly a government agent. There is an explosives test about to go off sometime in the next cycle and we can't get a hold of anyone who can help. That last test was close enough to cause trouble. This whole situation is a ticking time bomb."

"Please don't call it that," Julietta flinched. "The museum is safe, Charles. It's a sturdy structure full of knowledge if we only can find it. There are still displays and papers we haven't read. I'm sure if we just keep looking—"

"Some answers can't be found in the past, Julietta."

"Then where can they be found, Charles? In magic?"

Charles's eyes went wide. "Arcane!"

"You're delusional."

"I'm delusional? Just because I am worried about the future, I am delusional. What about you?"

"What about me?"

"Miss 'all the answers lie in the past.' You are so stuck in history you can't even see in front of your own nose."

"Excuse me, this museum has given us a lot of answers."

"It's also given us more questions."

"You are crazy."

"And you're just a stuck-up history snob who won't face the fact that history is dead and gone and can't be brought back."

"Is that what you think of my work? That it's useless?" Julietta growled, her eyes blazing with anger. "Says the magic man."

"ARCANE ISN'T MAGIC!" Charles shouted, breathing heavily. "I'm not—"

Julietta took a step back, shocked.

Realizing the heat and his frustration were getting the best of him, Charles took a deep breath making for the ladder. "I need to go—"

"Go?" she stepped between him and his exit. "What do you mean go? You are just going to abandon Penny and—"

"No!" He paused, once more, containing himself. "No, I am going to take a walk to cool off. Us shouting at each other is going to get us nowhere." He pushed past her heading down the ladder.

Her last statement echoing in her ears, Julietta froze, deep regret setting in. "Charles…"

He was filling his canteen at the sink.

"Charles, wait…"

"I need to go cool off. I'll be back later," he growled, grabbing his duster and putting it on.

She was about to protest when her eyes landed on the open loft door. "Penny?"

91

"What about her?"

"I told her to keep the door closed to keep the heat out." Julietta moved to the entryway, looking around desperately.

"She probably just went to the electronics exhibit for more radio parts," Charles mumbled.

Julietta turned back. Glancing over to Penny's bed, her heart dropped. "Her bag is gone."

Charles stopped dead in his tracks.

"Her bag and Nelson are gone."

"That's…" Charles's eyes went wide, his anger gone in an instant, replaced with dread. "I'll take the second floor, you start on the third. I'll meet you in the atrium."

Failing to find any sign of Penny on the second floor, Charles rushed through the first, finally meeting Julietta at the main desk.

"Any—"

"No!" Julietta panicked.

"She can't have gotten far."

The wind outside began to whistle, a sign of a dust storm inbound.

"We need to go." Charles ran up to the loft, Julietta trailing behind.

Tossing her a canteen of water, he grabbed his bag. "There are only two places I can think she'd go. She's smart, and wouldn't go too far with a storm incoming."

"The abandoned buildings on the south side of town and the rocky plateau." Julietta answered, breathlessly, finishing dressing and packing her bag.

"I'll take the rocks," Charles offered, worry plain in his voice. "We'll find her. I promise."

The storm had whipped into a frenzy. The only respite was the various outcroppings that occasionally blocked out the wind. Charles had already spent the better half of two hours searching the various caves in the rocky plateau. Knowing it would be foolish to continue to search in the peak of a dust storm, he reluctantly resigned himself to seeking shelter in one of the nearby caves. He was about to enter a fairly large one, when he heard a strange sound coming from one a bit further away.

Hope renewed, he battled the wind and dust, finding a smaller crevice hidden between two large rocks. Squeezing through into the dim cavern beyond the sound became clearer. It was a child, crying.

"Penny…" Charles got on his knees, crawling deeper in.

"Penny? Penny!" His heart leapt into his throat. Hidden in a dark corner of the rock outcropping, smartly out of the storm, sat Penny, curled up holding Nelson.

"Oh, Penny, thank the heavens." He breathed a sigh of relief, crawling closer, shielding the entrance from the raging wind.

Spotting Charles, Penny's eyes filled with tears as she crawled toward him and into his awaiting arms.

"It's all right Penny, I got you."

He sat holding her tightly, until the sound of the wind outside began to fade.

"We'll wait here for the storm to let up a bit more. Then I'm taking you home, okay?" He was crying.

Penny nodded, snuggling more into him, holding him as tight as her arms could.

After a few more minutes, the wind seemed to be dying down to a reasonable speed. "Thank goodness. Come on, Penny, let's—"

Charles's relief was short-lived, as a low rumble reached their ears. A heartbeat later they were both nearly knocked over as something shook the earth. The sound of rocks and soil being knocked loose echoed from above. Thinking fast, Charles pulled Penny in close, using himself to protect her from the falling debris.

As the dust settled, Charles groaned. "Penny?"

The little girl gazed up at him, eyes full of concern, but unharmed. Not wanting to wait to find out what it was that shook them, he quickly dusted himself off, maneuvering himself and Penny to a taller part of the crevice.

"Hang on tight." With a pained grunt, he scooped her up. With her secured, he undid his scarf to cover her head, hoping to keep most of the thankfully settling dust out of her face. "Let's go home."

CHAPTER 13

Julietta's heart was racing. There had been no sign of Penny in the abandoned buildings, and she had been forced to seek shelter until the storm finally began to let up. Hoping to the heavens Charles had better luck, she forced herself to head home if only to resupply before venturing out once more.

Arriving at the museum, her heart sank. No one was there. She was about to head up to the loft, when the museum door thrust open.

"Penny, Charles!" She was immediately to their side. "Are you both all right?"

"She's…fine…" coughed Charles, taking a pained step forward. "Just…frightened."

Realizing Charles was hurt, she took Penny from him. "Come on, let's get you two upstairs."

Julietta helped Charles over to the sink, turning on the water before setting Penny down on the bed.

"Are you hurt, Penny?" Julietta asked, her attention split between the girl and Charles.

Penny shook her head, pointing to Charles.

"I know sweetie, I'll help him in a second."

Penny shook her head more forcefully, pointing again to Charles.

Julietta grabbed some spare clothes she kept stored under Penny's bed. "I'm going to help Charles, you go get cleaned up and changed, all right? Come get me if you need me."

Penny took the clothes, giving one last pointed look to Charles before vanishing into the bathroom.

Charles was still coughing rather harshly. "Charles…" She grabbed a towel, wetting it.

"I'm fine…just a little…dust. Nothing serious." He spat some water into the sink before taking another drink. "That's…better," he sighed, sounding out of breath.

Without a word, she guided him over to a chair, starting to wipe the sand and grit from his face. "What happened?" She frowned, seeing a bruise forming on his cheek. "You're hurt."

"I found Penny in the rock outcroppings. Something shook it and knocked some rocks loose. I took the hit." Seeing the worry in Julietta's eyes, he gave a pained smile. "Important thing is, Penny is fine."

Julietta shook her head, biting her lip. "Just rest a minute."

Charles closed his eyes, remaining silent as she continued to gently wipe away the dirt from his face. Within a minute, however, she noticed him leaning more to his right, his face pained.

"Here, let's get you out of your duster." Helping him slide it off, her eyes went wide. From the back of his neck disappearing into his shirt were bruises.

"Charles…"

"They'll heal," he grunted, dropping his jacket to the floor. "Like I said, the important thing is Penny…"

Penny appeared, holding Nelson tightly, tears in her eyes.

"Penny…" Charles frowned. "It's all right, Penny, I'm okay."

Penny slowly approached. Setting Nelson on the table, she gingerly climbed into Charles's lap. Julietta noticed Charles wince as she settled herself, but he didn't complain, instead wrapping an arm around her back to steady her.

"Penny…are you all right?" Julietta crouched so she was at eye level with the girl.

Penny shook her head. Reaching for Nelson, she turned him on. "Hello, Miss Penny."

As usual, Penny whispered to Nelson, so quiet only he could hear.

"Miss Penny would like me to inform you she is not hurt but is very sorry. She didn't want Charles to get hurt. She didn't want anyone to get hurt."

"It's all right. I'm fine." Charles leaned back slightly in his chair. "The important thing is that you are home safe now."

Penny once more whispered to Nelson.

"Miss Penny says she knows it was wrong to run away, but she was scared and didn't know what to do."

Julietta took Penny's hand. "Scared? Why were you scared?"

"Miss Penny says that she heard you and Charles fighting about something. She heard her name and thought she did something wrong."

Charles and Julietta looked at each other, defeated.

"No, Penny, we weren't fighting because of you." Julietta shook her head. "Sometimes grown-ups disagree about things, and they argue."

"Miss Penny says she was scared because she heard Charles say he needed to leave."

Charles's heart sank. "Penny..."

Penny's eyes filled with tears.

"Miss Penny doesn't want Charles to leave. Miss Penny loves Charles and Julietta."

"Penny, I wasn't going to leave. Not for good." Charles grunted, mentally kicking himself. "I was going to take a walk to calm down. I felt bad for yelling at your mom and wanted to clear my head before we talked it out."

Penny remained quiet for a moment, Julietta reaching up and wiping her tears. "Sometimes, grown-ups say things they don't mean," she explained, giving a regretful look to Charles. "Sometimes they need a minute to think and step away, but they come back. Charles was never going to leave for good."

"Never, Penny," Charles echoed.

Penny whispered to Nelson again.

"Miss Penny is very sorry for scaring you. She just wanted everyone to be happy."

"Oh Penny," Julietta smiled sadly. "We are all right. Charles and I are all right."

"Of course we are." Charles winced a bit as he shifted slightly. "Your mom and I will always be all right."

Setting Nelson on the table, Penny leaned into Charles, resting her head on his chest.

Julietta moved to take her, but Charles shook his head. "It's all right." He rested his arm gently around the girl.

"Stay?" Penny asked, voice barely above a whisper.

Charles and Julietta froze.

Penny looked up at Charles sadly. "Charlie stay with Momma Julie and Penny?"

Charles looked at Julietta, tears in his eyes. Her expression was the same.

"Of course, Penny." He hugged her tightly as he dared. "I'll stay, so long as you and your Momma want me to."

"Of course, he is going to stay." Julietta laughed despite herself, tears streaming down her face.

"Miss Penny...would you like me to tell them?" Nelson asked.

Penny nodded, closing her eyes.

"Miss Penny wants me to tell you she loves you both. She thanks you for protecting her and making her feel safe."

Julietta stood, mindful of Charles's bruises, wrapping her arms around them. "We love you too, our lucky Penny."

"We love you too," echoed Charles.

Penny yawned, snuggling more into his chest.

He chuckled. "I think our lucky Penny needs a rest."

"Come on, Penny. You can sleep in my bed for now. Okay?"

After putting Penny in bed, Julietta turned back to Charles just as he was rising to his feet.

"Are you all right?" She whispered, deep concern in her voice.

Charles held up a finger to his lips, gesturing to the hallway.

Closing the loft door softly behind him, Charles leaned against the wall beside it.

"Are you sure you are all right?"

"I'm fine. Listen, Julietta, I—"

"Jul or Julie."

Charles raised an eyebrow. "I'm all right, Jul. Just need some rest. Bruises heal quick enough."

Julietta's gaze fell to the floor, one hand coming to hold her other arm at her side. "Thank you, for finding her."

"Of course. I'd protect that girl with my life."

"I know."

There was a silent pause.

"Jul, listen, I—"

"Charles, I'm sorry."

Charles remained silent, standing up a bit straighter.

"I...I don't think you are delusional." She rubbed the back of her head. "I don't think you are a lunatic or crazy or...any of those things.

97

I know you would never abandon us. It was a stupid thought. I was...I am...scared." She took a deep breath, shaking her head. "I lashed out at you, and it was wrong." Looking over to him she bit her lip. "Honestly, I love hearing about your Arcane theories. Cause deep down...there is a part of me that wants to believe that some things aren't meant to have answers. That there is wonder still in this world."

"I'm sorry too, Jul." Charles sighed, grimacing as he shifted on his feet. "I don't think you're a stuck-up history snob stuck in the past. I was...frustrated. More at myself than anything else. When you thought I was going to leave...I never meant to scare you like that. I'm scared too. As much as I love the unknown, it sometimes downright terrifies me." His gaze met hers. "That's why I love listening to you talk about the past and what you've learned, Jul. You really do bring it back to life."

Julietta took a step forward, Charles meeting her.

"Are...are we okay?"

He answered her by wrapping her in a hug. She reciprocated, a sigh of relief escaping her as she let herself relax into him.

"Charlie..."

Julietta froze, stepping back slightly, her arms still lightly around him. "Penny, she called you Charlie. I'm sorry Char—"

"You want to know why I never let anyone call me Charlie?" Julietta nodded.

"Back in Matson, everyone close to me called me Charlie. My parents, my friends, my colleagues...then they all—My parents died, my friends were taken, and my colleagues...When I was thrown out, I wanted to start fresh. I promised myself I would never let anyone call me Charlie again. I wouldn't let anyone be that close."

Julietta remained quiet, listening intently.

"I was Charles, a doctor, researcher, and wanderer." He closed his eyes, his hands resting on Julietta's arms. "I never thought I could let anyone call me Charlie. Thought I couldn't find that...trust and...comfort."

"Charles, I—"

"Charlie."

Julietta froze.

"Charlie," he repeated.

"Charlie..." Julietta echoed, voice shaking.

"I never thought I'd let anyone call me Charlie again, Jul." He opened his eyes, smiling. "And now I have two I want to."

The hold Julietta had on her tears broke. "Charlie…"

"I know I am not a perfect man, but I want you to know I care about you and your little girl. That I'd never let anything happen to either of you. I'd never leave unless you asked me to. I hope you—"

He stopped as Julietta's hands shifted, one coming to rest gently on his bruised neck, the other on the side of his face.

"I never expected you to be perfect. I'm certainly not; no one is." She shook her head. "You don't know how much it means to me to have you here. To see you with Penny warms my heart. I'm glad I asked you to stay when I did. Despite our fights and our differences, there is no one I'd rather have here with us than you. I…I want you to stay."

"Jul, I—"

Whatever Charles was going to say was lost as Julietta kissed him. Deepening the kiss, he wrapped his arms around her, holding her close.

"Charlie…"

"You do not know how long…"

"Probably as long." She chuckled, resting her forehead against his.

They stood there a moment, savoring each other's presence. "So about earlier…"

"Let's talk to Byron and Penny. This isn't something we can decide alone."

"Agreed." She relaxed, kissing him gently again. "So long as we are together, wherever we are, we'll be okay."

Charles brushed a stray piece of hair from her face. "Always."

The moment was interrupted by the sound of the loft door creaking. Looking over, they spotted little Penny peeking out, Nelson toddling out from behind her.

"Miss Penny heard your voices and wanted to make sure Momma Julie and Charlie were okay?"

"We are fine, Penny." Julietta laughed, looking deeply into Charles's eyes.

"More than," Charles smiled.

"Come on. I'll get you something for those bruises." Julietta took Charles's hand, neither one taking their eyes off the other, as they headed back into the loft.

CHAPTER 14

Weeks passed. As if to spite the lingering heat, the Dust season hurled itself in full force. Byron had come to visit the day after the storm. He was shocked to find Charles bruised, but was relieved once they shared what happened, knowing it could have been much worse. With him and Penny present, discussions began about Turner concerns, the lack of information, and the bomb threat. Byron agreed that leaving might be the best course of action, but he also pointed out the timing had to be right. It was concluded that for now, at least, they should continue their research while Charles recovered and Penny boosted the radio signal. By the end of the day, he'd left them with the promise to try to visit more often, and a list of frequencies for Penny to try in his stead.

And so, with a very loose plan, the three waited and worked. Charles, while continuing his studies, eventually stumbled across a small display about the human genome that pointed to a few other exhibits of related interest in the War Exhibit. With this breadcrumb, he followed the trail, finding himself spending his days scouring the War Wing for more.

Julietta's restoration projects kept her busy, including getting Charles's original gun working so they would have two. She had learned to shoot from Charles in the days following the incident with Mr. Turner.

It was another warm dusty day in Waterwealt. A few days prior, another storm had bore down on the poor town, leaving everyone stuck indoors until the night before. Charles had spent much of the evening digging out the front entrance, while Julietta tried in vain to clean up the ever-growing dust piles in the atrium.

Penny was sitting at her radio desk, tinkering away while Charles was still sound asleep on his mattress in front of the kitchen table.

Momma Julie had told her to leave him to sleep while she went up to the workshop to finish up something.

Placing another battery in the radio, she flipped the switch. Static, then nothing. Penny frowned, shaking her head.

"Another dead battery, Miss Penny?" Nelson, sitting on the desk beside her work, asked.

Penny nodded.

"That is the third one this week, Miss Penny. Do you think the batteries are too weak to handle the new modifications?"

Penny agreed.

"Are there more powerful batteries in the museum?"

Penny thought for a moment. Her exhibit was full of gadgets and gizmos run on battery power. Surely one of them had to have something strong enough.

"Maybe later you can get Julie and Charlie to help you search, Miss Penny."

Penny smiled, glancing over to where Charles slept. She was happy he had not left. He promised her he'd never leave. She shook her head, remembering how she misheard what the grown-ups had said. *Charlie and Momma Julie love Penny. They protect Penny. They will stay with Penny. They will help Penny.*

Kneeling beside his makeshift bed, Penny chuckled seeing how silly Charles's hair looked. Reaching out, she poked his cheek causing him to shift in his sleep, wiping a hand past his face before lying on his back.

Penny giggled. This time she placed her hand on his shoulder, shaking him slightly.

"So much dust," he mumbled, but did not wake.

Penny tried to shake him again.

"Pancakes..."

Penny found it very hard not to laugh. Sitting up a bit more, she attempted to place a hand on each of his shoulders when she slipped, falling onto his chest.

"Ah!" Charles startled awake. It took him a moment to realize it wasn't the roof coming down on his head, but Penny, who was giggling away.

"Oh, Penny," he sighed, running a hand through his hair.

Penny smiled at him, shifting so she rested her head on his chest more comfortably.

"You okay?" He yawned but smiled, brushing a piece of hair from her face.

Penny nodded, sticking her tongue out.

"Just wanted to wake me up, huh?"

She nodded again.

"Everything all right down there?" Julietta appeared at the open hatch to the loft.

"Yeah, Miss Penny here decided I needed to wake up," Charles chuckled, sitting up, Penny shifting to sitting beside him.

"Penny, I told you to let Charlie sleep."

"It's all right." He shook his head, looking up at the window. "What time is it?"

"About midday. You were exhausted so I figured I'd let you sleep."

"Thank you," he sighed, stretching.

"Since you are up, when you are ready, I have something to show you."

"I'll be up in a minute." He turned to Penny. "Mind moving my bed while I get myself situated?"

Splashing some water on his face, he looked up at the tall cabinet in the corner where Julietta had laid his knife and gun. Despite no immediate threat, Charles had still taken to sleeping with his knife beside him, the gun on the table. If Julietta got up before him, she'd always put them up there for safekeeping.

Slipping on his boots, he stowed the knife before grabbing the gun and holstering it. By the time he finished readying himself, Penny had pushed the mattress back under the table and folded the blankets neatly on it.

"Thanks, Penny," Charles smiled. "Let's go see what your mother's been up to."

Julietta was waiting for them at the far end of the workshop tables.

"Someone's been busy," Charles chuckled, noting the now very clean space.

"Needed to be done. There were so many bits and bobs everywhere I couldn't keep anything straight!"

"Bobs? Who's Bob? Should I be worried?" Charles teased, crossing his arms.

Julietta rolled her eyes, laughing. "The only thing you have to worry about, Dr. Hawthorne, is Penny trying to hide in that cabinet over there."

Turning behind him, he indeed spotted Penny trying to slip into one of the cabinets. "You, miss, are one little ninja."

Penny laughed, moving instead to stand beside Julietta.

"Now that we are all here, I have a surprise for you." Julietta opened a cabinet beneath the table and pulled out a small metal box. She had gone as far as to wrap some fabric around it like a bow.

He quirked an eyebrow. "A present?"

"What? Can't I get you a present?"

"What did I do to deserve such a thing?"

Penny stepped forward hugging Charles.

"I believe that answers that question," Julietta smiled.

He shook his head, hugging Penny back. "No gifts required for that."

"Regardless, open it."

Penny nodded her head furiously, stepping back.

"If you insist." He winked at Julietta, undoing the bow. His eyes went wide, however, as he opened the box. "Jul..."

"Surprise! I hope I did a good job. The scalpels and such were fairly easy. The magnifier thing, the oto—whatchamacallit—was a bit harder. Only one I am not sure is perfect is the stethoscope, I believe it's called?"

"Otoscope and stethoscope." He turned the various devices over in his hands, admiring them. "There is an easy way to find out." Setting down the otoscope, he placed the stethoscope around his neck. "Penny, how about a check-up?"

The girl jumped up and down with joy as he picked her up, sitting her on the table. Taking the otoscope in hand, he smiled. "All right, Miss Penny, let's see. Stick out your tongue and say 'ah.'"

Penny stuck out her tongue laughing, opening her mouth so he could look.

"Looks and sounds good," he smirked. "Now your ears."

Gently he turned her head looking into her right ear, then her left. "My, my, such a big brain you have in there. No wonder you are good at electronics."

This made Penny giggle more.

Setting down the otoscope he put the stethoscope in his ears. "Let's see now." He placed the circle piece on her chest. "Nice and strong. Do you want to hear?"

Penny nodded happily as he wiped off the earpieces before holding them by hers. Her eyes went wide hearing her own heartbeat.

Taking it back, he continued his exam. "Now for your lungs." First listening to her back then her neck he gave a nod of approval. "All sounds good. Now how about your head." Chuckling, he placed the circle on her head. "Hmm…interesting. You are thinking about chocolate chip cookies!"

Julietta at this point was finding it very hard not to laugh, Penny giggling away.

"How about your knees, hmm?" He pretended to listen to Penny's knees, then her elbows, making sure to tickle her there, causing her to laugh harder.

"Last but not least, the stomach!" Placing the circle on her stomach, he furrowed his brow. "Hmmm…Jul, I have a diagnosis!"

"Oh?" Julietta feigned concern.

"Yes. Miss Penny here is a perfectly happy and healthy child. BUT! I must insist you give her two CCCs."

"CCCs?"

"That's two chocolate chip cookies. Her stomach is growling at me!"

Any control Julietta had on her demeanor was lost, everyone laughing.

"If you think it will help, doctor," Julietta teased, shaking her head. "After lunch, you can have two CCCs, Penny."

Penny feigned pouting but couldn't hold the expression as Charles tickled her stomach.

"Speaking of lunch, why don't you go get the table ready, Penny? I'll be down with Charlie in a minute."

Penny looked up at Charles, waiting to be dismissed.

"All right, my little patient, you are free to go."

She hopped off the table, giving Charles and Julietta each a quick hug before heading for the ladder and disappearing into the loft.

Setting the stethoscope around his neck once more, Charles turned to Julietta, a bright smile on his face. "Thank you. They work flawlessly."

"Anytime." Julietta took a step closer. "Want to give me a quick check?"

He quirked an eyebrow. "I think we can skip the otoscope."

Julietta took the stethoscope, placing it in his ears before sitting herself on the table. "Do your worst, Dr. Hawthorne."

Stepping close, he placed the metal circle first on her back, then her neck, then her chest, his brow furrowing.

"Something wrong?" Julietta frowned, wondering if he actually heard something unusual.

"Your heart rate is elevated, and your breath is catching. It seems you have…Fallen-in love-itis."

"Why, you shameless flirt." Julietta stuck out her tongue. "Oh no, dear doctor, whatever shall I do?"

"Well, here is the thing. There is a worse part."

"Oh?"

"What you have is contagious." Removing the stethoscope from his ears, he cleaned it before placing it in hers. Taking her hand, he guided her to place the circle over his heart. "Cause I have it too."

Julietta stayed quiet for a moment, listening to the calming beat of Charles's heart. "Well doctor, tell me, what do we do?"

"There is no cure for it, but there are treatments we can try." A mischievous look danced in his eyes as he took the stethoscope from her, placing it once more around his neck.

"What treatment do you suggest we start with?"

He answered her by gently placing his hands on her face, kissing her tenderly.

Julietta sighed deeply into his lips, her arms moving around his neck as she returned the favor.

As they kissed, Charles's hands moved from her face, down her sides, to her hips. To his pleasure, she moved closer, letting his hands come to rest just under her shirt against her skin.

"Well, doctor, would you say this treatment is working?" Julietta moved her hands to his face, running a thumb over his cheek.

"That depends, how do you feel?"

"I don't know if I should tell you the truth. If I tell you I feel amazing, would you stop treatment?"

"Certainly not, that means the treatment is working," Charles lightly pressed his thumbs against her skin.

Julietta's eyes lit up. "Those are some healing hands you got there, doctor. I will say I've never had an exam quite like this."

"Neither have I."

Their moment was shattered by the sound of something hitting the floor in the loft. "Miss Penny, are you sure you need that bowl for a sandwich?" Nelson asked.

Both of them burst out laughing.

"That's our cue." Julietta slowly climbed off the table, only a hair breath away from Charles.

"Thank you, again." He kissed her cheek. "These will be extremely useful."

"You mean a lot to me and Penny. It's nothing." Julietta gave him a brief hug, before heading for the hatch. Just as she was about to climb down, she paused. "Would you say that I'm going to need a daily dose of that particular treatment, doctor?".

"Doctor's orders. Then maybe later on we can talk about more potent ones if needed."

"We'll see." Julietta winked as she began to descend the ladder leaving Charles to admire her gift to him.

CHAPTER 15

Finishing lunch, Penny, through Nelson, explained her need for a better battery. With not much else to do, they spent a few hours scouring for and successfully finding a few new batteries. By late evening, Penny had the radio running at higher frequencies.

The following day, after breakfast, they readied themselves for a visit to Waterwealt. It would be their first time going together since Turner had arrived.

"Penny, we are leaving in a few minutes. Hurry up!" Julietta shouted to the girl who was still in the washroom.

"Got everything?" Charles asked, packing his bag.

"Actually, I've been meaning to ask. Do you have a spare clip for the Sig Sauer?"

He paused, digging around in his bag for a moment before producing one. "Only spare I have. I take it you got the other one working?"

"Finished it a couple of days ago. Did a blank fire outside and it seems to be functional."

"Good. Let's hope you never have to use it."

She nodded in agreement, loading the clip and ensuring the safety was on before hooking it to her belt.

Penny appeared a moment later, dressed and ready to go.

The intense and almost weekly dust storms made the walk to town a bit more difficult and longer as they found themselves traversing rather unstable ground. Just as they reached the edge of town, they were surprised to run into Marisa.

"Julie, Charles, and Penny! What are you doing here?" Marisa's brow creased in concern.

"Stopping by Byron's, why?" Julietta replied, confused by her demeanor.

"But all three of you?"

"Yeah…" Charles shrugged.

"It's not safe." The woman shook her head. "Come with me to the bakery. I have much to tell."

At the bakery, Oliver was sitting on a chair beside the counter, looking rather exhausted. "Aren't you a sight for sore eyes. Been a while since I've seen the three of you together in town."

"Are you all right, Oliver?" Charles frowned, immediately taking off his bag. "You look ill."

"Just a bit tired."

"Mind if I give you a quick check? No charge."

He shrugged. Marisa gave Charles an approving nod. While he worked, she began to explain.

"Ever since the whole incident with Harrison the people 'round here have been on edge. Then Dust season blew in here as a nearly non-stop tornado makin' for bigger trouble. Folks 'round here are just all sorts of wound up."

"That's why we took turns coming in up until now." Julietta quirked an eyebrow. "But Penny's been patient and we figured it had been long enough since…"

"I thought the very same until a few days ago," Marisa huffed. "There have been strangers passing through town and they're askin' some strange questions."

Hearing this, Penny immediately clung to Julietta.

"It's all right," Julietta soothed. "What sort of strange things?"

"They seemed interested in some school over in Johani. A few asked if any of our town's children have been tested but everyone is keeping mum. Byron's been on alert day and night trying to keep 'em on the move."

"You say this happened earlier this week?" Julietta nervously bit her lip.

"Yes'm. The day after I saw you last. I know I said how much I missed seeing my little Penny and that maybe soon you could visit with her, but now—"

"Healthwise, he is okay. Bit of dust in the lungs but nothing too serious." Charles interrupted, having finished with Oliver. "Just need some more water and rest. What have you been up to?"

"Been helping Byron and the townsfolk with the dust. Doin' my best not to inhale it but, easier said than done."

"At this point, we all have some in our lungs." Charles sighed, shaking his head. "You need rest, Oliver."

"Don't worry, doc. I wasn't planning on going out today. Marisa was making sure of that."

"I told him what you told him, but he don't listen."

"You should listen to your missus," Charles chuckled, finishing packing up his tools. "She knows what she is talking about."

"Don't they always." Oliver winked.

"Here, let me get you three some sweet bread to go. You really shouldn't linger long."

"We are just planning on talking to Byron before heading home," Charles explained, glancing over to Penny.

Penny let go of Julietta, running over to him. He picked her up. The poor girl was shaking.

"It's all right, Penny. We'll just go see Byron and then head straight home, okay?" Charles soothed, giving Julietta a worried look.

"I'm sorry to frighten you, Miss Penny." Marisa looked crestfallen. "Here." She grabbed a few cookies and tossed them in the bag. "I really am sorry."

Julietta took the bag from her. "It's better we are all aware. Penny knows we won't let anything happen, right, Penny?"

Penny nodded her head, resting it again on Charles's shoulder.

"We should go. Thank you, Marisa. Take it easy, Oliver." Charles bid them farewell. Julietta echoed the sentiment as they headed out for Byron's, a feeling of uneasiness over all of them.

Byron was sitting at the front counter of his shop, looking rather haggard. Upon seeing the three enter, he shook his head. "Based on Penny, I am guessing someone has told you?"

"Marisa mentioned there have been people asking around about Johani," Julietta explained.

"Not just Johani, the children, Turner…seems you were right, Charles. People are coming looking."

"Wish I wasn't." He frowned, adjusting his hold on Penny. "What do we do?"

"That's what I've been wondering. Any updates?"

"I've been following a trail of displays regarding the genome. Started with a small exhibit in the far back of the medical wing. It pointed me to a few others in the war one. Apparently, in past conflicts, it wasn't unheard of for scientists to conduct human testing and forcefully cause genetic mutations." Charles paused, his stomach churning. "I won't go into detail, but let's just say I've had some sleepless nights after reading about those."

"I've been helping him with the documentation. It's…" Julietta grimaced. "I've also been working on restoring a few more things around the museum. Fixed up some better medical tools for Charlie. I have a working gun now. Also been collecting and repairing portable survival gear."

"You may need it, sooner rather than later at this rate." Byron leaned back in his chair, pensively.

Julietta's gaze fell, a part of her wishing that wasn't the case.

Charles nodded in confirmation.

"Question is, where and when do we leave?" He moved to lean on the counter. "Personally, with the bomb threat still lingering I am leaning more on the cautious side of waiting. On the other hand, with the townsfolk getting noisier by the day and travelers looking for Turner… and you, Charles."

His eyes went wide. "What do you mean, me?"

"A messenger came through with this. Said if I saw you to give it to you." He tossed an envelope on the counter.

"Penny, could you—" Charles didn't have to finish his statement as she was already shifting so he could set her down.

Grabbing the opened envelope he paused, noting the broken seal. "I presume you read it?"

"My apologies, but I wanted to ensure it was safe."

Charles nodded, pulling out a letter and three news clippings. His expression turned from confusion to upset as his eyes roved over them. "I can explain."

"I assume Julie knows?" Byron turned to Julietta whose face had paled.

"I told her about the former governor of Matson, about my failure." He swallowed a lump in his throat. "It was a case of lack of tools and resources."

"I trust you, Charles. You don't have to worry," Byron assured.

Charles said nothing more, replacing the envelope's contents.

"That being said," Byron continued, "Matson may very well be the location we head to. If the governor wants to see you, that could be an in for information. Question is, when do we leave?"

"You are serious?" Julietta crossed her arms.

"As serious as the day is dusty. I'll need time, at least a week or two to garner the necessary items for the journey. In the meantime, Miss Penny, I have some more frequencies for you to try once you've boosted the signal."

Penny, though still visibly shaken, nodded her head as he handed her a piece of paper with the frequencies.

"Penny wanted us to tell you she got the radio extension working last night," Julietta added, glancing over to Charles whose expression had gone blank.

"Then it won't be long," Byron sighed. "You better head out. I noticed another storm brewing on the horizon. It will likely hit tonight."

"Thank you." Julietta took Penny's hand, nudging Charles to follow.

"Thank you," Charles echoed numbly, his voice too soft as they departed, making for home.

"Penny, why don't you head upstairs and try those frequencies," Julietta suggested as they entered the atrium.

"Charlie…" she said, now sure the child had gone far enough ahead.

Charles leaned against the atrium desk, handing her the envelope. Removing its contents, she began to read. First was a letter from Governor Lisle Benedict. "She wants to meet with you to discuss your departure from the medical society?"

"Departure, more like forced removal," he sighed, finding a spot on the floor interesting. "Lisle Benedict was the person who got me ousted after…after I failed to save the life of Governor Archibald Winslow."

Julietta flipped through the news articles. The first was an article about Governor Winslow's death. It claimed he died of a gunshot wound, unable to be saved by the 'top doctor' of Matson. The article went on to question the merit of Charles, stating rumors of

Arcane methods being used rather than proper science leading to the Governor's death.

"Charlie, I'm so—"

"Keep reading."

She flipped to the next article. It was about the investigation launched after the governor's death by Governor Benedict. It talked about questionable methods used by Charles during the surgery. It also stated by the end that the accusations were deemed unfounded, and he was cleared of any wrongdoing.

"What did you do that they questioned?"

"There is one more article."

Scanning the last article, her face fell. Governor Benedict had taken great care with this article, painting Charles in a horrible light. Having known him now for nearly a season and a half, she knew none of the claims were true.

"These are all lies and exaggerations. I've heard you talk of these theories. They've been twisted and—"

"Do you want to know why Benedict claims I tried something Arcane?"

"Yes."

Charles shifted uncomfortably, his gaze still fixed on the floor. "When they brought Governor Winslow in, it was bad. Me and two other doctors, Henrietta Calhone and Victor Lawson, were called in to try and save him."

He shook his head. "Someone had gotten a hold of a working gun and shot him. Bullet gashed his arm and came to a stop in his side. He had already lost a lot of blood by the time we got to him. Lawson lost his nerve once I cut into Winslow's side to remove the bullet. Henrietta stayed but wasn't able to help much as she tried to keep Winslow breathing. None of us really knew what to do. I had read about gunshot wounds in books, but nothing could prepare me for the real thing."

Julietta moved to stand beside him, placing a hand on his arm. "Charlie…"

"I got the bullet out. Thankfully it had missed vital organs but by then he was fading fast. It would have taken too long to stitch him. I needed to stop the bleeding quickly, so I tried something never done before. I had come across in my various studies an explanation about a wound-sealing method called cauterization. You apply heated metal to the skin, essentially fusing it back together with a burn. Henrietta was against it but I knew it would be too late if I stitched him, so I went over her head. I used one of the lanterns in the room to heat a scalpel. At first, it seemed to be working, but before I could finish— we lost him. Too much blood loss." Tears sat on the surface of Charles's eyes. "He wasn't the first I'd lost. That comes with the territory. But his loss hurt the most."

"Sounds to me like you did what you could."

"Lisle didn't see it that way. With the gunman long gone, as far as I know never to be found, they needed an answer. When Henrietta admitted I tried a new method of wound closure that was their answer. I was brought up on misconduct, citing I used an untested medical procedure, accused of being Arcane by Lisle. Even after I showed everyone during the investigation the various medical books and old articles describing the procedure, some still didn't believe me. I may have been cleared of official wrongdoing, but the damage was done."

"You said yourself he would have died had you done the other method. You were desperate."

"Winslow was a friend and a good leader. I did everything I could." A few tears escaped.

"You did nothing wrong, Charlie. You tried to use actual medical procedures, whether they knew it or not." Julietta stood in front of him, placing a comforting hand on his arm. "I've spent enough time in the Medical and War Wings recently to know the procedure you are talking about. It was legitimate, just lost to time. It was just too late for him."

"Jul—"

"I've seen your notebooks and how you take care of people. I don't doubt for a second you made the right choice. You gave him the best chance. Unfortunately, time wasn't on your side."

"She wants to see me to discuss what happened." His voice broke, deep-seated fear within it. "Why? Why now?"

She reached up, wiping his tears. "I don't know. It does seem odd. The timing…"

"She's a governor, what if she heard about Turner? How did she even know I was here?"

"I—" She was at a loss for words.

"Jul, I feel—I feel like I'm putting you and Penny in danger."

"No, no you're not." Julietta embraced him tightly. "Don't think that, please."

He closed his eyes, taking a deep breath. "I am supposed to protect you."

"We protect each other." She rested her head on his chest. "If you go to Matson, we go to Matson. If you stay here, we stay here. We do this together, Charlie."

She felt Charles relax slightly, his arms wrapping around her. "Are you sure?"

"More than."

"I knew you would say that but I needed to get that off my chest." Charles's shoulders slumped as he opened his eyes. "But what about Penny? The wastes are dangerous for an adult, let alone a child."

"She is in danger whether we stay or go. She knows that, based on her reaction today."

"Poor kid." He shook his head. "What did she escape?"

"I don't know if I want to know."

"Somehow I think we will have to find out eventually." Charles kissed Julietta's forehead. "We should let her know what is going on. She may be only nine Dust, but she deserves to be kept in the loop, to a point."

"Yeah, better to let her process the idea of leaving than spring it on her." She let go of him, taking his hands. "You okay?"

"I will be." He gave her a sad smile. "Come on, let's go talk to our lucky Penny."

Entering the loft, both Charles and Julietta stopped dead in their tracks. Penny was sitting in front of the radio, crying.

"Penny, what—" Before she could finish, Penny flipped the switch on the radio, the dials set to an unrecognizable frequency.

There was brief static then…"bomb test…I repeat if anyone is list—there is…bomb tes—mid-Dust…unconfirmed loca—Skel..idge…I repeat…Skelter Ridge."

The room went silent as the broken voice repeated. There was another bomb test coming, likely within the next week, and it was heading for the rocky outcroppings Penny had hidden in—Skelter Ridge, far too close to home.

CHAPTER 16

C harles returned with Byron about a half hour later. "I know that voice." The older man's eyes lit up. "You've done it, Penny. You've found my contacts." He began fiddling with the radio, reaching for the voice transmitter. "Hello, hello, Ava? Can you hear me?"

The transmission repeated, still broken.

"It's not strong enough." Byron's brow furrowed.

"Bigger issue here is Skelter Ridge. That is only a few minutes from here." Charles frowned.

"I guess this means it's time to leave." He looked over at Penny who sat in Julietta's lap at the kitchen table. "We have to tell the town."

"We don't have to explain everything do we?" Julietta shifted uncomfortably.

"No, certainly not." Byron continued to fiddle with the dials. "Penny, you got any ideas to boost this?"

Penny thought for a moment, her eyes lighting up. Jumping off of Julietta she disappeared into the museum.

"What should we tell them?" Charles ran a hand through his hair. "We can't tell them about Penny or the school?"

"What if we tell them I was the one who found the radio and happened to find a working battery?" Julietta suggested.

"That sounds plausible to a point. The battery is a stretch, but most people don't understand your museum." Byron sighed, giving up on the radio.

Charles looked deep in thought. "Will they believe us that a bomb is inbound?"

"We have them listen to the transmission." Byron shrugged. "They make their own choice then. Simple as."

"What about us, then?" Julietta stood, placing herself beside Charles.

"Matson," Charles sighed, shaking his head. "It's only about a week and a half from here and is a large city. If who we are dealing with is smart, they wouldn't target a large city for a test. If this is the government doing this, then cities are the places to find information."

"Precisely," Byron concurred, giving Charles a sympathetic look. "I am glad to hear you agree."

Penny appeared a moment later holding what looked to be a small metal tree. Setting it on the table she turned on Nelson, whispering something to him.

"Miss Penny says this should work to boost the signal. It's called an antenna. The only concern she has is that it may cause problems with the battery."

"Worth a shot." Byron gestured to the radio as Penny hooked the piece.

Tuning once more to the frequency, Penny found the voice continuing its message, though much clearer.

"I repeat there is…bomb test. I repeat, if anyone is listening there is…expected mid-Dust. Unconfirmed location Skel..idge…I repeat… Unconfirmed location Skelter Ridge."

"Ava, this is B.G., do you read me?" There was static. "Ava, this is B.G. from Johani."

There was a bit more static. Then, "Byron? Is that really you?"

"Yes, it is."

"Orion."

"Canes Venatici."

"It is you…I—I thought you…dead."

"I wanted it that way," Byron grimaced. "Listen, Ava, we have a problem. I'm in a little town called Waterwealt not far from Skelter Ridge. I am going to get everyone out."

"Affirmative. Where…expect?"

"You are breaking up a bit, but I believe you were asking where to expect me. I'm heading for Matson. I have some allies with a child."

"A child?"

"I'll explain later."

"Los…connect…meet…Matson…Find…Daisy…Herb."

The radio sputtered and died.

"Ava? Ava?" There was no response.

Penny stepped forward, pulling out the battery. Almost immediately she dropped it, the heat hurting her fingers.

"Did you burn yourself?" Charles took Penny's hand.

She shook her head, frowning.

"Miss Penny, was that your last battery?" Nelson asked.

Penny shook her head again, holding up one finger.

"We won't be able to do that again, then." Byron headed for the door. "I'll call a town meeting for tomorrow afternoon. You three best start packing. I want everyone out of Waterwealt by week's end."

Charles stepped in front of him. "Won't that be too late?"

"Not if what I plan to do works. After the meeting, I'm going to need your help."

"You have an idea?" Julietta quirked an eyebrow.

"If they are going to set off a bomb in less than a week, supplies must already be arriving at Skelter Ridge. If some were to say go missing, we could buy ourselves some time." Byron smiled sadly. "I am already on borrowed time; they can afford to lend me a little more."

The sky was an ominous gray. The dust storm that should have hit seemed to be withholding itself as if wanting to watch what was about to play out. Julietta, Charles, and Penny spent the morning packing up essentials while making notes of what else could be needed. By lunchtime, however, they found themselves having to put that on pause as they made their way with the radio to Waterwealt.

Byron placed a table in the town center for the radio. While Julietta and Penny worked to set it up, he and Charles watched as the couple hundred residents began to gather.

"Nervous?" Charles whispered, a deep-seated feeling of dread sitting in his stomach.

"I would be mad not to be." Byron frowned. "You ready for later?"

"Nearly. Jul gave me some climbing gear she restored, and Penny gave me this." From beneath his shirt, Charles pulled out a small cylindrical device on a metal chain. "It's a flashlight."

"Works?"

"Penny gave it to me," he repeated. That was all Byron needed to know.

As the last few people trickled in, Byron moved to stand on a crate he brought. "Can everyone hear me?"

The voices of the crowd began to settle into silence.

"I know this was short notice, but time is not on our side," he began. "I received some rather disheartening news last night, a warning of an incoming bomb test near here."

Murmurs of concern rose from the crowd.

"I am sure many of you are wondering how we've received this news. While restoring one of the museum's radios Julietta happened to find one that had some life left in it. After some fiddling, a transmission came through."

Charles flipped the switch on the radio.

"I repeat…bomb test…" The message from the night before, though static and broken, still played.

More murmurs of concern.

"What do we do?" Ira's eyes widened.

"That's too close," Marisa spoke up.

"Are we sure that's even a true warning?" Marius asked.

More and more questions were vocalized before Byron silenced them. "I understand your concerns and have some suggestions. If this test is indeed to happen in a matter of days, our best bet is to leave Waterwealt."

The crowd went dead silent, the idea lingering over all of them like a wet blanket.

"I understand that sounds drastic, but it is not safe here. There are towns nearby that surely would not object to you visiting or settling in. Johani, Linden, and Harlington are all within a day or two journey."

"What about you?" A voice came from the crowd.

"Matson, about a week and a half from here. I plan to reconnect with some old friends there. These are just some suggestions. I cannot decide for you. If the transmission is correct, then we must depart by week's end. I am sorry."

They watched as some folks ran for their homes, likely to immediately start packing, while others lingered, seemingly lost. Byron stepped down from the crate. "I did my best. They have what they need."

Before he could continue, Marisa and Oliver approached. "Well, when do you all leave for Matson?" Marisa asked.

"What—what do you mean?" Julietta stuttered, surprised by her forwardness.

"Jul, I've lived over 40 cycles and seen plenty in my time. I know you, Charles, and little Penny here are going with Byron to Matson."

She stood dumbstruck, unsure what to say.

Byron quirked an eyebrow, grabbing the radio. "Let's go somewhere a bit more private."

Locking the door to his shop, Byron returned to the front desk where everyone had congregated.

"Well?" Oliver frowned.

Byron was about to speak but was interrupted by Marisa. "Now Byron, I've known you for five cycles. I don't want no lies. You, Jul, Charles, and Miss Penny have spent an awful lot of time together in that there museum. Now, I may not be a chemist or a doctor or a mechanical wiz, but I got brains. You are up to something, and it has to do with that Mr. Turner."

Julietta and Charles glanced at each other, exchanging looks of fear.

"Byron, you can trust us," Oliver assured. "You'd be surprised what we'd believe."

Byron looked to Julietta and Charles who shrugged. It was Penny, however, who did something unexpected.

Stepping toward the radio, she removed the battery. Turning to the adults, she smiled at Marisa as a soft blue glow appeared at her fingertips.

Marisa and Oliver's eyes went wide.

"Penny..." Byron frowned, taking the battery. "You shouldn't have—"

"My niece," Marisa chuckled. "Penny is like my niece."

He turned to Marisa. "You know about—"

"Kids with powers? Yeah, Marisa's sis had two little ones," Oliver shrugged. "The boy was normal, the girl, what do you call it, Charles?"

"That's why you were so worried about the children when Turner came." Julietta shook her head. "You've lost someone to the school too."

"Yes'm." Marisa crossed her arms, shoulders slumping. "My poor niece was taken, never to be seen again."

Penny approached Marisa, hugging her.

"We were trying to protect her. We're—" Charles stopped as Penny took her necklace from beneath her shirt, holding it out to the woman.

"You escaped the school, Miss Penny?" Marisa asked.

Penny nodded her head.

Oliver stood up a bit straighter, a look of determination on his face. "What can we do to help?"

"You want to help?" Byron couldn't stop a smile.

"I helped you bury a man, Byron. You think I wouldn't do more?" Oliver laughed.

"Could use a contact back here. The bomb testing, unfortunately, seems to be connected to all this. I would explain more but I have some things I need to do this evening."

"You'd want us to gather information?" Marisa suggested. "You'd be surprised what folk tell you when you offer them some baked goods."

Everyone laughed, breaking the tension in the room.

"That sounds like a good plan. Thank you, Marisa, Oliver. I'm sorry I didn't tell you sooner. Tomorrow, I'll stop by the bakery and give more details," Byron sighed, turning to Charles and Julietta. "I think we better get going. Need to get this radio back to the museum and discuss travel."

"I suppose we have something similar to discuss," Oliver smiled as Penny turned, giving him a hug. "We'll do our best, Miss Penny. Your secret is safe with us."

CHAPTER 17

The wind had begun to pick up by the time Byron and Charles dropped the girls off with the radio at the museum. Julietta had voiced her concerns about the coming storm, but both Byron and Charles agreed the sooner they checked out Skelter Ridge the better.

The two men had been climbing around for more than two hours when the storm started to hinder their progress.

"Won't be able to search much more. We'll need to seek shelter soon." Byron grunted as Charles helped him up onto another ledge.

"Need to be careful. The recent storms seem to be—"

The sound of rocks and soil falling reached their ears as a massive gust of wind blew through the area. Then, without warning, the ground beneath them began to give way.

"Look out!" Byron shouted, grabbing Charles's arm while also trying to grab for a sturdy hold. He was too late, however, as the two men went tumbling down with the landslide toward the ground below.

"Agh!" Charles groaned as he came to a stop in what seemed to be the bottom of a sinkhole wedged between two rather tall stone cliff sides. Giving himself a moment to regain his bearings he immediately sought out Byron.

"Over here," Byron coughed, slowly rising to his feet.

Aside from being very dusty, and most likely bruised, both men seemed to be all right.

"The universe sure has a sense of humor." Charles spat out some soil. "I was about to say the storms recently have been making this place unstable. It was already bad when I found Penny here."

"The universe also seems to have given us a lead," Byron smiled, shaking the dust from his hair. "Look there."

Just off to the side of the sinkhole was an opening into what looked to be a natural cave. What was not natural was the dim light coming from within it.

Charles quirked an eyebrow. "Let's go."

Walking along quietly, the two soon came across a carved-out hallway lit by dim oil lanterns.

"This looks recent," Charles whispered.

"Unless Mother Nature decided oil lamps are the newest thing to grow," Byron chuckled.

Charles rolled his eyes but said nothing as they ventured deeper in. The further they went, the fewer oil lamps appeared. They were replaced by what looked like a child's glow stick from the before times. A light haze in the air gave them an unearthly look.

"I wonder why—" Charles stopped, his heart dropping into his stomach as they entered a small open cavern space. This was no natural space. Surrounding the carved-out room were several sealed metal crates; in its center, what looked to be a set of tables with various old electronics upon them.

Byron un-holstered his gun, Charles mirroring. "This has to be it. Try not to disturb anything just yet," the older man whispered, starting towards the right side of the cavern.

Poking around the various crates and pallets on the opposite side of the room, Charles felt uneasy. With the dim light and the dusty haze, he struggled to make out the labels. Not that the ones he could read were any better at helping his stomach with words like 'cabling,' 'dangerous,' and 'contains acid' visible. As he approached another stack of boxes one, in particular, caught his eye. It was made of metal, with the label: Test Payloads: Handle with Care painted across it. Spotting a piece of paper taped to it, he tried to make sense of it, but in the dim light, he couldn't. His curiosity getting the better of him, he dared to holster his gun. Reaching into his duster pocket he pulled out a matchbook.

"Charles, wait!"

The man was too late as Charles struck the match. There was a bright flash of light, and the sound of soil and rocks being knocked loose, clanging onto metal boxes before the world plunged into darkness.

"Charles…Charles!"

Charles shook his head, trying to focus as Byron came into view pulling him to his feet.

"We have to go."

He stumbled after the man as he led him out of the cavern, rocks and soil raining down upon them.

"Charles…" Charles didn't remember falling to his knees or blacking out. "Thank heavens you're alive."

As his vision focused, he realized it was Byron leaning over him, blood dripping down the side of his face.

"What—what happened?" Charles coughed trying to sit up.

"Well depending on your point of view, you either did something really useful or really stupid."

Head clearing, Charles realized he was no longer in the small cavern but in the hallway outside it.

"I am hedging my bets on stupid. Was I out long?"

"Just a few seconds, thankfully." Byron chuckled, shaking his head. "It was stupid, but helpful. The haze, it wasn't just dust. I just realized it when you went to light the match. You should be counting your lucky stars there was only enough gunpowder in the air to basically be a flashbang."

Finally, back to his senses, he frowned. "You're bleeding."

"I'll live. I was more worried about you. That flash knocked loose a ton of rocks and such. Buried a good amount of the equipment in there. Managed to drag you out before you blanked and the cavern caved fully."

"I think I'm all right." Charles paused a moment, assessing himself. "Some minor cuts and bruises. Just was really stunned."

"You'll feel more than stunned in the morning, we both will," Byron winced, standing. "At least we've done what we've come to do. That cave-in should slow down whatever they were doing in there."

"Good." Charles slowly rose to his feet. "Now for the matters at hand. First, I want to get a bandage on your head, then how do we get out of here?"

Byron let Charles bandage his gash before they headed back toward the sinkhole entrance. They were relieved to find the storm had let up slightly but concerned as night had fallen.

"We aren't going to be able to get back in the dark, let alone climb this." Byron winced, taking a seat on the ground.

Charles shook his head, thinking. "We can't stay here either. This dust storm is likely to fill this sinkhole at the rate it's going." Rubbing the back of his head, his hand came to a stop as he brushed against the chain around his neck. "Penny..."

"Penny?"

Charles removed the flashlight from his neck. "She gave me this flashlight, remember?" Flicking the switch, he smiled. "Let's go home, Byron."

Julietta had been pacing the loft for the past three hours. The dust storm had been bad from what she could see from the loft window, but thankfully was letting up. That wasn't what worried her. Charles and Byron should have been back by now. They had promised to be home by sundown.

Penny sat on Julietta's bed holding Nelson tight.

"Miss Penny wants to know when Charlie and Sir Byron will be home."

"I don't know, Penny. Hopefully soon."

Julietta had begun to debate with herself how to go and search for them when the loft door flung open. In stumbled Charles and Byron, covered head to toe in dirt and dust, coughing harshly.

"Help, Byron." Charles coughed, heading towards the kitchen table.

"Penny, get—" Julietta didn't have to ask as Penny was already at the sink getting two glasses of water. "You're both hurt," she frowned, helping Byron into a chair.

"'Tis merely a scratch, my dear," he half coughed, half chuckled as Penny handed him a glass of water.

Charles had made it over to the sink, downing the water Penny had left him there before spitting sand into the sink.

"What happened?" Julietta asked, grabbing some medical supplies before tending to Byron.

While Byron explained, Penny walked over to Charles.

Pulling out a chair, she took his hand.

"I'm all right, Penny," he sighed, taking the seat, gratefully.

Penny shook her head, opening a nearby drawer and taking out a small towel. Wetting it she began to wipe the dust and dirt from his face.

"Thank you," he smiled, coughing slightly.

"You exploded a bomb site!?" Julietta gasped, her voice a bit pitched.

"Not intentionally," Charles winced. "But it did the job."

"Let's just say your boyfriend over there is lucky," Byron teased. "Once you've finished patching me up, I really should get back home. I have much to do tomorrow."

"You think I'm going to let you go back like this?"

"I've been through worse. Believe you me," Byron sighed, standing. "If it would make you feel better you can walk with me back to town."

"Here." Charles reached up, removing the flashlight Penny gave him and handing it to Julietta. "That little thing saved us." He smiled at Penny.

"Will you be all right? Byron said you blacked out."

"It was only a few seconds. I'll be fine," he sighed, leaning back in his seat. "I'll probably just get cleaned up then lay down for a bit."

Julietta looked worried.

"I don't have a concussion if that's your worry. No headache or nausea. I can breathe fine and my heart rate is normal. I hurt just about everywhere else, but the important things are okay." Charles assured. "You make sure Byron gets home okay."

Julietta relented. "Come on, Byron, let's get you home."

Julietta returned about 20 minutes later to a rather comical sight. Charles, having washed up and changed into a plain gray t-shirt and black sweatpants, was sitting on her bed. Penny was standing in front of him, trying and failing to wrap a bandage around his right arm.

"Penny, you've been a great nurse getting me water and such, but we can wait for your mother to get home for bandages. I really don't think I—"

"I see our spark plug is trying to be a good doctor," Julietta chuckled.

Penny turned to her, smiling.

"She insisted she bandage me up. I told her I could just lay down on my bed until you got back but she was persistent."

Penny nodded, once more trying to wrap the bandage around Charles's arm.

Unholstering her gun and retrieving her knives from her boots, Julietta set them beside Charles's on the cabinet. "You've done a good job my little nurse, but I can take it from here. It is past your bedtime. Why don't you go get cleaned up and ready?"

Penny pouted.

"Penny..." she chastised, taking the bandages from her. "I promise I will take good care of your Charlie, okay?"

Penny sighed, but relented, grabbing her bedclothes and disappearing into the washroom.

"You could have just told her no," Julietta chuckled, pulling up a chair before unwrapping the mess of bandages from Charles's arm.

"She was so worried. Figured I'd let her play nurse to keep her calm," Charles sighed, exhaustion settling over him.

Placing a hand on his neck, she checked his pulse. "You sure you're okay?"

"Just sore and tired. I'll live."

Feeling his pulse was good, she relaxed. "All right. I am just worried 'cause—Charlie..." She gasped, spotting the burns on his right arm.

"They aren't as bad as they look." He winced slightly as he shifted. "My shoulder is worse."

Reaching into the medical kit Penny had left open on the table, she pulled out some aloe cream. "Let me see."

Charles removed his shirt enough for Julietta to see the angry red patches of skin on his right shoulder and back.

"Charlie...why didn't you say anything?"

"I didn't want to scare you," he frowned. "They look worse than they feel honest."

Julietta shook her head, beginning to apply the cream. "For a doctor, you sure don't worry about yourself."

"That's cause I've seen so much worse. I know what is bad and what is survivable," he tensed, before relaxing as the cream took away the sting of the burns. "Though I must admit, you may have been right about applying that cream."

"Still no headache?"

"No, I am pretty sure I don't have a concussion."

"How can you be sure?"

"Finish applying the cream and I'll show you."

Helping him put his shirt back on, she washed her hands before returning to the chair, lit candle in hand. "Explain."

"First, you ask the patient to look at the light. Then, you watch their eyes as you move it around. If they keep up, they likely don't have a concussion. You also can carefully press on the patient's head, making sure nothing feels strange."

Julietta did as he instructed, using her other hand to gently check his forehead. After a minute she sighed, relieved. "You're fine, I think."

"I'm fine, Jul. Thank you." Charles smiled sadly.

Blowing out the candle she tossed it into the sink. "You going to be okay?"

"Something tells me you aren't talking about my injuries."

She moved to sit beside him on the bed, placing a comforting arm around him. "How long has it been?"

"Nearly four cycles, give or take. I left just as Damp started. I was 24 Cold."

"Did you ever think you'd go back?"

"I...I don't know. I was wondering for so long. Never could find a place I wanted to settle." He bowed his head. "Never felt welcomed anywhere until I met you. You know, when you offered me the job at the museum, I wanted to say yes right then and there but, I didn't want to seem hasty and scare you."

"To be honest, I was afraid you'd leave right then and there. Part of me selfishly wanted you to stay so I could get to know you."

"Well, I'm glad you did," Charles smirked, his gaze meeting hers. "As for Matson, I'll be all right. For Penny, I'll face it." He rested his head on her shoulder, his eyelids feeling heavy. "Today's been one heck of an adventure."

He attempted to stand, but Julietta stopped him. "Lie down, Charlie."

Charles looked at her confused. "Why?"

"With your injuries, there is no way a mattress on the floor will be comfortable."

"I'm all right, honest."

"Please? I would feel better if you did."

Before Charles could argue, Penny emerged from the washroom, looking sleepy. "Come on, Penny, let's get you into your fort." Julietta smiled, leading her over to her fort bed.

Charles watched, his heart warming, as Julietta tucked in Penny, the little girl almost immediately falling asleep.

"Your turn," Julietta teased.

Feeling exhausted and frankly very sore, he relented. Lying down he beckoned her over. "Just for tonight, okay?"

"Okay." She kissed him. "Rest, we have much to do tomorrow."

"That we do." He sighed, looking deeply into her eyes. "Jul, I—" He paused, the words he wanted to say lost to his exhaustion.

"You too," she whispered, the sadness in her eyes lessening a touch.

Walking over to the tall cabinet she grabbed her gun and a knife before heading for the table. Setting the weapon upon it, she pulled out Charles's mattress. Placing her knife beside it as Charles had done for the past several weeks, she paused for a moment. She would be the guardian tonight. Lying down, she took one last look over to Penny's fort, then her bed. Seeing her little family asleep, her heart felt lighter. Closing her eyes, she relaxed, finally allowing herself to fall into much-needed sleep.

CHAPTER 18

The following week was a flurry of activity. With the bomb test hopefully delayed, they focused on preparing to leave. Day after day, the
population of Waterwealt dwindled as folks made off for places known
only to them. Byron, keeping his promise, met with Marisa and Oliver
Healey the following day. They were a bit shocked seeing his injuries, but
given his explanation, they were relieved at the outcome. After some discussion, it was decided that the Healeys would go to Johani. They would
establish themselves there in an attempt to garner some information
about Rho-597 until Byron could contact them with further instructions.

Charles, Julietta, and Penny were equally busy. Every morning after
breakfast and every evening before bed, Penny would tune to the station
Ava broadcasted from. To everyone's relief, there had been no further
updates signaling a bomb imminent.

Charles was well on the mend, helping Julietta gather supplies.
They would be carrying two packs each, Penny one. Having only been
wandering the wastes himself a few months prior, he was a wealth of
knowledge when it came to potential hazards and the items they would
need. Taking a couple of days to clean out the medical wing of any easily
portable medical supplies, he then switched to creating food that would
hold until they could reach their first town.

Julietta continued repairing survival gear including a tent, some
camping cookware, and a portable water purifier. She also dug up four
sleeping bags and raided the home exhibit for any blankets to be safe.

"Food and medical supplies are split between all our packs. Each of
us has a sleeping bag and extra blankets. I got the more fiddly medical
equipment and my notebooks…" Charles continued to rattle off the
various items in each backpack on the kitchen table.

"I got my notebooks as well and a few multitools. Everyone should have a flashlight to keep on their person. Penny found some more batteries for them," Julietta smiled, showing off the small light now around her neck.

"Great." He zipped up each pack, securing them closed with a rubber band tie. "I think that's everything we will need. Well, at least everything we can carry."

"That's…good." She frowned, brushing some hair back from her face.

"You okay?"

"Just, so many things I wanted to do here. So much history that will never get restored." Her shoulders drooped. "I didn't even get to finish that painting."

"I know." He wrapped her in a hug. "I may have only worked here for a season and a half but…I see why you loved it so much."

She embraced him back, resting her head on his chest. "We've recovered a good amount. I take solace in that fact." Looking up at him she smiled sadly. "There will be other places, with more knowledge to unlock. We'll find a place."

"Together." Charles chuckled, kissing her forehead. "Once all this is behind us, we'll find a museum to restore together."

"I'd like that." She hugged him a bit tighter. "I—"

"You too."

Penny appeared a moment later carrying what looked to be three small boxes.

"What are those?" Julietta quirked an eyebrow.

Setting the boxes on the table, Penny turned on Nelson.

"Miss Penny found three portable radios. They are for short reach, but she thinks she can get them working while we travel."

"Not a bad idea," Charles shrugged, taking and placing them in Penny's pack. "Try this out for me?"

Slipping it on, she marched around a bit, adjusting the straps for herself.

"Comfortable? Not too heavy?"

Penny shook her head.

"Good. Jul, I want you to try yours." Charles reached for his own.

"Not too bad. I mean after a long day I probably will feel different, but I think it's manageable," she sighed, adjusting her straps. "Is there anything else?"

"I'm good." Charles shifted back and forth slightly, ensuring the pack sat just how he wanted it. "As you said, after a few days I may sing a different tune, but we'll cross that bridge when we come to it."

As the three set their packs back on the table Charles turned to Penny. "Just one last thing, Penny."

The girl looked up at Charles, confused.

"Your mom and I were talking. As you know, the wastes can be a dangerous place."

Penny nodded, frowning.

"That being said, we want you to be safe. Though you know we are going to protect you, we also want you to have something to protect yourself just in case."

Penny watched as Julietta pulled a small pocket knife from her duster pocket, handing it to Charles.

"You know this is not a toy." Charles knelt in front of her, holding it out to her. "This should be kept on your belt during the day and kept with mine and Jul's at night, okay?"

Penny nodded, looking nervous.

"Do you want me to attach it to your belt?"

Penny shook her head, taking the knife from him. She held it for a moment, pulling out a few of the small blades and tools before folding it up and attaching it to her belt.

"You okay?" Charles asked, concerned.

Penny hugged him.

"It's going to be all right." He reciprocated. "I promise."

"Charlie and I will make sure you are safe." Julietta comforted, kneeling beside them.

Penny reached out, pulling her into the hug.

They were interrupted by a knock at the loft door.

"Ready?" It was Byron.

Holding each other for a moment longer, Penny was first to let go, grabbing her pack.

"As we can be." Charles sighed, standing.

"Our first stop is Neilhem, three days north of here. We stick together. Travel only in daylight if we can help it." Byron's gaze fell as he adjusted his pack. "Everyone in town is gone. I…I let Harrison go last night. Gave him a pack and sent him off. Doubt he'll be any trouble."

Julietta and Charles nodded in understanding, the look on the older man's face speaking volumes as to the discussion that likely occurred.

Packed and ready, Penny grabbed Nelson from the table. Walking over to Byron, she took his hand, looking up at him with a smile.

"Ready, Miss Penny?"

Penny nodded as the group made their way out of the museum and into the unknown of the wastes.

Surprisingly, the first day of travel was smooth, all things considered. The weather was still unseasonably warm, but the dust seemed to have settled for the time being. Along the way, Penny happily pointed out different rock formations, using Nelson to tell the adults what they looked like. Some highlights included a unicorn, a dragon, and a rock covered in shaggy moss that Penny compared to Charles's hair. They stopped for the night in the shade of some hills, the three adults taking turns keeping watch until dawn.

It was nearing midday on the second day when the sky began to turn gray. With not much in the way of scenery and having walked way further than she ever had before, Penny was rather tired. Since they had stopped for lunch, she had taken to Byron's side. He was now carrying her as they approached the outskirts of an abandoned city, its name lost to time.

"You sure you don't want me to take her?" Charles offered.

"No, I'm fine," Byron chuckled. "I may be old but there is still plenty of life left in me to do this."

The dusty ground gave way to a patchy cracked asphalt road as they entered the city limits. Where once stood tall skyscrapers full of life and commerce in the before times, now lay ruin and rubble, much of the land reclaimed by Mother Nature's wrath. Those that still stood were little more than hollow shells, a monument to man's fall. Picking past the rusted cars and fallen concrete, there was an air of quiet sadness and grief that lingered over the group.

"Can you imagine working and living in a place like this?" Julietta asked as they moved past another dilapidated structure. "I heard there are a few scrapers left in the capital, but I doubt they compare to what these were."

"There are a few in Matson, but not as tall." Charles shrugged. "Most of the top floors were rubble according to some historians I spoke with. They only managed to save seven, maybe eight floors at most."

"Kentburg had one, the city center, where the government was housed," Byron explained. "I was only ever in it once, when they took my Francis from me."

Silence fell amongst the group, all eyes falling on Penny, who was asleep in the older man's arms.

"Never again," he muttered as they continued.

A mist began to fall.

"Rain?" Julietta quirked an eyebrow. "But it's Dust season. It never rains except in Damp."

"It's not supposed to be this warm either, my dear, yet the heat from Hot has not abated," Byron grunted, shifting his grip on Penny.

"Weather has been odd," Charles added, looking nervous. "If it's going to rain, we may have to stop early this evening."

Byron pulled up Penny's hood. "Let's press on for now and see what happens."

They managed to make it about halfway into the city before the rain began to pour. Soaked and tired they all agreed it was time to seek shelter.

"There looks to be some sturdier structures up ahead," Byron frowned, adjusting Penny's duster around her. "Let's see if—"

His words were lost as a loud boom echoed around them, the area suddenly brighter as the ground shook violently.

"Lightning!" Julietta spat, regaining her footing. "Too close."

Before they could react, another sound reached their ears, the sound of crumbling concrete. Looking back everyone's eyes went wide. The road they had just traveled was sinking, fast.

"Run!" Charles shouted, but it was unnecessary, as Byron and Julietta had already taken off down the street.

The rumbling grew louder, the slick street making it hard to keep their footing. Despite their best efforts, they struggled to outrun the slide as the earth continued to give way. In a last-ditch effort each made for a solid piece of ground. There was another boom, then silence.

Staggering to his feet, Charles found himself on solid ground, the road behind him wiped out. Glancing around he breathed a sigh of relief, Julietta and Byron had found similar luck, though they were all now separated by rubble and ruin.

"Penny and I are all right. A bit scraped up but nothing serious," shouted Byron. "There looks like a good place to seek shelter a few blocks up. I'll mark it. Meet us there!"

Charles looked over to Julietta who nodded as they went their separate ways, hoping to meet very soon.

Charles found the building not long after, Byron having marked the outside with a tied-off piece of fabric at its entry point. Climbing through the hole in the wall he found the man had already gotten Penny out of her soaked duster, wrapped her in blankets, and was now starting a fire.

"Are you both all right?" Charles asked, shaking off some of the water from his coat.

"Right as rain, aside from a few scrapes," Byron chuckled, lighting the fire. "Miss Penny is a brave girl."

Penny nodded, giving them a small smile.

"I didn't see Jul out there," Charles frowned. "Hope she is all right."

"Give her a few minutes. She was furthest out." Byron stood, removing his wet coat and tossing it beside Penny's.

"I think I'm going to go look for her. Just to make sure she gets here okay."

"Suit yourself."

Stepping back out into the pouring rain, Charles headed down in the direction Julietta should have been coming from. Walking a few blocks, his stomach began to turn. Surely, he should have run into her by now? As he approached what he believed should have been the street that led to the sink hole his heart nearly stopped. There was another one.

Deeply worried, he ran to the edge of it, his fears confirmed. Stuck at the bottom, water rising around her, was Julietta, struggling to free herself.

"Jul!" Charles called, desperately looking around for a safe way down. Not finding an immediate one, he hedged his bets on a portion that looked semi-stable.

"I'm stuck, my ankle." Julietta gritted, once more trying in vain to free herself.

Noting the rising water level, Charles pushed down his panic as he began to clear the rubble near her. A large piece of metal and concrete had collapsed into the hole, a chunk of it trapping her ankle beneath it.

"It's too heavy," she cried, panic in her voice.

Spotting a long piece of metal that had fallen loose, he thought fast. "One sec." Returning a moment later with the beam, he wedged it under the concrete. "On the count of three...one...two...three!"

Throwing his weight on it the concrete block moved slightly. It took three more tries for it to finally give just enough for Julietta to yank her ankle out with a pained cry.

"Jul..."

They didn't have time to think as another bolt of lightning struck nearby, the water in the sinkhole surging. He barely managed to get her to her feet as they scrambled over to the somewhat stable section he had slid down. With great effort the two climbed, having to stop a few times as the earth shook and shifted with the storm.

Finally, after what seemed like ages, they found themselves at the top. Flopping down hard onto the solid ground, spent, they breathed a sigh of relief. They were out.

"Jul..." Having caught his breath, he sat up, pulling Julietta into his arms.

Despite the rain, he could see tears falling down her face as she wrapped her arms around him tightly.

"It's all right, Jul, I got you."

Byron was to his feet as Charles stumbled in carrying Julietta in his arms.

"What happened?" He rushed over with a blanket as Charles set her down by the wall nearest the fire.

"Sinkhole, she was stuck. Her right ankle is hurt," Charles panted, pulling off his bags and wet coat before digging for his medical supplies.

Byron helped Julietta out of her soaked coat, wrapping a blanket around her. "I have some water boiling, use it," he instructed as he went to fill another pot.

Penny, having watched this happen, moved to sit beside Julietta, her eyes full of worry.

"I'm okay, Penny." She winced as Charles removed her boot. "Just my ankle."

Pulling up her pant leg and removing her soaked sock, Charles began his examination. "Gash isn't deep, once I clean it, I'll put some anti-bac on it. I'm more worried about the bone." He frowned. "This is going to hurt a bit."

"Do what you have to."

Slowly moving her ankle around, he checked for signs of a break. "Can you move it to the left and right? How bad does it hurt?"

"It hurts but I can."

He pressed on it a bit, causing her to yelp. "Sorry."

"It's fine." She sighed deeply, Penny, taking her hand.

"Considering you were able to put some weight on it and your range is good, not broken. Though, it is bruised and swollen. Definitely sprained, maybe a small fracture but I can't tell. Let me clean it up first then I need to figure out how to stabilize it."

Julietta closed her eyes, Penny squeezing her hand as Charles used the hot water to clean the wound. "I know it hurts, but I don't want it to get infected."

"I know," she grunted, opening her eyes, trying to relax into the stone wall behind her.

"Byron, you think we have anything I could use to stabilize her ankle? I didn't think to grab any splints from the museum."

Hearing the word splint, Penny's eyes lit up. She remembered in her brief visits to the medical wing seeing strange wood and metal contraptions called splints. She had an idea.

Reaching into her bag beside her she removed her two six-inch wood rulers, holding them out to Charles.

Charles, having finished cleaning and bandaging the gash, looked up with a smile. "Penny, did I ever tell you, you are a genius?"

The girl smiled brightly, Julietta placing a hand on her shoulder.

Using the rulers and some bandage wrap, Charles was able to make a decent splint. "That should hold it." He ran a hand through his wet hair, shaking his head. "Are you hurt anywhere else?"

"A few scrapes and bruises but I think we all have those. I'll live." She shivered as Penny moved to rest her head on her shoulder.

Charles placed the back of his hand against her forehead. "No fever, but the weather certainly has shifted. You were soaked."

"We all were." Byron frowned, handing Julietta and Penny cups of tea. "You may not feel it yet, but you will once you calm down."

Charles's face flushed. "I'm fine, Byron."

The older man handed him a cup as well. "Drink that. It's going to be a long night."

CHAPTER 19

B yron was right. Sitting by the fire on his slightly damp sleeping bag, adrenaline wearing off, Charles began to feel the chill. Having finished their tea, the two men had set to work trying to block up some of the drafty gaps while Julietta and Penny tried to dry out their gear. It wasn't until the sky drew dark with night that they finished. Eating a light meal and layering on what dry clothes they had, it was decided Charles and Byron would be the only ones to keep watch to give Julietta a chance to rest and recover from her narrow escape.

Byron had gone to sleep beside the fire a few hours ago, only a single blanket for warmth. Julietta and Penny were also asleep behind it. Ever the protective guardian, she had wrapped up the little girl in whatever blankets could be dried, using herself as a barrier to the wind that crept through.

Gun in his lap and knife beside him, Charles had kept watch for the past few hours, his mind struggling to maintain focus. The events of the day, the past week, and the past few months lay heavily over him, draining his resolve. So much had changed since he arrived in Waterwealt at Hot's start. Some of it was good, some bad, and some he wouldn't change for the world.

"Charlie?"

He turned to see Julietta was awake.

Crawling over, he set his gun within arm's reach before turning to her. "You okay? What woke you?"

"I'm fine."

His brow furrowed, his eyes scanning her for signs of illness or hurt. To answer his silent concern, she took his hand, gently resting it on her neck. Feeling her pulse strong and well he relaxed, breathing a sigh of relief.

"You need rest."

"I'll be all right. I want to give By—"

"You should get some sleep, son," Byron yawned, stretching as he sat up.

"Sorry, did we wake you?" Julietta frowned.

"No, I've been awake for a few minutes. The cold and these old bones aren't conducive to a good night's rest. Don't you worry though, I'm pretty spry for an old guy." He chuckled, placing his gun in his lap and settling in. "Julie's right though. You could use the sleep."

Charles nodded, turning toward his sleeping bag, only to stop as Julietta gently grabbed his arm. "Stay with me."

He looked confused.

"You gave up your blankets to Penny. You can't just sleep in that damp bag, you'll catch a cold or worse."

As if to prove her point, a cold breeze blew in through the cracks, sending a shiver up his spine. Shaking his head, he briefly glanced to Byron who gave him a look that said he would be stupid to disagree.

Charles smiled. "All right, Jul."

Moving his bag beside hers, he placed his gun and knife beside it. Lying down facing her, he shifted closer as she moved the blanket to cover them both.

"Warm?" she asked, her hand coming to rest against his bearded cheek.

"Yes, thank you," he sighed, shifting a bit closer.

There was a brief, comfortable silence.

"Jul—"

"Every time you hold my hand," she chuckled lightly, running her thumb over his beard. "Every time you take care of our lucky Penny, make me laugh, or teach me something new...every time you've made breakfast, kissed me, or reminded me to take a break once in a while..." She swallowed a lump in her throat. "Every night when you lay down to sleep, gun and knife beside you to protect us, you've said it. You've said it in so many ways, without saying the words."

"So have you." He gave her a tender kiss, the unspoken words held within it.

Taking his hand, she urged him a bit closer, resting it around her waist.

"Comfortable?" She rested her head against his.

"Yes..." He yawned, his eyelids drooping.

"Rest, Charlie," she chided, running a soothing hand down the side of his face as he closed his eyes.

As she closed hers, she heard Charles whisper, "I know I show it, but I still want to say it. I love you, Jul."

Her heart fluttered, her mind and body relaxing. "I love you too, Charlie," she returned as she drifted off into much-needed sleep.

Staring out at the finally dwindling rain, Byron sat in silence, his heart heavy. Glancing over to where Charles and Julietta lay, arms around each other, and little Penny sound asleep beside them, he couldn't help but feel a tug in his chest. He had put them in this situation.

It was he who brought little Penny to Julietta's front door. He had directed Charles to the museum, encouraged him to stay and learn, then convinced them to travel to Charles's home city, a place he knew very well may not welcome the doctor with open arms. He may not have originally known what his actions would have caused, but now he was tangled.

The words of love whispered between Julietta and Charles replayed in his mind. At least that was one good thing that came of his decisions. He'd given little Penny something she never had. He gave her a loving mother through Julietta, and now it seemed a loving father through Charles. Though he could not have known they would have fallen for each other, he couldn't be happier for it.

So there he sat, thinking. Pondering his choices, both made and unmade. They would hopefully be in Matson within a week or so. From there, more problems would need to be solved with varying outcomes. There was one resolution, however, he already made. He would protect this new-found family. He had only everything to lose if something should happen to them. He already felt he was on borrowed time, and therefore was more than willing to steal more of it, if it meant saving them and many others from harm.

The rain had stopped by morning, a cold fog rolling in. Everyone awoke just after sunrise, a bit chilled and slightly sniffly, but surprisingly rested.

Byron had already made some hot tea and was well on the way to cooking breakfast.

"How's the ankle, Julie?" he asked as the group sat around the fire eating.

"Sore, but mobile. I should be all right to walk."

He turned to Charles, who frowned. "I'll take a look at it after breakfast. As a doctor, I'd want you to rest it, but as someone who has traveled the wastes we can't afford to stop. Especially not after that freak storm yesterday."

"I am inclined to agree with the traveler side of you." Byron furrowed his brow.

As he said, Charles tended to Julietta's ankle after breakfast. "Gash is already healing well. No signs of infection. Not too stiff either from being supported?"

"No, I can move it, just hurts." Julietta winced. "I think I'll be all right. Won't know 'til I try to put weight on it."

He gently massaged the joint, trying to relieve some of the tension around it. "You'll need to lean on someone. We won't be able to move as fast."

Penny, who at this point was still a bit groggy, was walking around the space trying to wake up as the adults talked. She had heard enough to understand Momma Julie was hurt and needed help walking but didn't know how she could help. As she came to the far wall from where they had slept, her foot hit something hard. Looking down, she found what looked to be a short metal pole. Thinking back to the museum she remembered seeing things called 'canes' in some of the clothing displays that men would use to walk. Grabbing the rod, she ran back over to Julietta who was currently being helped to her feet by Charles.

Leaning heavily on Charles, she took a few staggering pained steps, then slowly some more stable ones. After a minute, she was able to walk mostly on her own.

"I won't be fast, but I'm mobile." She gave a pained smile.

Penny approached, holding out the rod to Charles. It took him a minute to realize what she was suggesting.

"Did anyone ever tell you, Penny, you are a genius?"

Penny beamed.

"Keep telling her that she'll wind up with an ego the size of Waterwealt," Julietta chuckled, taking the rod and testing it. "But she is very smart. This works. Thank you."

The girl hugged them both as Byron appeared, having finished packing up camp.

"Neilhem is still about a day and a half away, more likely two now with Julie's ankle and any damage that storm did. Best we leave now if we want to make some headway before dark."

It took three days to reach Neilhem. With Julietta's ankle and the road being a muddy mess, travel was slowed to a crawl. On top of this, it appeared little Penny had developed a cold from the rain and now consistently freezing temperature.

"How is she?" Byron asked Charles who was carrying Penny.

Shifting his grip on the girl, he placed the back of his hand against her forehead. "A little warm, but nothing serious from what I can tell. Once we get to Neilhem I can better assess. To be honest, I think she'll be all right after a good night's rest in a warm bed and some hot food. Her appetite is good, and when I checked her at lunch everything else sounded fine. She was a little sniffly of course. Likely a head cold."

"Good as to be expected I suppose..." Julietta winced. Despite her best efforts, she found herself walking slower and slower the past few hours.

"Your ankle could use a break too," Charles sighed, his own body aching. "We all could."

"Shouldn't be long now to Neil—" Byron stopped as the outline of a small city came into view.

Julietta quirked an eyebrow. "Something wrong?"

"There is no smoke." The older man's brow furrowed. "We should be able to see smoke from fires from here." On edge, he drew his gun, Julietta doing the same, moving to stand on Charles's other side. "Stay alert." He shook his head as the group continued forward.

Entering the city limits they were greeted with eerie silence. Not even the wind seemed to whistle as they slowly walked down the empty main street. Neilhem was deserted and, based on the broken wagons and various strewn-about items that littered the street, in a hurry.

Byron broke off from the group, cautiously approaching a building. Peering inside he found there to be no light, no signs of life.

"Empty."

He checked each building along the row with similar results.

"I don't like this," Julietta whispered, keeping herself close to Charles and Penny.

"There is an inn here," Byron beckoned. "Let's at least get ourselves situated. No sense in staying out in the open."

Having confirmed the inn was empty, he left Charles to take care of Julietta and Penny. Selecting a room on the second floor with two beds, a fireplace, and an attached washroom, Charles lay Penny on the one nearest the window.

"She is still warm." He shook his head. "Let me get a fire going then I'll check her. You better get off that ankle."

Julietta didn't argue, taking a seat beside the poor girl, helping her get settled under the blankets on the bed.

Fire going, Charles tossed his duster on the chair with Penny's and Julietta's before grabbing his medical bag. Giving Penny a quick check, he relaxed. "Heart and lungs sound good. Her nose is a bit stuffy like I suspected. Anything hurt?"

Penny shook her head.

"Head cold then. Some food and a good night's sleep will help that." Adjusting the blanket on her, he moved to the other side of the bed to tend to Julietta.

Unwrapping her ankle he winced, though the gash was well faded now and healing nicely the joint was covered in bruises. "Does this hurt as bad as it looks?"

Julietta nodded, leaning back against the headboard.

Charles shifted, resting her ankle in his lap. "It's still a bit swollen. Tonight soak it in the bath in there and keep it elevated." He gently massaged around it.

She nodded with a wince, closing her eyes. "The muscle is really tense."

"Too much walking," he scoffed.

Opening her eyes, she frowned, noticing the dark circles under Charles's. "How are you?"

"Surviving, best we all are." His shoulders slumped. "I hurt just about everywhere."

"If I wasn't in the same pain I'd try to help." She gasped slightly as he pressed on a particularly tense spot.

"Don't worry about it."

"Everyone okay?" Byron grimaced seeing Julietta's ankle.

"As we can be," Julietta replied, sounding exhausted.

"There is some food that is salvageable in the kitchen and the water seems clean enough. This place was likely abandoned only a week or two ago. I'd like to try and raid some of the shops nearby before dark."

"I can help." Charles carefully set Julietta's foot on the bed as he stood.

"Penny and I will be fine," Julietta added, noting a hint of concern in Byron's expression.

Grabbing a pillow from the other bed, Charles fixed it under her ankle.

"Stay off of it." He instructed before slipping on his duster. "We'll be back in a couple of hours."

The search through Neilhem yielded minimal supplies and no answers as to why the place was deserted. Most of the stores within a few blocks of the main road had been thoroughly emptied. Starting to explore the nearby homes, they were able to at least procure some warmer clothes for all of them. With the sun setting and only having searched a fraction of the city, Charles and Byron returned to the inn.

Once everyone had the chance to wash up and change, the men proceeded to the kitchen to cook up some dinner.

"Chamomile tea, perfect," Charles sighed as he dug through the rather lackluster pantry.

"For Penny?"

"From my research, this is a tried and true treatment for head colds. This and some soup will do her good."

"Poor girl. She's had it rough."

"I can only imagine," he frowned, grabbing a few more items for the soup Byron had on the go. "She still hasn't told us anything more but...part of me is afraid to know."

"You care a lot about her." Byron quirked an eyebrow, dropping some carrots into the soup.

"Don't we all?"

"You care about both of them."

"Of course," he furrowed his brow, a bit confused about where this conversation was going. "They are my girls."

"Did you ever think you'd have a kid?"

He paused, shaking his head as he filled a pot for tea. "Before I met Jul, I didn't think much about a family or my future for that matter. That all went out the window when I was kicked out of the medical society."

"There was no one special in Matson for you?"

He shook his head. "Spent most of my time working in the clinic and researching. Sure, I had friends I'd hang out with and co-workers but, no one ever interested me like that."

"Not 'til you met Julie," Byron chuckled. "At least that choice of mine seemed to pan out well."

"Didn't think when you said she owned a museum it was that giant building. Guess I should count my lucky stars I stumbled in during that storm."

"Penny loves you too. That much is obvious."

"I love her too, protect her with my life."

"She sees you like a father, did you know that?"

Charles paused, a smile appearing on his face. "I'd be honored if she called me that someday, but that is her decision and Jul's." He stirred the chamomile. "We've known each other for nearly two seasons now, though to be honest feels longer."

"What is time but merely a human's counting of the sun's rotation," Byron shrugged. "But I understand what you mean. I felt the same way when I met my Georgia."

"Be—Before we left Waterwealt I—I promised Jul, after all this is over we'd find a museum to rebuild together."

"I am sure you will, Charles."

"Charlie. You can call me Charlie."

The older man raised an eyebrow. "Julie and Penny love you, Charlie. You'll have that museum someday. I promise." He paused for a moment, his expression bittersweet. "Now, the soup is nearly done. I assume the tea is too. Best be getting this up to the girls before it gets cold."

CHAPTER 20

Dinner eaten and everyone settled in, Charles took the first watch, swapping with Byron around midnight. Despite the comfortable bed and the roof over his head, Charles found his mind couldn't help but dwell on what lay ahead. They were going to Matson, the last place he'd ever thought he'd return to. A million different scenarios ran through his mind. Most of them were bad. At some point, however, his exhaustion won out and he fell asleep.

The sun was well up, when he felt something poking his face. Groggily opening his eyes, he found Penny, sitting on the bed beside him smiling.

"Looks like someone is feeling better." He chuckled, running a hand through his hair.

"I told her to let you sleep a bit longer but she insisted." He heard Julietta laugh from the other bed.

"What time is it anyway?"

"Midmorning-ish."

Sitting up, he shook his head. "Why don't you grab my stethoscope and otoscope for me, Penny, and I'll give you a quick check-up?"

Penny almost immediately jumped from the bed, running over to Charles's bag.

"I think she is the only child in history who enjoys check-ups," he laughed, shifting so he sat facing Julietta.

"I think she just likes that you are the one who gives them to her."

Penny returned, sitting on the bed beside Charles, the stethoscope around her neck.

"Did you want to give me a check-up first?"

She nodded, putting the device in her ears like she'd seen Charles do before. Placing the silver circle on his chest she let him help her find the right spot to hear his heart.

"How does it sound?"

Penny gave a thumbs up, before shifting to kneeling on the bed, placing the circle on his forehead.

Charles and Julietta laughed. "What's he thinking about, Penny?" Julietta asked with a bright smile.

Climbing off the bed Penny went to grab Nelson.

"Miss Penny would like to inform you she thinks your heart sounds very strong," Nelson explained.

Penny whispered to Nelson again.

"She says you were thinking about kissing Momma Julie."

Charles quirked an eyebrow, finding it hard to not laugh. "Is that an official doctor's order?"

Penny smiled, sitting once more on the bed.

"Miss Penny says yes."

"Well now, what do we have here?" Byron chuckled, leaning on the door frame.

"Dr. Penny here wanted to give me a check-up before I gave her hers."

"Miss Penny is ready for her check-up now," Nelson added.

Checking Penny over, ensuring to also "listen" to her thoughts, knees, and stomach, he breathed a sigh of relief. "Everything looks and sounds good. Your nose will be a bit stuffy for a few more days, but that should clear up. I say you need a couple of the CCCs we brought with us after breakfast, and you'll be right as rain."

Penny hugged him.

"I think that can be arranged. I came to get some help bringing up breakfast. Want to help me, Miss Penny? Maybe I can sneak you a few extra CCCs before breakfast too." Byron winked.

Penny was immediately to her feet, practically dragging Byron out the door to the kitchen.

"She sure loves her CCCs." Julietta rolled her eyes teasingly.

"She sure does," Charles sighed, moving so he sat beside Julietta. "And how is Momma Julie?"

"Feeling all right. Ankle hurts but feels much better now that I've rested it."

He turned his attention to her ankle. "Looks and feels a lot better." He gently pressed around the bruising. "You soaked it, like I said?"

"Of course, Dr. Hawthorne."

Turning back to her he frowned. "I'm sorry, Jul, for last night. I know I was rather short tempered."

"You were worried and exhausted. I don't blame you."

"Still…"

"Charlie…"

"What?"

"I believe Dr. Penny gave you a prescription for something."

Charles smiled, moving closer. "I suppose she did."

"Plus, I don't believe we've had the chance to attend to our Fallen-in-love-itis much while we've traveled."

"Shall we rectify that?" He brushed some hair from her face before resting a gentle hand behind her head.

"Do your worst, doctor."

Charles leaned in, kissing her gently once, twice as she wrapped her arms around him, deepening the second.

"I love you, Jul."

"And I you."

"Well, Miss Penny, looks like they took your doctor's orders very seriously," Byron chuckled, holding two plates of food.

Penny was beaming, seeing Momma Julie and Charlie kissing.

Realizing they now had an audience, Charles and Julietta blushed.

"Um, yes. Of course, we followed Dr. Penny's orders," Charles smirked, rubbing the back of his head.

"Of course." The older gentleman's eyes twinkled with mirth. "Let's eat. I want to do some more exploring today for supplies. Think it might be wise to give ourselves another day's rest before we venture on."

Leaving Julietta and Penny to rest some more, Charles and Byron spent the rest of the day seeking out supplies, only taking a break to eat lunch with the girls. Having found little more than a few preserved foods, some more clothes, and a few bandages, they spent the evening after dinner rationing out what they could to hopefully get them to their next destination.

The journey to Cartsdale took three more days. After all their misadventures leading to Neilhem, they were pleasantly surprised to find the next leg of their journey relatively smooth. It wasn't until they were near the city limits that Mother Nature decided to change that.

They were within minutes of entering the city when the sky decided to turn a sickly green, the wind picking up significantly. By the time they hit the main road the dust storm was bearing down full force.

Byron, who was holding Penny tightly, glanced around desperately for shelter. Charles holding onto Julietta, was not far behind him. They managed to make it part way up the street when they heard a voice beckoning over the wind.

"Over here!"

Following the sound, they, to their relief, were ushered quickly into what looked to be a small cafe.

"Are you insane?" asked the woman who had called them over rushing to grab water.

"Wasn't our intention," Byron coughed, setting down little Penny on a chair at the nearest table. "Are you okay?"

Penny coughed slightly but nodded.

Charles led Julietta over to another chair. "That storm…came out of…nowhere."

"Here, this should help. Please sit," the woman gestured, her voice a bit on edge.

Once everyone had collected themselves the woman began her questioning.

"First off, who are you?"

"Brandon, this here's my son Nicholas, daughter-in-law Jessa, and granddaughter Josie," Byron explained, giving Charles and Julietta a sideways glance.

"I see," the woman frowned. "What were you doing out in the wastes, with a child no less?"

"Traveling to visit family in Allisburg," Charles replied with the lie that they had agreed to if anyone questioned them.

"Yes," Julietta coughed, keeping her face obscured, hoping the woman wouldn't notice she was too young for Penny to actually be hers. "My sister lives there. She's been writing to us for months about visiting her and her new husband."

The woman's eyes narrowed. "Well, you picked a fine time to travel with the crazy weather we've been having." Her expression softened a bit, glancing over to Penny. "Though, I suppose there really is never a good time is there? Name's Francine. This is my cafe. You are welcome to stay 'til the storm clears."

"Thank you, Francine," Byron sighed, shaking a bit of dust from himself. "You wouldn't happen to have a place my family and I can wash up a bit? Also, we are rather hungry." He reached into his pocket, pulling out about 10 coins. "This cover us?"

Francine's expression was blank as she took the coin. "There are washrooms at the back. I'll see what I can do about getting you a hot meal. There are some couches by the fireplace you can rest on."

Cleaned up, the group made themselves comfortable by the fireplace. Byron was sitting on one couch, little Penny lying down beside him, head in his lap, already asleep. Charles and Julietta took the other, Julietta resting her sore ankle beside her.

"Weather is getting worse. First the freak rainstorm, now this?" Charles shook his head, sinking back in his seat.

"At least we are all okay," Byron sighed, brushing a piece of hair from Penny's face. "We got lucky we didn't inhale much dust."

"Par for the course at this point," Julietta yawned, leaning her head on Charles's shoulder. "I feel like I'm half made of dust at this point."

"Tell me about it," Charles closed his eyes. "Everyone still feeling okay?"

"Feeling the same as when you checked us a few minutes ago," Byron smirked. "He really is a mother hen, isn't he, Jess?"

"I don't blame him," she closed her eyes as well. "I've learned enough and seen enough of what dust can do."

"I know. Just trying to keep things light."

"Sorry, Brandon." Charles smiled slightly. "Too tired tonight for jokes."

"Fair enough," He chuckled, taking the hint. "You should both try to get some sleep. We are safe enough here, I think."

"It is so strange, a man from the capital," came an unfamiliar woman's voice.

Byron awoke with a start upon hearing those words. He was still sitting on the couch by the fireplace, little Penny, sound asleep beside him. It seemed someone had placed a blanket over her during the night. Glancing up, he found Charles and Julietta sound asleep on the other couch, Charles's arm resting around her.

"From the capital?" He heard Francine reply. "What would the capital want with Cartsburg? We've only just reached what they consider 'medium city' status. Surely, they can't already be wanting to make changes."

"He's not here for renovations," the other woman said. "He is here to test the children."

Byron quietly crept over to Charles and Julietta, shaking them awake.

"What's—" Charles stopped as Byron held a finger to his lips. "Test the children? What for?"

"Some big school in the capital. If they are smart enough, they get sent there to learn and get government jobs or something."

"Well, there aren't very many children here in Cartsburg. I think the school only has about 15."

"They are looking for children about five to ten seasons old."

Julietta and Charles were to their feet, reaching for their packs while Byron woke Penny.

"Come on, we need to—"

"Oh good, you're awake. Storm is over." Francine approached.

"Yes, good thing too. Thank you for your hospitality. It was much appreciated," Byron smiled, picking up a rather groggy Penny. "We really should be going. Need to get supplies before heading to Allisburg."

"You should consider staying here for a bit," the woman smiled. "There is a man in town looking for children about your Josie's age, I think. Said something about a good school in the capital."

"No!" Julietta paused, realizing her abruptness. "No, thank you. We really should be going. My sister is expecting all of us in Allisburg."

"Suit yourself," Francine shrugged.

"You wouldn't mind not telling the capital man about us, would you?" Byron reached into his pocket, producing a couple of coins. "We wouldn't want our trip to be delayed by someone trying to convince us to send our little Josie away while we are away from home."

Francine's eyes narrowed on Byron. "I am not in the business of taking coins for silence, sir. If you don't want to stay in Cartsburg then by all means leave. I'm not fussed. If you get stopped on the road that's your problem."

"Very well, sorry," he sighed, giving Julietta and Charles a fleeting look of fear before exiting the cafe.

The next hour was a flurry of activity as the group went from shop to shop gathering what supplies they could without drawing too much suspicion. They had managed to purchase some preserved food along with one new blanket before they found themselves face to face with the one person they didn't want to find them, the capital man.

They had just exited another shop, having purchased some bottles of water.

"At this rate, we won't have enough supplies to leave until noon," Charles complained.

"Can't buy in bulk, Charlie. It will draw attention." Byron sighed, adjusting his hold on Penny.

"The longer we stay here the more I am worried—" Julietta's face fell, her heart dropping into her stomach as she spotted a tall lanky man in a 1950s suit round the corner.

"Oh no." Byron's eyes went wide as the man approached them.

"Well, hello there. I'm Mr. Turner, an ambassador for the Apolis Academy for the Future. I'm here in Cartsdale looking for children to test to attend this prestigious school."

Byron could feel Penny tense in his arms, burying her face into his chest. "Thank you, Mr. Turner, but we are just passing through." He moved to walk past him but was stopped.

"Oh, but you see, all children need to be tested. It is important. Certainly, your journey can wait a day more."

"It really can't." Charles butted in, placing himself between Byron and the man. "We really must go, sir. I am sure our daughter can be tested once we are back home." Grabbing Byron's arm, he pushed past Turner roughly, Julietta following right on their heels. As they did, Penny was jostled slightly, causing her to look up.

"E-165141425."

"Run!" Byron shouted, bolting down a side street, Charles and Julietta right behind him.

The sound of rushing footfalls reached their ears as they hurried along the various streets, hoping to lose their pursuers.

"We need to get out of the city, the far side should be just ahead," Byron panted, rounding another corner.

They had barely made it to the city limits when they heard the sound of a gun going off. Julietta and Charles immediately reached for their own. Another shot pinged off of a nearby rock as Julietta stopped for, turning back towards the city. Without hesitation, she fired.

There were more shouts, but no more gunshots followed as Charles grabbed Julietta running after Byron once more.

CHAPTER 21

They continued until well after dark, Penny's flashlights around their necks lighting the way. Spotting a natural formation of rock outcroppings, not unlike Skelter Ridge, they sought out a decently hidden cave before finally allowing themselves to stop.

"It's all right, Penny. We are safe now," Charles comforted, pulling another blanket over the trembling girl.

Byron, having set up the campfire, was keeping watch, while Charles and Julietta sorted their sleeping arrangements.

"It's okay. We won't let that bad man take you. You are safe with us." Charles frowned, gently placing a hand on the girl's face. "I promise."

Penny nodded, a few tears escaping.

He shook his head, wiping her face. "You've been very brave, our lucky Penny. We love you very much."

She gave a small smile through her tears.

Reaching into her bag, Charles pulled out Nelson.

"You don't have to turn him on. I know he makes you feel safe."

"Charlie, Sir Byron, and Momma Julie keep safe," Penny whispered, holding Nelson close.

"Charlie, Momma Julie, and Sir Byron will keep you safe," Charles smiled sadly. "Rest, Penny. You are safe now."

Having assured Penny was asleep, he turned his attention to Julietta who sat nearby, leaning against the cave wall.

"Jul?" His heart sank, seeing the silent tears running down her face.

Julietta didn't say a word.

Sitting beside her, he took her into his arms. "It's all right, Jul. Everyone is all right."

"I shot him, Charlie." She stated flatly.

"I know."

"I shot him in the leg."

"You did what you had to." He wiped a few of her tears with his hand. "He'll come back for us."

He held her a bit tighter, feeling her body tense. "Not yet. Not if we can help it."

"What you did today, Julie, was hard but necessary," Byron affirmed. "No one likes to hurt someone but…if you hadn't done that, no telling what would have happened. You only fired because they shot first."

"I—I couldn't let them hurt us. I had to do something."

"You did." Charles kissed her forehead. "You protected us."

After a minute more, Julietta's tears subsided, her body relaxing into Charles's arms.

"You okay?" he asked tentatively.

"I'm all right," she nodded, exhausted. "My ankle hurts something fierce, but I'll live."

Charles glanced down at her foot, debating if he should move, but Julietta stopped him. "Leave it be. Right now, I need you here more."

He nodded in understanding, shifting so her head rested against his chest.

Byron turned away, his heart aching. "You two should get some rest. I'll take the first watch. We leave at first light."

It was another four days to Matson, the damage from the sudden dust storms and the need to cover their tracks making travel more diffi-cult. Their lack of supplies only made the journey more miserable as food had to be rationed leaving everyone with grumbling stomachs. By the time they reached their destination, evening was drawing near. Cold, exhausted, and hungry they entered the city limits, Byron car-rying Penny.

Approaching the first inn they could find, Charles attempted to get a room.

"Identification card?" the man at the front desk asked.

"We just came into town. We don't have IDs," he explained.

"I'm very sorry, sir, but without an identification card, I cannot rent you a room. It's the law."

"Since when?"

"About a cycle ago, sir. All citizens of Matson were issued identification cards. Visitors are to report to the town hall to receive temporary ones before they can stay."

Charles shook his head. "Are you sure you can't just rent us a room for the night? We'll go get the identification in the morning."

"I'm sorry, sir. Please leave."

Defeated, they left, hoping to try their luck somewhere else. Much to their dismay, the story the first inn owner told them was true, as they received similar treatment from every place they stopped. Most were sympathetic to their state, but not enough to allow them to stay without identification.

"Guess we have no choice," Byron sighed, adjusting his hold on Penny. "The sooner we get those IDs, the better."

Making the long walk to City Hall, they reached it just as the sun began to set.

"I'm sorry, but City Hall is closed for the day." The guard at the door stated bluntly, blocking their way.

"But we need to get identification cards or we can't stay," Charles spat, exasperated.

"I'm sorry, sir, but the City Hall is closed. Come back in the morning."

"We can't wait until morning," Julietta argued. "We have traveled a long way to be here. Surely, you won't make us sleep in the streets?"

"If you do not leave, I will be forced to remove you from the premises."

"Please, sir," Byron pleaded, sounding weary. "We have a child with us. We just need identification so we can rest."

"I am sorry, but you must leave or—"

"Michael, what is going on here?" The door opened, out stepping a rather formally dressed woman.

"Governor, these folks are seeking identification but I've already told them that City Hall is closed. I was about to remove them."

Charles turned to Governor Lisle, his face falling.

"Charlie? Is that you?" Lisle smiled. "I was wondering if you'd come."

"You know them, ma'am?"

"Yes, please let them in."

Ushered into City Hall, they waited quietly as the Governor began to fill out the necessary forms. "Charlie...it's been so long."

"Charles, please Governor Benedict," he sighed, his voice weak.

"Charles, no need for formalities. We are old friends, after all, aren't we?"

Charles remained silent as Lisle filled out his form. "You are 27 Cold now, yes?"

"Yes."

"Now for your companions."

"Julietta Milard, 24 Damp," Julietta stated, keeping close to Charles.

"Byron Galigar, 59 Damp."

"And the little one?" Lisle asked, a tone of curiosity in her voice.

"Penny Milard, 9 Dust," Julietta answered, shifting uncomfortably on her feet.

Penny lifted her head, smiling at Lisle.

"Your daughter, I presume?" Lisle raised an eyebrow but didn't question further as Julietta nodded in confirmation. "Very well, here are your temporary identification forms. Please, allow me to escort you to one of our finest inns."

She led them to a place just down the road called the Snapdragon Inn. Entering, they were greeted by a rather jovial woman named Lynn.

"Lisle, to what do I owe the pleasure?"

"Evening, Lynn. These folks here are good friends of mine, Dr. Charles Hawthorne, and his...family. Please set them up with rooms, food, and anything else they may need. You can put it on my tab."

"Of course. If you would follow me."

Before Charles could leave, Lisle stopped him. "Spend tonight and tomorrow resting. I wish to speak with you in my office the day after."

The accommodations offered to them were rather comfortable, a small apartment with three bedrooms, a bathroom, and a kitchenette. Once they were settled, Lynn brought them food and some fresh clothes before leaving them to rest and recover.

Spending a full day recouping, the meeting was fast upon them. Having eaten breakfast, Charles, Julietta, and Byron were seated at the kitchen table while Penny sat in front of the fireplace tinkering with her portable radios.

"I suppose I should be getting ready for this," Charles frowned, taking a sip of his coffee.

"Do you want me to come with you?" Julietta offered, her eyes full of worry.

"Don't think Lisle will take kindly to that." He shook his head. "She may seem nice right now, but I don't trust it."

"Neither do I. But it's our best chance at getting information," Byron sighed, leaning back in his chair. "We wanted to talk to her after all."

"Just wish it was more on our own terms." Charles shifted uncomfortably. "Too bad you can't be a fly on the wall."

"Yeah," Julietta sighed. "I'd give anything to be that."

Penny bounded up to the table, smiling brightly.

"What's up, Penny?" Charles questioned, as she handed him one of the portable radios turning it on.

There was static noise as Penny turned on her own.

"You got the radios working?" Byron looked confused.

Penny pressed a button on hers, the static dissipating.

"What—" Julietta stopped as her voice echoed from the radio in Charles's hand.

"Those aren't radios," Byron grinned. "Penny, you little ninja. You knew those were handheld talkers, didn't you?"

Penny smiled mischievously.

"Handheld talkers?" Charles quirked an eyebrow.

"We used them at Rho. They are for short-range communication. These are older but should do the job. You press the button there to talk. That one there mutes the audio so we can hear you, but you can't hear us."

"I think our Penny has brought us a bit more luck than we thought," Julietta smiled.

"So, I just need to leave mine on and muted and you can listen to the conversation no problem?" Charles examined the 'talker,' sounding a bit relieved. "Penny, you deserve two CCCs."

"Three," Byron corrected. "One for each one she's fixed."

Penny jumped up and down, setting the talker on the table before climbing onto Charles, and giving him a big hug.

"Thank you," he hugged her back. "Now I suppose I really should get ready."

Sitting on the couch in front of the fireplace, Julietta held Penny in her lap, nervous.

"You okay, Julie?" Byron frowned, taking a seat across from her, talker in hand.

"We've sent him into a lion's den," she sighed, shaking her head. "Who knows what will happen?"

"He went willingly. You didn't send him to anything."

"He is doing this because of us."

"He is doing it because he knows it's our best chance to protect Penny and possibly save other kids like her."

Julietta frowned, holding Penny a bit tighter. "I know we agreed to help you, Byron, I just feel...responsible to some degree for this. I read those articles Lisle wrote about him. Charlie may act brave but—"

"I know. He is a good man, a tough man. He'll be all right." Byron relaxed back in his seat. "Though to be honest I think you could have asked him to walk a tightrope over a sinkhole and he'd do it for you."

"He might as well be." Her shoulders slumped.

"Julietta, what you are feeling is completely normal. You love Charlie. He has been a wonderful father figure to little Penny and a loving partner."

Penny looked up at Julietta, a sad smile on her face.

"He has—wait, you've been calling him Charlie."

"He told me his story while we were searching in Neilhem and gave me permission while we cooked dinner that night."

"He trusts you, Byron."

"Just like he trusts you."

"I love him." Julietta sunk back into the couch a bit more. "He feels—"

"Like the piece that was always missing that you didn't know was missing." The older man smiled. "Like my missus was to me."

"I just want him home safe." Julietta felt Penny snuggle more into her arms. "We both do."

"We all do." Static crackled from the radio in his hand.

"I'm here to see Governor Benedict," came Charles's voice.

"Right this way, sir," stated the guard. Having relieved Charles of his knife and gun, he led him down the maze of hallways to a door labeled Governor Lisle Benedict.

Knocking, the guard let Lisle know of Charles's presence.

"Come in," Lisle beckoned.

Stepping into her office, Charles stood just at the entrance as the guard closed the door behind him with an audible click.

"It's nice to see you, Charlie. It's been a long time. Nearly four cycles if I remember correctly."

"Charles, please Governor Benedict."

"Charles, why so formal? Please, have a seat."

He sat in one of the two chairs in front of Lisle's desk.

"Comfortable? Would you like some tea, or—"

"I am guessing it took an awful lot of effort to make sure that letter and those articles found me. How exactly you managed it I don't know. You must have something pretty important to tell me so let's cut to the chase. Why do you really want me here, Lisle?"

Lisle's face fell, along with all pretense of formality. "Because, Charles…I need your help."

Chapter 22

"Excuse me? I must have misheard. You need my help?" Charles looked very confused.

"I'm sure your friends in your pocket would love to hear this," Lisle frowned, leaning back in her chair.

Raising an eyebrow, he removed the radio from within his duster, setting it on the desk in front of him. "Do I want to know how you knew?"

"I wouldn't trust me either, if I were in your boots."

"What do you want, Lisle?"

"What I want to do first is apologize."

Charles stared blankly at her.

"I know at this point this probably means nothing to you, but I'm sorry. What I did to you four cycles ago was...inexcusable," Lisle sighed, brushing a loose strand of blond hair from her face. "I was young, scared, and grieving. Victor and I had just agreed to a union when Archie was brought in that morning. I was already overwhelmed when the news broke that he didn't make it. Suddenly, my plans of marriage and starting a family were dashed to the side with the weight of losing a friend and being thrust into the governor position before I was honestly ready. I panicked. The people wanted an answer, and I gave them one, at the cost of a good friend. I should have just taken the hit, admitted we lost the culprit, and dealt with the fallout. Instead, I took the easy way out, the young and stupid way out."

He quirked an eyebrow, crossing his arms as Lisle continued.

"The day you left Matson in unwarranted shame I—I was a mess. If it wasn't for Victor, I probably would still be a mess. I regret that day, regret my actions. Matson didn't just lose a doctor. The world lost a doctor, and I lost a friend."

"You expect me to believe you? It's been four cycles. No one would take me. You must really be in a bind to think I'd—"

"I have a child with Victor."

He paused, his senses on edge. "And?"

"It seems you have one as well, though Penny is obviously not biologically yours or Julietta's."

Grabbing the radio, he immediately made for the door. "This conversation is over."

"Charles, wait!"

He opened the door.

"I have another child like Penny."

He stopped, his back to her. "Penny is just an ordinary kid."

"You and I both know that is a lie."

"Think what you want."

"I know the truth about Apolis, the real dark truth."

The sound of papers hitting the desk stopped Charles in his tracks, debating if he should turn back.

"Please, Charles, I don't want any more children taken. Not mine, not Penny, not anyone's. Not after Nicolas."

To her relief, he closed the door, walking back over to the desk. On it, he found several marked-up papers.

"Please, read."

Setting the radio back down, he took the papers in hand, his eyes widening.

"It's not the government, but a private research lab…"

"For those with Arcane powers. A place dedicated to understanding them and…'fixing' them." Lisle's voice quivered. "The government has no idea."

"So much has been redacted." Charles frowned. "J.H., who's—"

"Allow me to explain." Lisle gestured to the chair. Charles paused briefly before taking it.

"About a cycle ago, a child was left on my doorstep. The poor boy was sick and injured. The only identification on him was a necklace with a nickel engraved with strange markings and a piece of paper that gave his name as Nicolas."

The memory of Julietta's description of Penny when she first found her flashed through his mind. "How did you get these papers?"

"About a week after he appeared, a woman showed up at my door. She gave me the name Daisy Herbert."

Charles found it hard not to react to the name. If he were to hedge his bets, that was the name Ava had tried to give them on the radio.

"She gave me these papers. Explained she worked for a group called the Constellation. They were trying to save these kids from J.H."

Charles shook his head. "These papers state that J.H. believes anyone with Arcane powers is dangerous and that he is the cure. That's absurd."

"I would have thought this all absurd had Daisy not explained to me what she knew about J.H. Apparently he is Arcane himself, a powerful one at that."

"Yet, he—" He stopped, not wanting to reveal more. "What do you want from me? Why did you bring me here? How did you even find me?"

"Daisy, her Constellation has many informants. One happened to pass through Waterwealt and spotted not only you, Julietta, and little Penny, but Byron, a former contact. When they notified Daisy, she asked me about you having seen the articles. I told her the truth. She wanted to see Byron. I wanted to see you. Everything was confirmed when Byron contacted Ava a couple of weeks ago."

"You still haven't answered why you wanted me."

"It's Nicolas. Please, follow me."

Lisle led Charles to another room towards the back of the city hall. Entering, he found Victor, sitting and playing with a little girl of about four if he were to guess. What drew his attention, however, was a boy who looked to be about seven sitting and staring out a window, a woman, who he recognized as Henrietta, seated beside him.

"Victor, could you please take Maya outside for a bit?"

The man picked up the little girl, giving Charles a nod of recognition before departing.

Henrietta approached them. "Charlie?"

"Charles, please." He frowned.

"Charles, it's—been a long time."

He simply nodded.

Lisle broke the silence. "Henrietta has been taking care of Nicolas for me during the day. He is a bit…quiet."

"He hasn't spoken a word since he was left here a cycle ago," Henrietta sighed, adjusting her glasses. "He doesn't play. He doesn't read. I have to basically force him to eat. All he seems to want to do is stare out that window."

"He's been through something traumatic." Charles' shoulders slumped.

"No doubt in my mind." She nodded in agreement. "I am just worried about his health. He is nine Damp from what I could get out of him, but he's so small."

Penny is small for her age too. "May I give him a check-up?"

"You can certainly try." She stepped out of the way, allowing him to approach the boy.

"Nicolas?" He took a seat beside him, but Nicolas didn't react.

"My name is Charles, Nicolas."

The boy turned his head to him but did not answer.

"I am a doctor. I am here to give you a check-up, if that is all right?"

Charles went to reach into his bag. The boy bolted from his chair, moving to hide behind the sofa against the wall. Not wanting to frighten the boy further, he slowly closed his bag, taking his time walking back to Lisle and Henrietta.

"He is scared. I won't force him."

"He barely lets me near him, let alone anyone else," Lisle frowned. "Once he was healed, even Henrietta found it hard to get him to interact."

"We can't force him. Based on his reaction, he's been through a lot." His brow furrowed. "I have an idea, but…"

"Let's continue this conversation in the hall. Henrietta, see if you can calm him."

Closing the door, Lisle leaned against the wall. "Will you help us?"

"Yes, but—"

"You want assurance. I respect that. What do you want from me?"

"First, I want to be allowed to bring Julietta, Byron, and Penny."

"Done."

"Second, we will not be disarmed. I can promise you everything will remain holstered and hidden on us so as not to frighten Nicolas, but I have to ensure everyone's safety."

"Of course."

"Lastly, you will set up a meeting with Daisy for us."

"As you wish."

Charles was shocked at Lisle's willingness to comply; a thought that he apparently could not keep off his face.

"I know you don't trust me, Charles. If I was in your shoes, I would expect nothing less." Reaching down she pulled a small knife from her boot, ensuring she kept it pointed at herself. "All of us have something to protect. I won't let harm come to my Maya or Nicolas and you won't let any come to your Penny."

"You assume they are my family. When you checked us into the Snapdragon you said as much."

"I knew you from before. You wear your heart on your sleeve. I saw it when you showed up at City Hall, and I see it in your eyes now." Lisle smiled sadly. "We've both grown and have families now. It's all we have in this wretched world. We'd protect it with our own lives if we had to." She relaxed, replacing the knife. "You can collect your things as you leave. I expect I shall see you tomorrow?"

Charles felt confused, but nodded. "Tomorrow."

Returning to the apartment, Charles was greeted by Penny running up to him. Picking her up he held her tightly as he stepped into the room.

"Are you all right?" Julietta asked, placing a gentle hand on his shoulder.

"He's like Penny." He shook his head, hugging Penny tighter.

The girl snuggled into him, resting her head on his shoulder.

Byron set some tea on the coffee table in front of the fireplace. "Come sit. We have much to discuss."

Once everyone was settled, Charles explained everything they could not see. "He was small for his age, like Penny. He wouldn't let me give him a check-up. Reacted poorly as soon as he caught sight of my medical bag."

"Penny was like that at first." Julietta frowned. "She always hated the Medical Wing."

Penny, who was sitting between them, shifted closer to Charles, resting her head on him. He placed a comforting arm around her shoulders, shaking his head. "It's all right, Penny. You and little Nicolas have been through a lot."

"If he was in any shape like she was…" Byron shook his head, his voice fading.

"Penny, can I tell Charlie about the day I found you?" Julietta asked gently.

Penny nodded, snuggling more into Charles.

"There had been a dust storm," she began, taking a sip of tea to steady herself. "I happened to be cleaning the atrium when I heard a faint knock at the door. There was Penny, covered head to toe in dust and dirt. She was scratched up, bruised, and looked as though she hadn't eaten right in a while. She was burning up something fierce."

Charles wrapped his arm a bit tighter around Penny.

"Once I got her cleaned up and bandaged, I did my best to treat the fever. Thankfully after about a day it broke. Then she slept for nearly three days, only waking when I went to feed her and change her bandages." A few tears escaped her eyes. "Much to my relief, after about a week she was awake more than asleep and slowly began walking after that. She wasn't 100 percent until about a month later. By then she had warmed up to me and Marisa who came by often once she heard."

Penny shifted to Julietta's lap, giving her a hug.

"My Penny," she sighed, kissing the girl's forehead. "It hurt my heart to think someone would do such a thing to a child."

Byron and Charles both wiped tears from their eyes.

"It's why I joined the Constellation." Byron bowed his head. "I don't know how Penny and now Nicolas came to be in their situations but…I don't want anyone else to go through it."

"I convinced Lisle to set up a meeting with Daisy, in exchange for me helping with Nicolas." Charles ran a hand through his hair. "I would have helped, regardless if she said no, but figured—"

"What is your idea, Charlie?" Julietta shifted, allowing Penny to rest more comfortably against her.

"Nicolas is like Penny; he doesn't speak. Unlike her, however, medicine still terrifies him. I don't think he will listen to an adult on these matters as it was adults who did this to him."

Penny nodded in agreement.

"Are you suggesting he'd listen to Penny?" Byron quirked an eyebrow. "I know you asked Lisle if we could come and that we'd be armed but..." He paused, thinking. "Then again..."

"I—I know you'd never put Penny in danger, but I don't know if I am fully okay with this." Julietta quirked an eyebrow. "What if Lisle is lying? Using poor Nicolas."

"That's why I asked for the ability to protect ourselves, as well as having all of us there." Charles sunk back in his seat. "I can't just let that little boy—"

"No, of course not," she interrupted. "I understand why you think what you do. Don't think me—"

"Never," he assured. "I know you want to help him as much as I do. You just want me to know your concerns."

She relaxed. "Thank you."

"Now I think there is one more person we need to ask before we go through with this plan." He looked over to Penny who was smiling. "Miss Penny, will you be this doctor's nurse and try to help me with Nicolas?"

"Penny Charlie nurse," Penny cheered.

"Then it's settled," Byron chuckled. "Tomorrow, we go back to City Hall together and hope your little negotiation holds true."

They arrived at the town hall after lunch. As promised, they were not searched nor relieved of their hidden protections as Lisle led them to the playroom. Henrietta was there with Nicolas, who was still sitting at the window, unmoving.

Byron placed himself firmly at the door while the others hovered nearby.

"Go on, Penny." Charles encouraged Penny, who was holding his hand. She let go, approaching the boy with Nelson.

Looking back at the adults, she gave them a smile as she turned Nelson on, whispering to him.

"Hello, Nicolas. My name is Nelson. I am friends with Miss Penny. Miss Penny tells me you are a friend too?"

Nicolas didn't move.

"Miss Penny wants me to tell you it's okay if you are a bit scared. She was too the first time she met Momma Julie and her Charlie, but they are good people. They protect Penny. They love Penny."

Nicolas looked over to them, his expression blank as Penny took the seat beside him, setting Nelson on the window ledge.

"Miss Penny wants to know if you are okay?"

Nicolas nodded.

"Miss Penny wants to know if you are scared?"

He nodded again.

"Miss Penny says she understands, but her Charlie only wants to help Nicolas. He wants to give Nicolas a check-up."

The boy shook his head, looking frightened.

"Miss Penny wants to know if you want her to go first. Would that help Nicolas?"

Nicolas paused for a moment, thinking, before nodding yes.

Penny smiled at Charles, beckoning him over.

Kneeling by the chair, Charles took his time giving Penny a check-up ensuring Nicolas saw exactly what he was doing and how he was doing it. He explained everything to the boy as he had done for Penny. He even did his silly checks that made Penny laugh.

As he finished, Penny pointed to the stethoscope around his neck. Charles nodded in understanding, cleaning it before placing it in her ears. Taking the metal circle in hand she placed it on his chest as he had taught her. He watched as her eyebrows rose, likely hearing just how nervous his heart was beating.

Turning to Nelson, Penny whispered something to him.

"Miss Penny wants to know if Nicolas is okay with her checking him too?"

Nicolas turned to face Penny, letting her check him.

"Miss Penny says your heart sounds loud and strong. She thinks it would be better if her Charlie checks though, just to be sure. Are you okay with that?"

Nicolas looked at Charles.

"Are you okay with me giving you a check-up like Miss Penny?"

The boy nodded.

Taking the stethoscope from Penny he began his exam.

Once he finished, he reached into the outside pocket of his bag where he had stored a few chocolate chip cookies. "Both of you sound healthy. I think you deserve some CCCs." He smiled, handing the cookies to Penny before rising and heading back over to the others.

"Well?" Henrietta bit her lip, nervous.

"Physically, everything seems all right at the moment, though he definitely needs to start eating more. His reflexes are a bit slow indicating a nutritional need."

"We've tried...but—" Lisle stopped watching the two children.

"Miss Penny wants to know if you want a CCC?"

Nicolas eyed the cookie warily.

"Miss Penny says not to worry. Momma Julie and her Charlie only give her good food. Not like school."

He took the cookie, biting it with a small smile.

"Miss Penny wants to know, do Miss Lisle and Miss Henrietta give you good food?"

The boy paused, thinking.

"Miss Penny wants to know, have you been eating the food they give?"

He held up his hand, indicating a little.

"Miss Penny asks, have you had nightmares from it or felt funny like in school?"

He shook his head.

"Miss Penny thinks the food is safe then like Momma Julie and her Charlie's."

He nodded in understanding.

"Miss Penny says you should ask Miss Lisle to make the sweet toast like her Charlie makes for breakfast. It is delicious!"

Upon hearing this the adults chuckled.

"It seems your Penny may have gotten through to my Nicolas." Lisle sounded relieved.

"Our little nurse." Julietta took Charles's hand. "She learned that from you, Charlie."

Charles breathed a sigh of relief, seeing a smile now on both the kids' faces as they continued to talk through Nelson. "I am just glad they are both all right."

Byron moved out of the way as Victor and Maya appeared.

"Momma, what's going on?" Maya asked.

"Nothing, dear," Lisle assured, picking her up. "An old friend of mine, Dr. Charles, was just checking on your brother Nicolas for me. He says he is going to be all right."

"Does that mean Nic will play with me now?"

"Why don't you go try to talk to him and Penny?"

Maya nodded as Lisle set her down. As she walked over to Penny and Nicolas the adults smiled seeing Penny have Nelson introduce her and offer Maya a cookie.

"If only adults could be like children." Lisle shook her head. "We could learn a thing or two from them."

"Don't we already?" Byron chuckled.

"I think I agree." Victor placed a hand on his wife's shoulder. "Daisy messaged. She'd like to meet everyone at sunset. The usual place."

"Looks like you got your meeting." Lisle rubbed the back of her head.

"Thank you, Lisle." Charles held out a hand.

Lisle took it. "I know one act of trust does not fix cycles of mistrust. I hope to someday earn yours back."

"I accept your apology and maybe someday you will," he nodded. "We have to start somewhere."

"Daisy's place is about a half-hour walk from here. We can let the kids play a bit before I take you all over there. Sound good?"

Wishing her new friends goodbye, Penny took Julietta's hand as Lisle led them through the city streets to the shopping district. It wasn't long after she stopped in front of what looked to be a small tea shop called Auriga's Tea Palace.

Byron and Charles entered first, hands resting on their hidden guns just in case as Julietta and Penny followed behind them. Their concern was short-lived and unfounded, however, as they approached the counter.

"Daisy?" Lisle knocked on the counter. "It's Lisle. I have the folks that wished to see you."

The sound of wheels against wood echoed through the small shop as the curtain that led to the back of the shop opened, a woman wheeling herself up to the counter.

Byron's jaw dropped. "Ola?"

"It's been a long time, my old friend."

CHAPTER 23

"Cygnus," Byron stated breathlessly.

"Corvus," Ola replied, smiling serenely. "Please sit. We have much to discuss."

As they took seats at the cafe tables, Ola laid out a spread of cookies and biscuits with some tea. "You look well, Byron, though I must say your mustache is a bit grayer than before."

"I can blame you for that," he chuckled, stroking it.

"I suppose I am partially to blame, given what happened when we last met." She frowned a moment, before once more putting on a neutral demeanor. "And E-165141425, I am happy to see you as well."

Penny, who was sitting in Charles's lap, shifted uncomfortably at the use of her former designation.

"She goes by Penny now," Byron corrected.

"Sorry, Penny," Ola nodded, before addressing Julietta and Charles. "I suppose I should introduce myself. I'm Ola Hampton, co-founder and current head of the Constellation."

"Charles Hawthorne." He extended a hand.

She shook it briefly. "The infamous Dr. Hawthorne. Lisle told me a good deal about you."

"I see." He frowned, leaning back in his seat.

"I assure you, she has told me the truth of her misdeeds. From one doctor to another, I found what you did to try to save Winslow inspiring." She glanced at Julietta. "Am I to assume this is your wife?"

"Girlfriend, Julietta Milard; I'm a restorer, mainly mechanical."

"She says that, but you should have seen the painting she was restoring in Waterwealt." Charles reached for a cookie and handed it to Penny.

"Julie did well in her restorative ventures in Waterwealt. Even helped me out with some bigger projects around town. Her museum is where we found the radio, which Penny fixed, that got us in contact with Ava," Byron explained. "Charles, aside from being the town doctor, was documenting the Medical Wing. More recently, however, he helped me sabotage a bomb testing at Skelter Ridge."

"I see." Ola's gaze roamed over them thoughtfully. "I am to assume, then, you both wish to help the Constellation in its work?"

"What is the Constellation, exactly?" Julietta questioned, taking a sip of her tea.

"A fair question." The woman sat up a bit straighter. "The Constellation is a secret organization, founded by Byron and I about 12 cycles ago whose sole purpose is to bring an end to J.H.'s plans and free the Curied. Byron and I were its founders."

Julietta and Charles both quirked an eyebrow at the older man, but said nothing as she continued.

"Currently, we have small outposts near each of the 24 institutions with Matson being our current main base of operations."

Penny visibly shirked at the mention of the Curied.

Charles placed a protective arm around the girl. "I think Penny is a bit uncomfortable with all this."

"I'm sorry, Penny," Ola frowned. "I know this subject holds horrible memories for you."

The little girl nodded, holding Charles a bit tighter.

"If your parents are all right with it, how about I take you next door to the toy store for a bit?" Lisle offered, glancing over to Charles and Julietta.

Penny looked up at Charles who turned to Julietta.

"I'm okay with that if Charlie is."

He gave Lisle a stern look but agreed. "Go on, Penny. It's okay."

Penny climbed off his lap taking Lisle's hand. "We'll be back in about 20 minutes." Lisle smiled warmly, leading Penny away.

"She—she hasn't told us what happened to her at Rho and we haven't pushed." Julietta shook her head. "She barely speaks as is and we don't want to lose what progress she's made. We were honestly shocked when she revealed her powers to us back in Hot."

Ola's brow furrowed. "Can't say I'm too surprised."

"She usually talks through a small toy robot she fixed up named Nelson," Charles added.

"A bright child, if I recall from my brief interactions with her at Rho." Ola's eyes reflected her turning mind. "So small for her age. I hated to see—"

"So, what exactly are J.H.'s plans?" Charles interrupted, not comfortable with the information Ola was likely to reveal. "Obviously something to do with the powers children like Penny have and lately, it seems, a bomb?"

Sensing his tone, she dropped the subject. "As of now, our intelligence is limited. We know, initially, these schools, if you can call them that, were established to understand why children were, for lack of a better phrase, manifesting Arcane powers. At least that is what we are led to believe. They are put through various tests. I can't speak for all the students, as I dealt with ones like Nicolas."

Julietta quirked an eyebrow, curiously. "Which means?"

"He's a telekinetic according to his recovered file. He was rescued by one of my Constellation members from Lambda-158. As far as we know, however, he hasn't revealed this ability. Lisle knows all this, if you are wondering."

"You mentioned you are a doctor?" Charles questioned.

"Yes, emphasis in psychology and the human brain," she shrugged. "That's how I ended up forcing my way into Rho-597."

Julietta shifted in her seat. "Byron mentioned you both working there. Told us about how you attempted an escape after seven cycles of work."

"What exactly happened to you, Ola?" Byron leaned on the table, hands clasped. "That day we were caught, I saw you being dragged away. There—there was so much blood."

"Yes, yes, there was." The woman's face fell. "To make a long story short, I was captured. They dragged me into one of the lower labs and locked me in a room. It was only the guilt of one of our supposed allies, Johan, that I am sitting here. I was barely conscious when he came for me. He got me out, somehow, and left me on Ava's doorstep nearly dead. When I finally returned to consciousness, I found I could no longer walk and the Constellation was in shambles. I spent a cycle recovering before attempting to reestablish the movement and finally moving here to Matson."

"You said there are 24 now?" The older man sank back in his seat. "There were only about 15 when I lost contact and only five outposts with Johani as the main."

"We've been busy in your unfortunate absence." Ola bowed her head. "Despite our best efforts, we've made little progress, only freeing a handful of Curied each cycle."

"These aren't government schools, surely you've reported them?" Charles asked, sounding frustrated.

"Money talks, as does a fresh coat of paint and strategic visits. We've tried to prove the truth but have been thwarted at every turn." Ola sunk further into her chair, looking exhausted. "After 12 cycles the Constellation is running thin. People are still too scared, too far removed, from one another to help."

"What can we do?" Julietta asked, determined. "How can we help?"

"You realize the risk you take helping us? If discovered…"

"It's a risk we are willing to take, for Penny…for Nicolas…for all the kids." Charles' eyes narrowed. "I won't let anyone take her. I can't stand by and let these kids—" He felt Julietta's hand on his arm. "We can't let this continue."

"That's all I needed to hear." A sympathetic smile appeared on Ola's face. "I should have known Byron wouldn't just let anyone help him. All right, you are both in. Now as for your first assignments…"

"Already?" Byron interjected. "Surely you aren't expecting them to jump in head first. We've only just arrived a few days ago! We aren't even established here."

"I can help with that," came Lisle's voice as she and Penny appeared.

Penny was holding a small plushie robot, looking very happy.

"What do you have there, Penny?" Julietta admired the small toy as Penny climbed into her lap.

"She spotted that almost immediately and became attached," Lisle chuckled. "I think it reminds her of her other robot friend."

Penny reached into her backpack, and pulled out Nelson, setting both robots on the table.

"Hello, Miss Penny, who is this?" Nelson asked curiously.

Penny whispered something to her little friend.

"I see Miss Penny, is Margie a friend for me?"

Penny nodded.

"Thank you, Miss Penny, for the friend," Nelson replied, sitting beside Margie.

"Thank you, Lisle." Julietta chuckled. "How much do we owe you?"

"Nothing. Seeing Penny happy is payment enough." Lisle took a seat beside Ola. "As for your living here, I am sure I could find you work and set you up with a place. It's the least I can do if you are helping the Constellation."

"Problem solved," Ola concurred. "If I may be so bold as to make a suggestion of jobs?"

"By all means."

"Byron, you said Charles documented the Medical Wing of the museum in Waterwealt?"

"Yes?" He crossed arms, leaning back in his chair. "He has his notes with him I believe."

"Then I see no reason he couldn't possibly work on publishing those. Maybe doing more medical-based research?"

"I don't think—" Charles paused, glancing over to Lisle. "My name in the medical community—"

"Shall be redeemed," Lisle interjected. "I will endorse any publications and sponsor you for reinstatement in the medical society."

Ola peered over her glasses at Charles. "Does this sound suitable for you?"

"That's...fine. What would I do for the Constellation, then?" He bit his lip, letting the idea pass over him.

"You would be our head doctor here in Matson. Not to mention any research in the medical field is of great value to us as it is to the world at large."

"I can accept that."

"Now for Julietta," Ola furrowed her brow. "I have a much more, shall we say, unusual request of you."

"Yes?" She shifted nervously, an action not unnoticed by Penny in her lap.

"One of the issues we have right now is getting information from the school near here: Iota-795. We have a field agent on the inside who goes by the alias Cartier Smith. As of two weeks ago, we have heard nothing from him. We sent in another agent last week, Joyce Handel. She too has not reported back."

Byron's face fell. "Ola, you aren't suggesting..."

"Yes, though not covertly as we previously have anyway," she answered. "It has come to our attention that a position for a low-level machinist has opened up in Iota. I am suggesting we get Julietta the job and have her snoop while there."

"Why not send me in too?" Charles offered, sounding worried. "I mean, not that Jul can't handle it alone, but…"

"You are too recognizable," the older woman stated flatly. "Your name is known in Matson."

Charles shrunk back in his seat, running a hand through his hair.

"That's an awfully tall ask for someone you barely know." Julietta held Penny a bit closer. "You want me to get hired at that horrid school and try to find your two missing members? You barely know me…"

"That's the beauty of it. Charles has a name here. Byron used to work at Rho as have I. Many of our agents have made waves. We need a new face."

"Turner man…" Penny whispered, snuggling into Julietta's arms looking frightened.

"Turner man?" Lisle looked confused.

"If I may, Miss Penny." Nelson stood toddling over to Ola. "Miss Penny refers to the strange man who nearly took her from her Momma Julie and her Charlie months ago. He was disposed of by Byron only to be seen again in Cartsburg. He recognized Penny. He's seen them all."

"Remarkable," the woman mumbled, admiring the small robot before her. "Nevertheless, she is still the least recognizable out of all of us. Therefore, I ask you, Julietta, if you'd be willing? I know this is a tall ask and a dangerous one, but think of the children you can potentially help, the families, if you can get us our information. Right now, we are at a severe loss and with the bombs…"

"What do you know about the bombs?" Byron raised an eyebrow.

"Our intel is limited at best." Her expression darkened. "I get reports from our auxiliary, or satellite, locations bi-weekly via radio. No agents have reported back anything of interest since the discovery of the bomb test trial at Johani, the one you managed to intercept the warning about. It was a fluke they found the plans. Since, we've put out a watch for any other information, but most facilities seem to have minimal information regarding bombs."

"Penny did tell us about some things she overheard at Rho." Charles frowned, looking to Penny who gave him a nod to continue. "Iso-210, HL-138, and genome…When I looked those up in the museum, I found some information about genetic testing. It wasn't pretty."

"All the more reason to send someone in." Ola shrugged.

"I'll do it," Julietta stated flatly.

Penny remained quiet in her arms.

"Are you sure, Julie?" Byron looked upset.

Julietta turned to Charles, a sad smile on her face. "I can do this. If it means making this world safer for Penny and the other kids, I'll do it."

"I know you can." Charles placed a hand on her knee. "Just be careful. Please?"

"I promise not to explode anything like you did," she teased.

The tension of the moment broke as Byron and Charles burst out laughing, Ola and Lisle giving the two men a strange look.

"It's a long story." Byron rolled his eyes. "But I guess that means we are staying in Matson for a while."

"Byron, you'll work here with me at the tea shop," Ola added. "It's a functional shop, but mainly gets used for covert messaging."

"I'll arrange for your stay at the Snapdragon Inn for now until a more permanent placement can be arranged," Lisle chimed in. "As for Penny, I'd like to offer her the chance to be tutored privately with Nicolas. Three days a week Henrietta works with him on reading, writing, and such. The other days she can spend with whomever."

"I mean, it couldn't hurt?" Charles shrugged. "We hadn't really had the chance."

"I think that is a great idea." Julietta echoed.

"Then it is settled. I'll get an application into Iota for you, Julietta, in the morning." Ola smiled brightly. "Should have you working within the week."

CHAPTER 24

The week following their meetings went by slowly. Penny had begun her lessons with Henrietta; she, Nicolas, and Maya becoming friends. They would spend their off time playing together in City Hall, at one of the offices at the nearby medical clinic with Victor and Charles, or 'helping' Byron and Ola serve the meager customers that actually came in for tea and cookies. While waiting for her application to be processed, Julietta worked with Charles on his medical publications, organizing notes and proofreading for him. By the end of the week, they received word she had been hired by Iota. She was to start on the first day of the following week.

Julietta stood nervously at the edge of town where she was to meet her new supervisor. That morning both Charles and Penny had stayed back at the apartment in the Snapdragon to see her off. Reaching up, she grasped the small gear that now rested on her necklace with the flashlight Penny had also given her, a gesture of good luck. Charles had given her his own form of good luck that morning with a kiss before he left her at the meeting spot.

Finally, after what seemed like ages, a woman appeared. "Jessa Lynn?"

"Oh, uh, yes. Sorry, just some first-day jitters."

Standing before her was a very foreign looking woman, with pale skin and equally pale eyes. She was a far cry from the usually tan wasteland inhabitant. Her clothes were unusual as well. Her black boots, black jeans, and brown shirt, though common, were too clean. It was her jacket, a stainless pure white long coat, and the goggles that rested on her black hair, however, that unsettled Julietta the most. They reminded her of the ones found in the Medical Wing in Waterwealt, the ones that scared Penny.

"I'm afraid I'm going to have to see your identification card. Can't be too careful." The woman started almost robotically.

"Of course." Julietta pulled out the fake identification card Lisle created for her.

While she was working at Iota, she was to be Jessa Lynn, a mechanic who moved to town a few weeks ago to live with her sister and seek employment in the big city after living in some no-name town for several cycles fixing water pipes. It wasn't a complete lie, but a deception all the same.

"Very well, Jessa, if you would follow me."

Julietta followed the still-unnamed woman for a few minutes to a rocky hill. "Um, may I ask your name?"

"Danni."

"Okay, Danni. What is it you do?"

"Research."

"Research on?"

"Classified."

Julietta's brow furrowed. Before she could ask anything else, they rounded the hill. There sitting at the bottom of it was what looked to be a rover of some sort, not unlike those pictured in the Space Exploration section of the Waterwealt Museum. This one, however, had a covering over it, likely to keep the passengers from getting too dirty when traveling.

"Please be seated," Danni instructed, getting into the driver's seat.

Realizing she didn't have much of a choice, Julietta got in. As she sat down, she moved her backpack into her lap, secretly wishing she had brought one of the talkers with her. Charles had suggested it that morning, but Byron warned them about bags being searched.

They zoomed along at a reasonable pace, the solar-powered cart sailing rather smoothly over the rock and dust-covered land. It made her wonder if this was what it was like when the astronauts landed on the moon and explored. After about a half hour a building appeared on the horizon, Iota-795.

Stopping just in front of its looming metal gate and barbed wire-topped fence, Julietta's heart felt like it would leap out of her chest. What horrors would she see behind these gates? Stepping out, Danni walked straight for a panel beside the door, scanning the ID that she now wore around her neck. "You will be given an encrypted identification card at the end of your orientation."

The metal gate slid open; Danni once more striding ahead without a second thought for Julietta, whose legs seemed to have rooted themselves in place making walking a feat of the mind rather than the body. After a moment of stealing her nerves, she followed, trying to act as unconcerned as possible as the gate closed behind her.

The building itself was made of a thick dull gray concrete. Approaching a second set of metal doors, Danni once more scanned her ID. "Once you enter, you will be searched as per security protocol. Please do not resist." She stated robotically as the doors slid open.

Stepping into the atrium, Julietta suddenly felt a chill run through her. The room was stark white, the floors spotless. Ahead of her was an archway that was lit up with lights, and to the right of it, a table with another machine she didn't recognize. On either side of these were guards holding batons with what looked like a metal coil on the end. Just beyond all this was yet another set of metal doors.

"Please remove your shoes and place them along with your identification cards and any bags or weapons on the table," boomed the guard at the table.

Danni didn't even flinch as she removed her now slightly dusty black boots, placing them on the table before stepping into the archway. She held her arms up facing the other machine for about 30 seconds before the guard on the other side waved her through.

"Please remove your shoes and place them along with your identification cards and any bags or weapons on the table," the guard repeated, eyeing Julietta suspiciously.

She hesitated a moment before removing her backpack and setting it on the table with her identification. Sliding her knife out of her boot she placed that beside it before removing them too. During all this her eyes watched the guard intently for any indicator of what he thought.

"Step into the detector please," the guard commanded, sounding bored.

Taking one last look at her items, Julietta obeyed, stepping into the strangely lit archway. Before she could walk through, however, another guard stopped her.

"Stay and face the dot, arms up."

Turning in the direction she had seen Danni face, she spotted the dot the guard spoke of, raising her arms. After about 30 seconds she heard the guard say. "Step out, please."

The first guard rifled through her bag before sending it and her shoes through the strange machine beside the archway but her knife remained on the other side.

"What is that around your neck?" The guard questioned, pointing to Penny's flashlight.

"Just a flashlight," she shrugged.

The guard stepped forward, making the hair on Julietta's arms stand on end. She remained completely still as they reached for the flashlight, pressing the button on it.

"Confirmed," they grunted, stepping back. "You may collect your things. Your knife shall be labeled with your name and returned to you upon leaving. It is recommended you do not bring weapons or tools to the facility as we will provide you with anything your job requires as well as protection."

"Understood," she nodded, collecting her things. Once she was put back together, she joined Danni at the metal door.

"You will be taken to the decontamination room next. There you will find washrooms with showers. All employees are expected to shower prior to entering and exiting the facility. There you will also find a locker with your name. This is your assigned locker which can be locked and unlocked with your encrypted ID. It's unlocked already for now. Your uniform is inside. No personal items are allowed in the facility proper without prior authorization. You are expected to remain in uniform until you leave the facility. All uniforms must be returned to the laundry at the end of the day. A fresh uniform will be placed in your locker prior to your arrival each morning."

Scanning her ID, Danni strode into the hallway beyond, leading Julietta to a door on the right marked 'Women's locker room.'

"No men are allowed in here," Danni ushered her in.

Julietta's uniform was similar to Danni's, but instead of a brown shirt hers was light gray. Once she had cleaned, dressed, and stored her belongings she met up with the strange woman whose clothes were once more pristine.

"You should leave that flashlight in your locker next time," Danni chastised, shaking her head. "I'll allow it this time because we are nearly late. Come."

Exiting the locker room, Julietta was led down another hallway of doors to yet another large metal door.

"Through this door is the facility proper."

"What about all the other doors we passed?"

"Staff quarters for those who live onsite," she answered, not missing a beat. "The facility is split into three main sections, the student space, the school, and the laboratory. You will have limited and assignment-necessitated access to these three spaces. Today I will give you a short tour of each before showing you to your main workspace."

Since she'd entered Iota, she hadn't had time to think, as Danni scanned her ID for the umpteenth time, proceeding into the facility proper.

If the white walls and floors of the previous rooms had not already made Julietta feel uncomfortable and cold, the main facility certainly would have. The main hub was a large circular room, devoid of any furniture save the signs on the walls directing toward the three offshoots' doors. Each one had two guards stationed nearby. The room felt so clinical, so wrong, she thought as she followed Danni to the first hallway on the right labeled 'Student Space.'

"This is where our students live. The youngest are dormed near the front, the older the back." Danni explained as they briskly made their way past various rooms labeled simply with identification numbers. "There is a cafeteria that connects to the school side on the far left. You won't be spending all too much time in here unless something breaks in one of the dormitories."

Leading her down the far left hallway, they arrived at the cafeteria. Here, Julietta was surprised to find adults, dressed none too dissimilar to herself save the shirt color, but no children.

"Here is where you can get food. Breakfast is served from sunrise till noon, then lunch and dinner from noon till sunset. There is no assigned seating, but we do request you spend no more time than necessary here. Too much work to be done," Danni huffed, leading her almost immediately to a set of doors labeled 'School Entrance.'

"What do all the different color shirts mean?" Julietta dared to ask.

"Team and rank designation." She paused in the hallway just outside the second door to the school entrance, turning to Julietta. "Reds are medical staff, blue instructors and professors, green researchers, and neutral building staff. You are entry-level building staff therefore light gray. Once you've satisfactorily proven yourself, you'll graduate to gray staff, then if you are fortunate brown supervisor, then black manager. Now, if you'd kindly refrain from any more questions until the tour is concluded."

Julietta nodded without another word as they continued. The 'school' was little different from the dormitories from the outside and just as silent. Its hallways were lined with metal doors leading into rooms with covered observation windows. The major difference was the increased security with guards stationed at each crossway.

"There are specialized machines in each room that tend to need a tune-up weekly. Once you are trained on them you may be put on call for this maintenance." Danni gestured to one of the open classrooms.

Stepping inside Julietta's heart sank. The 'classroom' was a small windowless room, save for the observation one on the hallway wall. It contained two desks with chairs, a few strange machines on the far left wall, and locked cabinets. It resembled an interrogation room more than a learning space.

"Those are the machines. They are used to monitor students'…learning. They help us ensure they are meeting expected markers."

Learning her lesson from earlier, Julietta simply nodded.

"Come along, there is just the laboratory left. That is the building you will spend the majority of your time in anyhow."

The laboratory was shockingly the liveliest of the three buildings. No sooner had they entered they were greeted by various researchers, guards, and instructors hurrying to and from various locked-off labs.

"The maintenance wing is in the basement of this building, but given the number of machines and devices in here you'll end up topside more often once you get established," Danni explained, heading directly to the center of the space.

Unlike the other two buildings, this one had a large round desk at its center, at which an elderly gentleman sat.

"Melvin? Where's Joyce?"

"Running late, again," the old man grumbled, shaking his head. "For a new employee, she sure is irresponsible. At this rate, she'll be released well before her probationary period is over!"

"Hard to find good workers nowadays." Danni shook her head. "Speaking of new workers, I have one here. Jessa, this is Melvin, one of our archivists. He's usually in the archive but it seems the receptionist is late again."

"That is unfortunate," Julietta replied, trying to sound sympathetic.

"I assure you, Jessa, we don't take actions like this lightly," Melvin frowned. "Has she gone through orientation?"

"Not yet. We are heading to my office now. I just came to pick up her encrypted identification."

"Of course." Melvin handed Danni a manila envelope. "All her paperwork should be in there."

"Good. I'll see you at lunch."

As the two turned to leave, a young woman, not much older than Julietta, came rushing in looking rather frazzled, her red hair in disarray. "Sorry, I'm late."

"Joyce Handel," Melvin boomed, as he stood. "Meet me in my office at the end of the day, please."

"Of course, sir."

Julietta didn't have time to react as she felt Danni grab her arm and drag her to her office.

"I'll need you to sign these." Danni yawned, sounding as though she was all too ready to have this over with.

"What is this?" Julietta questioned, nervously as she sat down at the desk.

"Required employment forms. The first is non-disclosure. While working here, you are not permitted to discuss what you see here with anyone outside of the facility. This includes but is not limited to government officials, family, friends, and other employees, not on the property. Failure to follow this may result in termination."

She raised an eyebrow but didn't reply, flipping to the next page.

"That is your employee probationary agreement. It states should we feel you are not a good fit for our facility we reserve the right to either transfer or release you."

"Okay…" She cringed slightly, flipping to the next page.

"That form details that you understand your expected hours of work and that delayed transportation is not a valid excuse for being late.

There are dormitories available to any level of worker past their probation. These can either be permanent housing or requested on an as-needed basis."

"People live here? Aside from the students?"

"This facility has full-time care staff staying on property for the students. However, many of the longer-term and higher-ranking employees have decided to reserve permanent places here."

"Do you live here?"

"That's a rather personal question."

"I'm sorry." Julietta's gaze dropped.

"You will do well, Jessa, to learn not to ask too many questions. It will be better for you in the long run."

"Yes, of course." Grabbing a pen, she started to fill out the forms.

Once all the necessary paperwork was completed, Danni handed her the encrypted ID. "Don't lose that. If you do, there will be severe consequences. That ID must be scanned at every door you enter or exit, no exceptions. Even if someone is holding the door open for you, you must scan in. Understood?"

"Yes, ma'am."

"Good. Follow me."

Entering back into the central laboratory, Julietta spotted Joyce sitting at the desk watching her intently as they strode by. Averting her gaze, she and Danni had nearly made it to the stairs when the doors that lead to the school burst open, a young man of about 15 rushing towards them.

"Please, don't let them take me back. Help me!" The boy cried as he ran from two rather burly guards.

Julietta didn't have time to react as the boy barreled right into her, sending them both tumbling to the floor.

The wind knocked out of her, she looked on helplessly as the two guards grabbed the boy harshly, dragging him off her. A moment later she heard static and a cry from the boy. By the time she regained her bearings, the boy was on his knees a few feet away with stone manacles around his wrists.

"Are you all right?" Asked a feminine voice, Joyce, who had come out from behind her desk to check on her. Everyone else had ignored her, including Danni who stood by the stairs looking rather bored with the spectacle.

"Yeah, I think so." Julietta rubbed her lower back, slowly checking the rest of herself. "Just winded."

"Here let me help you up." Joyce extended a hand, helping Julietta to her feet.

"Thank you."

"You're the new girl, Jessa, right?"

"Yes."

"Keep your nose clean and eyes on the stars," the young woman winked, returning to her desk.

"Ahem," Danni interrupted, looking rather impatient. "Now that this little spectacle is over, shall we continue?"

Julietta glanced over to the boy, catching a glimpse of his sad, pale face as the two guards dragged him away.

"Is he—" She stopped, remembering the warning about questions.

"This is not a usual thing. Most students are quiet. This one must have just been…overstressed. Rest assured, he will be taken care of accordingly." Danni answered calmly, as though rehearsed. "Come now. We are late getting you to your station. You have much training to get through today."

It was very late, the sun long since set, when Julietta arrived back at the Snapdragon Inn. Upon entering, she was surprised to find Charles sitting on the couch asleep. Penny was in his arms also asleep. After the day she had had, it was the sight she needed to see.

Approaching them she gently placed a hand on Charles's shoulder. "Charlie…"

"Jul?" Charles stirred, eyes blinking open. "Sorry, I tried to stay awake. Poor Penny had a nightmare and woke up a couple of hours ago. She was worried about you. I told her she could sit with me and wait." He yawned, shaking his head. "I knew she would fall asleep again but didn't think I'd join her."

Julietta chuckled, kissing him on the cheek. "I'll take her to bed. You should get some sleep."

Tucking Penny in, Julietta sighed sadly, the image of the young boy still playing in her mind. Kissing her on the forehead, she brushed a stray hair from her face before retreating to her side of the room to change.

Still feeling uneasy, she made for the kitchen. Entering, she wasn't surprised to find Charles sitting on the couch, with a mug of hot tea now in front of him.

"I figured you'd need it." He walked over to her.

Julietta wrapped her arms around him, resting her head against his chest. "Charlie…" Her voice broke.

Taking her in his arms, he held her close. "Let's talk." Gently, he guided her over to the couch. Handing her a cup of tea, he rested a protective arm around her. "What happened?"

Julietta took her time, taking sips of tea in between her retelling of the day, her voice and heart feeling heavier and heavier.

"Nothing Byron told me could have prepared me for that boy. After witnessing that I felt empty. The rest of the day was just going through the motions." A few tears rolled down her face.

"I was afraid of what you'd see." Charles reached up, wiping them away, gently. "It seems they tried to hide what we already know."

"I—I don't know if I can handle this, Charlie."

Taking the empty mug from her, he set it on the coffee table, shifting so she could more comfortably sit in his arms. "You know I am not going to force you to go back there Jul, but you also know as much as it hurts in the morning you will get up and go back there. You'll do it because of that boy."

Julietta sighed, leaning her head against Charles's chest. She paused for a moment, listening to his familiar calm heartbeat. "I know…I just need to…"

"Process." Charles ran a hand up and down her shoulder soothingly. "Take your time."

It couldn't have been more than an hour since Penny had heard Momma Julie go back to the kitchen, she and her Charlie talking about Iota. It hurt Penny to hear Momma Julie upset. She wanted to help Momma Julie and tell her and her Charlie about Rho, but she was too scared.

Hearing the door creak open, Penny once more pretended to be asleep. Through half-closed eyes she watched her Charlie carrying Momma Julie, laying her down on their shared bed. She could hear them whisper goodnight and share a small kiss before her Charlie vanished back into the apartment, closing the door behind him.

Her Charlie had taken care of her Momma Julie. He had helped her sleep. Her Charlie was always brave and kind. She wanted to be like her Charlie. She wanted to be brave like him. Turning to her bedside table she reached for Nelson. Turning him on she gestured to him to be quiet.

"Something wrong, Miss Penny?" Nelson whispered.

Penny shook her head and began to talk.

CHAPTER 25

It was nearing the expected end of Dust. In an effort to fulfill Penny's one request of being a normal kid, Julietta and Charles decided they wanted to celebrate her turning 10 Dust. Nelson explained that she wanted a tea party at Ola's shop which she had come to love over the past few weeks.

Ola, with Byron and Lisle's help, brewed all sorts of delicious teas and laid out a variety of sweet treats for the occasion. Penny, Maya, and even Nicolas, who still rarely showed emotion were all smiles enjoying their 'dessert for dinner' party. As the evening drew to an end, Penny was even surprised with a few presents!

"A toolkit, specifically for electronics, so you can work on Nelson without worrying about damaging him." Julietta smiled as the girl hugged her tightly in thanks.

Charles knelt to Penny's level, holding out a small newspaper-wrapped gift. "It's not as cool as an electronics kit, but I hope you like it."

Unwrapping the present, her eyes went wide. Inside was a small bronze compass on a metal chain, its edges engraved with flowers. Turning the compass over in her hand she spotted another engraving on the back, this one made more recently than the rest. The words 'To Our Lucky Penny, Our Spark in the Dark' were inlaid above a set of three stars.

"I will admit I had a bit of help from your mother restoring it. Took a bit of research but it works correctly." He smiled. "See if you turn it this way, it points north, but if you apply your sparks and turn it this way..." He helped her position her hands, before she let her sparks dance. "It points to the Snapdragon Inn, towards home."

Penny smiled brightly, letting her powers fade before holding out the chain to him in request.

Charles clasped the chain around Penny's neck. "There, how does that feel?"

She answered by wrapping her arms around him, hugging him tightly.

"You're welcome, Penny."

"I also have a present. Though this one is not as cool," Byron chuckled, holding out two tiny hats. "One for Nelson and one for Margie. I overheard you mentioning to them about the cold. Now they won't get cold!"

All the adults laughed as Penny took the caps, happily placing them on robots before turning Nelson on.

"What's this on my head, Miss Penny?"

Penny whispered to him.

"Oh, I see. Thank you, Sir Byron. Now my Margie and I will be warm."

"Tank you, everyone." Penny blushed shyly, feeling happier than she had in cycles.

Weeks passed. Unlike Hot, the Cold season wasted no time barreling in. Practically overnight, the temperature dropped from chilly to downright freezing. The people of Matson were in a tizzy for days rushing to find warmer clothes and the necessities they thought they'd have time to prepare for. Eventually, however, things settled even as the temperature continued to drop further and further.

It was the day before Charles's presentation to the medical board. With he and Lisle busy with last-minute preparations, Julietta stuck later at work, and Victor taking Nicolas and Maya to visit their grandparents, Byron had agreed to keep an eye on Penny for the evening.

Having had dinner at a cafe nearby, Byron brought her to Ola's tea shop for dessert. While Penny enjoyed her tea and cookies at a nearby table, Byron chatted to Ola at the counter.

"Can't believe she is 10 Dust already." Byron stroked his mustache, pensively. "Seems like just yesterday I was assigned to her and promised to get her out." He paused, a flash of memory passing over his eyes. "You know my boy would have been about 27 now, a grown man."

"I know." Ola placed a comforting hand on his arm. "I know it still must hurt all these cycles later."

"16 cycles…" He glanced around at the empty shop. "The Constellation has come a long way in that time. By the way, I've been meaning to ask. When did you discover it was this J.H. person? When we last spoke at Johani, you and I were certain it was the government behind it all."

"About a cycle ago, around the time we established the last of our Constellation satellites. One of the agents in Apolis intercepted some papers. It was correspondence with a J.H. and the current head of the Apolis Academy asking about any students of interest. Turns out these schools are technically government-funded but their true nature is hidden. Apolis Academy for the Future is a legitimate institute. There are actually students there learning and growing to become great leaders. J.H. has just been siphoning off those with powers. He paints the picture of taking the 'brightest' students in to prepare them to be scientists and engineers. He's even had government agents tour Alpha-156 to ensure them it was legit. He's pulled the wool over their eyes and the eyes of the public."

"Then why not tell someone? You have Lisle, a government contact. You could just…"

"If J.H. was able to fake this for 20 plus cycles, who's to say anyone would believe us? It would be their word against ours. We need concrete evidence. The catch is getting it."

"They wouldn't listen to a child's story, nor would I want to put one in that position." Byron frowned, thinking. "You were able to convince Lisle, though, with the papers and Nicolas."

"Lisle is open-minded and knows nothing of Apolis Academy. She is a smart woman. The powers that be may not be so receptive even in the face of evidence due to status quo bias." Ola leaned back in her chair. "J.H. has established trust, 20 plus cycles of it."

Byron nodded in understanding, looking grim. "Speaking of agents, I think I've recruited a few more. Been casually chatting with various folks around the city. Some have heard of us through the grapevine, mainly those who've lost a child in the family to the schools. They want to help. Told them to stop by here if they are interested."

"Understood, just be careful. Yes, we can use all the help we can get, but we must be cautious."

"Of course, do you not trust me?"

"I trust you, Byron." Ola smiled, sadly. "Speaking of trusted folks, your friends, the Healeys, they've made contact with our outpost in Johani. They are both safe and are establishing a bakery which they've offered to let us use for any of our needs."

"I can tell you that the bakery will be a gold mine of information if Marisa has anything to do with it." He chuckled. "But I am glad they are safe. Please send them a message from me that I appreciate their help and to be safe."

"Of course."

Byron looked over to Penny who was happily eating a cookie while playing with Nelson and Margie. "It's the kids who suffer the most in all this. Torn away from their parents or guardians, made to do endless tests like lab rats."

"If only we could teach them instead, teach them to use their powers for good."

"Teach them that they are normal, Ola, that they can lead normal happy lives."

"But they aren't normal. Penny can charge batteries with her hands; Nicolas levitates small objects...that's not normal."

"But they are people nonetheless and deserve to have the same freedoms as everyone else." He turned to Ola, giving her a stern look. "Have we learned nothing from our past? Nothing from the stories written about those with unique abilities? If treated differently than anyone else, forced to be something they are not, they are prone to make drastic decisions. Any person would be that way."

Ola looked as though she wished to say something but paused, thinking.

"Don't become what you fear, Ola." He shook his head. "Be better."

Dressed in a borrowed suit coat from Victor, a nice button-up shirt Julietta bought for him, and his usual pants and boots, Charles found himself unable to sit still. The last time he stood in this same room was four cycles ago. At the time, he was facing the same medical council, but for a vastly different reason.

"Why hello, doctor." Julietta teased, closing the door behind her. Charles had been permitted to bring one guest to this presentation aside from his sponsor. Julietta was the obvious choice. "Lisle is doing a good job of schmoozing out there as your sponsor. She really wants to make it up to you."

"Yeah, I guess so," he chuckled nervously, continuing to pace the small office that acted as the presenter's holding chamber.

Stepping in front of him, she stopped him. "Charlie…" She placed a comforting hand on his chest over his heart, the other coming to rest on the side of his neck. "Take a deep breath. It's going to be okay."

Charles reached up, resting a hand against hers on his chest. "I've been here before, Jul. Many, many times before I sat in this very room excited to present. The last time I was here, however…" His hand took hers as he closed his eyes. "I was in handcuffs."

"Unrightfully so." Giving his hand a squeeze, the other brushed a gentle thumb against his chin. "You know that. The council knows that, and once your paper on the human nervous system is published, the world will know that."

"What if they don't—"

"They will. They'd be stupid not to accept it and not accept you back in."

Taking a deep breath, he opened his eyes. Staring into Julietta's before him, he felt that flutter in his chest he had come to recognize as his love for her. "Thank you, Jul…Thank you for being here for me."

"Of course." She gave him a light kiss on the cheek. "So long as you'll have me, I'll be here for you."

"Always. You have me, and I you." Charles smiled brightly. "Wonder what our Lucky Penny is doing right now?"

"Probably sitting in front of the fireplace with the talker in hand waiting anxiously to hear her Charlie give his presentation," she chuckled. "Byron pinged me a few minutes ago on mine, she was so excited she didn't even touch the two CCCs he gave her."

"Oh Penny," he shook his head. "Must be really excited to not eat her CCCs."

"She loves her Charlie." Taking the hand from his neck, she reached into her pocket. "She wanted me to give you this." She held out a small piece of folded paper to him.

Carefully undoing it, his shoulders relaxed as he saw what was drawn upon it. The words 'My Family' were scrawled in shaky handwriting with five stick figures: one small one holding an even smaller stick figure and three taller ones, one with what looked like goggles drawn on its head, one with a curly mustache, and the last holding what looked like a stethoscope in the shape of a lopsided heart.

"I guess those lessons with Henrietta are going well." He admired, a tear coming to his eye.

Their moment was interrupted as Lisle entered the room. "It's almost time."

Standing to the side of the room, Charles put on an air of confidence. Despite the deep-seated pit in his stomach, he waited patiently for Lisle to finish her commendation of him. Observing the various faces around the room, he couldn't help but wonder what was going through the council members' minds. He recognized most of them. All of the ones that were there during his trial were present, but there were a few new faces that Julietta had let slip were scientists at Iota. He had warned her to stay clear of them, but it was little needed as no one seemed to notice his guest, fully engrossed in side conversations amongst themselves. The biggest change to the council, however, was its new leader, a man named Morgan Cone. He was an older gentleman, rather large and balding. He gave off an air of importance, commanding the attention of the room with the slightest move of his hand. Charles had asked Lisle about him before the meeting, but all she could tell him was he took control about a cycle after he was dismissed.

"Therefore, I, Governor Lisle Benedict, hereby sponsor Charles Hawthorne for the publication of his paper on the Human Nervous System as well as his reinstatement into the Medical Society of Matson."

With that Lisle stepped out of the way, gesturing for Charles to take the floor. It took every ounce of his willpower to get himself moving, and even more to start speaking.

For two hours Charles spoke, explaining his research at the Museum of Waterwealt. Describing the various diagrams and displays he meticulously documented, he elaborated on the medical journal references that allowed him, with his prior knowledge, to rediscover the details of how the human nervous system worked. He went on to draw the connection that it was not so dissimilar to wiring and electricity, with signals being sent to various locations in the body, which then respond. He rattled off the various diseases that afflicted such a system, many of which were still present today along with variations, and how they were treated in the past and should be now. Eventually, he came to a close.

Following this was another hour of questions. Though many were out of curiosity, some were more pointed as if testing if his knowledge would waiver. He remained firm and confident, however, stealing glances at Julietta who, despite having heard him practicing his speech into the wee hours of the morning, was attentively listening. She knew he knew what he was talking about. He knew this information had to be shared if the world was to ever recover, if they were ever to put a stop to J.H.'s schools.

As the questions came slowly to an end it was Dr. Cone, who up to this point had merely stared at him rather pointedly, who spoke.

"Thank you, Mr. Hawthorne. If you would kindly return to the waiting chamber, I believe the council would like to discuss this further." Dr. Cone smiled widely, an expression that sent a chill down Charles's spine even as he left the room.

Julietta appeared a few minutes later, finding Charles sitting at the desk with his head in his hands. "Charlie?"

"I'm all right, Jul. Just tired," he replied, not looking up.

Moving to stand behind him, she placed her hands on his shoulders. "From what I was hearing, the majority loved your work."

"Majority, but Cone will have the final say. The lead doctor always gets the final say."

"He would be nuts not to accept you back."

"Even if he does, he may regret it when he hears what I plan to research next." Leaning back in the chair, his head resting against Julietta behind him.

"It's sure to raise a few eyebrows, but it's our best shot." Wrapping her arms around his shoulders, she kissed the top of his head. "We'll be fine, Charlie. We have to be."

They stayed there in comfortable silence, letting the weight of the day wash over them as the voices from the other room grew quieter and quieter. Finally, the door opened. Lisle beckoned them both back.

Standing once more in front of Dr. Cone, Charles struggled to maintain his composure. A minute passed, two minutes…what was Cone waiting for? Finally, after five agonizing minutes, the domineering man stood.

"Hawthorne, after much consideration and debate, I, Dr. Cone, would like to formally accept your paper on the human nervous system for publication by the Medical Society of Matson. It shall be published a week from tomorrow and sent out to the other medical societies including Apolis's. In light of this achievement, as well as the evidence brought to light by Governor Benedict regarding your past and present endeavors, we would also like to reinstate your membership in the society."

As claps arose from the scientists about the room, Charles let out a deep breath he didn't realize he was holding. He had been accepted back; the first part of the plan was in motion.

With a wave of his hand, Dr. Cone silenced the room once more. "With this reinstatement, of course, comes the expectation of research and publication within reasonable time frames. Therefore, I ask you, what is the subject of interest for your next endeavor?"

This was the moment he had been dreading as he straightened himself up, looking to all the world as a confident and excited man. "My next subject of research shall be the human genome. Having briefly touched upon it in my previous studies, I feel it may be of use to explore going forward given the mutations the medical community has encountered since the great war in not only the nervous system but the human body as a whole. It is, after all, the core of our human existence. What determines our predispositions to disease and illness."

The room was silent, not even a sneeze could be heard. The pause was laborious, Charles keeping his gaze locked with the head of the society.

"Very well, I am sure everyone here is as interested and encouraged by your selected endeavor. Thank you for your time, Dr. Hawthorne. We shall meet again soon, I am sure."

It was near the end of Julietta's fifth week working at Iota. Since she had started, she spent every workday down in the basement of the laboratory slowly learning about the various machines and contraptions. Despite her best efforts, however, she wasn't permitted any significant amount of time on any particular one to parse its exact functionality. In addition to this training, Danni seemed determined to keep her deep within the facility away from anything more than the mundane. She even went with her to every meal, making sure to keep her away from anyone more than her rank.

Julietta, of course, did her best to glean what information she could for the Constellation, drawing up partial sketches and gathering lists of names overheard. However, it wasn't enough. They needed her to make contact with Joyce, if only to discover what became of Cartier. If she had any guess, based on what little she had heard, she had a sinking feeling it had something to do with release or termination.

It was nearing late afternoon. Julietta was busy once more fixing an electrical box on yet another strange machine when suddenly there was a loud bang and a rumble that shook the whole workshop, knocking her off her feet.

"What on earth?"

"Stay down here, Jessa," Danni ordered, not sounding the least bit shaken as she disappeared up the stairs.

Dusting herself off, she slowly rose to her feet. What could have happened that could have rocked the entire building like that? She hadn't felt anything like it since—her thoughts stopped short as she heard a small squeak coming from the back of the workshop.

Listening closely, she found the source, a loose board near the back corner. Pulling it back, her heart dropped. Staring back at her were two small eyes and a terrified face. It was a little girl, no older than four or five cycles by her stature, dressed in a faded gray long-sleeve dress, well-worn and too big for her. Looking her over, she found it hard not to cry seeing how thin she looked, a hunger in her eyes. What drew her attention the most, however, was the chafing on her wrists and bruising on her hands.

"Hey..."

The child shrunk back, silent tears running down her face.

"Hey...it's okay. I'm not going to hurt you."

The girl hugged her legs tightly, burying her face in her knees.

"Do you have a name? Do you—"

"Jessa?"

Julietta immediately was to her feet, pulling the board back into place swiftly. "I'm here, Danni. I'm just picking up some things that fell during the shake."

"Well, come along. It's nearly the end of lunch hour, best we go get some food."

Not wanting to draw attention to the hidden child, she followed obediently, hoping she could get back to help her later.

Stepping out of the workshop and into the atrium, Julietta stopped short, spotting what had caused the shaking, and its aftermath. There had been an explosion in one of the laboratories, collapsing a wall that was now black with scorch marks. However, this wasn't what turned her stomach upside down.

Lying on the floor, haphazardly covered with stained sheets, were what looked to be three bodies. She watched in internal horror as these poor souls were kicked to the side by various scientists rushing to their labs without a second thought. Those who did make any note of them looked rather annoyed, tutting how this would delay their progress or how this would be an inconvenience before storming off in another direction. It was as if nothing mattered to anyone but their work.

"An accident, a rarity," Danni answered flatly, reading the unspoken question on her face. "Thankfully, no serious loss. No students or important equipment."

Swallowing the bile that had risen in her throat, she followed silently as Danni led her away toward the cafeteria.

Returning to the workshop after, Julietta snuck back toward where the girl was hidden. Much to her concern the child was gone, however, from what she could tell it was of her own volition. Taking the cookie she had squirreled into her pocket from her mostly uneaten lunch, she set it on a napkin in the space.

The rest of her day was spent in complete focus, trying to act as calm and unconcerned as possible. Much to her surprise and secret relief, near dinner time she was stopped by Danni.

"It appears the accident caused a bit more damage than expected. Please clean up your things. Everyone is being sent home. You are to report to work, as usual, tomorrow morning. I have a meeting to get to. I assume you can see yourself out?"

"Yes, of course." She plastered on a smile, hoping to hide her true feelings. "See you tomorrow. Bright and early."

She waited a moment longer, ensuring Danni was gone before once more returning to the hidden hideaway. Pulling back the board she was slightly concerned to see the cookie had vanished, a small piece of paper in its place. Reading the paper her heart dropped. On it, written in crayon with a childish scrawl, were the words 'tank you.'

198

CHAPTER 26

It was relatively late. Charles had just put Penny to bed and was now sitting in front of the fireplace drinking coffee and discussing Constellation business with Byron when they heard the door to the apartment open.

"Jul?"

Julietta bolted to the bathroom.

"Jul?!" He rushed in after her, finding her kneeling in front of the toilet relieving herself of what she managed to stomach at lunch that day.

"Julietta?" Kneeling beside her, he placed a hand on her back, rubbing it.

For a brief moment, she turned her head towards him, tears streaming down her face.

"Something happened at Iota…"

She nodded, coughing before another wave of nausea hit her.

"It's all right, Jul, take your time." He gently pulled back her hair.

Byron appeared a minute later, carrying Charles's medical bag. "What's wrong?"

"Something happened at Iota."

"They're—they're monsters," she spat, her stomach finally empty.

"You want to sit?" He helped her reposition to lean against the cabinet while Byron got her a wet washcloth and a glass of water.

"I'll go get her night clothes," the older man offered, leaving them alone.

Once Julietta had cleaned up a bit and rinsed out her mouth, Charles began his exam. "Are you hurt?"

She shook her head, leaning it back against the cabinet and closing her eyes.

"Your heart is racing, but other than that everything else seems fine, physically."

"Everything all right? What happened?" Byron asked, setting the clothes on the counter.

Pulling out the girl's thank you note from her pocket and handing it to Charles, she slowly began explaining about the accident and the child, silent tears once more running down her face.

"Three people had died, yet everyone acted as though it was a minor inconvenience. They talked over the bodies as if they were merely dust on the floor." Opening her eyes, she struggled to maintain her composure. "And the poor girl. She...she reminded me of Penny. I couldn't do anything...I was powerless...I..." She couldn't finish the thought, her heart too heavy.

Charles glanced up at Byron, whose face was somber.

"I'm sorry, Julie. I know...there was...I didn't know how..." He stopped, tears sitting in his eyes. "There was nothing I could have told you to prepare you for that. I knew back when I worked there that some people were rather apathetic but, it appears that mentality has spread."

"Jul..." Pushing his bag off to the side, Charles moved closer to her. Gently he wiped her tears, his heart matching hers. "Why don't we get you out of your dusty clothes? Maybe get you some light food or tea?"

"Okay." She bowed her head, her voice barely a whisper.

"Byron, can you—"

"I'll go make her some tea." He closed the door behind him as he left.

"I'm going to help you up, Jul, hold onto me."

As he helped her to her feet, she felt so light to him. It scared him. "Jul..."

She didn't reply, simply wrapping her arms around him in a tight embrace.

"I know." He returned the embrace, tears in his eyes. "I'm sorry you had to see that. I couldn't imagine—" He hugged her a bit tighter. "Come on, let's get you more comfortable.

Byron was already ready with tea sitting on the other couch by the time Charles had gotten her situated. They sat in silence for a moment, all trying to process what Julietta had seen.

"I have to go back tomorrow. Danni said it was a fluke they let us go early." Julietta's shoulders slumped as she took a sip of her tea.

"If I were you and I had a choice I'd never want to go back there." Charles' brow furrowed. "But—" He paused, feeling her hand come to rest on his leg. "I know, just stating what we are all thinking."

"I know." Shifting closer, she rested her head on his shoulder. "Thank you, both of you, for helping me."

"Of course." Byron sank back in his seat. "When Ola said she wanted to send you in I was afraid of what you might see. It was bad when I was there. I can only imagine—"

The sound of a door creaking open caught everyone's attention. Turning, they found little Penny approaching them.

"Penny, sweetie, you should be asleep." Julietta smiled sadly. "Everything is all right."

Penny shook her head, setting Nelson on the coffee table.

"Did you have a nightmare?" Charles asked gently. "Do you want some tea?"

She shook her head again, turning on Nelson.

"Miss Penny is sorry Momma Julie had to see all that."

Everyone's faces fell.

"Miss Penny knows how bad school can be."

"I'm all right, Penny." Julietta sighed. "Charlie and Byron helped me."

Penny shook her head again, tears on the surface of her eyes.

"Miss Penny wants to help the Constellation. Miss Penny wants to be brave like Momma Julie, her Charlie, and Sir Byron."

"You are very brave, Penny." Charles assured her. "You've been so brave."

"Miss Penny knew you would say that. That's why Miss Penny has something to tell you." There was a slight pause as Nelson looked to Penny for confirmation. When she nodded, he proceeded. "Miss Penny is ready to tell you her story. Miss Penny wants you to know what happened to her in Rho-597."

Penny moved to sit on the coffee table beside Nelson facing Julietta and Charles.

"Miss Penny, are you ready?"

Penny nodded.

"Momma Julie and her Charlie?"

They nodded, Julietta, taking Charles's hand in hers.

"Then I shall begin." Nelson shook his mechanical head from side to side. "Miss Penny doesn't remember much from before living in Varington. She doesn't remember her parents or even how she got there. Miss Penny was about three or four Dust when she was taken from the house where she lived in Varington. She was living with two women, who took care of different kids in the cycle she had lived there. While she was there, she was required to wear gloves. Miss Penny didn't know why at the time, but thinking back she thinks the ladies that took care of her didn't like her sparks she made.

"Miss Penny just stayed quiet most days, cleaning her room and trying to find something to play with. Then Mr. Turner visited. On that day, Miss Penny was taken into one of the woman's offices and sat at the big desk. Mr. Turner showed her cards of things, and asked questions. All she had to do was point to the card with the answer. Before Penny knew it, she was being taken to the capital in a strange moving thing that looked like the space car in the Waterwealt museum with only a backpack containing the few dresses she had been allowed to own.

"Once in the big city, Miss Penny was taken to a large glass building. There they took her backpack. That's the last time she saw it. Mr. Turner brought her to a room where a lady in a skirt and blouse told her she was safe and took her to yet another room. This room was smaller than the one at the house in Varington, but somehow felt scarier. Miss Penny was told to sit on a metal chair and take off her gloves. Miss Penny didn't want to, but the lady told her it was okay to take them off, that she wanted to see her sparks.

"Miss Penny was excited, someone wanted to see her sparks, so she showed the lady how she made sparks with her hands. The strangely dressed lady smiled but said nothing. Then a few minutes later another strange lady entered the room, this one wearing a long white coat over clothes like Momma Julie's. This lady wasn't so nice. She took Miss Penny by the hand and led her to a small room with only a bed, desk, chair, and dresser with a gray dress, shorts, and underclothes on the bed. Miss Penny was told to change into the clothes on the bed and wait for someone to come to get her for dinner. Miss Penny was scared so Miss Penny listened."

As Nelson continued, Charles could feel Julietta tense beside him, her thoughts aligning with his own.

"No one came to get Miss Penny for dinner. Miss Penny went to bed hungry. Miss Penny didn't know what she had done wrong to not get dinner. Miss Penny went to bed sad. Then the next morning came. The strange white coat woman returned. She brought Miss Penny oatmeal. Miss Penny thought it tasted funny, but Miss Penny was hungry. After Miss Penny ate, she felt tired again and went to sleep.

"When Miss Penny woke up again, she was in a space car. The white coat lady was sitting beside her. She told Miss Penny she was almost at her new school: Kappa-139. Miss Penny had never been to school. Miss Penny could barely write and read her letters. The ladies in Varington didn't teach her. Miss Penny tried to tell the white coat lady that, but she yelled at her to be quiet. Miss Penny didn't talk again.

"Miss Penny was taken into a big concrete building and brought to a doctor's office. The doctor there was not nice like her Charlie. The check-up he gave her made her feel sad. He poked her with something that made her arm hurt and no CCCs were given. After that Miss Penny was led to another small bedroom and told to stay there. Miss Penny started to cry. The white coat lady gave Miss Penny a candy. Miss Penny was so happy she ate it. Miss Penny doesn't remember much after that. When Miss Penny woke up again, the white coat lady was taking her to another place. This time she was taken to a big room with strange machines. There was another white coat lady and the doctor man from before. They stuck sticky circles on Miss Penny's arms and made her make different sparks for hours. Miss Penny was really tired, but they made Miss Penny keep going until Miss Penny cried. Then they yelled at Miss Penny. Miss Penny wanted to go home."

Charles did his best to hold back his tears. Penny had trusted him to give her a check-up after experiencing all that, and Nelson wasn't done.

"This continued to happen every day for several days. Eventually, Miss Penny was told she was to be sent off to another school and that this school wasn't for her. Miss Penny was terrified but stayed quiet as they took her, and others, into another space car to her new school: Rho-597.

"When Miss Penny arrived at Rho they gave her the penny necklace with the strange marks on it before taking her to her room. It was the same as the others. Again, Miss Penny was told to wait. This time

Miss Penny didn't cry, Miss Penny stayed quiet. Every day, Miss Penny did the same thing. Miss Penny was woken up before the sun came out and taken to the doctor who poked her and gave her icky medicine. When she got back to her room there was food on her desk for her. It always tasted bad, not like the sweet toast her Charlie makes, or the choco-pancakes Momma Julie makes."

Charles glanced briefly over to Julietta whose eyes were filled with tears as Nelson continued.

"After breakfast, Miss Penny was taken to what was called a class-room. This is where she met Sir Byron. Sir Byron would come in with a big case of tubes filled with strange liquid that he would put into the strange machines. Sir Byron always smiled at Miss Penny. Sir Byron was nice to Miss Penny."

Byron bowed his head, ashamed.

"Once Sir Byron left Miss Bell would come in. Miss Bell would attach the sticky things to Miss Penny and have her use her sparks to make the tubes change color. If Miss Penny couldn't do it Miss Penny was yelled at, hit on her hands and arms with a ruler, and told she wouldn't get lunch. Miss Penny learned quickly how to make colors change. Miss Penny missed a lot of lunch. After class was done for the day Miss Penny was taken back to her room. Miss Penny saw lots of other kids but was not allowed to talk to them. When Miss Penny tried, Miss Penny didn't get dinner. Miss Penny was forced to stay in the room after dinner. Miss Penny was scared and lonely. Miss Penny did this for many months. Miss Penny remembers the night Sir Byron and Miss Ola tried to get her out. Miss Penny was punished.

"The person who took Sir Byron's place was mean to Miss Penny. He never smiled at her and often yelled at her. Miss Penny was forced to wear heavy bracelets that made sparks not work when not in class. After Sir Byron left there were new teachers with scary-look-ing wands that could make sparks like Miss Penny. Miss Penny only saw it spark once. An older boy and girl were running in the hallway when Miss Penny saw teachers chase them with spark wands. Miss Penny never saw the older boy and girl again. Miss Penny noticed older kids would disappear from time to time. Younger kids too, but not as often."

By this point, Julietta and Charles both had tears running down their faces, hearts heavy as Nelson pressed on.

"Miss Penny learned to be silent and listen. After about three cycles, Miss Penny was woken up one night by a strange lady. She was dressed in all black with a set of stars drawn on her shoulder that looked like a bird. She told Miss Penny she could help her out. Miss Penny was terrified she would be punished again. The night lady said that Constellation would help her. Miss Penny went with the lady. Miss Penny heard many scary wands as the night lady carried her out. A few teachers with wands hit night lady but Miss Penny kept her eyes closed so she didn't see much. When Miss Penny opened her eyes again, they were outside Rho, somewhere in the dusty lands."

Penny shifted a bit but said nothing as Nelson finished.

"Miss Penny and the night lady slowly walked away. The night lady was hurt but Miss Penny couldn't help her. The night lady said she was taking Miss Penny to Harlington but a dust storm stopped them. The night lady put Miss Penny in a rock cave and stayed guard. Miss Penny was very tired and felt sick. When Miss Penny woke up, the night lady was on the ground. Miss Penny couldn't wake up the night lady. Miss Penny was scared. Miss Penny then spotted buildings. Miss Penny ran towards the buildings, where she found Sir Byron.

"Sir Byron told Miss Penny he couldn't help her, but there was a nice lady who could. Sir Byron carried Miss Penny to the museum where Momma Julie found her. Sir Byron came a bit later with Miss Marisa to help take care of Miss Penny. That's how Miss Penny found her Momma Julie."

The room went silent, Nelson's words laying over it like a shroud.

"Penny..." Julietta's voice cracked. "Do...Do you remember your name?"

Penny shook her head, tears in her eyes.

"Miss Penny doesn't remember her name or much else before Mr. Turner. Miss Penny doesn't know why."

Tears running down her face, Penny moved to sit between Julietta and Charles. Immediately both wrapped their arms around her in a hug.

"You were so brave," Charles managed, his voice breaking.

"Penny safe now." The little girl sniffled, hugging them both back.

"Yes, Penny is safe now," Julietta whispered, hugging her tighter.

"You will always be safe with us." Charles kissed the top of her head.

"I'm...so sorry Penny." Byron bowed his head. "I...I didn't know they punished—"

"Penny is safe now." The child yawned. Crawling into Charles's lap, she sat facing her momma Julie, before resting her head on his chest.

Julietta shifted closer, brushing a stray hair from Penny's face as the girl closed her eyes. "Our lucky Penny."

Wrapping his arms around Penny, Charles shook his head. "This explains...a lot. Why she rarely speaks, why she is so attuned to other's emotions...she had to be."

"She is safe now. That's what's important." Byron sniffed, wiping the last of his tears.

They sat in silence for a time, letting Penny rest, letting their minds absorb what they had been told.

"I'm going to go put Penny to bed," Charles finally whispered, carrying a sleeping Penny out of the room.

Returning to the living room, Charles was surprised to find Julietta and Byron in a rather heated discussion. Stopping just before the two couches he said nothing as the two continued to argue.

"How can you honestly expect me to go back there, Byron?" Spat Julietta, tears still staining her face. "I was fixing the very machines they use on those poor kids."

"You have to go back," Byron grumbled, crossing his arms. "The Constellation needs information. If we don't get the information, everything we've worked for will be lost."

"And what have we been working for? From where I am sitting it looks like the Constellation hasn't gotten anywhere with the mission of putting an end to these schools."

"They've gotten some kids out and are working on getting more."

"But what about the ones you can't get out? What about that poor boy who was trying to run, or that little girl who was terrified of me hiding in a wall, or those kids Penny said disappeared? What about them, Byron?"

"If you don't go back, you are dooming them by not getting us information."

"I am dooming them by fixing the very machines they use to study them like lab rats. There has to be another way!"

"There is no other way! Either you go back, Julie, or you fail your task and we have to start over with someone else who can handle it."

"THAT'S ENOUGH!" Charles shouted, silencing the two. Both turned, suddenly realizing his presence.

"Charlie, will you please tell Julie she is being unreasonable?" Byron sighed, shaking his head. "I worked at one of those facilities for seven cycles and dealt with it. She couldn't handle a few weeks?"

Charles glanced over to Julietta whose face fell, growing pale. He could read her like a book. She was starting to blame herself.

"Clearly things have gotten worse since you were last there. After what I heard from Jul and Penny this evening, I wouldn't want to set foot in that place either."

"But Charlie, the mis—"

"You didn't let me finish." He held up a hand taking a step toward Julietta. "Yes, the Constellation needs information and yes they've made a few rescues but there could be more that can be done so we are not aiding, while information hunting. Jul has a point about not wanting to add to the problem by fixing the very machines we want to destroy."

"So what are you suggesting? That we just barge in and destroy everything? That's sure to get people killed."

"I am suggesting, if Jul is willing to go back, that she does two things. First, she has to stay under the radar and break no rules. Second, she continues to fix the machines but she does it through malicious compliance."

"What do you mean?" Julietta frowned.

"I mean you fix the machine as asked, but then make it fall slowly further into disrepair, maybe its power levels are inaccurate or it turns off intermittently. Nothing dangerous, just annoyances that keep machines from being used for longer and longer periods of time…"

"So sabotage, and what happens when they trace the fixes back to your Julie?" Byron grumbled.

"They can't." Julietta's eyes brightened. "They purposely try to keep us in the dark about what the machines actually do. There is no way to mark who has fixed what machine. They all look alike and are repaired as and when with no real note other than if it is in working order. All orders are shredded at the end of the day. So long as I don't only 'fix' one machine and I spread the wealth, make things break intermittently so a machine could go through multiple fixes or uses before it starts to degrade…"

Byron looked confused. "Can you even do that?"

Charles glared, his eyes like daggers. "Jul, if you remember, is the one who helped fix the water pump, helped you with your purification process, restored dozens of machines and devices in that museum…if anyone could 'fix' a machine to break at the right time and not cause injury it's Jul."

The old man held up his hands. "All right, all right."

Realizing his anger, Charles rolled his shoulders, turning his attention back to Julietta. "It's your choice, Jul. I won't force you to go back. I wouldn't have forced you before I knew all this. All I can say is yes someone needs to be there collecting information, but also you are right to not want to be complicit. I hope my suggestion gives us the best of both worlds."

Leaning back into the couch, she seemed to relax. "If I can sabotage the machines, then maybe I can handle it. It's just, having to see what they do…"

"That I can help with." He frowned, rubbing the back of his head. "As much as I hate to admit it, as a doctor you kinda learn to hold back emotion at the moment and process it later. It's necessary to get through our work with some of the direst cases."

"You do that?"

"Why do you think I was so calm in the museum facing Turner?" His gaze dropped to his feet. "I cried when you went to sleep."

The memory of Charles holding Penny crying flashed in her mind. "I've done it too, just not to this capacity."

"I can help you." He offered again, giving her a small smile. "I already wait for you every night. We can talk when you come home if you need it. I can spare a few more hours of sleep."

"Charlie…"

"I'm serious. If it makes it easier for you to deal with the day-to-day, it's the least I can do."

"Then, I'll go back," she sighed, her face betraying her exhaustion. "For Penny, for Nicolas, and all those kids I will." Looking up at Charles, a tired crooked smile appeared on her face. "Malicious compliance, that I can do."

"You've had a long day. You should get some sleep," Charles chided. "You feel all right?

Yawning, she slowly rose to her feet, walking over to him. "I will be. Thanks to you." She kissed him on the cheek, heading to her and Penny's room and closing the door behind her.

Only once he was sure Julietta was gone did Charles address Byron. There was a pregnant pause between the two men. A million words running through their minds, but none were the right ones to say.

"Charlie—"

"I won't let anything happen to them," he stated firmly, though his exhaustion weighed heavily on him. "I will do everything it takes to protect my girls." He said nothing more as he retired to his room, shutting the door.

Byron sat in silence, Charles's words washing over him. Thinking back on what he had said to Julietta his stomach turned. How easy it was to send someone else into the lion's den. How easy it was for him to fail himself. His face fell, his hands coming to hold it. Had he not chastised Ola the other day for her idea about the children, and here he was doing no better with those he had come to care for? He had to be better. He would not become what he feared most.

CHAPTER 27

The next day at Iota was long and brutal for Julietta. Arriving early, despite her tumbling stomach, she was determined to do what Charles had suggested. Going through security with only the clothes on her back and none of her usual personal items on her, she went directly to the locker rooms. Cleared and cleaned she made a bee-line for the basement, strolling past the blackened wall and across the bleach-cleaned floor without a second glance. She would need to take a shower when she got home, she thought, to scrub away the guilt, but for now, she had to press forward. Entering the basement she found Danni at their assigned station near the front, looking surprised to see her there early.

"Well, I see the little incident didn't dampen your spirits. Good. We are backed up on machines topside, so I'll be upstairs most of the morning once I hand out assignments. There is a machine already at your station. See that it is fixed by lunch."

"Yes, ma'am," she nodded with conviction as she headed to her station, a small mischievous grin dancing onto her face once she was out of the line of sight.

Keeping her head down, she kept herself busy until lunch. A part of her wished she could just stay in that basement, away from the wicked and unfeeling people in the laboratory above, but she knew if she were to complete this mission and prove Byron wrong, she'd need to do exactly as Charles had said: malicious compliance.

As she worked on each device, she fixed the issues that were listed. However, she also found ways to introduce new problems, ones that wouldn't be seen until after the machine had been used a few times.

Danni returned towards the end of the lunch period, pleased to see Julietta had completed her work on the machine. Switching it on briefly she checked all the lights. "Well done, Jessa. Seems you are mastering these fixes quite quickly."

"Just doing my best, ma'am," Julietta replied, wiping some grease from her face, breathing a small sigh of relief that Danni didn't test further to discover her little secret.

It wouldn't appear as an issue for at least a couple of uses, but by then the machine would need at least a couple of days of down-time. It was a small compromise, she reasoned, to let the machines be used for a few days here and there, for them to be taken out in the long run.

Returning from lunch, this time some apple slices squirreled into her pocket, Julietta found a different machine at her station. With instructions from Danni, who once more disappeared into the upper facility, she found herself sneaking over to the hidden hovel in the wall. Leaving the apples, she vowed to check again after dinner.

After another machine 'fixed' and dinner with her supervisor, she returned to her station again, finding a different device awaiting her.

As soon as Danni disappeared, she checked the hole. The apple slices were gone. Setting some crackers in it, she once more returned to work. The sun was well set when Danni returned to find Julietta cleaning her workstation.

"I am happy to see this, Jessa, even more so given why I came to talk to you." The pale woman smiled, a gesture that made Julietta's skin crawl.

"Something wrong?"

"Our typical probation for new employees is about half a cycle, however, after the unfortunate events of yesterday there has been an influx of requests. Starting next week, you will be off probation and allowed on the facility floor. You will report to me in the morning for your task list. You must manage your own time and return to me at the end of the day with your list complete or a very good reason why it wasn't. Understood?"

This is what Julietta had been waiting for and dreading. "Of course, ma'am. I will see you first thing in the morning at the start of the week."

"Then you are dismissed. Enjoy your weekend, Jessa, and rest up. You'll need it."

Danni wasn't kidding. Arriving early on her next workday, Julietta was handed a laundry list of fixes to make around the facility. Tapping her ID on the pad next to her supervisor, she watched as the woman keyed in her permissions for the day.

"That should do it. While in the facility remember you are to act as though you don't exist. Do not speak to anyone unless spoken to. Understood?"

"Yes, ma'am."

"Good. See you at the end of the day, Jessa."

Her first assignment was in one of the classrooms. She noticed the guards stationed nearby each door, carrying metal rods with a cage on top. Based on Penny's description, and what Julietta had witnessed, she had come to the conclusion they were some sort of shocking device, not unlike tasers from before.

Reaching her destination, she was surprised to find a woman there. Dressed in black flats, a plaid gray skirt, a pale blue blouse, and a stark white lab coat, the woman looked as though she stepped out of one of the stock doctor photos from before the war. The only thing that looked out of place were the two thin black bracelets around her wrists. Julietta was still getting used to the system of clothing, but from what she could remember this was a low-level instructor in training.

"Hello," the woman smiled broadly, brushing a stray piece of black hair from her face. "Are you the one to fix my machine?"

"Yes," Julietta answered flatly, remembering Danni's many warnings about addressing those in other departments.

"Good," the woman replied cheerily. Standing from the desk, she approached Julietta, her hand extended. "I'm Miss Bell."

The name alone was enough to send a chill down her spine, what made it worse, however, was the face she now saw clearly before her. If she didn't know any better this 'Miss Bell' looked like a very young Marisa.

"Jessa." She shook the woman's hand. "Which machine?"

"This one over here. My trainer and I noticed it was skipping a bit," Miss Bell replied, her smile unwavering.

"I see. I'll get right on it."

"I'll leave you to it then. Miss Bell is waiting for me. She just wanted me to make sure it was getting handled."

Julietta stopped in her tracks, a question dancing on her lips. This Miss Bell was nice enough, would she tattle? "Your instructor is also Miss Bell?"

"Yes," Miss Bell replied, looking slightly confused. "Is there something wrong?"

"No, no. Just wanted to know who to report completion to."

Miss Bell shook her head. "You must be very new, dear, to think you'd have to report to Miss Bell. You just mark it on your sheet and turn it into your supervisor's box in the laboratory and they'll send someone to test the fix."

"Oh yes, silly me," she chuckled. "Sorry, this is my first day outside the workshop. My supervisor did mention that."

"Very good. Have a good day, Jessa," Miss Bell chirped, closing the door behind her.

With 'Miss Bell' gone, she breathed a sigh of relief. That could not be a coincidence that Miss Bell's instructor was also named Miss Bell, could it? Filing that thought away for later, she set to work on the machine, making sure to hide her adjustments before turning in the slip to Danni's box and heading out to her next fix.

With the amount of work assigned to her, Julietta barely had time to eat lunch let alone squirrel away anything back to the workshop. It was nearing dinner time when she was making a fix on a heat sink on a machine in one of the laboratories. Lost in her work, she did not hear someone entering the lab.

"So, they finally let the new girl out of the dungeon."

Jumping to her feet, she turned to face the voice. It was Joyce.

"Sorry to startle you. Name's Joyce. I'm a new secretary here. My supervisor sent me in here to pick up some papers."

"I see. Sorry," Julietta smiled slightly, turning back to her work.

"Your name is Jessa, right?"

"Yes." She continued working, not looking at the young woman.

"I heard through the grapevine you have a thing for stars."

The hair on the back of her neck stood on end. "You could say that. Spent a lot of time traveling to get here. You really get to see the stars clearly out in the wastes."

"True," Joyce shrugged, fiending looking for the papers that were on the desk in front of her. "Orion was always a favorite of mine."

"Canes Venatici is one of mine."

Joyce picked up the papers from the desk. "You know a lot of the new folks around here rarely get to speak to each other. I learned all the names of course being a secretary. It is so strange. This one researcher, oh what was his name, last name Smith. Such a common name. He just stopped showing up one day."

"That doesn't sound productive." Julietta snorted, giving Joyce a quick glance as if to say continue.

"No, it was not. Heard he was terminated, though, haven't seen the papers for it. The few terminations they've had me handle the paperwork for were…difficult. Not as bad as being released though. That takes more time."

"I see."

"We aren't supposed to talk about those terminated or released though. Confidentiality, of course, so you didn't hear that from me."

"Hear what?"

Joyce walked over to the door. "Well, I better get these papers to my supervisor. Maybe we'll chat again sometime if the stars align."

"When the stars align."

Finishing up the machine, Julietta felt rather hungry. Grabbing a quick dinner, she managed to shove a cookie in her pocket without anyone noticing before heading back to the workshop.

To her relief, it was empty. It seemed the other maintenance staff were either on a job or grabbing dinner. Not wanting to waste time, she headed for the hidden hovel. She was surprised to find the board slightly askew. Carefully pulling it back, instead of finding the little girl she had met briefly before she found a slightly older boy, maybe seven cycles, staring back at her. Much like the girl, he wore gray plain fabric, a pair of long pants with a long-sleeved polo. He looked hungry and sad, tears staining his face. Unlike the girl, however, he had on what seemed to be two thick black stone bracelets.

"Hi…" Julietta whispered, looking back to ensure no one had come in. "Who are you?"

The little boy stared but didn't answer.

"I'm not going to report you, if that's what you are worried about. In fact…" She reached into her pocket, pulling out the cookie. "Here."

The little boy's eyes lit up, taking it. "You gave sis cookie."

Her heart broke. "Yes, I left a cookie for the little girl who was hiding here a few days ago."

"You work days, not ends?" The little boy frowned.

"Yes. I don't work on the weekends."

"Sister was taken to school away from me."

"She's been transferred?"

The boy nodded, holding out his identification necklace. "Dimetre, sister Nicole."

She noted the dime with an alchemy symbol around his neck, wondering for a moment what his real name was. "Could I see your bracelets?"

Dimetre held up his wrists, letting her examine the stone around them.

"Could you tell me more, Dimetre, about this school?"

Dimetre nodded. "Yes, not now. Need go back. Bring more food?"

"I'll try, around the same time tomorrow."

He smiled sadly. "Thank you for help, Dimetre. Thank for giving Nicole cookie for one of last days with brother."

Julietta nodded, leaving Dimetre to make his escape. Cleaning up her workspace she fiddled with a few of the machines in the backlog of repairs until Danni appeared to dismiss her.

"You did well today, Jessa. Completed all tasks and even worked on the backlog. I'm impressed. See you tomorrow."

Dismissed, she made for the locker room, remaining calm as she completed her evening decontamination before heading for the rovers. Thankfully, she only had to wait a few minutes for a transport to be available and was back in Matson just after dark. Entering the apartment at the Snapdragon Inn, she was relieved to find Charles waiting up for her.

Closing the door behind her, she stood there a moment as he approached.

"Need to talk?"

Without a second thought, she wrapped her arms around him letting all the pain of the day fall from her eyes as he embraced her tightly.

"I'm here, Jul. I'm here."

It was just after the lunch rush when Byron found himself and Ola finally able to talk. The week had been a busy one for the Constellation. With Julietta off probation since the start of the week, she was coming back with information daily, taking to writing up her findings each night for Byron to bring to Ola the next day.

The shop was unusually busy that morning, likely because it would be closed for the evening after lunch for 'taking inventory.' That was the story they had maintained. In reality, there were to be new recruits arriving that evening.

"Ola?" Byron called, having finished washing the last of the teacups. "Shop's clear."

Ola rolled out from the back of the shop, looking grim.

"Something happen?"

"Ambleton satellite, Eta-165," she sighed deeply. "They've been discovered. Word came in from Ava in Apolis about 20 minutes ago. Survivors arrived in Johani this morning. Only five, nine others are confirmed dead, and thirteen missing."

He bowed his head. "How'd it happen?"

"No word as of yet. From what they could glean from the survivors, it was a raid. Someone slipped up somewhere and the hideout was attacked during their weekly meeting. Originally, eight had made it to Johani but three succumbed to their injuries overnight."

"A great loss." He shook his head. "It's getting more dangerous."

"You're telling me." She leaned back in her chair. "I contacted Ava this morning about check-ins. She hasn't heard anything from Omicron-753, Tau-059, or Chi-560 yet. Their last correspondences are scattered at best. With Eta being taken down…" Her voice broke. "I am worried."

"We all are. Every morning when I watch Charles take Julie to her stop, I wonder sometimes if I'll see her in the evening."

"A sacrifice we all make, for the good of the cause."

"Speaking of people helping the cause, I need a favor."

"Really, Byron? Now?" she huffed. "What is it?"

"I need a message sent to Johani to Marisa Healey."

"About?"

"Her niece, who was taken as a child. Julie ran into a woman at Iota, an instructor in training, who bore an eerie family resemblance."

"And?"

"And...what if that was her niece? She called herself Miss Bell, which happened to be her teaching instructor's name and the name Penny gave us as her teacher's name."

"Three Miss Bells? That seems, not a coincidence."

"Precisely why I want you to ask Marisa about her niece. What was her name? What did she look like? Did she have any identifying characteristics?"

Ola pondered for a moment this information, her face giving no indication if she had found a reasonable explanation. "All right, I'll ping Ava and have her send the message. This isn't something that can wait for a courier."

Before anything more could be said, the bell on the shop door chimed. Henrietta entered.

"Such a day I've had. First, I had to make a house call, then I just saw a very strangely dressed man."

Julietta was busy working on yet another machine in one of the classrooms when Danni appeared.

"Something wrong?" Julietta frowned, noting it wasn't even dinner time yet.

"Finish up your work, you are being dismissed early."

She raised an eyebrow but did not argue. "Yes, ma'am?"

"It's nothing wrong, if that's what you are thinking. Some important higher-ups are visiting this evening. Security protocol dictates only necessary staff may be permitted to be in the facility. This does not affect your scheduled return at the start of the work week."

"Of course." Finishing tightening the last bolt on the panel she was fixing, she stood. "Done."

"Good, please return to the workshop and depart as soon as possible."

Julietta was all but rushed out of the facility by security. She barely had time to return her tools when guards ushered her and the other low-level maintenance to the locker rooms and out the door.

Standing outside waiting for transportation, she couldn't help but wonder just who was coming that warranted such secrecy. The answer to her question arrived just as her rover pulled up. Across the way, another transport had arrived, out of which climbed six Mr. Turners.

Hoping no one could see the fear in her eyes, she boarded her rover, heart pounding. Six identical people in the same suit she had last seen Mr. Turner in Cartsdale in, and in Waterwealt she realized. There were two Mr. Turners? Eight now? These questions and more flooded her mind as she rode in silence back to Matson. As soon as she disembarked and was sure she was clear of any onlookers, she ran toward Ola's.

Charles had a long day. With Julietta working at Iota, Byron helping Ola set up for the recruiting meeting that evening, Lisle getting city hall ready for an upcoming visit from the Governor of Ambleton, and Henrietta out on house calls, he and Victor had taken turns keeping an eye on the kids at the clinic.

Victor had taken over child duty a couple of hours prior, given the lack of patients that day, allowing Charles the time to continue his research on the human genome in the clinic's laboratory undisturbed for a bit.

He was just finishing up writing some notes from an old medical journal that had been recovered when he felt a small hand pull on his sleeve. Glancing from the corner of his eye, he found Penny.

"Is it dinner time already?" He smiled, not looking up from his work. "I'll be ready in a minute.

Penny pulled on his sleeve harder.

"I know you are hungry Penny, but I need to finish this. We'll head to Ola's right after I—"

"Papa Charlie!"

Charles froze, partially from the shock of hearing Penny call him Papa, but more from the tone she had used. Penny sounded terrified.

Immediately dropping his work, he turned to find her along with Nicolas who was hugging Maya tightly all gazing up at him panicked.

"What's wrong? Where's Victor?"

"Turner man," Penny cried, shaking.

Immediately, he was on his feet. A moment later he heard something that made his heart drop. Coming down the hall were slow methodical footsteps with a pronounced limp.

CHAPTER 28

"What do you mean, a strangely dressed man?" Byron frowned.

"Well, there was a man, tall, lanky, and pale. He was wearing a suit right out of the before times, fifties style, I'd say." Henrietta shrugged. "Walked with a limp. Asked me where the nearest clinic was so I directed him to ours."

The bell on the door chimed again, this time Julietta rushing in. "Turners…" She gasped breathlessly.

"Turners?" Ola asked, confused.

"Six of them just arrived at Iota."

"The one you shot in Cartsdale is here," Byron's face paled, rushing for the door. "Heading for the clinic!"

"The kids!" Julietta rushed after him, Henrietta right on their heels confused but concerned, leaving Ola to figure out what exactly just happened.

"Stay under there and don't move," Charles instructed the children, pulling his knife from his boot and facing the door just as Mr. Turner appeared.

"Well, what do we have here? E-165141425 and T-14931512119, with a little one I haven't had the pleasure of meeting."

Charles could hear the children behind him shuffle a bit under the desk, terrified. "Leave, Turner."

"Now, why would I do that? Surely you want these Curied back where they belong, with their own kind."

"They're with their families, where they should be," he spat back, part of him wishing he had time to get the children out. In this tight office, he reasoned, his gun would be too dangerous, more likely to ricochet. His knife would have to do.

"They are dangerous, these Curied. They need to be trained."

"They are children who need a childhood." Stepping forward he forward, brandishing his knife defensively. "Now I believe I asked you to leave. This clinic is private property."

Mr. Turner chuckled, the sound of it unnatural. "You will give me the Curied."

Charles began to sweat. Mr. Turner's words seemed to echo in his ears, physically hurting them. It took every ounce of willpower not to flinch.

"Oh? A mind not so easily bent? Maybe you'll be a more worthy opponent than the last." He grinned manically. "Give me the Curied."

Charles's head began to hurt, each word like a dagger in his mind. "Leave."

"Give me the Curied."

The pain became more intense, but he did not take his eyes off Mr. Turner. "Come any closer and you'll force my hand."

Mr. Turner took a step forward.

There was no hesitation as Charles immediately pounced. The pain in his head seared as he reached the man, attempting to grapple him. There was a brief struggle. Mr. Turner managed to catch both of his wrists just before he slammed him into the wall beside the door.

"Foolish man," Mr. Turner chuckled. "Let me show you just what a Curied can do when properly trained."

The pain was blinding, sapping his strength. He couldn't fathom what was happening to him and didn't have time to as Mr. Turner's power overwhelmed his senses. Despite his best efforts, his strength buckled for a moment; it was all Mr. Turner needed. In a flash of movement, he had disarmed Charles, swiping the knife down his arm, gashing it badly.

Unable to handle the pain, he fell to the ground clutching his arm, his mind on fire.

"Pitiful," Mr. Turner spat, tossing the knife out of his reach. "Now, my Curied…"

In a deft movement, he was upon them. Penny, seeing this, moved in front of Nicolas and Maya, hands out.

"Come now E-165141425 let's get you and your fellow—AGH!" As soon as Mr. Turner reached out to Penny, she acted. Sparking her fingers, she grabbed his arm hard, sending a burning shock to it.

The man stumbled back, patting his smoldering sleeve. It was enough of a distraction to allow Nicolas, who had now moved beside Penny, to use his telekinesis to send various books, containers, and other small objects flying toward their assailant.

SLAP. A book slammed him in the face, despite his best efforts to shield himself from the tossed projectiles. As it hit, he lost his concentration.

That was all Charles needed. The pain in his mind lessening briefly, he staggered to his feet. Quickly scooping up the tossed knife, he charged once more at Mr. Turner. After another brief skirmish, he managed once more to grapple the man, this time from behind, holding the knife to his throat.

Nicolas halted his assault, not wanting to hit Charles, but held a few objects aloft, just as Penny kept her sparks dancing on her fingers.

"Now, you are going to leave," Charles spat, slowly dragging the man towards the door.

Mr. Turner, however, wasn't fazed. About halfway across the room, he regained his bearings, elbowing Charles hard in the ribs. Though briefly stunned, he somehow maintained his grip, using the pain to fuel his strength as he twisted Mr. Turner around, running him into the glassware-laden table in the center of the room.

CRASH

Fast as lightning, Mr. Turner grabbed some of the broken glass, swinging, his mind assault renewed.

Charles cried out as the shard cut into him, but held firm, managing to pull Mr. Turner away from the table. Blows were traded, knife and glass, until they had disarmed each other, the only difference in strength diminished to the now constant mental blows from Mr. Turner. Mustering up his strength, Charles slammed his attacker into one of the sturdy bookshelves near the desk, the force of the immovable object, however, giving Mr. Turner more momentum than expected, sending both men to the ground.

Despite his throbbing head and weakening body, Charles pressed on. The sole thought of protecting the children fueled him, keeping Mr. Turner's power from breaking him. Pinning the gangly man briefly to the ground once more, he caught a flash of movement out of the corner of his eye. Maya had moved from beneath the desk to the side of the bookshelf above them. Confused, he watched in shock as she easily began to tip the shelf that had taken both him and Victor to move only a week ago. Realizing what was about to happen, he rolled off of Mr. Turner who chuckled as he flipped onto his stomach.

"Had enou—AGH!"

The bookshelf hit its mark, trapping the vile man from the waist down. Charles did not hesitate, grabbing his fallen knife.

"You will not take my daughter." With that he brought the back end of it onto Mr. Turner's head, knocking him out cold.

The strangling pain in his mind released almost instantly, leaving behind a deep throbbing one. He did not have time to address it, however, not with the children still nearby.

"Penny..." Charles panted. "Get me those zip ties." He pointed to the tube of zip ties Nicolas had thrown that now lay near the overturned glassware table.

Dropping her sparks, Penny retrieved them, while Nicolas, who also dropped his powers, went to check on Maya. Zip-tying Mr. Turner's hands, he found himself finally able to breathe a sigh of relief.

"Are...are you all okay?" Charles breathed, his head spinning as Penny, Nicolas, and Maya approached him.

The three children nodded just as they heard footsteps rushing down the hall.

"Nicolas! Maya!" Lisle shouted heading straight for her children.

Byron immediately went to the unconscious Mr. Turner, while Julietta knelt beside Charles and Penny.

"Charlie..." Julietta gasped seeing the blood coating him.

"Papa Charlie stop Turner man." Penny cried, tears staining her face.

"Dr. Charlie protect us," Nicolas sniffled, looking up at Lisle.

"I...knocked him out...he...tried to take the children...has... powers..." Finally safe, Charles could not handle the pain any longer, fainting, Julietta catching him.

"Charlie!" Laying him down carefully, she checked his pulse while trying to rouse him. "Charlie..."

Lisle pulled Penny to her, while Byron rushed over to the medical kit on the wall. Grabbing the smelling salts he returned, waving them under Charles's nose. After about a minute, to everyone's relief, Charles stirred with a groan.

"It's all right, Charlie, you're all right." Julietta breathed a sigh of relief.

Charles coughed, his eyes still closed. "Sorry…Jul."

She shook her head. "Don't be."

"Let's get him to Henrietta." Byron frowned, glancing over to Mr. Turner. "And get Turner locked up."

Henrietta, with Julietta's help, patched up Charles. Once he was coherent, he was able to explain what had happened, including Mr. Turner's mental powers and Maya's seemingly unnatural strength.

Not wanting Mr. Turner to be able to use his powers again, Henrietta suggested sedating him while Byron went to see if they had any of the black cuffs from rescues that Julietta had recently discovered were used to suppress the kids' powers.

It was late in the evening. Julietta was in bed beside Penny who was sound asleep. They had brought Charles back to the apartment to rest only a few hours ago with the agreement to talk more once everyone had recovered. She, however, was still worried, her mind unable to rest. Ensuring she wouldn't wake Penny, she quietly crept out of the room.

Cracking the door open, she peeked into Charles's room. He was, to some relief, asleep. It hurt her heart to see him so banged up. The mental attack on Charles had left him with a painful migraine, but thankfully no concussion or further damage. Of his cuts scattered across his arms and torso, his right forearm had been gashed the worst. There had been a bit of concern about the blood loss from this injury, but after cleaning him up and administering some medication, Henrietta found it unwarranted.

Mr. Turner had also managed one good slice across his right cheek before Charles had disarmed him, a mark that likely as not would leave a scar. From how he was breathing she could tell his ribs were still very sore and bruised. She was just thankful they had not been broken. The only other injury that he sustained was a left knee sprain. Henrietta had assured Julietta he would make a full recovery; it would just be a bit of time.

Though still worried, she turned. "Jul?"

"Sorry, Charlie," She opened the door, stepping into the room. "Just making sure you're all right."

He smiled but didn't open his eyes. "Stay a bit?"

She didn't hesitate to approach. Reaching for the washcloth she had laid on his forehead before he went to bed, she frowned. "One minute, let me get you a fresh one." Returning with a fresh damp cloth she sat beside him, gently wiping his face and neck. "How do you feel?"

"Better than earlier," he sighed, letting the cold soothe his aching head. "The meds and the cloth help the headache. Barely a throb now. I hurt just about everywhere else but...at least the kids are safe. How's Victor?"

"He tussled with Mr. Turner like you but was knocked out a bit quicker. Similar, lingering migraine but Henrietta said he should be fine in a couple of days."

Charles's eyes fluttered open. "I'm sorry."

"Sorry?" She quirked an eyebrow. "Sorry for what?"

"For scaring you, when I passed out. The pain was—"

"Charlie...it wasn't your fault you fainted. Yes, I was scared but... you are fine now."

"I wasn't going to let him have them. Not on my life." He swallowed a lump in his throat. "He almost had them. I wasn't strong enough to hold him off completely. If Penny and Nicolas hadn't—"

"Sshhhh..." she chided, running the cloth down the side of his face, wiping away a few tears that had begun to form in his eyes with her other hand. "You fought him, Charlie, and won. The kids are safe. Our Penny is safe."

"She...she called me Papa Charlie."

"Yes," she smiled, placing the cloth on his forehead. "She loves her Papa Charlie."

"You are okay with—"

Charles's words were lost as Julietta placed her hands on his face, bent down, and kissed him. "More than." She pulled back slightly, looking him in his eyes as her thumb gingerly ran over the gash on his cheek. "I couldn't ask for anyone better."

"Our Penny..." Charles lightly placed his hands on her arms, smiling. "I love you both."

"I love you too." She brushed some stray hair from his face. "And our beautiful daughter."

"She has bright eyes like you, you know." He teased, eliciting a laugh from Julietta.

"If we are going on that logic, then she has your crooked smile, full of mischief."

It was his turn to laugh, though shallowly given his aching ribs. "Our daughter not by blood, but our daughter, nonetheless. I wouldn't change that for the world."

"Charlie…Would you…would you maybe someday…"

"Want one of our own?" He raised an eyebrow curiously.

"Give Penny a little brother or sister, with your crooked smile."

"And your beautiful eyes." He reached up, running his hand through her hair gently. "When the world is right, and we have the museum…"

"When we have the museum…" She blushed, kissing him once more. "Everything will be all right, Charlie."

Charles relaxed, gazing into Julietta's eyes. "Jul?"

"Yes?"

"Do—do you think Penny ever wonders about her birth parents?"

She furrowed her brow for a moment, thinking. "She's…never said anything. From what she told us she lost them very young. I do sometimes wonder…"

Both stopped, Julietta, sitting up as the door creaked.

"Penny?"

Penny approached, climbing into Julietta's lap so she was sitting facing Charles.

"Papa okay?"

They exchanged a smile as Julietta wrapped her arms around Penny.

"I'm okay, Penny." Charles rested a bit further into his pillow. "I'm going to be okay."

"Momma take care, Papa?" Penny looked up at Julietta.

"Yes, Momma was just checking on Papa."

Penny looked down at her hands, frowning. "Penny dangerous?"

Julietta and Charles's faces fell.

"No, Penny," Julietta shook her head. "Why would you think you are dangerous?"

"Turner man say Penny dangerous. Penny sparks hurt Turner man."

Charles's held out a hand, Penny taking it. "Penny, remember when I gave you that pocketknife before we left Waterwealt? How I told you it was not a toy but a tool to be used?"

Penny nodded.

"You've seen Momma and I use knives before, right?"

She nodded again.

"We used them to cut sandwiches, cut materials for some projects, and also to defend ourselves, right?"

"Yes," the girl answered, looking a bit confused.

"A knife was also used to hurt me today."

Penny frowned, tears in her eyes.

"But it was also used to protect me. Do you see what I am saying?"

Penny wiped her tears, looking at her Papa thoughtfully. "Knife good and bad?"

Julietta nodded, realizing what Charles was getting at. "The knife is neither good nor bad, Penny. A knife is just a tool. What makes it good, bad, or dangerous, is the person who uses it."

Penny looked down at her hands again. "Penny good?"

"Penny is very good." Charles ran a thumb over her hand. "Our Penny is an intelligent, beautiful, and good girl. You used your powers today to help me and protect your friends. You've used your spark before to power the radio that warned us about the bomb that protected the people of Waterwealt. You also used it to bring our little friend Nelson to life."

"Penny's sparks good?"

"Penny's sparks are good because you are good and decide to do good with them. That is your choice." Julietta hugged her slightly. "We love your sparks and trust you to make good choices with them."

"They are beautiful sparks, Penny." Charles shifted slightly, wincing as Penny pulled her hand away. "Nothing to be afraid of."

She looked at her hand thoughtfully, letting a few sparks dance on her fingertips before letting them fade. "Penny good. Penny want good. Penny sparks good cause Penny want good."

"Exactly," Charles smiled brightly. "I love you, my little spark."

"Penny love Momma and Papa." Penny smiled. "Penny safe."

"Penny safe." Julietta kissed the top of the girl's head. "Come on, we better let your Papa get some rest."

Penny hopped off of Julietta's lap but stopped. "Momma stay with Papa."

Julietta quirked an eyebrow. "Of course, we all stay—"

Penny shook her head. "Momma stay with Papa to sleep."

Julietta glanced over to Charles who looked amused. "You want me to sleep here?"

"Penny brave. Penny have Nelson and Margie. Papa need Momma. Momma worried about Papa."

"Papa is hurt, Penny. I—"

"If you stay on my left, it should be fine." Charles chuckled. "Dr. Penny's orders."

"Make Penny happy," Penny smirked, sticking out her tongue.

"Well, when you put it that way." She chuckled, giving a look to Charles that secretly wondered how much of their conversation Penny had heard. "I'll be right back."

Returning, having settled Penny in, Julietta went to lie beside Charles.

"You can be closer. You won't hurt me," he smirked, using his good arm to pull her lightly towards him.

His left arm around her, Julietta settled herself facing him, resting her own lightly over him.

"Momma Julie protects Papa Charlie?" he teased, kissing the top of Julietta's head before closing his eyes.

"Yes, Momma Julie protects Papa Charlie just like he protects her and their Penny." She sighed, closing her eyes. "Momma Julie loves Papa Charlie, and feels safe with him."

CHAPTER 29

The plan was to meet at Ola's the next evening, giving Victor and Charles at least a day to recover. Thanks to Henrietta's treatment and Julietta's care, Charles was already back on his feet and ready to go.

"Are you sure you'll be all right?" Julietta frowned as they began walking, Charles, leaning on her, limping. Penny was a few feet ahead of them, happily twirling.

"I'm fine, Jul. 'Tis merely a scratch," he chuckled. "The headache is completely gone. I'm just a bit sore is all."

"All right, but if you need a break, you let me know, okay?"

"Of course, Dr. Milard."

She shook her head, sticking out her tongue. "Cheeky."

They arrived at Ola's about 30 minutes later, having to stop a couple of times for Charles to rest. Upon entering, they found Byron already there.

Penny waved hello to Byron before running over to the table that had been set up with some paper and crayons for her, Nicolas, and Maya, immediately setting to work on something.

"Well, you won't win any beauty contests, but at least you're mobile." The older man teased.

"Speak for yourself," Julietta scoffed, leading Charles over to a chair.

"It's all right, Jul," Charles smirked, mischievously. "He's just jealous my misadventure will leave me with a cool scar."

"Oh yes, that's sure to attract the ladies."

"Only the right one." Charles placed an arm around Julietta's waist.

Julietta relaxed, brushing a gentle hand over the healing gash on Charles's cheek. "Makes you look more rugged. Better than a curly mustache." She gave Byron a pointed look.

He burst out laughing. "All right, you two win. Joking aside, glad you are here, Charles. You look better."

"Feel better. Henrietta came by this morning. You'll be happy to know my headache is gone, and no lingering issues there. Seems Turner's power, aside from manipulation, is just giving people the mother of all headaches."

The sound of wheels on wood reached their ears as Ola rolled in from the back room, Henrietta following carrying a tray of tea and cookies. "Good, you're here," Ola greeted, as Henrietta set the tea on the table in front of them. "Byron explained what happened. I have two of our most trusted people guarding Turner in the basement. Henrietta has kept him mellow and the bracelets are doing just what Julietta mentioned. I plan on having Byron look further into the others we retained to see why that is exactly."

A few minutes later Lisle, Victor, and the children appeared. Nicolas and Maya gave Julietta and Charles a quick hello before joining Penny at the art table. From what they could tell, Victor was a bit worse for wear, a bandage above his right eye, his left black. He too walked a bit slower but seemed in good spirits as Lisle helped him to the seat beside Charles.

Charles held out a hand, Victor taking it, shaking it as a silent understanding and thank you passed between the men. They had protected each other's children and were grateful.

"Glad to see you are on your feet, Victor." Julietta stood behind Charles, placing her hands over his shoulders. "And thank you for protecting our Penny."

"Same to Charles." Lisle nodded, sitting beside her husband. "Nicolas and Maya couldn't stop talking about how Dr. Charlie saved them."

"I did nothing more than what any of us would," Charles shrugged. "I refuse to let any more children be taken if I can help it."

"Agreed." Victor leaned a bit further back in his seat. "I'd take another hit to the head if I had to. Speaking of, did your headache finally go away? I swear I was seeing double until breakfast."

"Only double?" Charles chuckled. "Kidding, but yeah, mine faded this morning. That was one whopper up 'til then though."

"I had three of our members, Barbara, Colin, and Jens, keeping watch on Iota for signs of any other Turners the past few days. They should be here in about an hour with today's report. I wanted to talk with all of you first to decide what we do." Ola glanced over at the children who were busy playing and enjoying the cookies she had left out for them. "For starters, we have Turner. Odds are Iota knows he was meant to be in Matson, and based on what Julietta said when she burst in here yesterday, he is not the only one."

"We first encountered 'Mr. Turner' back in Waterwealt," Julietta explained. "He came to town claiming he was from Apolis and wanted to test the children. The Mayor fell for his ploy, and he tried to take Penny. Byron shot him dead."

"And you are sure he was dead, Byron?" Ola quirked an eyebrow.

"As a doornail." Byron crossed his arms. "Oliver and I buried him ourselves. He wasn't coming back."

"This one that we have, however, you said was not from Waterwealt, but Cartsdale?"

"Yeah, we sort of had a run-in with another Turner looking to test kids. This one recognized Penny. Called her by a number rather than a name. At the time we didn't think about it, just ran. Julietta shot him in the leg as we escaped." Charles felt Julietta, who was now sitting beside him, take his hand under the table. "Didn't register then that he was identical to the one from Waterwealt."

"The ones I saw at Iota were spitting images from what I could tell." Julietta shook her head. "It's like they are duplicates or twins of one another."

"Whatever they are, they pack a punch," Victor snorted. "I thought he was splitting my skull open with his powers."

"You and Charles are lucky," Henrietta chimed in. "I was worried when I saw you both that something worse could have happened."

As they continued to discuss the oddness of Mr. Turner, Julietta's eyes drifted to Charles, whose face showed deep thought.

"Charlie?" She whispered. "What's wrong?"

"Twins, duplicates, not duplicates, but…" His eyes went wide. "He's not human."

The discussion came to an abrupt halt.

"What do you mean, Charles?" Lisle looked deeply concerned. "He sure looks human."

"He's human, but not in the traditional way. If I were to hedge my bets, Turner's a clone."

"A clone?" Victor raised an eyebrow.

Henrietta shook her head. "That's Arcane, Charles."

"Is it, though?" He sat up, leaning on the table. "You all thought cauterization was Arcane when I did it, yet now I find many papers discussing its effectiveness as a wound-sealing method. In fact, from what you've both told me since my departure it's become a more common practice in dire situations."

Victor and Henrietta both averted their gaze, realizing their mistake.

"You are studying genetics right now, correct?" Ola raised an eyebrow. "Have you come across cloning?"

"I have, though most papers from the past talk about its failure. There were too many complications, not to mention the morality and ethical issues surrounding it."

"Given what I've seen in Iota, I don't think morals or ethics is an issue," Julietta scoffed. "That being said, then who's to say someone in these schools hasn't figured it out?"

"When Ola and I worked in Rho there were some geneticists, but they were looking at the kid's DNA." Byron's brow furrowed. "I always thought they were trying to figure out where the powers came from."

"Turner claimed to be a Curied and had powers like one." Charles' shoulders slumped. "Never said he was the original owner of said powers."

"Charles!" Henrietta chastised. "That's horrible, who in their right mind—"

"They are not in their right mind, Henrietta," Ola chastised. "Why do you think I am in a wheelchair?"

"What about Nicolas, Hen?" Lisle added. "Think about how he was brought to us."

"Think about what he did to Charles and me," Victor coughed, his voice fading.

Henrietta sat in stunned silence.

"This, of course, is all pure speculation." Ola looked deep in thought. "We need concrete proof."

"We have potential proof locked up in the basement," Byron smirked. "You can thank Charles for that."

Charles winced slightly at the mention of what he had done. It was not that he regretted it, not by a long shot. He did what he had to do to protect the children. It did not mean he had to enjoy that fact. "He won't talk."

"What makes you think that?" Lisle questioned. "He has no other options, does he?"

"He sure wasn't up to talking when he came into the clinic," Victor replied, gesturing to his black eye.

"Whether he is a clone or not, he is clearly trained for one sole purpose, to find and collect Curied." Julietta shook his head. "Doubt you could reason or threaten him into talking."

"It's still worth a shot," Byron argued. "He can't use his powers and is tied up. We have limited time before someone comes looking. Better to try to get something out of him now before we have to dispose of him."

They all gave each other uncomfortable looks, except Ola who seemed unfazed. "Do you want to do the honors, Byron?"

"Sure, if no one objects?"

No one said anything.

"Then that's settled." Ola shrugged. "Tomorrow, Byron you can work him over. Now onto the next matter, what do we tell people?"

"What do you mean?" Julietta looked confused. "No one saw what happened in the clinic."

"No, but people saw Turner in town. People also come to the clinic and will see Victor and Charles." Lisle shook her head. "Not to mention the medical society will want Charles's updates soon. Dr. Cone is interested in your current research."

"We tell them we had a bit of a wild patient, someone who had a psychotic break. Came in from the wastes and gave no name, just attacked." Victor suggested. "Surely no one will ask questions."

"Average person might not, but Cone sure will." Julietta crossed her arms, a thought turning in her mind. "What does Cone do, Lisle?"

"He's the head of the medical society."

"I know, but what's his day job?"

Lisle paused for a moment, thinking. "I...I don't know. I don't keep track of all the medical society folks."

"He's—he's a researcher," Henrietta piped up, sounding frightened. "Doesn't work in any of the clinics though. His workplace is considered a private office on record."

"You don't think..." Lisle's voice faded.

"I haven't seen him, but I haven't been at Iota long. I know there are quite a few researchers on the board. I recognized them when Charlie had his presentation." Julietta shifted nervously.

"That's why you wanted him to research genetics, Ola? To draw out Cone?" Lisle looked appalled.

"Partially, I wanted him to research it because it was of use to us, and I knew it would raise some eyebrows with those who worked at Iota. Cone is just a mere bonus."

"You knew?" Charles sat up straighter, eyes wide. "You knew he was a higher-up and that it would put a target on my back? When you told me to make that my next paper, I thought it was just to rattle the Iota members and get them to potentially reveal information to me, not draw out someone who likely as not—"

"It's fine, Charles. It was a risk, but a necessary one. The Constellation needs to start pinpointing heads, people who have power who—"

"It's bad enough I have to be sent into the lion's den, but now you want to send Charlie? Julietta spat, clearly annoyed. "What if they wanted him at Iota?"

"All the better," Ola stated. "We could use a researcher there since we lost our last one."

"Ola, I am usually on your side about these things, but even I think that was a step too far." Byron looked genuinely concerned. "Why didn't you just tell us this was the case?"

"Because you would react like you are now, against me," she grumbled. "What's done is done."

"No, this is not done. This put Charlie at risk!" Julietta growled. "What were you planning on next? Sending Victor or Henrietta in?"

"Maybe…"

Everyone's eyes were on Ola, staring daggers.

"I trusted you." Lisle stood. "When I agreed to help you, you promised me that you would do your best to keep everyone safe. This is downright reckless."

"What would make you think this is even remotely okay?" Charles grunted, his body tensing.

Victor shook his head. "You could get any one of us killed."

"It's a calculated risk," Ola replied, sounding nervous.

"It was too much of a risk." Henrietta stood, making for the door. "I can't do this."

"Henrietta, please." Ola moved to follow.

Lisle moved to help her husband stand. "Unless you can tell me why you are so willing to risk—"

"BECAUSE OF MY BROTHER."

The room froze, even the children stopping for a moment to see what the commotion was.

"Your brother?" Byron looked confused.

"That's why I was at Apolis, and why I wanted to help you, Byron. My—my brother was a researcher there. He—he got roped into working in Alpha then eventually transferred somewhere else. That was around the time you showed up. You were looking for your son and I was looking to get my brother out. They brainwashed him into thinking he was doing good, but when he told me what he was being made to do…I had to get him out. I needed to find him and get him out. Then seeing all those poor kids…"Tears formed in Ola's eyes. "I'm sorry. It's just…I feel like some days it's a losing battle, especially after yesterday with the Ambleton satellite."

Henrietta walked back over as Lisle sat down. "Ambleton?" Lisle asked, concerned. "I'm supposed to meet the governor of Ambleton in the next couple of weeks."

"The Ambleton satellite was destroyed. Of the 27 members, only five survived. They are in Johani now recovering."

It was as if the air was let out of the room, everyone sinking back into their seats.

"I'm sorry, Ola," Julietta finally spoke, breaking the silence.

"You couldn't have known." The older woman shook her head. "I don't blame you for being angry with me. I should have told you the plan in case it went sideways. I didn't think."

"Well, we know it now so…" Charles leaned on the table, taking his head in his hands, starting to feel the strain of his injuries. "At least we can plan for it."

Seeing this Byron stepped in. "Enough business talk. Why don't we all just relax for a bit until the others get here?"

"I'm okay with that." Victor leaned back in his chair, closing his eyes.

Julietta gently rubbed Charles's back. "You feeling okay?"

"I'll live." He relaxed to her touch.

"I'll go get some more tea," Ola offered. "Henrietta, do you mind helping?"

As Ola and Henrietta disappeared, the kids ran over. Placing Nelson and Margie on the table, Penny smiled, turning her robot friend on.

"Hello everyone," Nelson greeted.

"Hello, Mr. Nelson," Lisle chuckled. "And how is our favorite metal friend?"

"I am fine. Miss Penny and Master Nicolas wanted to show you all something."

"Oh?" Victor opened his eyes.

"Is everyone ready?"

"Sure." Charles smiled, Julietta, nodding in agreement.

The adults watched as Nicolas held out his hand, Margie rising to her plush feet. Nelson stepped forward, taking Margie's hands in his, and began dancing. Everyone was all smiles.

"That is wonderful, Nelson." Byron smiled sadly.

"Miss Penny and Master Nicolas said this is what Miss Lisle, Dr. Victor, Miss Julie, and Dr. Charlie should do."

The two couples looked at each other chuckling.

"Maybe once Victor and I have healed up a bit we'll take our girls dancing," Charles smirked, giving Julietta a wink. "What do you say?"

"I think that's a brilliant idea, Charles." Victor chuckled, taking Lisle's hand in his. "In all honesty, we could use a break from this madness."

Penny smiled at her Papa Charlie and Momma Julie. "One more ting."

"Oh?" Julietta smiled.

Turning to Maya, Nicolas and Penny each took a piece of paper from her. Setting them on the table the three smiled brightly.

"Tank you Dr. Victor and Dr. Charlie," Nicolas blushed.

"Thank you to Papa and Charlie!" Maya cheered. "I'm a strong girl!"

Everyone laughed, though their eyes held happy tears seeing the stick figure pictures each child had drawn. Across the three pages, they had attempted to draw them all sitting at the table.

"Yes, you are, Maya." Lisle wrapped an arm around her kids as they went to stand between her and Victor. "Our strong girl with an amazing telekinetic brother."

"And our beautiful spark," Charles added as Penny went to join him and Julietta.

Ola and Henrietta returned with the tea and cookies. Seeing the drawings on the table they both smiled.

"Your motor skills are improving." Henrietta chuckled. "The three of you are turning into some real Picassos."

"Miss Henrietta much nicer than Miss Bell." Nicolas smiled.

"Miss Henrietta teach good," Penny added.

All the adults glanced nervously at each other at the mention of Miss Bell. Their thoughts were further interrupted by the sound of the bell chiming at the door. Barbara, Colin, and Jens entered, each holding up another person.

Henrietta, Lisle, and Julietta were to their feet, grabbing chairs for the injured while Byron ran for the medical kit.

"What happened?" Ola asked, wheeling over to them.

"We were heading over here when we spotted these three," Barbara explained, voice shaking. "They are from the Ciysea satellite. Chi-560 was evacuated about four days ago. Ciysea is gone."

"Gone? What do you mean gone?" Byron asked, handing the kit to Henrietta.

"Flattened." Colin frowned, "Blown off the face of the planet."

Jens, who at this point was visibly shaking, could no longer hold back their frustration. "It was a bomb, Ola, a frickin' bomb."

CHAPTER 30

"Are you ready for this, Byron?" Ola frowned as he entered the shop. "As I can be. After everything that's happened over the past few days, I can't say I look forward to doing this."

"I spoke with the three surviving Ciysea members brought in last night, Lea, Jon, and Xavier. Apparently, Ciysea was bombed five days ago. They managed to get here quickly cause they found an abandoned rover outside Chi. It broke down about a day from here, so they walked the rest of the way."

"I still don't know how we didn't get any indication," he furrowed his brow, heading toward the back room, Ola following right behind.

"I mean, Ciysea is…was about a week or so journey on foot, so distance-wise we wouldn't have seen a mushroom. Then again, there was that freak dust storm a couple of nights ago. Likely as not that could have been the fallout."

"Maybe." Byron sighed, stepping into the makeshift lift to the basement. "Just, all those people, Ola."

"Are why we are doing this." Ola started up the pulley system that took them down to the hidden basement. "How's Charles?"

"He's all right as can be expected. Spent most of the day in bed, resting. Julie is taking good care of him, though she is a bit nervous about having to leave him tomorrow for work." Byron smiled slightly. "Penny's been quite the little nurse too. She has brought him at least three CCCs today, though I think that's cause she gets one too."

"CCCs?" Ola quirked an eyebrow.

"Chocolate chip cookies, it's a joke name Charles made up. He gives Penny CCCs when he gives her a check-up."

Ola chuckled. "You found that girl a loving family."

"I just hope—" He paused, not wanting to finish the thought. "Penny's lost so much already, and we are putting Julie and Charles at great risk."

"No more than anyone else," Ola shrugged, a deafening silence following.

Reaching the bottom, they both hesitated for a moment.

"Why didn't you tell me about your brother?"

Ola bowed her head. "I…I didn't think it was important. You were so worried about your son and the other kids. My brother is a grown man. He made a choice."

"We all make choices. Some we live to regret." Byron headed off to the left, past the various rooms that acted as offices, barracks, and the like for the Constellation, toward the room where Mr. Turner was being held.

"You sure you don't want me to be with you?"

"No, I want to talk to this man alone. It's better this way." Byron nodded to the two guards, Holly and Martin, who unlocked the door.

"Be safe, Byron," Ola smiled. "I look forward to your report."

The room Mr. Turner was being held in was small and dark, with one single bed and a soft chair. Entering the space, Byron flipped on the lights. Mr. Turner was sitting in the soft chair in the far-right corner from the door, looking rather pleased with himself despite his situation. Henrietta had done him a service patching up the various injuries Charles had inflicted on him while also giving him something to dull his powers. Byron's eyes landed on the black stone cuffs around his wrists and ankles, the latter binding him to the seat. He hoped they were actually doing their job of stopping his powers and it wasn't just an act or the drugs keeping him in check.

"Well, if it isn't Byron Galigar," Mr. Turner chuckled, his words slightly slurred. "Come to finally deal with me."

"You seem rather happy for a man on death row," Byron growled, stealing his face into a look of cool indifference.

Mr. Turner continued to laugh, the sound unnatural. "Be that as it may, at least I'm not the one hiding in the shadows with no one to take my place as I fall."

Byron began to pace a distance away. "Tell me, Mr. Turner. What are you?"

The strange man just laughed, shaking his head.

"I asked you a question, Turner. I suggest you answer it."

"And why should I? You'll just kill me either way."

"Maybe I will and maybe I won't. That all depends on your compliance. Now tell me, what are you?"

"I am me."

He closed the gap, slapping the man across the face. "We can do this the easy or hard way, Turner. What are you?"

"I'm an agent, a powerful one at that. My sole purpose is to seek out Curied and bring them to the facility where they belong." The prisoner grinned, looking like a madman. "You, my friend, are harboring not one, but two fugitives, and now it seems a third new one."

Byron's heart raced, every part of him resisting the urge to do more harm to the shell of a man in front of him. "An agent who is also a Curied, as you call it. Someone with powers."

"I am Curied, yes. My powers are a gift," he replied, his voice like oil.

Byron didn't like the tone with which Mr. Turner said that. "You are not the only Turner, however."

"You speak of my...brothers. You've run into one before, haven't you? That's why you ran in Cartsdale. Of late only TV12 never reported back from Johani. Did you have something to do with that?"

He refused to answer, keeping his face blank. "You are a twin of sorts?"

"Your refusal speaks volumes." Turner grinned wider, almost comically. "Yes, a twin of sorts. Not that it matters. Soon enough things will change."

"What do you mean?"

Turner just laughed.

Byron pulled out his gun, pointing it at the vile man's chest. "I asked you a question."

"I shouldn't be the one you are asking questions to." Mr. Turner laughed harder, the sound grating in Byron's ears. "The person you really should be questioning is that woman."

"What woman?"

"The one who runs this little operation. The one with the wheels for legs. Just how does she know so much about our lovely schools?"

Byron adjusted his grip. "Your manipulation is fried Turner. Those cuffs stop it. Your voice alone is powerless."

"Be that as it may, my voice speaks the truth. It is your choice, Byron Galigar, to decide if it is I or Ola Hampton who is the liar."

Byron stood motionless, his mind returning to the argument the night before.

"Pity, E-165141425 had so much potential. It was a great loss to the institute when your pirates stole her away from Rho. Her powers would have made a lovely addition to our collection once she—"

BANG

Byron was shaking with rage, Turner dead before him, blasted through the chest. This man was a menace. J.H. was a menace. He would not let anyone take Penny or any other children, not on his watch.

The door behind him flung open. Holly and Martin entered, knives drawn.

"Uncuff him from the chair and lay him on the bed," Byron ordered, putting the safety back on his gun, and holstering it. "Ask Ola about what we want to do with the body."

With that he turned, heading straight for his private office on the opposite side of the basement. Taking a seat at his station, he retrieved the black cuffs that Ola had made sure to deliver. Turning them over in his hand, he scoffed as he set to work identifying them.

How much time had passed Byron did not know or care to know when he heard the door to his private office open, wheels entering.

"Byron? Why didn't you come to talk to me? Holly told me you killed Turner."

"I did," he answered, flatly, continuing his analysis of the cuffs.

"Well, did he say anything?"

"Not much. He admitted he is a twin of sorts. Said his powers were a gift, but I don't believe a word of it."

He heard Ola stop behind him. "Byron, what happened?"

"Nothing, he wasn't compliant. Just like everyone thought."

"Byron..."

"I have nothing to say."

Ola sighed, shaking her head. "I had Henrietta draw blood from him this morning. She is going to run some tests. Once Charles is well enough, she wants his help looking at it. Thinks maybe Turner's DNA might hold some answers, given our discussion last night."

"Very well." Byron huffed, not looking up from his work.

"I'll have Holly and Martin take care of the body. I'll leave you to your work." Ola's brow furrowed as she turned, wheeling towards the door.

"Ola…"

"Yes?"

Byron set down his work. "Turner mentioned you. Said I should have been questioning you, not him."

Ola looked upset. "Byron, you don't think—"

"As I said, I didn't trust anything coming from that man's mouth." He turned to face her, catching a glimpse of fear in her eyes. "You know you can tell me anything, right?"

"Of course."

"No more secrets."

"No more secrets." Ola smiled slightly, turning and leaving the room.

Byron hesitated, watching her go. He knew that smile, there was something hidden in it. He just hoped whatever it was that Ola decided she needed to keep from him, it was worth the risk.

It had been a week since Mr. Turner had appeared, a week of surprising quiet. Much to Julietta's relief, but also unease, upon returning to Iota on the first day of the work week, she saw no sign of the other Mr. Turners, nor was she willing to ask about them.

The work she was assigned for the week kept her fairly busy, with multiple machine fixes that forced her to stay her way later than expected. However, all these late nights kept Danni pleased with her, so much so that she suspected nothing when about halfway through the week the first machine 'Jessa' had fixed after her probation ended started to fritz out.

Unfortunately, all this heads-down time also kept her from gaining much in the way of helpful information for the Constellation. Even Joyce, it seemed, was too busy keeping her nose clean to try and contact her. They barely exchanged eye contact a handful of times, let alone spoke. Dimetre had vanished for the time being, though the small food offerings she left in the hidden hovel did, in fact, disappear. She was more than ready to call it a day when Danni finally let her go for the weekend.

Entering the darkened apartment at the Snapdragon, Julietta leaned against the door as she closed it, exhausted. Before she could move, however, she spotted something that made her smile. She could see the top of Charles's head peeking out over the back of the couch. Despite his still healing injuries, he was up waiting for her, as he had done every night since she first started at Iota.

Shedding her outerwear, she made for the bedroom to change, returning a few minutes later to Charles still lying on the couch sound asleep. She shook her head, taking a seat beside him. Brushing some hair from his face, her hand came to gently rest on his now scarred cheek. "Charlie…"

"Good, you're home." Charles's eyes fluttered open as he smiled groggily. "Sorry, Jul. I must have dozed off."

"It's all right, Charlie. You should be resting. You're still healing."

"Eh, I'm okay. I've had a good doctor and two great nurses take care of me." He smirked, wrapping an arm around her waist. "Plus, Henrietta gave me the all-clear today to return to work next week."

"Did she say anything else?" She quirked an eyebrow, running a hand through his hair.

"She said my arm is healing fine, no permanent damage. Most of the bruising is gone. I'll have the scar on my face for life, but something tells me I will be quite all right with that." He yawned, relaxing to her touch. "My knee still is on the mend, but if you were able to walk on a sprained ankle for miles, I can handle it."

"You've stayed up every night waiting for me since I started working at Iota. You must be exhausted."

"And you aren't?"

"You have a point." She sighed, her true exhaustion painted on her face. "But—"

"Come here, Jul."

Charles shifted so she could lie with him, his arms around her, her head on his chest. "Would it help if I told you I couldn't sleep in the first place?"

"What do you mean?" She yawned, relaxing into him.

"I worry about you," he sighed, gently rubbing her lower back. "I need to know you are home safe before I can sleep. And I promised Penny I'd stay up and wait for you. Doctor's orders, she told me."

"Well, if it's Dr. Penny's orders," she chuckled, shaking her head. "And just what else has Dr. Penny ordered?"

"Well." Charles smirked mischievously. "She ordered at least three CCCs a day for both her and I...and Momma Julie needs to kiss Papa Charlie."

"Oh?" She looked up at him, biting her lip. "And did you already have your prescribed CCCs?"

"Oh yes, which leaves just one more prescription to fill."

"Shall we then?"

"Doctor's orders," he teased, kissing her once, twice, three times.

"I think my Fallen-in-love-itis is flaring," Julietta whispered breathlessly, smiling into his lips.

"I could think of a few procedures that might help."

"And what do you propose, Dr. Hawthorne?"

Before Julietta could find out, the door to the apartment opened. Untangling themselves quickly, both sat up to find Byron standing at the door.

"Byron? When did you leave?" Charles rubbed the back of his head, slightly embarrassed. "I thought you went to bed a couple of hours ago?"

"Ola called me on one of the talkers. I gave her mine since we keep Julietta's at the house. She wanted to talk. You were asleep. There's been a development."

Sitting at the kitchen table, a cup of coffee in hand, he began to explain.

"We've received news from Johani, that the satellite monitoring Omicron-753 in Evrine has fallen, with only two survivors. Constellation still hadn't heard from Tau-059 in Vexledo. The closest city to them is Sleburn where Pi-023 is. Ola's sent a message to them to dispatch an agent over but given recent developments..."

"Another satellite down..." Julietta sank back in her seat. "That's three in a matter of days. Not to mention Ciysea..."

"Do we know what happened to the people at Chi?" Charles asked, his voice low.

"Chi was evacuated, and the students and scientists of importance sent off to other schools." Byron scoffed. "The rest weren't so fortunate."

"That leaves 23 schools still operational, 21 satellites." Julietta shook her head. "And with Tau up in the air..."

"The Constellation is still strong, Julie. This is just a blip. I assure you, Ola will see that things get re-established." Byron stroked his mustache. "There is something else. We've heard from the Healeys."

"About Miss Bell?" Charles quirked an eyebrow.

"Yes, Marisa gave a detailed description. If Miss Bell is in fact her niece, she'll have a distinct scar on her inner right arm, a burn she got as a child on accident from grabbing a hot pan. It is about an inch above her wrist, and curves like a quarter moon towards it. Powerwise, Marisa never found out what she could do, just knew she had Arcane abilities."

"I'll have to see if I can run into her again." Julietta sighed, looking rather tired. "Anything else?"

"Well," Byron turned to Charles. "Henrietta has done some analysis on the sample of Turner's blood. She wants your help looking into the DNA side of it."

"She mentioned that to me, and gave me the all-clear today to start back working after the weekend."

"Good. The sooner we can figure out what we are up against, the better." He grimaced. He had told Julietta and Charles about his encounter with Turner and how he killed him, but he had conveniently left out the part about Ola.

Charles crossed his arms, his mind turning. "What about the bomb?"

"Ola sent out a message to Bragas. They are the closest. Reports indicate they felt a rumble and were later hit with what they realized was a fallout dust storm hours later. The rumble caused some serious damage, not just to the city, but to the school, Epsilon-182. Not even a day later engineers from Apolis were spotted heading that way. The timing doesn't add up for their arrival, but no one is questioning given they've agreed to help the city as well. The satellite plans on investigating Ciysea within the next couple of days."

"Apolis is at least a couple weeks from Ciysea based on old maps from before. There is no way they would have made it there that quickly even with rovers." Julietta leaned back in her chair, feeling defeated. "Too much has happened in such a short time. I'll have to try and contact Joyce somehow, let her know what's going on."

"That would be ideal, but don't put yourself at additional risk. With satellites dropping like flies, we need to keep ourselves out of sight and mind." Byron stood, placing his coffee cup in the sink before heading towards his room. "It's late. You two should get some sleep. We can talk more in the morning if you wish."

Charles took his and Julietta's cups to the sink, needing a moment to think. Returning, he stood behind Julietta, resting his hands on her shoulders. "Anything you need to talk about?"

She shook her head, closing her eyes.

Gently he bent down, kissing her forehead. "Then let's get some rest, Jul. We all need it."

CHAPTER 31

"Jessa?"

Julietta was busy working on another fix, making sure to add her adjustments discreetly, when Danni walked in.

"Something wrong, Danni?"

"How much longer on that machine?"

"Just need to adjust this and…seal it up."

"Good, I have a few more jobs for you."

Julietta tried to hide her annoyance. For the past two days, all Danni had were additional jobs for her. "Of course."

"Look, I know I've given you a lot of work this week so far but for good reason. Just know that if you keep going at this pace soon enough you will be pulled for special assignments like Ken."

"I'm taking on Ken's tasks today?" She asked, forgetting herself for a moment. "I mean—"

"I'll give you that question given I am interrupting you." Her supervisor frowned, looking nonetheless disappointed. "Ken has been pulled for some important work, so I need you to take on his jobs, which includes a hotfix for the machine in room 103."

"Hotfix?" She quirked an eyebrow, finishing closing up the panel.

"There will be a student and instructor in the room with you. You are to go in, fix the machine, and leave. No speaking unless spoken to. You are not to engage with the student in any way, understood?"

The hair on the back of Julietta's neck stood on end. She would be witness to the training Penny had warned her about. Danni was letting her be a witness. "Yes, ma'am."

"Good. Normally I wouldn't send in someone with less than a cycle under their belt, but we are short-handed as of late and given your work ethic and clean record I'm allowing it."

"I appreciate the opportunity."

"Room 103, report back to me immediately after for the rest of your additional jobs."

Julietta had been given a few classroom fixes since her probation ended, however, most of them were in empty rooms. Upon entering room 103, she immediately felt uneasy. Sitting at the large desk was a man dressed in the colors of the instructors, his blue button-up shirt and white lab coat pristine. Across from him sat a young teenage boy, dressed in student gray.

"Ah, you must be the mechanic. This machine here…" The instructor gestured to the device a few feet away. "It's on the fritz, won't stay on. Think you can get it working for me?"

"Yes, sir," she replied, immediately setting to work, averting her gaze.

"Now, where were we…ah yes. Have you been practicing your lessons W-172191435?"

Julietta could hear the boy mumble some reply.

"Excuse me. What did you say?"

"Yes."

"Yes, what?"

"Yes, Mr. Bell."

Hearing the boy's voice, sad and defeated, broke Julietta's heart but she remained focused, letting no emotion show as 'Mr. Bell' continued to question the boy. It had occurred to her over the past couple of weeks that Bell was the name for all the instructors, whether in training or otherwise. Why this was, she couldn't say, though she had a theory given the black bracelets around their wrists.

It didn't take Julietta long to find the problem; she had been the one to cause it, after all. Finding the wire she had purposely loosened to fail, she quickly tightened it, making sure to loosen another to do something similar in the near future.

"That should do it." She stood, waiting for a reply.

"Very good, if you would please wait for me to test." Mr. Bell smiled, a gesture that made Julietta wish she could run and hide. It took every ounce of willpower to watch indifferently as Mr. Bell attached leads to the boy, turning on the device. "Ah good. You can pack up your things then and inform your supervisor." Mr. Bell reached into the desk, handing Julietta the ticket to turn in.

"Yes, sir," she replied flatly, packing up her things as Mr. Bell began his lesson.

"Now W-172191435, let's see how well you do today."

Julietta watched out of the corner of her eye as Mr. Bell flipped over a small hourglass he had on his desk. The sound of the machine clicking in reaction to whatever the boy was doing filled the space. It couldn't have been more than five seconds later, however, when Mr. Bell spoke again. "You have to do better than that, W-172191435. You are nearly 16 cycles now. You don't want to be released from the program, do you?"

Those words were enough to send Julietta's stomach tumbling. Quickly as she dared, she finished packing up her things and headed straight out the door, wanting to put as much distance between her and Mr. Bell as possible. Lost in her thoughts, however, she barely made it to the first crossway when she ran right into someone.

"Ouch!" A female voice came as Julietta dropped her tool case, its contents spilling out.

"Oh, I am so sorry."

"That's all right, mistakes happen," said a familiar voice.

She had nearly retrieved all her tools when an arm came into view holding one of her wrenches. On this arm just above the wrist was a crescent moon-shaped scar. Daring to look up briefly, she found herself face to face with the Miss Bell she had first met. If that scar was anything to go by along with the familial resemblance, she was looking into the face of Marisa's niece.

"Thank you, again, sorry," Julietta replied hastily, taking her wrench and shoving it in her bag before quickly but somehow calmly heading back to the workshop as Danni had instructed, her head and stomach reeling.

After retrieving her further assignments from Danni, Julietta took her lunch break during which she spent the majority of the time in the bathroom trying not to be sick. Miss Bell was Marisa Healey's long-lost niece, a former student. She was being trained to be an instructor, likely by another former student. At 16, students were taken out of the program. If they failed out, they were released, which, if Joyce's coded message was anything to go by, wasn't a good thing.

STEPHANIE VACCARO & LOUISE ALLEN

Sneaking some food into her tool case, she made a quick stop at the hovel in the workshop before heading to her next set of tasks which were thankfully fixing various equipment around the laboratory and not the school.

"Well, someone is looking a little green around the gills."

Julietta had been so focused on reassembling the circuit board in the machine in front of her, she hadn't heard Joyce walk in. Still trying to hold down her lunch, she did not verbally answer, shaking her head.

"Was it the sushi at lunch today? Should have warned you that it could give you indigestion."

"I'm fine." She managed to whisper, her hands starting to shake.

Seeing this, Joyce took a step closer, putting herself between Julietta and the door. "See anything interesting in the stars lately?"

She had been waiting for that question and had been thinking of ways to tell Joyce in the similar cadence she used before. "Yes, the past few weeks have had some sporadic sights. Gemini made an appearance. Been a few since I've seen it. Saw three shooting stars as well."

"That must have been something."

"Yeah, it's a shame when you think about what they really are, asteroids or long-lost space tech streaking back to earth only to fall apart in our atmosphere."

She could hear Joyce swallow hard, clearly getting the message. "Anything else?"

"Not really, though I was a bit disappointed that one night we had the freak dust storm. Blocked out everything for miles. Really made an impact on what you could sightsee."

"I'd imagine so." Joyce's voice broke slightly. "Sounds like you've been doing a lot of stargazing. To think, most of the stars are from the big bang."

"Yes, whole galaxies were thrown out into space by the big bang."

Julietta could hear Joyce's footsteps stop beside her. "You like puzzles?" She whispered, dropping a piece of paper in Julietta's tool case.

"As much as anyone."

"Sometimes puzzles are best solved when looked at from a different perspective. You need to bend the rules to get—"

"Joyce? What are you doing?" Melvin, the archivist Julietta had met on the first day, asked as he entered the room.

"Oh, I was just looking for something I dropped in here earlier."

"From where I am standing it looks like you are keeping Jessa here from working."

"No, no, I'd never do that."

As if to prove the point, Julietta had just finished replacing the now 'fixed' circuit board in the machine. "That should do it. Sorry, Joyce, but like I said, I haven't seen any notebooks here. Then again, I've been staring at this machine for the last two hours."

"Very well," Joyce shrugged, "Figured it couldn't hurt to ask. I bet you anything I probably left it in the lunchroom."

"You better hope you did." Melvin frowned. "What did I tell you about losing your belongings? We will talk about this later."

With that, Melvin left. Joyce followed behind him, leaving Julietta hoping that their ruse had held up, and the puzzle that had just been dropped into her bag would be easy enough to solve.

Julietta didn't see Joyce the next day, nor the morning of the next. She had brought the puzzle home that night, squirreled away as usual in a hidden pocket in her scarf that no one noticed. She had left it with Byron who ended up giving it to Penny who solved it in a matter of minutes. By folding the paper a certain way and viewing it in a mirror you could see the connections between a color and a title. Joyce had figured out what each of the clothing sets meant in the institute, giving the Constellation a better chance of spotting authority on the inside.

Despite her nerves regarding Joyce's sudden disappearance, Julietta continued her work for Danni, which seemed endless. It was towards the end of the last day of the week when she found herself finally in the workshop alone.

Hoping for some better luck, she headed for the hidden hovel. To her relief, Dimetre was there.

"Hey, are you okay?" She frowned seeing the small boy nibbling at the apple she left at lunchtime.

"As can be." Dimetre shrugged as she handed him some cookies. "Not caught."

"Good. I was beginning to worry. You hide here from the Bells?"

Dimetre nodded. "Hide from Bell. School breaks, after school, Dimetre needs hide for safety. No caught thanks."

"I understand," she shook her head. "Are all your teachers named Bell?"

"Miss Bell, Mister Bell not nice."

"How old is the oldest student?"

"Old 16 cycle, once 16 go to Apolis for train."

"Train for what?"

"Train or release," Dimetre shrugged.

Julietta's heart sank hearing that word. "Do…Do you know what release means?"

Dimetre shook his head. "Lots words don't know what mean. Dimetre must go. Bring more food for Dimetre and friends? Hide food in other place?"

"There are other hiding places?"

Dimetre nodded.

"You have friends that hide in those places from the Bells?"

Dimetre nodded again.

The gears in her head were turning. "If you can get me a list of locations, I'll be sure to try to drop some food for them. Also, maybe have your friends help others go to these spots sometimes. That way everyone can have some treats. Sound good?"

"Dimetre, thank you," Dimetre smiled. "Dimetre see soon?"

"I'll try to stop by in the evenings when I can. The lady called Danni keeps me busy."

"Danni lady not nice." Dimetre frowned.

"No, Danni is—"

"Jessa?"

Julietta held up a finger to her lips. Dimetre nodded in understanding, waving goodbye to her as she covered the hovel once more.

"I'm here, Danni. Figured since I was waiting I'd clean up a bit. It's a tad disorganized as of late."

Danni was standing beside Julietta's workstation, eyes trained on her. "Very well. I appreciate your…initiative. I must say you've done well this week keeping up with the demand. I heard from the instructor that your fix was swift and accurate. No issues."

"Yes, ma'am."

"Keep this up and maybe I'll give you more interesting tasks."

"Thank you, ma'am."

"You are dismissed for the day. As always you are expected back on the first workday, early."

"Of course."

Packing up, Julietta headed for the locker room to get changed before leaving. As she placed her clothes on the side table provided in the private shower space, a small piece of folded paper fell out. Heart pounding, she opened it. It was from Joyce.

It took Julietta a minute to decipher what was written but she got the gist. Joyce was okay. She had been moved to the archives for further 'training.' She wouldn't be able to speak to her anytime soon, however, she had a plan for communicating.

Joyce had an apartment in the facility, giving her access to certain places late at night. She would leave any correspondence in one of the listed locations based on a code left in Julietta's locker in the morning. She'd hide the message in her clothes for her to read when she went to the private showers, one of the few places with little risk of being seen. If Julietta had something to give her, she was to leave it in one of the locations based on the day of the week.

It would not be easy, and downright dangerous should they be caught. If either was caught, the other would not be able to help. But what other choice did they have? Their communications may not be elegant, but they could provide crucial information required for them to save the children.

CHAPTER 32

"I've double, triple, and quadruple-checked my findings. Would you like the readout?" Henrietta smiled, looking quite pleased with herself.

Henrietta had been analyzing Mr. Turner's blood sample periodically over the past two weeks. Only this week, with Charles and Victor back in the clinic, did she finally have time to run a full analysis. She was counting her lucky stars. It was Cold season, so she could keep the blood preserved until now.

"Of course." Charles set down his pen. He had hit the ground running the first day of the week, and now on the last workday, he was determined to have results. "What do you have?"

"Turner was human, but not a healthy one. His cholesterol was out of whack, his blood counts low, not to mention the presence of elevated white blood cells."

"I can confirm that." He gestured to the microscope. "Take a look."

Henrietta peeked into the microscope beside him. "Yep, he had some sort of infection."

"I mean, he was shot not long ago." He shrugged. "Anything else?"

"His metabolic panel was interesting. He must have had to eat a ton to keep up with these numbers."

"That explains why he looked so gaunt, but doesn't explain how he was so strong." He shook his head, turning back to his work. "At least the results paint the picture we sort of expect, and point out anomalies."

"Any luck with the DNA analysis?"

"Not much. My little sparring match with Turner destroyed some things I could have used. That, coupled with the fact that clinics are not really equipped for DNA testing nowadays, I'm stuck with what I can see and conjecture."

"Well, cut yourself some slack. You've only been back a week."

"Only thing I have to show for it is the visual analysis of the blood. Extra white blood cells and the shapes are…off."

"Off?"

"They are almost too perfect. Especially given the blood is a couple of weeks old. There should have been some loss by now."

"What would cause such a thing?"

"Nothing in common DNA, but mutated maybe…"

The two stopped, hearing the usually quiet Victor coming down the hall talking loudly to someone.

"I assure you, Dr. Cone, everything is back in working order. The clinic is now operating at full capacity once more."

It was a warning. Immediately they began to hide their Turner analysis, pulling out Charles's previous genetics research to take its place. They managed to hide all read-outs and the container of blood Henrietta had been working on just before Dr. Cone and Victor arrived.

"Charles, Henrietta? Is now a good time?" Victor asked.

Charles looked up from his desk where he was feigning reading something. "Oh, hello, Dr. Cone. Didn't expect you to visit." Grabbing the cane Henrietta had given him to use while his knee was still healing, he limped over, shaking Dr. Cone's hand. "I've been very busy today, so please do not mind the mess."

"I heard about your and Victor's little mishap with a wandering vagabond. You are both lucky to have recovered so quickly, relatively speaking." Dr. Cone gave a pointed look toward the cane Charles leaned on.

"Merely a precaution. I should be back to full mobility by next week. Henrietta insisted I use one, though I protested."

Dr. Cone chuckled, "Doctors do really make the worst patients, don't they, Dr. Calhone? You must have had your hands full with not one but two of them."

"Yes, sir," Henrietta nodded, feigning disinterest as she shuffled some papers on the central table.

"Dr. Lawson here has assured me that everything is back to working order, which is only part of my reason for visiting. I've come to see how your research is going." Dr. Cone strode over to the desk where Charles had been sitting, his eyes scanning over the papers scattered about it.

"It was going well until I got injured. I hit the ground running, however, when I return this week, I hope to not fall too far behind."

Dr. Cone's expression remained blank, his eyes landing on the microscope. Charles's heart leaped into his throat as he watched him bend down to peer into it.

"A blood sample of yours?"

Charles glanced over to Victor and Henrietta whose expressions were the same as his, terrified. "Yes, I—"

"It's from when he was injured," Henrietta blurted out. "I mean, I took a sample from him and Victor to ensure they were all right. Charles thought it an interesting idea to analyze it for his genetics research."

"There are quite a bit of white blood cells in this," Dr. Cone frowned.

"No infection now," Henrietta assured, hoping he wouldn't call her bluff.

"Of course," Dr. Cone rose, grinning, an expression that made everyone's skin crawl. "Looks like you are doing good work, Charles. Though I can't help but wonder if you could do more with a more…advanced setup."

"Advanced setup?" Charles furrowed his brow.

"You see, Charles, I work for a research institute and engineering school just outside Matson. It's a branch of the Apolis Academy for the Future, specifically for children who are gifted in the engineering fields. I am the head of genetics research, hence my interest in your work. I require a new researcher, as mine has moved on to greener pastures as of late."

Charles thought back to the night Julietta had come home sick due to three deaths at the institute. "Am I correct in understanding you are offering an interview?"

"I am offering you the position," the doctor chuckled. "You are a smart man, Dr. Hawthorne. I could use you on my team."

Charles froze, not sure how to respond. To his surprise, Dr. Cone expected this.

"I don't expect an answer right this moment. After all, you are still recovering. How about you let me know in two days? I'll have you on the list to be let onto a transport to Iota on the first workday. If you come, I'll be happy to have you. If not, well I wish you the best of luck in your endeavor, though I highly suggest you take me up on this offer. As you know, things move quickly in our line of work. Opportunities like this only come once."

"Of course, Dr. Cone." Charles managed, hoping his voice did not betray his fear.

"I'll leave you to it then." The doctor sniffed, turning back to Victor. "Thank you for your hospitality, Dr. Lawson. I take my leave."

"Absolutely not!" Byron growled. "You can't be serious!"

It was the day after Dr. Cone's visit. Byron, Charles, Julietta, and Ola had gathered at the tea shop to discuss the 'offer' Charles had been given.

"I am," Charles frowned, leaning up against the counter. "Jul and I talked about it last night. We both think it's a good idea."

"Julie? You can't be serious."

"Believe me, I had the same reaction as you when Charlie told me," Julietta averted her gaze, picking at the biscuit on the table in front of her. "However, after some discussion and given some of the information I discovered this week, as much as it pains me to say it, it wouldn't be the worst idea to have him at Iota with me."

"What about the fact that you yourself only a few weeks ago didn't want to go back?" Byron spat.

"If I recall, Byron, you wanted me to go back."

He didn't answer, stomping towards one of the windows.

"Byron, if Julietta and Charles are both willing to be at Iota, I don't see why we shouldn't let them," Ola shrugged, taking a quick sip of her tea. "If Cone is indeed a head, this might just be the big break the Constellation needs. Not to mention Julietta's discovery of the students being trained as instructors and your research on the lead cuffs."

"Lead?" Charles quirked an eyebrow.

"Byron told me this morning." Ola smiled. "The bracelets are lead with a protective coating on them. Took him forever to chip away at it but he figured it out."

"Why lead? That's…dangerous." Julietta sunk back in her seat. "That could do so much harm if not handled right."

"Hence the protective coating," Ola stated.

"We are not here to talk about bracelets. We are here to discuss Charles's idiotic plan!" The older man grumbled.

"It wasn't idiotic to send me in. Why is it for Charlie?" Julietta spat back.

"And what does Lisle think of this?" Byron asked, ignoring Julietta's question.

"I talked with her, Victor, and Henrietta this morning. They all agree with me," Charles replied, looking pained. "They know it is risky, but there is a chance with me in there we can—"

"What about Penny?"

"We already talked with her," Julietta bowed her head. "If neither of us survive this, she is to go live with Lisle and her family. We figured she is far enough removed from the Constellation that she could keep her safe and Penny would have Nicolas and Maya with her."

Charles moved to stand beside her, placing a comforting arm around her. "She was upset, of course, but understood. She knows why we have to do this."

"She's lost so much already." Byron's face fell, but he did not turn to face them.

"We've talked about it. If either of us should…" Julietta paused, swallowing the lump in her throat. "The other will stop, and run with Penny."

"I mean, I suppose that would be the best course of action should something happen." Ola's brow furrowed, sounding a bit disappointed. "Can't make you stay in that case."

"I can't condone this, but I also can't stop you. If you want to risk your life…I will not have your blood on my hands." Byron stormed out of the shop, leaving everyone in stunned silence.

Charles followed, limping behind as fast as he dared. "Byron…"

The man kept walking.

"Byron, please."

He did not stop.

"Byron, argh!" Charles cried out as his knee nearly gave out.

He immediately stopped, running back to him.

"Charlie?"

"I'm fine. Just pushed my knee too far." Charles grunted, leaning heavily on the cane.

Anger abated, he shook his head. "Come on, let's go back and I'll explain."

Helping Charles sit down beside Julietta, Byron apologized. "Listen, I know I haven't always been exactly right in my choices, especially with how I treated you, Julie, after the accident at Iota, but…" His shoulders slumped. "But I know I made the right choice giving Penny to you and sending Charlie your way. It…warms my heart to see you as a family, and breaks it knowing how much danger I have put you in."

He dared to look up at them, their expressions blank.

"Penny deserves to grow up happy. You both deserve to be happy. You shouldn't have to wait up every night pacing the floor wondering if she will come home. Julie shouldn't have had to hold you bleeding and unconscious hoping you'd wake up. Penny shouldn't have to wonder if she'll end up in another school—"

"Byron…" Julietta's voice stopped him. "You are right, but you do not shoulder the burden of our choices. Yes, you brought us into this when you told us about the schools and the Constellation, but it was our choice to stay in it."

"Jul's right," Charles sighed, leaning back in his chair. "We could have run with Penny, could have tried to hide out somewhere. But we all know that's no life for a kid and odds are that eventually we'd be caught. So, we made the choice instead to help, to give Penny a place somewhere relatively safe and the chance to be free. To give all those kids a chance to be free."

Tears rolled down Byron's face. "All right, I…I understand Charlie, but please…both of you…if at any point suspicion is thrown on you, at any point you feel it becomes too dangerous. Please, come tell me so we can get you out. Okay?"

"Agreed." Julietta took Charles's hand.

"Agreed," Charles echoed.

"Then I suppose you both better head back to the apartment and get some ice on that knee, Charlie. I'll pick up Penny from Lisle's. It's going to be an awfully short weekend, I feel."

CHAPTER 33

Despite everyone's premonitions, the next few weeks went by like clockwork. Lisle's planned meeting with the Governor of Ambleton, Robert France, went as smoothly as could be expected. The only point of concern was Governor France's mention of a 'Mr. Turner' approaching him a few weeks back. From what he told her, Lisle put two and two together that 'Turner' visited around the time Ambleton's satellite fell. Unfortunately for her, she could do little to convince him that sending any of the children to Apolis regardless of their scores may not be in the city's best interest. She did, however, persuade him to hold off for a few weeks once the results were in to allow the parents to strongly consider what was offered.

Charles arrived at Iota for his first day the workday following the offer. To say Dr. Cone was pleased would be an understatement, as his first day consisted of him being put to work in record time in comparison to Julietta. He immediately set him out on remapping the human genome based on current-day samples from 'volunteers.' The way the volunteer part had been emphasized made Charles's skin crawl, a clear indicator to him that these volunteers likely were not so willing.

While Charles played his part, Julietta set into motion the necessary flow of contact between him, her, and Joyce in the hopes of throwing off anyone who would become suspicious. Within a week of Joyce's new system being used, they were informed that Joyce would continue to work in the archives, a place surprisingly useful for knowledge collection. It turned out the archives were not as old as one would think, containing data not only from Iota's start but data from only a few weeks ago.

Sadly, this led to the discovery that Cartier Smith had, in fact, been terminated. The reasoning on the file: Failure to comply with proper communication protocols and restrictions. He had been caught collecting and sneaking out information to the Constellation.

While Joyce continued collecting any information from the archives and Charles plotted to find out what Dr. Cone was actually researching, Julietta continued her covert operations. Aside from sabotaging the machines she fixed, she set to work mapping out all the hiding locations Dimetre and his friends provided to her. Utilizing Joyce and Charles, they would each try to visit a set and leave a bit of food when possible. This led the three of them to get to know quite a few of the students at the school.

Many were quite young, barely five or six cycles. They were often quiet and spoke much like Penny. The older ones' speech was better, but still rather subdued. It was the teens, particularly the few closer to about 15 cycles that were the most vocal, passing on information about what sorts of training they were being put through in the hopes that they would somehow be able to get out. It was heartbreaking but necessary work.

Charles and Julietta found themselves in a difficult routine, constantly worried about getting caught. Since Julietta had been at the medical society presentation as Charles's guest, there was concern that Dr. Cone might recognize her. To prevent this, precautions were taken. They would take different transports to and from Iota, never interact, not even make eye contact if they ran into each other, and sat on opposite sides of the room with their own departments if they were at any meal together. It was difficult for them to act as strangers, seeing the strain on the other's face when they were having a particularly rough day and not being able to comfort them until later that evening. It was almost as bad as the lack of time they got to spend with Penny.

They had talked with her about all this before Charles agreed to take the position. They explained that both Momma Julie and Papa Charlie would not be home until late most nights and be tired in the mornings. The girl, however, seemed to take it in stride. She went as far as to ensure she was up early with them to share breakfast and leave notes on the dinner table in her ever-bettering scrawl on the nights she could not wait up for them. Penny was smart, but also wise beyond her cycles. It made them hug her that much tighter when they wished her goodbye every workday and drove them to make the weekends with her count. It hurt them to have to leave her like this, but they knew as well as she did it was so they later could be together without fear.

Charles, now fully healed from his encounter with Mr. Turner, had spent a decent amount of time working on his genome mapping while also learning Dr. Cone's routine. He knew the doctor likely did not believe Henrietta's lie about the blood on the slide. It was more a question of if he recognized where it was actually from. The first day of the work week, in what should have been the dwindling weeks of Cold, Charles finally got the chance he had been waiting for to investigate.

"Hawthorne."

Charles looked up from his work to find Dr. Cone standing beside him, his Cheshire grin wide. "Yes, doctor?"

"Based on your latest report, it seems you've made quite a bit of progress. The samples were satisfactory?"

"Yes. So far, I've identified the standard 46 chromosomes and noted each of their variations from the original mapping, particularly marking samples with larger than standard deviations, of which only one or two seemed to have them. My next steps are to dig further into the four known nitrogen bases in the nucleotides and confirm they are as expected or..." He continued to ramble on about his research for another few minutes, watching the man closely for any sign of certain interest.

"Very good, Hawthorne. You've already been much more proficient in this task than my last researcher. They barely scratched the surface on 10 of the chromosomes before they moved on to green pastures."

He nodded in reply, his stomach turning slightly. He had asked Joyce for information on Dr. Cone's other researcher. She had been killed in that accident Julietta had caught the aftermath of. "Is there anything else, sir?"

"I am off to a meeting with some other heads of the departments. I won't be back before shutdown time. I trust that you'll be leaving on time, yes?"

"Of course, sir, not a minute sooner."

"Good. I'll leave you to it then." The doctor smiled once more, a look that sent shivers down Charles's spine.

Dr. Cone was a smart man, but also vain, to the point of fault. Charles quickly learned his research labs were originally on the first floor, but after the accident moved to the second, which, up to that point, was reserved for the heads' individual private labs. The man had claimed to anyone who would listen that he got permission to move it right off his private one 'for safety' but from the eye rolls and murmurs of the other less tactful researchers, it was so he could show off to the other heads how he had been given this 'privilege' due to the nature of his most important work.

Thanks to this vanity, he had been able to watch the esteemed doctor as much as the doctor watched him. With a little help from Julietta and Joyce, Charles had managed to get the access code to Dr. Cone's private lab loaded onto his ID card which would register as the man himself for a few scans. After waiting about 30 minutes to ensure Dr. Cone would not return, Charles cleaned up his work, closing the shutters on the lab window and the lights before scanning his badge on the door to sign out, making sure to close the door fully. He waited a few minutes, then scanned again, this time as Dr. Cone. Jamming the door as Julietta had described to him so it registered as closed without locking, he made for the doctor's private lab.

Scanning his ID, he waited a breathless moment, then a beep. He was in. Taking out Penny's flashlight from beneath his shirt, which he had managed to squirrel past security that morning, Charles headed straight for his first priority: Cone's desk.

The top of the desk was empty, save a few empty beakers and books that Charles himself returned to Dr. Cone not a few hours ago. The drawers on either side were also rather lackluster, containing some scholarly articles he had seen before along with a few other communications from the facility itself about changes in electricity priority and the like. Opening the last drawer, however, he became a bit nervous. Contained within, were files with various names, two of which made his heart skip a beat: Kendrix Wilham, Dr. Cone's previous researcher, and Charles Hawthorne. Pulling his own file, he found various articles pertaining to his work dating even before the late Governor Winslow's death. To his relief, however, it seemed that was the only information held within. No mention of Penny, Julietta, or anyone else in the Constellation. Were these simply for personal reference for Dr. Cone as to the works of those under his employ or something more, Charles did not know. All he knew was it was something to make note of as he returned the file exactly as he had found it, closing the drawer.

Disappointed, he shook his head. Surely there must be more than just these expected items. Working the desk over once more, he was about to give up when he found a groove just on the underside of the desktop. Jackpot. Reaching into his pocket he pulled out the lockpicking tool Julietta had snuck him from the workshop, something he'd return before he left for the night. Fiddling with the groove, the very top of the desk popped open, revealing stacks of papers and notebooks.

Taking out the first notebook, he thumbed through it quickly. Unlike the general genetics research that the man openly talked about and shared with Charles, this contained far more darker works. Its pages held marked-up notes and taped research articles about designer babies, a concept from the before times that Charles had seen discussed in the Waterwealt museum. According to it, and most of society, it was a field of study not looked at for long given its morally and ethically gray area.

Feeling uneasy, Charles pulled out a small notebook of his own, noting down some of the more prominent ideas from Dr. Cone's before moving on to the next. The next few, to his relief, were filled with general knowledge of DNA and its base components, more or less the basics of what he himself was researching. The last two, however, proved more fruitful, and terrifying. The first contained research regarding cell growth, its enhancement, and how to combat the complications. Not something Charles had looked at, but nothing out of the ordinary. The last, however, was far more disconcerting. Pages upon pages of DNA combinations and lists of genetic traits and their sequences, some crossed out in red ink, others circled in blue with IDs of TV with a number after it, methodically composed as a data log. Charles had heard of this identification number style. Byron had been the one to mention it a few weeks ago. Mr. Turner had mentioned the 'Turner' in Waterwealt was TV12; the numbers in this log went up to TV53.

Hastily writing down some notes, including a few IDs and their sequences, Charles moved on to the papers. Most were articles involving designer genetics, cloning, and the like. There was one page, however, that stood out as different. On the Iota facility marked letterhead was a list of identification numbers that, if Charles were to hedge his bets from what he'd seen, were student identification numbers. Next to each of these was a set of letters RO, EB, or BO. After searching a bit more, he found nothing. Defeated, he wrote down the IDs with their letters in his notebook before finally packing up the desk as it was before.

Glancing up at the clock on the wall Charles frowned. He was already nearly an hour into this endeavor. If he was to get out the way he got in, he would need to finish up quickly. Thankfully there was only one other place he wanted to search. Assuring everything was back to its former position , he headed over to the cold storage cabinet. Picking the lock, he had it open relatively quickly. The contents were as expected, various vials of blood and tissue samples. What was unsettling were the labels. It seemed Dr. Cone had sectioned the cabinet off into five areas: untouched samples, used samples, experimental in test, experimental failed, and ready. Each was labeled with an identification number and a date. For the untouched and used the IDs looked to be students; the experiments were labeled with TV.

The realization of what he was potentially seeing hurt his head. Student blood samples, and DNA, were being used somehow with the Turners. The Turners were not clones but designer humans. It was impossible, unethical, morally objectionable...Arcane. Yet all the evidence pointed to it. Enlightened with this knowledge, he felt sick to his stomach. Dr. Cone was having him map the genome so he could better conduct these experiments, so he could build a better human.

He managed to steal himself long enough to write down some of the identification numbers before closing the cabinet and locking it tight. He had to be wrong. Surely no one would attempt such a thing. History had shown them it was wrong to play with such concepts. Feeling sick, wanting a second opinion, and running out of time, he made to leave but stopped. On a table near the door was a microscope.

Every part of Charles was telling him to leave then and there, but a small part of him knew he had to take a look, to confirm his suspicions. Once more stealing his nerves and stomach, he peeked in for a moment. It took every ounce of willpower not to become ill. On the slide was a blood sample with cells far too perfect mixed in with high concentrations of white blood cells. It was a Turner's blood.

Julietta was already worried when Charles finally arrived back at the apartment, more so when she saw how pale and shaky he looked. After a cup of very strong coffee, he was able to explain what he discovered to her and Byron who had waited up for them. By the end, they all agreed that the best course of action was to have Joyce see if she could confirm any of the IDs with records in the archives, a plan they put into motion the next day.

It was the last workday of the week. Julietta had been on edge since Charles's discovery. Thankfully, at least for the time being, no one seemed any the wiser about their ploy. However, as more and more machines malfunctioned due to her 'fixes,' she could not help but wonder when something would give.

At dinner time, Julietta managed to sneak away for a few moments. Muffin hid in her bag, she headed towards the workshop, as she had told Danni she would. But before reaching it, she made a small detour towards one of the supply closets near the far back of the main atrium of the laboratory. Quickly slipping in, she moved the few boxes that covered the loose boards that led to one of the larger hiding spaces. There she found who she was looking for, a girl of about 16 cycles who had given the name Quinn.

"Hey, everything okay?" Julietta frowned, handing Quinn her muffin. There were dried tears on the girl's face. Quinn had only recently started hiding in the closet hovel about a week ago. In that time, however, she had been very vocal to Julietta about her training once she realized she was not going to be turned in.

"It's my turn." She shook her head, hugging her legs. Despite being nearly 16 cycles, if Julietta did not know any better, the teen could have been only around 13 at that moment given her size.

"Your turn?"

"Quinn made a friend called Paige when Quinn was brought to Iota. Paige was about five cycles older than Quinn. Paige acted like a sister. Paige was taken to Apolis when Paige was 16 cycles. Quinn thought Quinn would never see Paige again. Then about a season ago, Paige turned up dressed as a Miss Bell in training. Quinn was happy to see Paige, but Paige did not remember Quinn. Paige didn't remember Paige either. Paige said they were Miss Bell, but Quinn knows Paige was not named Miss Bell. Paige called Paige."

Julietta's heart sank. "You are afraid they will take you like they took Paige?"

"They are going to take Quinn. Miss Bell told Quinn this morning. At end Cold Quinn to go to Apolis. Quinn don't want to go to Apolis. Paige lost Paige in Apolis. Quinn already lost self once. That's why

Quinn called Quinn now by friends in school instead of…whatever Quinn was before. Don't want to lose self again."

"I'm sorry, Quinn," she sighed, holding back tears. "I promise. I will try my best to get you out of here."

"Promise?"

"Promise."

CHAPTER 34

Having spent the remainder of the workday fixing various machines around the laboratory, Julietta's mind was turning as she walked back towards the workshop to drop off her tools. Quinn was about 16 cycles, and her friend Paige would be about 21. Children were sent to Apolis at 16, some of which had returned to schools at 21 as Bells with no recollection of who they were before. Were all the children converted to Bells? If not, what happened to those not turned?

Finally arriving at the workshop, she was relieved to see that she was the last one to turn in for the evening, allowing her to check on the hidden hovel unseen. Not to her surprise, the hovel was empty at this hour, though the apple she had left after lunch was gone. She had just closed up the space when she heard the doors to the workshop slam open.

"Jessa…"

"Joyce? What are you—"

"I don't have time," the woman hissed, shoving a notebook into her hands. "I'm done."

"Done?"

Hurried footsteps were heard coming down the steps.

"Quick! Hide!"

Before she could react, Joyce had shoved her into the hovel, covering it over.

"Whatever you do, don't come out!"

She took a shallow breath as her body adjusted to the cramped nature of the space. From the position she had been shoved in she could barely see out a slightly larger crack in the wood.

"There she is," came a female voice. "Don't move, Joyce."

She watched as Joyce raised her hands, two guards coming to grab them and handcuff them behind her back.

"You are to come with us immediately. You have been found in violation of your contract and thus shall be terminated, effective immediately."

Her heart leaped into her throat as her accomplice was dragged away. Waiting for the workshop door to close, she extracted herself from the hovel. She had to know what was going to happen to her. Cramming the notebook into her inner lab coat pocket she ran towards the exit.

Emerging out into the atrium, she spotted a flash of movement in the direction of the far hallway. Following, she acted as naturally as possible as various researchers darted past her, thankfully paying her no mind, as they rushed to finish their day. Reaching the hall, she peeked around the corner. There at the end, the guards were dragging Joyce into a metal door that Julietta had never been behind. She waited a minute for them to vanish before approaching the door. Unlike the laboratory ones, this was key-locked. Counting her lucky stars that she had learned to pick locks at a young age, she reached up into her hair, pulling out a small lock pick pin she had taken to using to hold it back at work.

Picking the lock, she quickly slipped in before ensuring it shut silently behind her. Greeting her was a set of hallways. One straight ahead led to another metal door, the faint smell of burning coal emanating from behind it, another turning left led to familiar voices of guards. Heading down the left one, it was not long before she came upon the room where Joyce had been taken. Much like the laboratories, the room had a window, with a slatted shade pulled over it. Crouching in front of it, Julietta peered in.

Joyce was seated in what looked to be some sort of examination chair, her arms and legs clamped to it. On either side of her were guards, another standing at her feet holding one of the spark wands guards typically carried. Behind them was a man, his back to them working on something at a table.

"Joyce Handel, 29 cycles, hometown of Crecwood, hired as a receptionist mid-Dust. Had many infractions for being late, interrupting various employees for idle chat, and recently caught copying down archived files." sneered the guard with the wand. "According to these records, you should have been terminated a long time ago." The sound of static filled the air as the guard activated the wand, touching it to Joyce's leg.

The woman pulled against her restraints, crying out in pain as the electricity from it shot through her body.

"Yet, here you are. So, before we proceed with the termination, we have a few questions for you. The sooner you answer, the sooner this is all over."

Joyce shook her head, willing her face into cool anger.

"Who are you working for?"

She remained silent.

"Defiance will not help you, or your friends, whoever they are. We'll flush them out soon enough, just as we found you," the guard spat, touching the shock wand to her again, eliciting a cry of pain. "Who are you working for?"

"Like I'd tell you, heartless bastards." She spat, breathing heavily.

Julietta closed her eyes, hearing another cry of pain, her heart racing.

"You do yourself no favors. I'll ask one more time. Who are you working for?"

"Fuck you."

A scream of pain then silence again.

"Pitiful."

Tears ran down Julietta's face, as though Joyce's pain were her own.

"If you won't talk, then you are of no use to us. Terminate her."

As if this was nothing more than a day in the office, the man at the desk turned to face the helpless woman, a syringe in hand. Julietta watched in horror as he emotionlessly grabbed her arm, jabbing it with the needle, pushing the plunger in without a second thought.

Joyce cried out just before her body went limp, her breathing ragged. A moment passed, two, her breathing slowed, then stopped as her head lolled to one side, unmoving. The man retrieved a stethoscope from the desk, placing it on the woman's chest, listening. Grabbing her wrist, then checking her neck, he confirmed what Julietta's own heart had already realized. Joyce was dead.

"Strip the body of its things then dispose of it." The guard ordered, turning off her shocker. "Termination complete."

"Let me get this straight, the children are trained to get them to their most powerful, then…" Lisle furrowed her brow, going over once more the notebook in front of her.

After watching Joyce be murdered, Julietta somehow managed to steel herself enough to leave Iota quietly. It was not until she was home and the door locked, that she finally relented in telling Charles what happened.

Wired and unable to rest, she and Charles had spent the remainder of the evening reading the notebook. It was Byron who found them in the morning, Charles asleep at the kitchen table, Julietta staring at the notebook, dried tears on her face. Before he could even ask, she had requested a meeting, immediately. It was not even noon by the time they found themselves in Lisle's office at city hall with Ola and Victor, the kids in the playroom with Henrietta who would be caught up later.

"According to what Joyce found, the primary reason the children are taken is to not only be studied for their gift or 'Curie' but to be trained in it. Upon entering the system their memories of before are slowly wiped, until they don't even remember their names. Once they turn 16 cycles, they are then sent back to Apolis for further training until they are 21, either to later brainwash them into a Bell to help train the next generation of 'Curie' or to have their ability perfected. This is determined before they are sent. Those set to become Bells may or may not have some DNA harvested through blood draws, depending on their ability," Julietta explained, her voice sounding almost hollow.

Victor quirked an eyebrow. "And they are harvesting the DNA for..."

"For the Turner program, the secondary reason for the schools. The best traits found among these children are harvested from the DNA samples and used to..." Charles paused, taking a deep breath, "Used to create Turners. The Turners are designer humans, superhumans. The ones Jul saw have been sent out to their next targets for finding more kids. They only stopped to be refreshed. Apparently, they haven't been perfected yet."

"But why create these superhumans?" Lisle crossed her arms, deep in thought. "What happens to those children not turned into Bells?"

"This relates to the third and final reason for the schools." Julietta sighed, her voice shaking slightly. "Students at 21 who were deemed too dangerous to be a Bell are...released. Their DNA is harvested and they are then terminated, as Joyce was. They are building the Turners because they aim to make it so only the Turners will have Curie abilities."

"That's impossible." Byron shook his head. "Curie are born at random. It's a genetic fluke."

"A genetic fluke J.H. intends to remedy with the bombs." Charles bowed his head. "The bomb that destroyed Ciysea was an accident."

"But the agents who visited the remnants of Ciysea did not find anything of interest. Said it looked like a normal bomb site." Ola furrowed her brow.

"That's because the payload failed." Julietta took Charles's hand, taking a deep breath. "The bomb was intended not to wipe out the population, but genetically alter it. There was a miscalculation on its trajectory, according to what Joyce found. It was supposed to land and disseminate its payload immediately. The chemical load is not very stable and disperses quickly once in the air."

"Chemical payload?" Victor looked at Ola and Byron. "Did you—"

"No, I never worked with anything other than machines," Byron replied, shoulders slumped. "This payload is meant to genetically alter folks, how? Turn them into Curie?"

"The opposite." Charles squeezed Julietta's hand. "It's meant to prevent further Curie from being born by either preventing folks from passing on that genetic trait or, in extreme cases, making them infertile completely."

"Why would anyone want to do this? Children are few and far between as it is…" Lisle leaned back in her chair defeated. "Those poor children, raised like cattle."

"I don't believe it." Ola mumbled. "He'd never—"

"Who'd never?" Byron quirked an eyebrow, all eyes falling on Ola.

The woman paused for a moment, collecting her thoughts or something more no one was quite sure before she replied. "My brother, I just can't see why he would want to get himself mixed up in all this."

"We have a bigger issue." Julietta leaned back in her chair, her sleepless night beginning to catch up with her. "There are plans to drop another one of these bombs, the next iteration of them on Matson at Cold's end. Joyce intercepted intel from Apolis regarding how and when they plan to move the kids. Iota should receive the payload a few days before the end of the season. By then the kids would have been moved and it is as simple as setting off the bomb they have located in the basement."

The room went silent.

"Well, that settles it then." Lisle sat up, placing her hands on her desk.

"Settles what?" Ola frowned.

"The Constellation will just have to stage a rescue and destroy Iota before the payload arrives," Lisle replied, sounding matter-of-factly.

"And how do you expect us to do that?" Ola spat. "We already lost three satellites recently. Two of our agents have been killed within Iota's walls. Matson is not exactly the biggest—"

"Ola?" Byron's eyes narrowed. "Since when have you ever been against a mission?"

"We don't have the intel, Byron."

"We do, actually." Charles glanced over to Julietta who was slumping further and further into her seat. "It was…one of Joyce's last gifts. The last few pages of that notebook contain the IDs of every kid in the place. There are 273. She also got the schedules for deliveries to the facility. Jul and I already built up a repertoire with some of the kids who have secret hiding places around the building."

"I suppose by telling me all this, you hope to convince me of a plan you've concocted?" Ola quirked an eyebrow.

"The next shipment of goods should arrive in two weeks on the last workday, three days before the students are set to start being moved, and five days before the payload drop off. According to these notes, the shipments arrive at night. We intercept some of these and drop our own shipment with people, trojan horse style. Once in we simply sneak the kids out," Charles explained.

"Trojan horse style?" Ola scoffed. "You spend too much time reading history."

"What other choice do we have?" Julietta spat, sounding exasperated. "Joyce gave up her life so we could have this information. I risked my life for it, so these kids can have a chance, so Matson won't befall the same fate as Ciysea."

There was silence once more in the room. Julietta locked in a staring contest with Ola, neither woman willing to bend. Finally, after about a minute it was Ola who relented.

"All right, you have a point. If we are going to do this, I'll need to send word to the other satellites and see if they can get us some help within the next couple of weeks. In the meantime, I trust you and Charles to get the kids at Iota ready."

Julietta nodded, leaning on the desk in front of her, head in hands.

Charles placed a hand on Julietta's back. "Thank you, Ola, Lisle, Byron, Victor…I think Jul and I better head home to rest before we figure out how we want to handle our end of things. No sense trying to figure it out with muddled minds. We can get everything fleshed out later."

CHAPTER 35

The next two weeks were a flurry of covert activity. Ola immediately contacted the network, the nearest satellites sending people and supplies. While awaiting backup, those in Matson set out to prepare themselves. The more mechanically minded worked on fixing up some rovers to be used to transport the children once they were freed. The others prepared the base, creating a makeshift hospital and clearing a more convenient entrance into it. Ola had explained the base used to be part of a skyscraper before the war. The underground space was what was left. The second entrance, which was now being fixed up, was a street over in a construction zone that never seemed to be finished.

While the Constellation prepared, so did Charles and Julietta. First and foremost, they informed the children of their plan, having them spread the word with the promise to keep quiet. It did not take much convincing, given they all had learned that keeping quiet was the best way to stay hidden. Julietta also taught them how to jam their doors for that evening so they could slip out to the hiding places at the designated time. For the children who would not be able to, she had designed a modified lock pick that Constellation members would use to retrieve them from their rooms.

The plan was simple. She and Charles would go to work as usual, then when clock out time came, they would find themselves conveniently near the shipping and receiving bay of the facility where several boxes of Constellation members would be waiting. Once they could ensure the all-clear the members would split into three groups.

The first would immediately seek out the hidden hovels, spiriting away the children back to the drop-off to be loaded onto vehicles headed back for the base. The second would make their way toward the apartments to retrieve the younger ones unable to spring themselves from their prisons. The third was information retrieval. They were to loot the archives first before making their way to the labs if there was time. Julietta was to be a part of the first group, focusing on the spaces nearest the workshop. Charles was to be a part of the third, his main goal to retrieve the files he'd found in Dr. Cone's office. Everyone was to be out of the facility by dawn. If they were caught at any point they were to get as many children as they could out before retreating.

The goal was to leave Iota in a position where Apolis would not send the payload and be devoid of students, or at the very least Apolis would think twice about sending the payload. In the event the payload was still in play, Lisle would put out the call to abandon Matson.

It was late when Julietta crept out of the room she and Charles shared and into the main living space. The apartment was quiet at this hour, so different from the beautiful sound of laughter she, Charles, and Penny had shared not a few hours ago making a pillow fort. They wanted Penny to have a happy memory of them as a family before the events of tomorrow evening, just in case.

With Penny sent to stay with Lisle's family until the planned extraction was over and Byron at Ola's finishing up last-minute preparations, Julietta had understandably found herself unable to sleep. Tomorrow she and Charles would go to work as usual, but would likely not leave unscathed.

Lost in her thoughts, she jumped slightly as the door to the bedroom creaked open.

"Can't sleep?"

"Not really," she frowned, turning to Charles. "Sorry, Charlie. Did I wake you?"

He approached her, wrapping his arms around her. "I wasn't asleep either. Hard to sleep, I know…"

Embracing him, she rested her head on his chest. "Charlie, promise me…promise me that if something happens to me, you'll run with Penny?"

She could feel him take a deep breath.

"Jul…"

She looked up at him, a pleading gaze that broke his heart.

"Of course. I'd—I'd want you to do the same." He hugged her tightly. "But it won't come to that. I promise."

"I wish I could believe you," she sighed, a few tears rolling down her face.

He shook his head but said nothing as they held each other, hearts heavy. Just as he felt as though the weight of the world had come to rest on his shoulders, a strange sound drew him back to himself. After a few minutes, he perked up slightly. "Do you hear that, Jul?"

Despite her own heavy heart, she listened closely. Somewhere from one of the apartments below came the sound of a guitar being played. "Lynn must have guests tonight."

"Sounds like it," Charles chuckled lightly, beginning to hum to the tune of the guitar, a hand gently brushing through Julietta's hair. "I recognize the tune."

"Where from?"

"From my childhood, when my friends and I would sneak off to spy on those fancy dress parties. This was one of the waltzes." He began to sway her slightly, a silent invitation.

Without missing a beat, she joined him, closing her eyes and letting him lead, letting herself be lost to him.

"Penny always wanted us to dance," she whispered, a sad smile appearing on her face.

"To be honest, when she suggested it I half wanted to stand up right there and start. Wouldn't have been smart with my knee at the time, but…"

Julietta opened her eyes, gazing into his. Shifting her arms around his neck she smiled. "My Charlie, always the charmer."

He answered her with a gentle kiss as they continued to sway to the muffled melody. They danced together for a while, even as the guitarist changed to another waltz. Slowly Julietta moved a hand to his scarred cheek, the thoughts of what happened the day he earned it and what may happen tomorrow suddenly clouding her eyes.

He shook his head, a glint of mischief in his eyes. "You like it? I personally think it makes me look more manly."

"You shameless flirt." She couldn't help but laugh, despite herself.

"Only with you."

She ran her thumb over the scar. "You got this protecting our daughter."

"I'd do it again in a heartbeat."

"I don't doubt it." She pulled him a bit closer.

Echoing the movement, his hands fell to her waist, coming to rest on her hips as they kissed once, twice, three times.

"Charlie...I...I never thought I'd find someone like you. Someone who...who makes me feel safe, feel loved."

"I never thought I'd find you either."

"I just wish—"

He stopped her with a kiss. "We will. When this is all over, we'll have that museum."

"With an apartment like this?"

"With a workshop attached, a bedroom full of toys for our Penny, a kitchen where I'll make you sweet toast, and more besides."

"A home for our family."

"One, I hope, we can grow someday."

"A sibling for Penny," Julietta bit her lip. "With your messy hair."

"And your beautiful eyes," Charles chuckled, his thumbs pressing lightly against her hips.

"Those are some healing hands you got there, Dr. Hawthorne," Julietta teased, once more wrapping her arms about his neck as she kissed him deeply.

"It's a good thing you are kissing me, I feel breathless."

She paused for a moment, her eyes lightening, "Shall we...move this little dance back to the bedroom?"

He quirked an eyebrow, grinning. "As you wish, Miss Milard."

As Charles closed the door behind them she continued in, stopping just at the end of their bed. "Now, where were we?" She stuck out her tongue as Charles approached.

"That depends entirely on you," he smirked, eyes bright. "You seem to like my scar. Would you care to see the others?"

Taking the hint, she bit her lower lip as she removed his nightshirt. Tossing it on the floor she placed a hand on his bare chest, feeling his thundering heartbeat. Letting her gaze roam over him she couldn't help but feel a tug on her own rapidly beating heart.

"I've shown you mine. Care to show me yours?" Charles teased.

She replied silently, taking his hands and placing them on the hem of her shirt. It was a matter of seconds before it and her undershirt joined his on the floor.

"Beautiful." Charles breathed, moving to take her in his arms. He stopped short, however, seeing a flash of hesitation on Julietta's face. "Jul?"

"Charlie…"

"It's all right. If you—"

He paused as she stepped into his arms. "I want you, Charlie. I've… never wanted anyone before. Never been with—"

"Me neither. Never wanted, never been…" He bowed his head, wrapping his arms around her waist tightly. "Until I met you."

"Until I met you." She echoed, pressing herself closer so their bodies touched. A moment later he had lifted her off her feet, setting her down on the bed before joining her.

Kissing turned to touch as hands roamed any exposed skin, caressing it as if to burn the memory of it into their palms. After a few minutes of this, Julietta grew bolder, one hand slipping into the front of Charles's pajama pants.

"Feeling naughty, are we?" He chuckled into her lips, pressing a bit closer, allowing her to feel just what she was doing to him.

"Charlie…" she mumbled into his mouth as she slowly began to work his pants and shorts off of him, eliciting her name from him.

Free of his formalities, he shifted her onto her back. Gazing down at her he smiled as though waiting for permission, even now letting her choose.

She answered him by taking his hand, placing it just inside where her pants sat against her stomach.

Kissing her lips, then her neck, her chest, and down her body, he painstakingly but lovingly removed the rest of her night clothes until she too was free of all formalities. Kissing each of her hips, she fell open to him, as he repeated his loving trail back up her. Once more gazing into her eyes, he sighed deeply. "My beautiful Jul…" The unspoken words were lost as Julietta pulled him into a kiss.

"My Charlie…always."

"Always," he echoed as he completed their connection. Julietta gasped, for but a moment, before smoothly falling into rhythm with him, thoughts of what lay beyond the dawn lost to the night.

It was just before sunrise, when Julietta awoke, her internal alarm clock waking her before the one on the bedside table. She was lying just as she had fallen asleep, wrapped in Charles's arms. They had talked, after making love, about the future, about the beautiful museum they would restore together, about the family they would grow there. Gazing up at Charles, she brushed a piece of stray hair from his face before her hand came to rest on his bare chest over his heart.

She loved Charles and he loved her. He was the father to Penny, their daughter. Today would not change that. No matter what, Charles would always be hers, and she his.

"You okay, Jul?"

"No."

Charles's eyes fluttered open as he pulled her closer, removing any space between them. "Everything will be all right. We know the plan. We know what to do if things go south." He shook his head, kissing her forehead. "I won't let anything happen to you."

"And if something does?"

"I will, as will you," he sighed, the unspoken promise resonating in those words. "I don't want to think about it."

"Then I won't either," she frowned, resting her head against his chest. "You are right. We'll be all right."

The sound of the alarm clock on the bedside table rang, but neither moved to silence it. "You'll always be..."

"Always, Charlie," she echoed as they untangled themselves from one another to prepare for the day ahead.

Picking up her discarded night clothes, she glanced over to Charles who already had started to dress. Only one thought permeated her mind. She could only hope that last night had not been their last. Based on Charles's expression, he shared her sentiment.

CHAPTER 36

The day seemed to drag despite the endless amount of work that needed to be done. Julietta had been sent to fix machines all over the facility with barely a chance to stop and eat. Meanwhile, Charles had been heads down working, ensuring he kept up his pretense with Dr. Cone who lately had started a nasty habit of looking over his shoulder when he least expected it. It would not matter after tonight, they both thought. Tonight would end their work one way or another.

As the sun set and clock-out time drew near, Julietta had made sure to double and triple-check her station was clean, prolonging her stay until she knew it was no longer reasonable for her to do so without suspicion. Tapping her ID on the workshop entrance, she could not help but smile. All her work, all the sabotage was over. She would soon be free of this wretched place.

Exiting the workshop, she made a small detour, feigning the need to use the restroom. Entering the one nearest the back of the institute she went straight to the stall at the far back. At the top of it was a vent, her ticket to the loading bay. Using the toilet as a step stool, she clamored into the duct. Crawling through the dark space, Penny's flashlight lighting the way, she hoped no one would hear her. To her relief, it seemed no one had as she reached the other end undiscovered. Pausing a moment, she listened for any sign of disturbance. Instead, she was greeted by silence.

Taking the flashlight in hand she waved it through the grate once, twice, an agreed upon signal that, to anyone unsuspecting, would look like one of the rare light bulbs flickering with its limited power. She waited a minute before repeating the process. This time, she heard footsteps coming her way. She held her breath as a figure appeared before the grate.

"Well, if my eyes don't deceive me, I believe someone has left the world's greatest treasure in this vent." It was Charles.

"Shameless flirt," she puffed, rolling her eyes teasingly, as he helped her out of the vent.

"Only for you," he winked, retrieving her gun from his waist and her knife from his boot. Byron had ensured both their weapons had been squirreled in with a trusted Constellation member. "Everyone is readying over there. They also brought a change of clothes."

Slipping into an all-black affair of jeans, shirt, zip-up sweater with hood, duster, and hat, Julietta's stomach began to turn with anticipation. They would wait another 30 minutes for the weekday staff to fully depart, leaving only those who lived on-site and the children inside.

"I'll see you back at the base, all right?" Charles sighed, kissing her on the forehead.

She nodded, holding back tears as she embraced him. "See you on the other side."

Iota was strange after hours, the cold clinic feel replaced by a dark and more sinister one. Due to the electricity rules of Matson, the corridors were now only lit by pale emergency lights, giving the whole place the air of a long-forgotten tomb rather than a school. Once inside the main atrium, the groups split off to their respective destinations, nods of understanding passing between them before each vanished into the darkness.

Charles was headed for his laboratory on the second floor with the information retrieval team who were beelining toward the archives. Having doctored the door when he left for the day, he slipped inside without delay.

Making straight for the inner lab, he reached into his pocket, producing Julietta's modified lock pick for overriding ID locks. He paused but a moment to admire his woman's handy work, a silent wish that she was all right as he pushed it into the small pinhole in the lock. After a few quick turns, he was in.

Racing over to the desk he easily found the same groove as before, again using the lock pick to open it. To his relief, the notebooks and papers were still there. Scooping them up, he tossed them into the black backpack he had been given before shutting the desk with an audible click.

His success was short-lived, however, as he turned to leave. In his haste to get the target items he had been caught unawares, for standing at the door, was Dr. Cone.

"Well, what do we have here? Working a bit late, aren't you, boy?"

Charles's hand went to his gun at his waist, but he did not draw it. "You are up awful late yourself. I would have thought a man of your caliber would be sound asleep by now."

"Oh? And miss your little raiding party?" The rotund man grinned, laughing. "Did you really think you'd get away with it? Breaking into my lab and reading my notes? Who are you working for, boy?"

Charles glanced around the room, looking for a way out.

"Nervous? You should be. We have a special procedure for people like you, like your friends down below."

As if on cue an alarm could be heard coming from the main facility.

"Ah, it seems they've arrived. Don't you worry. It will be all over soon!"

Quicker than he expected Dr. Cone was on him, knife in hand. In the short scuffle, he managed a good slash on Charles's left shoulder. With a cry of pain, Charles shoved him back hard, pulling his gun.

"What's that little toy you got there? Don't you know guns don't work any—"

BANG

Dr. Cone gripped his shoulder, eyes wide and ravenous as they darted between Charles, his backpack, and the gun. "No, you will not take my research."

BANG BANG

Charles stood in stunned silence as his assailant's knife clattered to the floor at his feet, Cone's body hitting the floor a moment later, unmoving. The man had meant to kill Charles, a knife to the heart, but he had a gun. Counting his lucky stars, the old adage about bringing a knife to a gunfight held true, he gave the lab one last sweep for anything of importance before bounding out into the main facility and the chaos that awaited him.

Julietta had managed to get three children to the vent and into the awaiting arms of her fellow Constellation members before she was confronted by guards. In the weeks leading up to this raid, she had the various students she left treats for tell their friends about hiding in the forty-some-odd hidden places about the institute. Some were only big enough for one child while others could hold multiple. The two she kept checking, as the dormitories were emptied, were singles: the one in the closet where the older ones would often meet her, and the one in the workshop.

Thankfully the guard that caught her was rather inept in the dim light. She managed to avoid being shocked, only taking a couple of hits from the butt of their spark wand before disarming them, knocking them out, and locking them in a nearby closet. She would have to be more careful. It took a few more tries and run-ins with guards that either ended in the guard being stuffed in a closet or her hiding for a few minutes before she found a safe path for her to take the children.

She had just dropped off her 17th child when the Constellation member on the other end stopped her.

"We are starting to clear out. Some of the kids have been taken by the scientists, spotted by one of our scouts on the outside driving away in rovers with them. There is little left we can do."

Julietta frowned. They had failed to get everyone out. However, that did not mean they could not try for a few more.

"I'm going to make one more pass."

"Suit yourself. Be quick. We won't wait long."

Stealthing back toward the closet she found no children. Undeterred, she made for the workshop, hoping to at least save one more. Upon entering it, however, her heart leapt into her throat. The hovel cover was shattered on the ground, signs of a struggle obvious, leading towards what was once a concealed door, now fully open.

Joyce's last gift had mentioned a basement where bombs and research of the like were stored. This must be one of the concealed entrances. Julietta had a choice. Retreat now and hope no child had been taken or risk a peek. She could not live with herself if she did not confirm there was no child.

Taking a deep breath, she made her move. The door led to a small hallway that ended in a darkened stairwell. Hugging the wall, she slowly crept down, hoping beyond all else she'd find nothing. Her wish was not granted. As she reached the last landing before the bottom she heard it, the faint whimpering of a child and a familiar voice shushing them.

"I said shut up! If you don't shut your mouth, I'll make sure when I bring you to Apolis you are put up for release!" Danni hissed at her captive just as Julietta appeared at the bottom of the stairs, face covered, knife in hand. "Who are you?"

"Give me the child," she spat, her voice strong despite the tug on her heart as she realized the captive was Quinn.

"Stay back," the woman huffed. "There are enough explosives down here to send this whole place sky-high in an instant."

Sure enough, behind Danni were barrels with powder spilling from them.

"You don't have to do this," Julietta pleaded, holding up her hands.

"I...I recognize that voice. Jessa?"

She dared to lower her scarf, revealing her face. "Just let me take Quinn, Danni."

"Quinn? Oh, you mean the experiment."

"Her name is Quinn."

"Her name is Quinn as much as your name is Jessa," she spat back, taking a step toward a string on the ground behind her. Not a string, Julietta realized, but a fuse.

"Don't do it, Danni. You'll not only kill yourself but everyone else in this building."

"You think I'd let myself die before my life's work was saved?"

"Don't light the fuse."

"Or you'll what?"

Julietta dared a step closer. "Just give me the girl."

"You know what, you can have the girl. If you live."

Without warning she pounced. Catching Julietta slightly off guard, she knocked the knife from her hand as she slammed her into the ground. As they tussled, Julietta desperately began seeking a way out as her opponent continued to pummel her.

SLAM

Julietta had managed to wrestle free for a moment, dragging Danni to her feet. It was a short-lived triumph, however, as the slippery woman twisted from her grip, injuring her right wrist in the process. Crying out in pain, she pushed through it, managing to knock Danni back against one of the walls, hard. It was enough to take her breath away for a moment, giving her the time she needed to reach for a blunt object from the nearby workbench.

Danni crumpled to the ground, bleeding, but breathing. Julietta did not have time to think about what she'd done when she heard Quinn say, "Fuse go boom soon!"

Glancing over, her heart sank. It had all been a bluff; Danni had already lit the fuse. Despite her injuries, she retrieved her knife, cutting Quinn free of the bonds around her wrists and ankles.

"Come on, we need to get out of here."

Counting their lucky stars the blast had been intended to be delayed, they were able to reach a rocky outcropping some distance from Iota when the earth shook, sending them to their knees as the sky above rained with soot, and the world around filled with dust.

Charles had been back at the base for all of an hour when the earth shook. After his confrontation with Dr. Cone, he ran straight for the archives, helping the Constellation members there deal with the guards, earning himself some electrical burns before they were able to safely retreat from the facility. Once he arrived, he dropped off his intel to Ola before Byron whisked him away to be treated by Henrietta and the other volunteer medics who now were assessing the Constellation members and the children they brought with them. Bandaged up, despite protests from Byron, he began helping with medical care. He had just cleared another child to be brought to the barracks where they were keeping them, for now, to eat and rest when the earth had moved.

There were screams, then silence as the underground building creaked and shook for a moment before settling back seemingly unscathed. They would get their answer to the unspoken question on everyone's minds a few minutes later as various other members and transports trickled in. Iota had exploded.

Charles's heart leaped into his throat. He hadn't seen any sign of Julietta up until now. Unable to leave his post as another child was brought to him, he asked Byron to look for her as he dashed past with more medical supplies.

An hour passed since the shake, Charles getting more nervous with each person that was brought before him. Still, no sign of Julietta, nor of Byron who had seemed to vanish.

An hour more. He convinced another medic to switch with him so he was helping those brought in closer to the entrance in the hopes of spotting her himself.

An hour later with no sign of her, he was struggling to focus, his eyes flitting towards the hallway entrance to the medical space, trying to will Julietta to appear with just his mind.

Over four hours had passed before the flow of patients trickled to only a handful. Finally relieved of his duty, his own injuries starting to plague him, he sought out Byron who had positioned himself near the construction entrance door.

"Where is she? Has she arrived?" he asked, pleading.

He did not need to wait for a verbal response, Byron's face said it all. "I'm going after her."

"No, Charles, you can't." The older man stepped in front of him. "The dust still has not settled from the explosion and you're hurt."

"Jul could be out there hurt."

"You can't go. Think about Penny! It's bad enough—"

The sound of the construction entrance door grating open silenced the two men. The sight that appeared was a cause of great relief and concern. Coming down the stairs was Julietta, being held up by a young girl of about 16 cycles.

"Henrietta, Kendra!" Byron shouted, both doctors appearing a moment later.

"We're all right." The young girl coughed as Kendra led her away.

Charles was immediately to Julietta, accessing her. "Jul?"

Breathing heavily, she managed to give him a small weak smile before collapsing into his arms.

CHAPTER 37

The final count of the rescued was 192 children. Byron had spent most of the night and well into the morning sifting through intel, counts, and the like with Ola while the rest of the Constellation recovered. He had briefly slept around noon, exhausted, awakening just in time for dinner. After meeting with Ola once more to get the final counts, he took his leave, wanting to check on Charles and Julietta.

Entering the small bedroom off his workshop, he was relieved to find both Charles and Julietta asleep, Julietta on the bed, Charles on the couch across from her. They had the fright of their lives when Julietta collapsed, thankfully only unconscious. Byron had immediately ushered them to his workshop bedroom, bringing Charles and Henrietta anything necessary to treat her.

Setting down the tray of food and glass of water he brought for Charles, he glanced over to Julietta with a sigh. They were alive. Hurt, but alive.

"She's stable Byron, but not out of the woods yet," Charles mumbled, shifting onto his back.

"I brought you some dinner. Has she been awake much?"

"A few times, never really lucid." His eyes fluttered open. "Henrietta gave her something for the pain last night. Should be wearing off soon." Grunting, he sat up. "I didn't mean to fall asleep."

"You aren't a hundred percent yourself, son."

"I'll live," he huffed, taking a seat at the desk, and starting to eat.

Assessing him, Byron shook his head. "When did you last change your bandage?"

"Henrietta changed it this morning when she came to check on Jul and me," he answered, not looking up from his meal.

Without another word, Byron left, returning a few minutes later with the necessary supplies. "Finish your dinner. Then I'll see to your shoulder."

Removing the younger man's shirt, he set to work cleaning and rebandaging the nasty gash Dr. Cone had left on him. He was lucky, Byron thought, given what Charles had told him and the injuries he had seen come through the door last night.

"How many?"

"192. The others have been confirmed alive, though we are not sure where they have been taken. If I were to hazard a guess, Apolis or another facility within a few days of here. The only bodies found in the rubble were thankfully staff."

Charles winced as Byron touched a particularly sensitive bruise on his side.

"You look like you've been through the wringer."

"They are just minor burns and bruises, they'll heal quickly enough." Charles rested his head in one of his hands, thinking. "How...how many did we lose?"

"Of the 53 volunteers that went in, 11 in total. Five were still in Iota when it went up, three were found on the streets this morning, and three died overnight from their injuries. The rest are alive, albeit in various states of health. No one seems to be on the verge any longer."

"Good...what's the plan looking like?"

"Charlie, you really should—" The man stopped, seeing the pain hidden in Charles's body language. He needed the distraction. "Ola and I've been talking about going to Apolis. Once everyone is healed, we can discuss this further, but many are already in agreement. It is time to cut the head off the snake."

Cleaning up his supplies, he took Charles's empty tray with him. Returning a few minutes later, he found him sitting on the bed checking Julietta over with his stethoscope, his shirt still tossed over the desk chair.

"Something wrong, Charlie?"

"Her vitals are good, was just checking," he sighed, placing his stethoscope back in his bag beneath the desk.

Byron bowed his head, an ache in his heart. "I'm going to Ola, see if there is any other news. I'll send Henrietta later to check on you both."

Alone, any sense of bravado deflated from Charles as his eyes continued to access Julietta. Gone was the doctor, replaced by the man in love. Shaking his head, he brushed away some hair that had fallen in front of her face.

A moment later, she began to stir. "Charlie…" she groaned.

"It's all right, Jul. I'm here." He leaned down, kissing her forehead. He had not meant to wake her before she was ready.

Her eyes fluttered open, to his relief, clear and lucid. "Charlie…" She frowned, seeing his various injuries on display. "You're hurt."

"I'm all right," he breathed, feeling a weight lifted hearing her voice. "It's just a scratch."

She shook her head, smirking. "Doctors are the worst patients."

"I suppose we are," he chuckled, lightly. "How do you feel?"

"My throat feels on fire." She coughed, slightly sinking a bit further into the pillow.

Reaching for his glass of water, he helped her drink. "You had a lot of dust and soot in your lungs. I had to do the same procedure I did on Marisa back in Waterwealt…" He set the glass back on the desk. "You were struggling when we brought you in. Took a bit to get you coughing. I was so—You were—We managed to—" He stopped as Julietta raised her bandaged right hand, resting it on his bare chest.

"I'm all right, Charlie." Taking his hand in her other, she brought it to her chest, letting him feel her heartbeat strong and calm. "I'm alive."

Taking her hand against his chest, he kissed it, letting his pent up tears fall. "We are alive."

"I'm sorry if I frightened you."

"Don't be. Quinn, she told us about Danni."

Julietta's expression darkened. "I killed her, Charlie. I knocked her out and left her to die."

"She lit the fuse and attacked you."

"I…I know. I don't regret, but—"

"I know," he assured, moving his hand from her chest, running it instead through her hair pensively. "I feel the same way about Cone."

"Cone?"

Charles explained how he had come across Dr. Cone and shot him.

"Charlie…" She moved her bandaged hand to his bandaged shoulder. "How many?"

"192. The rest are alive though."

"What was the cost?"

"11, with many injured as you are."

289

She closed her eyes for a moment, letting the information wash over her. "A price paid, to make a change. Any plans?"

Charles hesitated, a part of him wanting her to not worry and rest, but another part understanding why she needed to know. "Byron says Apolis is likely next."

"I'm not surprised. Time is running out with bombs dropping." She sighed deeply, opening her eyes once more, a deep sadness held within them. "Yesterday was merely a battle in a larger war."

He shook his head. "Does anything else hurt?"

"Everything does. I feel I could sleep for a month and still be tired." She relaxed a bit further into her pillow, though the pain in her eyes lessened. "My wrist hurts and I definitely feel the bruises, but I'd rather that than not feel anything at all. Speaking of which, how long was I out?"

"Only about a day. Henrietta gave you something for the pain once we stabilized you and got you cleaned up. Your wrist most likely is fractured, but not completely broken. You have about as many bruises and burns as me. It was the dust that really got you. Now that you are lucid, I can give you a full dose of that tea for your lungs. You came to a few times and we were able to give you some to start the healing, but you likely don't remember."

"I remember hearing your voice," she smiled sadly. "You kept telling me it would be okay. That you had me."

"I was right, wasn't I?"

"That depends…"

"Depends?" His brow furrowed, concerned. "On what?"

"That depends," she chuckled, coughing a bit. "Now that I am officially awake, I can get some treatment for my Fallen-in-love-itis."

Charles burst out laughing. "Why, you shameless flirt."

"Only with you," she echoed, gently pulling him towards her.

Leaning in, he placed a gentle hand behind her head as she placed her own on his face as they kissed.

"Thank the heavens above you are all right." Charles sighed, placing his forehead on hers. "Henrietta kept telling me you'd be fine when you woke up, but…"

She ran a soothing thumb over the scar on his cheek. "Such a mother hen."

"I was so scared I was going to lose you."

"I was afraid of losing you too, but it's over for now. We are alive. We are recovering."

"Yes, we are," he yawned, his true exhaustion taking hold.

"You should rest, my love. A battle has been won."

"A battle won; something to celebrate I suppose." He shrugged, kissing her once more before sitting up.

"Stay with me? I doubt you could hurt me any worse than I am." Too tired to argue, he smirked. "As you wish."

Julietta carefully shifted herself over, allowing him to comfortably lie down facing her, a protective arm draped over her waist. "Sleep, Charlie. I'll be here when you wake."

Charles closed his eyes as she did, both relaxing into the comforting presence of the other, falling into much-needed restorative sleep.

Though Cold season should have ended by anyone's measure, it was the coldest day by far. The sun had not yet risen when Julietta and Charles, holding a bundled-up and sleeping Penny, found themselves patiently waiting beside the rover for Lisle, Ola, and Byron. They were doing one last sweep of the former Constellation base.

In the week that followed Iota's destruction, a great many revelations had come to light as heavy decisions were made. The first decision was regarding the 192 rescued children. Thanks to the members who raided the archives, files on each of them had been found which included information such as their powers, hometown, parents' names, and even their real names. Immediately, the Constellation set to work reaching out to the families through the radio network, hoping to reunite the children with a blood relative. If they were found, groups were established that, by Cold's end, would depart to return them to their families. For the children unfortunate enough to find themselves orphaned, they would be taken in by trusted families in Matson.

The second decision to be made was where to go next for those not sent on reunions. This at first seemed like a daunting subject to approach given the myriad of ideas offered. Some people suggested traveling to other satellites, helping them stage their own raids and take out the schools one by one. Others wanted more covert operations, intending to hunt down the other Mr. Turners whose next orders were discovered amongst the intel. There were a few other, not as calculated ideas that sprung up, but soon they were all silenced as the last universally accepted choice came to the forefront. With bombs and payloads ready, the end would be sooner rather than later. They need to go to the source: Apolis.

Lisle was the first to emerge from the base. "Ola and Byron are just confirming a couple of last-minute things. Making sure no one left anything behind."

Charles and Julietta chuckled, both shaking their heads. The rest of the Constellation had cleared out a couple of days prior. There was little chance of anything being left behind.

"Short of breaking into walls, I doubt they'd find much of anything left." Charles chuckled, adjusting his grip on Penny.

Lisle frowned, placing a hand on his shoulder. "I suppose this is goodbye then."

"I suppose it is."

"I—I know we haven't exactly been on good terms until more recently but, I want you to know you are always welcome back here in Matson. A place like this could really use good people like yourself and Julietta. Maybe by the time you finish with J.H., I'd have finally found a permanent place for you and your family as I promised."

"You gave us plenty, Lisle. Thank you for everything." He glanced over to Julietta, a twinkle in his eye. "Maybe we'll take you up on that offer."

"I'd be delighted." She turned her attention to Penny who was now awake, though barely. "Goodbye, Miss Penny."

"Goodbye, Gov. Lis. Tell Penny friends Nic and Mai Penny miss them?" Penny whispered, sounding sad.

"I'll make sure to tell them. Hopefully, you and your parents can come back and visit us soon."

She smiled, closing her eyes again, snuggling more into Charles's arms.

Lisle extended a hand to Julietta. "Julietta—"

"Julie."

The governor raised an eyebrow but smiled. "Julie, I can't thank you enough for what you sacrificed for my city. What all of you did."

"It was what I could do." She shook her hand.

"You be careful, now. I know you already take really good care of your daughter, but I think you'll have your hands full more so with your husband." Lisle chuckled.

The night prior Charles and Julietta had wed in Lisle's office, Victor, Nicolas, Maya, Henrietta, Ola, Byron, and Penny present. Though it was more a symbolic gesture, it meant the world to them knowing they were officially husband and wife. Afterward, a small celebration and farewell dinner were had before they revealed one final surprise. Not only had they been wed, but Lisle had the papers written up for them, with Penny's permission, to officially adopt her. No longer could anyone say she was not their daughter. They were a family.

Julietta looked over to Charles, her husband, holding their daughter Penny, smiling. "I'll be sure to take good care of him."

"And you better take good care of her as well, Charles," Lisle teased.

"Don't you worry, I think this little miss here in my arms would have something to say about it if I didn't."

"Penny make sure Papa Charlie and Momma Julie behave," Penny stated groggily, eliciting laughter from the three adults.

Ola and Byron emerged from the base.

"Well, that's everything, not a speck of dust or crumb left. No way to track us." Byron sighed. "What's so funny?"

"Miss Penny here was just telling Lisle how she intends to make sure Charlie and I behave ourselves." Julietta chuckled, wrapping an arm around Charles's waist.

"Is that so, Miss Penny?"

"Penny make sure Sir Byron behave too," Penny replied, sticking out her tongue, eyes still closed.

Everyone once more burst into laughter, all tension about the trip released.

"We better get going," Ola said, turning serious. "We need to be out of city limits before dawn. Byron, could you help me into the passenger seat?"

Lisle watched as the five slowly boarded the rescued rover from Iota, that would hopefully get them to Apolis in two weeks if it held.

Climbing into the back, Charles lay Penny on the left soft bench, tucking a blanket around her. "Sleep, Penny. We'll wake you for breakfast."

He did not have to tell the girl twice as the child quickly nodded off.

Julietta climbed in after him, sitting on the right bench. "Are you sure you are all right on the floor?"

"There are plenty of blankets on it. Plus, it's better for your lungs to be up higher."

STEPHANIE VACCARO & LOUISE ALLEN

"My lungs are fine, Charlie, my cough is nearly gone. And don't you say my wrist is still hurt or I am more bruised. This morning when you were showering, I heard you yelp from that one bruise on your ribs."

He shook his head, smirking as he closed the door before sitting on the blanketed floor. "All right, how about this? You sleep there until breakfast then we switch. That way we both get the benefits of a slightly more comfortable rest."

She debated arguing back but as the rover began to pull away all the fight left her. He was right that she was still recovering, but they all were. The whirlwind of the last week settled into her further as Lisle began to turn into nothing more than a silhouette in the darkness.

"All right, you win." She sighed, lying down, pulling a blanket over herself.

Charles did the same. Turning his head to face her he reached up a hand. "My beautiful wife."

"My pain in the butt husband," she replied teasingly, her eyelids drooping. "I almost forgot with the strange weather, happy cycle Charlie."

Charles chuckled. "I forgot myself."

"28 Cold. How does it feel?"

"Well, considering I'm married to the love of my life and have a beautiful daughter with her…" Charles yawned, his hand letting go of hers, instead playing with the end of her hair that spilled over the seat. "I'd say it feels pretty good."

Shifting closer to the edge of the bench, her eyes gazed into his. "I love you, Charlie. Always."

"I love you, Jul."

She leaned over the seat, him sitting up to meet her with a brief kiss. "Rest, Charlie. We have a long journey ahead of us."

Lying back down, closing his eyes, he drifted off almost instantly. Julietta took one last look at her sleeping daughter and husband, a feeling of relaxation coming over her before she too closed her eyes and fell into much-needed rest.

Hours had passed. The sun barely crested the horizon as Byron drove the rover over dusty hill after dusty hill, everyone else getting much needed sleep. They were heading to Apolis, a place he had not been since he lost his son. Charles and Julietta were still alive, despite the risks they had taken. They had been lucky. He had been lucky.

Images of their journey began to flood his mind. He recalled how Charles and Julietta protected poor Penny hidden away in a cabinet from Mr. Turner. He remembered Charles lighting the match that accidentally exploded the hidden bomb site at Skelter Ridge. Snatches of their trouble ladened trip to Matson tugged at his heart, the visions of Charles carrying an injured Julietta into the damp, cold, dilapidated skyscraper he had found for them as a shelter and the image of Penny sniffling and terrified as they faced yet another Mr. Turner, bringing back the same pain as they had then. Julietta holding Charles, unconscious in her arms at the clinic, the bullet he put in the Turner they had taken prisoner, and Julietta collapsing into Charles's arms not a week ago after helping to rescue so many kids. These images pulled at the edges of his conscious mind, threatening to overwhelm him. He stayed the course, however, keeping the rover moving forward.

He would keep his promise. He would take down J.H. and his horrid schools. He would ensure Charles, Julietta, and Penny's safety even if he couldn't do the same for his own son. It was time to cut the head off the snake. If it meant his time would finally run out, then so be it. He had been lucky, after all. He was always on borrowed time.

CHAPTER 38

Penny Milard-Hawthorne.

Penny smiled reading the name she had written on her notebook decorated with flowers she drew. She was a Milard-Hawthorne. It had been about a week since she, her parents, Sir Byron, and Miss Ola had left Matson and her new friends. She was a bit sad to leave but understood why. It was why she now had this notebook, a journal Gov. Lis had given her to write down her travels so when next they met she could tell Mai and Nic all about it.

Julietta Milard-Hawthorne. Charles Milard-Hawthorne.

Penny carefully penned their names beside her own on the cover, drawing a heart-shaped stethoscope beside her Papa Charlie's and goggles with heart-shaped lenses beside Momma Julie's. Penny had been very happy when Momma and Papa told her they wanted to marry, even happier when they told her they wanted to become her Momma and Papa officially so no one could take her away again. They had asked her what name she wanted, Momma's or Papa's? Penny had wanted both. Momma and Papa liked that idea, so they had Gov. Lis write that on the paper that said Momma and Papa now are Penny's.

Momma and Papa love their Penny. They promised their Penny they would always protect her. Penny trusts them. Penny loves them.

Looking up from her journal, the girl smiled. Momma was sleeping on the bench, her head on Papa's lap. Papa was sitting up but also

had fallen asleep. Momma and Papa had slept a lot while they traveled in the space car Sir Byron drove. Momma and Papa had driven
the space car a few times during the week, but Sir Byron said he didn't
mind driving most of the time to give them time to rest. Penny knew
why. They had gotten hurt when they freed kids like her from scary
Iota. She had heard them talking about a few of them. One named
Quinn had been sent to live with an auntie in Sirie. Another named
Dimitre was adopted by Miss Henrietta, just like Penny was adopted
by Momma and Papa. Penny was happy her Momma and Papa were
helping kids like her even though it was hard. Penny was proud of her
Momma and Papa.

Having spent some time writing down her thoughts in her journal, Penny found herself eventually staring out the window at the
various dilapidated buildings and skyscrapers they passed. They were
traveling through another abandoned city. Most of the trip had been
through dusty hills and fields that made Penny sleepy. Penny liked
it better to see the cities, both working and abandoned. She liked to
imagine what it would be like to live in tall buildings. As she watched
the world drift by, she noticed a few drops of water hit the window.
Momma had said it was supposed to be Damp season now, and this
was the first rainfall.

She continued to write in her journal, writing about how Sir Byron
had found a shortcut the other day that took them past an old mining
town, about the food Miss Ola had brought with them, about wondering
what Nic and Mai were doing, and about how she had been practicing
her letters like Miss Henrietta told her to.

Miss Henrietta had helped Penny learn to write better in Matson.
Momma and Papa had taught her back in Waterwealt some basics, but
she had not really focused on it until Miss Henrietta started teaching
her. Penny loved to show Momma and Papa what she wrote. She liked
how it made them smile.

Tired of writing, Penny set her notebook on the bench behind her
before moving toward the front of the rover where she had sat Nelson
with Margie.

Adjusting the blankets Papa Charlie had laid on the floor for her
to sit on, she got herself comfortable before picking up Nelson and
turning him on.

"Hello, Miss Penny. How are you today?"

"Penny good. Nelson, Margie okay?"

"That's good, Miss Penny. Me and Margie are fine," the mechanical man replied.

"Penny work on letters again. Penny want show Momma and Papa when awake."

"I think they'd love to see your letters, Miss Penny. You are improving very much."

There was a flash of light, a low rumble filling the air a few seconds later. Penny had heard thunder before and seen lightning. It did not scare her much.

"Rain start," she sighed, shaking her head. "Penny maybe work on numbers. Papa showed Penny how to count between thunder."

"Yes, it seems the rain has started. That is expected during Damp season, Miss Penny. Though from what I heard your Papa say it is still Cold."

Penny nodded. "Cold at night. Penny extra blankets to sleep."

"Of course, Miss Penny."

Setting Nelson down, Penny yawned. "Stretch legs, Nelson."

Nelson began to walk around a bit, bending his legs this way and that. While Penny watched, her hand came to the compass around her neck. Unclipping it from the chain, she held it in her hand with a smile. Momma and Papa had given Penny the pretty compass for her tenth cycle. It was her favorite gift.

Touching her pointer finger to the words engraved on the back, her other fingers came to rest on the other three as her thumb held it steady on the side. Carefully she let a bit of her power flow, sparks dancing along the flowers etched into the sides. She smiled as she shifted her fingers slightly, the compass pointing exactly where she expected. She shifted them again, again pointing where she expected. She did it once more. Letting her power fade, she watched as the compass settled on North. This was her favorite gift because it would always point her way home like Papa Charlie taught her.

She clipped the compass back on her necklace just as another flash of lightning lit up the sky. She began to count, one elephant, two elephants, three elephants, four—there was a roll of thunder.

"How many, Miss Penny?" Nelson asked, walking back over to her side beside Margie.

"Four elephant."

"About four miles away then. We will probably be in this storm awh—"

There was a loud crack, not of thunder, but of metal snapping as the rover suddenly lurched forward sharply.

"Argh!" cried Charles and Julietta as they were sent to the floor, Penny tumbling a bit forward.

"Is everyone okay?" Byron asked through the internal window that led to the front part of the vehicle.

It took the three a minute to right themselves. "Shaken but not stirred," Charles grunted, his attention immediately on Julietta and Penny.

"I'm okay," Julietta frowned, rubbing the arm that she landed on. "Probably get a bruise on my elbow but I'll live."

Penny crawled over to Julietta, holding Nelson whose arm was slightly bent. "Penny hurt Nelson."

"Oh no, it's all right Penny. That wasn't your fault." She shook her head, taking Nelson from her. "You couldn't help landing on him."

"Her hand is scratched up." Charles crawled forward to be beside them.

"Penny okay." Penny sighed, seemingly more concerned for Nelson.

"I'm okay Miss—Miss—Miss Penny. It was an acc—acc—accident," Nelson assured.

"Might be a wire loose. I'm sure you'll be able to fix him." Julietta handed him back to the girl. "You and Ola all right?"

"As rain," Ola chuffed. "Which has started just in time for the rover to break down."

"Sounds like one of the treads might have snapped," Byron grumbled. "Julie, mind lending a hand?"

While Julietta and Byron checked on the rover, Charles's attention went to Penny's hand.

"Does it hurt, Penny?"

She shook her head, holding out her hand for Charles to see. Upon closer inspection he confirmed it was just a surface scrape.

"Might want to clean and bandage it up for tonight though if we are staying here. Just for precaution."

"Nelson hurt."

"Yes, but I think Dr. Penny can take care of him after we take care of her hand, okay?"

Penny nodded just as Julietta climbed back into the rover, soaked. "Well, we've managed to slide it back into place, but it won't last long.

Byron's gonna try to limp it to that house over there with the garage. Then he and I can hopefully get a better fix."

Byron managed to limp the rover within a couple of hundred feet of the house before it slipped again, this time unable to be temporarily patched. The rain, as if to spite them, was now coming down in buckets. Charles carried Ola into the house, leaving Penny with her while he, Byron, and Julietta pushed the rover the rest of the way into the garage before unloading all their gear. Drenched, he insisted everyone change into dry clothes before letting Byron and Julietta loose on the vehicle.

Laying out Penny's sleeping bag and wrapping a blanket around her shoulders Charles sighed. "You okay, Penny?"

"Yes, Papa."

Ola, who was seated beside Penny on her own sleeping bag, smiled. "At least it's dry in here. Hopefully, Byron and Julietta can get the rover fixed."

"Jul will figure it out." Charles shrugged, setting to work collecting wood before attempting to start a fire.

The house Byron had picked was indeed dry, for the most part, the central room, which looked to have been a kitchen and living space, determined the most suitable for temporary shelter. The roof had a few small leaks and the windows had some cracks, with one being now a sizable hole where a glass pane once sat. It, however, wasn't anything they could not patch up for the night if needed given the debris around.

"We may be dry but the wood sure isn't," Charles grumbled, having tried and failed to get the wood to light with the fire sparker.

Penny watched curiously, thinking. "Penny help?"

"It's all right, Penny, I'll get it working."

The girl frowned, crawling up to the edge of the stone-lined fire pit Charles had made. "Penny help Papa spark." She let a few sparks dance on her fingers.

Charles stopped, a curious expression dancing across his face realizing what Penny was suggesting. "All right, but be careful, as soon as you see smoke pull your hand away."

Penny placed her hand over the driest part of the wood, letting sparks come to dance between her fingers. Once she felt she had enough, she carefully began to manipulate them to fall around the wood, producing a little more with each pass until embers began to form.

"That should do it," he instructed, moving to stoke the embers. In a matter of seconds, there was a warm fire.

"Penny make fire!" Penny cheered.

"Yes, Penny make fire," he chuckled, a glint of pride in his eyes. "Thank you."

She hugged Charles before moving back beside Ola.

"That was unique," Ola quirked an eyebrow. "Where did you learn to do that?"

"Penny watch Papa. Papa make sparks like Penny, but Papa sparks not as hot. Penny burn before so Penny think Penny make fire if try."

"Penny has burned things before?"

"Penny burn Turner man when try to hurt friends," Penny frowned, looking sheepish. "Penny did what needed."

"That was…smart, I suppose."

Charles, who had started cooking dinner, was about to intervene when Penny piped up. "Penny only burn to defend not hurt. Papa and Momma told Penny gift is good if Penny use good. Penny try be good and want good. Gift is tool like knife for cut pancakes."

Ola looked over to Charles who was grinning from ear to ear. "Your parents are teaching you right, Penny."

"All right, my little spark, now that you got a fire going and I have some water boiling for cooking, mind if I take a look at that hand of yours before you start working on Nelson?"

Penny nodded, holding out her hand. Charles did not take long cleaning and bandaging it. "It's not bad, but I don't want it to get infected while we travel. You have to keep it clean and tell me if it hurts worse, okay?"

"Yes, Papa." Penny smiled, sticking out her tongue slightly. "CCCs help?"

"Yes, CCCs may help." Charles kissed Penny on the forehead. "But *after* dinner."

Penny pouted, crossing her arms.

"Penny…" He raised an eyebrow, smirking.

Penny could not keep up her charade and began to laugh.

"That's what I thought." He shook his head before turning his attention to Ola. "Ola, you got the food for tonight in your bag, right?"

"Yep, I have tonight's rations, some bread, and soup."

"Perfect. Mind if I—"

"By all means."

While Charles continued on dinner, Penny took out her tools and started to work on Nelson.

Ola watched in awe as little Penny easily repaired the minor dents before adjusting Nelson's wires, assuring they were tight before closing the robot back up and turning him on.

"Ah, that feels better. Thank you, Miss Penny."

"Welcome, Nelson." Penny smiled, putting her tools away.

Nelson walked over to Ola. "Greetings, Miss Ola."

"Greetings, Nelson. I see your creator takes good care of you."

"Miss Penny is my friend. She takes good care of my Margie and me."

"I see. Just how did Miss Penny create you?"

"Penny found in museum in Watwelt," Penny replied, shifting a bit closer to Ola.

"You found him in a museum? But how did you bring him to life?"

"Penny learn pictures in museum how to wire. Penny slowly learn read from Momma and later Papa. Then Penny read. Make sense like sparks."

Ola looked over to Charles incredulously.

"She's telling the truth. Julietta can attest to it. I believe it also has something to do with her gift. Most of the children in Iota were like her. Depending on their gift they had a…knack for a particular subject. There was one student I talked to a bit who could manipulate liquids, you should hear what he had to say about art and color. I bet if he had the chance, he could be an amazing art restorer and artist."

Ola smiled sadly. "If he only had the chance."

"Miss Ola tink of brother." Penny looked up at the woman curiously. "Miss Ola miss brother?"

Charles frowned. "Penny, you shouldn't ask—"

"No, no, it's quite all right, Charles. Yes, I was thinking of my brother. How did you know?"

"Miss Ola sad." Penny hugged Ola. "Miss Ola sad when tink of brother."

"Yes, Miss Ola is sad about her brother," Ola sighed, a tear in her eye. "That's why Miss Ola helped start the Constellation with Byron. To help her brother and other kids like Byron's son and you."

Penny quirked an eyebrow. "Miss Ola okay?"

"Miss Ola is okay."

Penny nodded with a yawn, whatever she was thinking lost to exhaustion as she shifted to lying down, her head in Ola's lap. "Penny nap now."

Charles moved to grab another blanket. "Sorry, I can move her."

"No, no. Just cover her with a blanket. I don't mind." Ola brushed a piece of hair from Penny's face.

Placing a blanket over Penny, he handed her Margie. "I'll wake you up for dinner, okay?"

Penny nodded, her eyes landing on Charles's scarred cheek for a moment, a flash of understanding as to why he had it in her eyes. "Love Papa."

"Love you too, my little spark."

Dinner was nearly ready when Julietta and Byron returned.

"I think I got it." Julietta smirked, wiping her forehead and accidentally smearing some grease on it.

"I'd say she did. Might even run better than before." Byron chuckled. "You have one heck of a mechanic for a wife, Charlie."

"Both my girls are amazing." Charles beamed, walking over to Julietta with a small towel, and wiping the grease from her forehead. "Penny got the fire going. Oh, and I bandaged up her hand as a precaution from earlier. Nothing to worry about, just with the weather and travel…"

"That's my girl and good call doctor," Julietta teased, kissing him on the cheek. "Thank you."

"Even more reason not to go back out in the rainstorm tonight. Wouldn't want to waste this beautiful fire Penny made." Byron relaxed, taking a seat beside Ola. "Even with the fix, I'd rather head out when the ground isn't a swamp."

"Definitely." Julietta sat down beside the fire while Charles began dishing up food.

Smelling the soup, Penny stirred. "Dinn dinn?"

"Yes, dinner is ready." Ola chuckled.

"CCCs after?" Penny sat up, giving Charles a pointed look that made everyone laugh.

"Of course, Penny, Doctor's orders."

CHAPTER 39

Curied.

Small for their age.
Stunted growth partially due to malnutrition.
Possibly due to daily medicine mentioned?

Speech is non-existent or very immature for their age.
Trained to be silent. Not allowed to socialize.

Refers to self in the third person.
Aware the name they use is not their name.
Cannot remember real names.
Names are given by other students?

Hyper Intelligent.
Special interest in a subject related to their power.
Protégés?

Hyper Aware of body language.
Learned behavior as a survival tactic.

How can anyone do this to children?

Charles's brow furrowed, his mind turning. It had been nearly two days since the rover had broken down again, this time near a set of rocky outcroppings. With rain inevitable, they had been forced to seek shelter in a nearby cave up a slope, leaving the rover to be drenched and sink into the now swampy ground. Once the rain had stopped, he, Julietta, and Byron spent the better half of the next day pulling it out of the mud and to higher ground. With still at least three days of travel by rover between them and Apolis, things were not looking great.

The Human Genome - Designer Humans - Curied?
Iso-210 -> Isotope 210?
HL-138 -> Half-life 138?
Polonium?

Why such an unstable material?

Turner's genetics seemed to be a combination of traits found in Curied.

Turners need to be 'refreshed' due to rapid cell growth side effects.

Is this causation or correlation?

Having returned to the cave to relieve Ola from watching Penny for a bit, Charles worked on his extrapolations of Dr. Cone's notebooks. Given the ample time to read while traveling, he had begun piecing together a theory regarding why the children had the powers they do. Lost in his thoughts, he almost did not hear Penny approach.

"What Papa write?" Penny asked curiously, taking a seat beside him.

"Well, Papa is writing down some ideas he's had since we left Matson."

"Ideas for new med?"

"Not exactly." He frowned, debating slightly whether to tell Penny. "While I was working at Iota, I found some notebooks that had some rather scary things written in them. I took them before Iota was destroyed and have been reading them to try to understand what exactly the purpose of the schools is." He hesitated, unsure how Penny would react to his next piece of information. "Based on what I've been reading, I think I may have an idea as to why you can make sparks."

"Scary notebooks from school explain Penny?" Penny frowned, looking down at her hands. "Penny scary?"

"No, no sweetie," he shook his head, placing an arm around Penny and kissing the top of her head. "The science of the person whose

305

notebooks I read was scary. It has nothing to do with you specifically. You are beautiful, Penny. Your sparks are beautiful."

"Penny gift good if Penny good. Penny try be good. Penny learn be good from Momma and Papa."

"Exactly, Penny." His shoulders slumped. "I'm sorry, Penny, I never want you to think that your—"

"You say might know reason Penny have gift?"

"Yes, I have a theory."

"Teory Arcane?"

"Yes." He chuckled. "An Arcane theory."

"Tell Penny?" She looked up at him, eyes wide.

"You sure you want to know?"

The girl nodded, smiling slightly. "Penny brave."

"Well, a long time ago, way before any of us, there was the Great War."

"Bomb rain," Penny frowned, snuggling a bit closer to Charles.

"Yes, the bomb rain." He held her a bit tighter. "During the rain of bombs, there were some that had some dangerous components to them aside from the boom ones."

"Bomb not just boom?"

Charles shook his head. "No, there were some bombs that had other things in them. Things that were bad for people to be near. These things affected people medically speaking. Over time those effects were passed down through what is called DNA and started to be more…pronounced in those people's children."

"Penny power from parents?"

"To a degree, yes. Your powers were given to you by your biological parents."

"Gov. Lisle no powers. Mai powers. How?"

"Well, DNA is funny like that. Sometimes things show and sometimes they don't. Now this is just a theory, a logical guess. I don't exactly have a way to prove it true. I'm making these ideas from what I've read and seen."

Penny sat up slightly, her head tilting to the side. "Penny power from parent. Penny see other kids' power different. Other kids don't know parent." She scrunched her nose. "Penny don't remember before. That why Penny, Penny. Penny called Penny by student secret talk in Rho. Penny name necklace coin."

"I'm sorry, Penny." Charles shook his head. "I didn't mean to upset you."

She furrowed her brow. "Penny not upset. Penny tinking. School use strange tings to read and stop power. Why?"

"That's what we're trying to figure out."

"Penny wonder lots tings from school, but Penny happy not in school. Penny like learn from Papa and Momma instead." She smiled. "Penny love Momma and Papa."

Just at that moment, Julietta appeared looking frustrated.

"I can't fix it," she huffed, sitting down beside Charles and Penny.

"What happened? Where's Byron and Ola?"

"Discussing how we can possibly get to Apolis now," she grumbled, kicking some rocks. "I couldn't fix it."

Penny shifted to sitting between her parents. "Momma okay?"

Julietta looked over to Penny, frowning. "Sorry, Penny. I am upset, I can't fix the rover."

Penny tilted her head slightly. "That otay, Momma. Not fault rover broke, like when Penny broke Nelson."

"Oh, Penny." Her shoulders relaxed slightly as she shook her head. "Problem is we still have a long way to go to Apolis."

"I am sure you did everything you could. Unfortunately, it was a bad time and place situation," Charles shrugged. "We don't exactly have a workshop around here."

"No, I suppose not."

Penny moved to grab her bag, pulling out Margie. "Momma hug Margie. Make Penny feel good." She held out Margie, a crooked smile on her face.

Julietta chuckled slightly, taking the plush robot and hugging it. "Thank you, Penny. Now how about a hug from you?"

Penny moved to sit in Julietta's lap, hugging her tightly. "Now Momma kiss Papa?"

Charles and Julietta burst out laughing.

"Penny serious," the girl pouted.

"All right, if you insist." Julietta kissed Charles on the cheek. "Better, Penny?"

Penny stuck out her tongue slightly. "Now CCCs?"

"Penny…" Charles shook his head, laughing. "CCCs are for after dinner."

"Otay," she sighed. "Penny go check Sir Byron and Miss Ola?"

"Yes, you can go check on them," Julietta agreed. "But be careful."

They both watched to be sure Penny got down the slope to where they could see Byron and Ola still were.

"Jul?"

She turned back to Charles, her smile falling. "I know Penny tried, but—"

"I know." He shook his head, brushing some hair from her face. "But don't beat yourself up about it. We'll figure it out. Right now, I think your mind needs a break. You've been working on that rover since late yesterday."

"Right as always, doctor." She leaned back against the cave wall. "Honestly, between fixing the rover and my nerves about Apolis, I'm fried."

"You and me both." He moved in closer. "Come here."

He shifted beside her, letting her rest her head on his shoulder, a protective arm around her.

As they sat in comfortable silence, Julietta felt Charles's hand on her side begin to fidget with the fabric of her duster. "You're thinking about the notebooks, aren't you?"

"That obvious?"

"Any new ideas?"

"A few. I was telling Penny I have a theory as to why she has powers."

"Oh?"

"Radiation. The bombs from the Great War had radiation. Cone's notes talked about it. It mutates DNA. With the passing cycles, it may have mutated to the point where you have people with powers like Penny."

"The polonium…an interesting theory…wait! Didn't Turner call himself…Curied? As in—"

"Madame Marie Curie? I remember reading about her in Waterwealt."

"Same. She researched radiation. Discovered polonium if I recall."

Charles pulled Julietta in close. "Did I ever tell you, you are a genius?"

"You could stand to tell me more, Dr. Milard-Hawthorne." She chuckled teasingly.

"I could stand to do a lot of things, Mrs. Milard-Hawthorne. Although most of them, I have a feeling, would end with us lying down."

She shifted in his arms, resting a hand on his chest before running her fingers playfully across it. "You know, we haven't had much chance to tend to our Fallen-in-love-itis."

THE LUCKY PENNY

"I know," he smirked, pulling her fully into his arms. "Not since that one small town just before the rover broke down. The shower…"

"Then the bedroom." She bit her lip, running a hand down the side of his face. "We were lucky the walls weren't so thin that anyone could hear."

"I don't know about that…Byron was smirking at me the next morning."

Julietta's eyes went wide. "Tell me you are joking."

"Maybe…"

"Charlie…"

"Jul…" He stuck out his tongue. "I am teasing."

"You dirty scoundrel." She made a face.

"I love it when you scrunch your nose when you are angry."

"Charlie, I—"

Whatever she was about to say was lost as Charles leaned in close, his eyes staring into hers.

"Yes?"

She couldn't keep up her charade. She smiled. "I love you."

"Love you too, Jul," he smirked as he kissed her, Julietta reciprocating, deepening it.

"Charlie…" She sighed, as he pulled away slightly. "I—Do you— When this is all over…Do you want to go back to Matson?"

"I've thought about it. Lisle did offer to find us a place there."

"There was a museum, an abandoned one we walked past almost every day."

"I saw it too." He raised an eyebrow. "Maybe?"

"Maybe." Julietta chuckled, closing her eyes. "I'd love it."

"I'd love any place, so long as I'm with you and our Penny." He kissed her forehead, relaxing back completely against the wall. "Rest now a bit. We have a long journey still ahead of us."

CHAPTER 40

After a break, Julietta figured out a plan for how to help Ola: a modified wheelchair. Using some of the smaller treads from the rover and some ingenuity, she, with Charles's help, was able to line the wheels so they could handle the rough terrain with Charles and Byron agreeing to help carry her over the worst of it if needed. Spending one day more to distribute the rest of their gear amongst them the best they could, they set off the following morning.

It was near sunset when they reached Apolis, a whole three weeks since they left Matson. The final leg of the journey certainly had not been easy. The Damp season was living up to its name, a near-constant drizzle now soaking them to the bone. This was made worse by the random storms that would start without warning, sending them running for the nearest form of shelter. By the time they entered the city, they were extremely tired, hungry, muddy, and feeling none too well.

"Is she all right?" Byron coughed, pushing Ola's wheelchair through the rather narrow streets.

Julietta placed her hand on Penny's forehead. "She's okay, I think. Not too warm or cold. Just a bit sniffly."

"Once we get to the Constellation, I'll make sure to check her over." Charles, who was carrying Penny, sighed, shaking his head. "Honestly, I don't feel all that great myself. A full meal, hot shower, and warm bed sound lovely right about now."

"Penny tired," the little girl whispered softly, snuggling more into Charles's shoulder.

"I can hold her for a bit if you want?" Ola offered. "I don't mind her sleeping in my lap."

"No, it's all right," he smiled, giving Byron, who looked exhausted, a sympathetic glance. "It's better we keep moving."

"This is it." Byron's brow furrowed, looking around the dim alleyway. It was well after dark when they reached the rendezvous point, Penny's flashlights lighting the way. "I didn't expect a welcoming committee, but I'd hoped it would be more obvious where to go." Locking Ola's chair, he began to explore the area for a sign of what they were to do.

"Jul, can you adjust Penny's hood? It's slipping," Charles asked, turning slightly toward her.

"You okay, my little spark?" Julietta asked as she adjusted her hood.

"Penny sleep." Penny coughed. "Penny want CCCs."

"I know, Penny. You haven't had any CCCs in a few days. I promise we'll get you some soon," she frowned, kissing her forehead.

"I am inclined to agree with you, Penny." Ola sighed. "I am tired and starving." Unlocking her wheels, she turned toward Byron. "Any luck?"

"Nothing so far…I—"

"Hold it right there."

Everyone froze.

"Hands up."

Byron immediately raised his hands. Ola, and Julietta followed suit as five figures dressed in black appeared, surrounding them.

"We mean no harm, we just—"

"Sir, they have a child with them," said the masked figure nearest Charles, the voice of a woman.

Penny visibly shirked away as Charles tightened his grip on her. "She's our daughter."

"Likely story," spat the masked man in front of Byron. "Grab her."

The masked woman, who had pointed out Penny, reached for her.

"No!" Julietta immediately pounced, grabbing the figure while Charles attempted to flee, unfortunately finding himself blocked in by another masked opponent.

"Grab them!"

There were shouts, hands roughly grabbing Byron and Ola, the former forced to his knees. Julietta, having succeeded in pulling the figure from Penny and Charles, was now in a grappling match. Charles, backed into a corner, placed Penny between him and the wall, using his body as a shield before drawing his gun.

"Cygnus and Corvus are in Retrograde!" Byron shouted.

The masked assailants froze. The silence that followed, deafening. "Boötes are about," the masked man in front of him stated, warily. "Lupus shall rise," the older man replied, sounding weary.

There was a moment's pause. "They are friends."

The masked figure who was grappling Julietta let her go. Julietta stumbled back toward Charles.

"Jul!" He gasped as she slumped against the wall beside him.

"I'm…okay…" she panted, though he could see a bruise forming on the side of her face.

"I'm so sorry." The masked woman pulled down her duster revealing her face.

Charles lowered his gun but kept it in hand as the woman knelt in front of them. "We've had some trouble lately and—"

Julietta shook her head. "It's fine. I'm fine."

The other masked figures all lowered their dusters, two men and two women. The man in front of Byron helped him to his feet. "I'm sorry, Sir Byron, but things have gotten worse since we last had contact. I'll have Ava explain. Come, let's get you all to the base."

The Constellation base, much to Julietta's delight, was in an abandoned art and history museum. Lead past various exhibits of ancient civilizations, the rise of man, and the eventual peak before the fall, Charles could see a child-like wonder in Julietta's eyes that he had not seen since they left Waterwealt. It made him smile.

"We've moved in here a couple of cycles back," explained the man who introduced himself as Thomas. "It's not slated for restoration yet by the administration but is a protected site. Makes it the perfect place to hide."

Being so late there was nearly no one around, save a few members who were on night shift keeping watch, each giving the group a sympathetic look as they passed. They had seen people like them before, dirty, tired, and weary.

Taking them to an exhibit on the government from the before times, Thomas elaborated on how they had, over time, retrofitted the museum to their needs. "The offices are now sleeping quarters, the cafeteria is back in use, and this exhibit is where the radio operators work, and Ava keeps herself."

Entering the replica of the pre-war government offices, they were met by a woman with auburn hair seated at a large desk. She looked to be no older than Charles, maybe a few cycles his senior. Her green eyes however held deep sorrow and weight. Beside her was a rather large radio and stacks of papers.

"Corvus, Cygnus," the woman stated, with no inflection in her familiar voice.

"Pyxis," Byron smiled. "It's good to finally see you, Ava."

"It is, my friend. Please, be seated."

Thomas briefed Ava on their unfortunate initial meeting while everyone situated themselves. Ola rolled up to the desk, setting her brakes, while Byron took the cushioned seat beside her. Julietta flopped down into another cushioned seat opposite him, Charles giving her Penny who immediately curled up in her lap, tired. Charles himself, however, still on edge, leaned on the arm of the chair, his arms crossed.

"You can sit, Charles," Byron frowned. "No need to be rude."

"It's quite all right. Given what Thomas just told me, I don't exactly blame him for being defensive," Ava sighed, sending Thomas away as she took her seat. "I am truly sorry about that. As I am sure you've been made aware, there have been problems."

Charles relaxed his shoulders. "Yes, we've heard but not been given details."

"Allow me to enlighten you then." She leaned forward on the desk. "We've lost contact with the network."

"What?" Ola's face went pale, an expression shared by everyone. "What do you mean?"

"Did you ever discover how you were caught at Iota? During your last transmission, you mentioned they knew you were coming."

"An unfortunate slip." Julietta sunk into her seat. "Someone overheard a couple of agents talking at the clinic about our plans and warned them." She gave a glance up to Charles, a silent understanding of why she did not name Henrietta as the slip-up. The poor woman had suffered enough after the fact when it was discovered someone had overheard her.

Ava shook her head. "That was the only accident then."

"How many, Ava?" Byron's voice quivered.

She opened her desk, pulling out a clipboard. "Statuses as of the last 24 hours...Varington Beta-763, no response. Rinby Gamma-732, no response. Krine Delta-951, no response. Bragas Epsilon-182, abandoned after researching Ciysea's destruction. They found evidence suggesting they were next."

She continued to rattle off names and facilities. In total, of the 24 Constellation outposts, six were confirmed abandoned including Matson, their members scattered to the winds with a few now working with the Apolis satellite. One of them, Horidge Psi-990, managed to destroy its institute rescuing 149 kids before abandoning. Aside from Ciysea and Ambleton, four more satellites had been completely wiped out: Crecwood three surviving members, Evrine two, Sirie none, and Vexledo none. The other 10 had not responded, including Johani.

"We are preparing for the worst. Sleburn contacted us first a couple of days into Damp. They discovered Vexledo before abandoning their own post. Hinburg contacted the next day, discovering Sirie. Then it was Akacaster, their agents all killed in Lambda-158. We made the decision to send out a warning...then the lines went silent." Ava's voice grew quiet, sounding almost on the verge of tears. "As far as we know, only Apolis stands."

The room was silent. The weight of the news covered everyone like a wet blanket. Even Penny, who was half asleep, found herself sitting up, a deep sadness on her face.

"Con—Const—Constellation still here," the little girl stuttered. "Constellation save Penny. Constellation save Nic. Constellation save gift kids." Penny looked over to Ava and smiled. "Constellation here."

"Yes, Penny. The Constellation is still here," the woman smiled sadly. "And we will do everything we can to save the kids like you."

Julietta hugged Penny. "Always, Penny."

Charles held out a hand to the girl. She took it immediately. "Exactly, my little spark."

"A child wise beyond her cycles." Byron sighed, rubbing his face with his hands. "Ava, this all has been very heavy, and we have come very far."

The woman's face flushed, for the first time realizing the state of the people in front of her. "Oh, yes, of course." She reached for a talker that she had lying on the desk. "Karrie, could you come up to my office? Tell Parker to come as well, please."

A few minutes later, Karrie, the woman who bruised Julietta appeared looking sheepish. "Miss Ava, I can explain."

Ava quirked an eyebrow. "Explain?"

Before Karrie could reply Julietta spoke up. "No hard feelings. I understand why you did what you did. You didn't know. You were only worried about my child."

Karrie relaxed, still looking embarrassed. "It won't happen again, miss."

"I can assure you it won't." Ava's brow furrowed. "Karrie, would you please see these good folks to their rooms? The ones reserved for Sir Byron and those traveling with him. I've already sent Thomas to make some food. It should be ready in the cafeteria when you are done getting yourselves settled."

"Thank you, Ava." Ola smiled, everyone, echoing the sentiment as they made to leave.

Before they reached the door, Ava beckoned to Byron. "Byron, could you wait a moment?"

The older man waved everyone forward. Once they were gone, he turned back to Ava. "Yes?"

"Psi-990. That was where your son was taken."

"Yes," he frowned. "Did…did you find something about him?"

"We found his file."

He leaned against the side of one of the chairs, looking defeated. "He's dead, isn't he?"

"Not exactly."

"He's a Bell?"

Before she could respond a young man appeared in the office space. "Miss Ava, you wished to see me?"

"Yes, Parker. I'd like you to meet Sir Byron Galigar."

Byron watched Parker's eyes grow wide, his green eyes.

"Byron, I'd like you to meet Parker West." Ava swallowed, nervously. "I think you two need to have a conversation."

After cleaning up and changing into some fresh clothes, Julietta, Charles, Penny, and Ola were escorted to the cafeteria where Thomas had laid out a decent spread of food.

"I'm sorry it's not much. The food during the day is better when made by our resident chef," he explained.

"It's perfect. Thank you." Charles smiled, relieved to just have a hot meal.

"Tank you!" Penny agreed, taking a big spoon of mashed potatoes from the bowl on the table. "Potatoes yum!"

Everyone chuckled as they began to eat. They were nearly finished by the time Byron appeared, a young man by his side.

"Byron, we were wondering what happened to you." Ola sighed, taking a sip of tea.

Julietta quirked an eyebrow as she turned her attention to him. "You okay? You look like you've seen a ghost."

"Everyone this…this is Parker West," Byron replied, his voice a bit shaky. "I knew him, a long, long time ago."

"Pleasure to meet you, Parker." Charles raised an eyebrow. "How do you know Byron if you don't mind me asking?"

Parker glanced at Byron, giving him a nod.

"The last time I saw Parker was more than 16 cycles ago. Back then he went by a different name." He placed a hand on Parker's shoulder, giving a sad smile. "Everyone, I'd like you to meet my son…Francis Galigar."

CHAPTER 41

Charles dropped his fork, Ola set down her teacup with a clatter, and Julietta dropped the roll she just grabbed back in the basket. Standing in front of them was Francis, Byron's son.

Without missing a beat, Penny reached for a chocolate chip cookie from the plate in front of her. "CCC?" She smiled, holding it out to Parker.

"Why, thank you," he chuckled, taking the cookie. "Based on everyone's reactions, I suppose I have a lot to explain."

Taking a seat at the table everyone waited patiently for Byron to fill his plate and start eating before Parker began.

"I should start at the beginning." Parker sighed, his hands clasped nervously in front of him. "I will say, I don't remember much from before I was taken. Like most, my memory was taken. It was about 17 cycles ago. I was around nine or ten. I remember Apolis, and a strange dressed man."

"Turner man." Penny frowned.

"Yes, Turner…that was the name. He brought me to be tested more. It's a—a blur, to be honest. I remember my things being taken and given a uniform, all gray. The next thing, I was in a new place, Rho, I think. That was my first school."

Everyone remained silent as the young man went into detail regarding his time at Rho. His story was eerily similar to Penny's. Charles and Julietta's gaze fell to Penny who sat quietly, her eyes locked on Parker.

"Doctors poked and prodded me. I was hooked to machines and forced to use my powers under the watchful eyes of Mr. Bell. It was…"

"We know," Julietta sighed, taking Charles's hand. "Sorry, continue."

The man nodded, a sympathetic look on his face. "I lost any sense of myself when I entered Apolis. Any left, buried at Rho. I was not Francis but L-1611811518, Curied, an experiment, not even human."

Parker paused, taking a necklace out from beneath his shirt. "I was given this coin to identify me. It's a penny coin, I believe. Marked with what I was told was an alchem symbol for sub-li-mation."

"Penny has Penny too." Penny held out her necklace.

He gave her a sad smile. "You were called Penny by those in your dorms?"

The girl nodded. "Parker called Parker by Rho secret friends?"

"Yes, I was Parker by my fellow classmates." He sighed, shaking his head. "Those kids were the reason I didn't completely lose myself. Without them...I was transferred about three cycles later, Psi. By then, I was thin and silent. I was lost. I existed and that's it. Then, a few weeks into Psi I overheard something. Some staff talked about a rumor. Apparently, people were starting to de- defect from the school's work. I knew they were telling the truth. That's my power. I am a human lie detector. It was enough to give me hope. From that moment on, I—I started to listen to the people around me and think of ways I could escape. I refused to just exist. I wanted to live."

By this point, Byron had finished his meal and was sitting silently. His head bowed.

"I listened for anything that could get me out of Psi. Eventually, news of a secret group forming reached my ears, but it was not near Psi. As I was near my 16th cycle, I was told of being sent back to Apolis. I knew I had to escape then. In my snooping and listening in, I learned about the location of the truck drop off. The night before I was to be shipped back to Apolis, I snuck out in one of the trucks heading for Horidge. The minute it stopped I ran. The drivers nearly caught me, chasing me for blocks. I thought I was done when a man grabbed me and pulled me into the storage room of his shop. The man's name was Calvin West."

"It turned out he and his wife, Amelia, had been watching the trucks from school and had seen me run. They were part of the upstart group called the Constellation. I fell ill the next day; in wi—withdrawal, I was told. The next few weeks were a blur as Amelia took care of me. Once I was able, we moved to Ambleton to join the Constellation base being established there. It would be safer, given my history."

The memory of Penny, sick and injured, flashed through Julietta's mind. Withdrawal had been the illness the girl had suffered from.

"Without any memory or ID, it was easy for them to claim I was their son and get the papers for it. Once I was nearly recovered, I began working at the general store in Ambleton, the front for the Constellation there. They also helped teach me the things I should have learned in school. Then when I turned 18 cycles, they offered me the chance to work for the group itself as an in—interrogator and information retriever. I accepted."

"All this time, you were a part of the Constellation…" Ola sat wide-eyed. "You had no idea it was your own father who started it…looking for you."

"Yes." Parker smiled at Byron, placing a hand on his shoulder. "I worked with the Ambleton group for many cycles. Of course, none of my missions sent me to schools, but I did my best with my b—boundaries. I didn't start putting two and two together about my real father until after I arrived at Apolis. The night we were attacked, Calvin and Amelia were not there. They had been tasked with something in the city. I found them later that night after I escaped and informed them of what happened. They were heading to another city last I heard to warn. I chose to come here in the hopes of helping out more. It was about a week after I arrived, I heard Byron's voice on Ava's radio talking about Julietta and Charles in Iota. There was a part of me that knew the voice, though my mind had lost the memory."

Penny moved to sit in Charles's lap, snuggling into his chest as he wrapped an arm around her.

"I asked Ava about him. She explained he was one of the founders who had lost his son Francis long ago. It was as if a light switched on in my head. Some part of me deep down knew Byron was my father. I didn't say anything, instead I spent some time mulling this over. Eventually, I told Ava my theory and asked if there was a way to prove it and there was. Byron, in his wisdom, had someone at Johani run a DNA analysis on him. The re—results were given to the Constellation in the hopes that someday someone would find me. It was confirmed a few days before you arrived."

The room remained silent as Parker finished, no one quite sure what to say.

"I…I never stopped looking for you." Byron shook his head, tears in his eyes, as he looked at his son. "I hoped beyond all else you were alive."

"I'm alive and here to help." Parker took his father's hand. "I've heard from Ava all about you and your amazing friends." He glanced over to Julietta, Charles, and Penny. "And now that you are all here, hopefully, we can finally put an end to all this madness."

"Yes," Charles hugged Penny, who had fallen asleep on him, a bit tighter. "Hopefully we can end all this."

Julietta squeezed Charles's hand, resting her head on his shoulder. "Tonight we rest. Tomorrow we plan."

"Agreed." Byron leaned back in his chair. "The hour is late and though I usually don't play this card, I am getting old," he chuckled. "Three weeks of travel takes it out of you."

"Three weeks of travel would have taken it out of me too," Parker laughed. "Tomorrow, afternoon, Ava will see you all. For now, let's get some rest."

Byron and Ola immediately began planning out the next steps for the Constellation. Charles, Julietta, and even Penny were put to work. Charles was given full access to the medical wing of the base both for research and in anticipation of more satellites arriving. In the interim, he would continue his work on genetic research as well as help those looking into methods for reversing the damage done to those in the schools.

Julietta, along with lending her first aid skills when new satellites arrived, began fortifying and modifying the base for the influx of members. Penny found herself spending most of her time with Ava and Karrie, modifying the radios and fixing up other small electronics for future use. However, whenever a new set of survivors arrived, she would join medical, learning some basic first aid as she delivered supplies and occasionally helped bandage someone up.

When Parker's adoptive parents appeared, he introduced them to Byron who thanked them for taking care of his son. Day after day, one by one, the fate of the remaining satellites came to light as their surviving members arrived at Apolis battered, bruised, and broken. Stories of attacks, bombs, and mysterious illnesses became the norm as slowly the remaining number of the 23 original satellites ticked down further and further.

It had been two weeks since arriving in Apolis, two days since the last satellite arrived, leaving only Johani as missing. With those who had arrived a few days ago well on the mend, Charles found himself in his office digging through some more of Dr. Cone's notes in the hopes of answering a curious question that had been nagging at the back of his mind for months. Lost in his work, he almost did not hear the sound of small mechanical feet walking toward him.

"Hello, Dr. Charlie."

Charles looked down to find Nelson standing beside him.

"Well, hello, Nelson." He looked confused, glancing around for Penny. "Uh, where's Penny?"

"Penny is with Julie at the moment. She sent me ahead to check on you."

"Oh, okay," he chuckled. "I'm quite fine, thank you. How about yourself?"

"I am doing good, Dr. Charlie. Margie and I are very happy with our current arrangement."

"I'm glad to hear it."

"What are you working on? Could I take a look?"

"Sure," Charles carefully picked up the robot, setting him on the desk. "I am looking into the genetic sequence that gives children like Penny their powers."

The mechanical man walked along the desk to the notebooks in front of Charles. "This one is yours, the other Cone's?"

"Yep. Cone was digging very deeply into this, but from his notes, he was flawed in his thinking. No wonder he was interested in my work."

"What will you do when you figure this out?"

"Well, honestly, I am not fully sure." He paused, his brow furrowed. "I do not intend to release this information with J.H. still around, that's for sure. Research like this needs to be handled delicately so it is only used for good like understanding and treating diseases or, in the case of powers, understanding where they come from so they can better be handled medically speaking going forward. There is no reason to fear these powers people have. They are a natural progression based on my research."

"What do you mean by handle medically?"

"The powers come from genetic changes. Much like how a person's hair or eye color is a predisposition based on their parents, powers too could act like that. If the parents carry the gene, the child may have powers. If that is the case, then we can assure them that they are normal and can live a healthy life. I am looking into whether this gene can cause any problems, but thankfully so far it seems it just manifests powers and not disease."

"That is good, I think." Nelson puttered, taking a seat on the desk. "Speaking of genetics, when are you and Julie going to give Penny a sibling?"

Charles burst out laughing. "What a question..."

"Miss Penny tells me she'd love to have a little brother or sister."

He leaned in, smirking. "Well, don't tell Penny this, but I'd very much like to give her a little brother or sister. The only thing is it isn't really safe right now. Hopefully soon though."

"Noted. I will not tell Miss Penny that."

"No, he won't, though she already heard it," came Julietta's voice from behind him, chuckling.

Charles turned to find Julietta and Penny at the door. Upon seeing him turn, Penny ran up to him, taking a seat on his lap. "Penny want brother or sister."

"How long have you been standing there?" He chuckled, wrapping an arm around his daughter.

"Not long." Julietta shrugged, leaning on the desk. "Actually, we heard your whole conversation from the apartment space."

"Huh? How?"

She pulled out one of their talkers. "Penny's been messing with the radios."

"Nelson mobile ear!" Penny cheered.

Charles turned to Nelson. "You were spying on me?"

"Miss Penny said it was not spying but scouting the area."

Charles turned back to Penny who was sticking out her tongue slightly. "Why, you little ninja!" he teased, tickling her. "Now you know that you can't use this feature all the time, correct?"

Penny nodded, giving him a crooked smile.

"Don't worry, I've already read her the riot act about what happens if she uses this out of turn." Julietta rolled her eyes teasingly, catching a glimpse of Charles's notes. "From what I heard, research is going well?"

"Yes, very." He paused, a silent concern passing across his face.

Julietta shifted slightly as her eyes came to rest on a highlighted piece of notes. "Comparison samples?"

"Yeah, I've been looking at my own DNA." Charles gestured to the microscope on the desk. "Could use a few more fresh samples to compare to the combinations found in Cone's notebook, but I don't feel comfortable—"

"You want mine?"

He quirked an eyebrow. "You'd be willing?"

"If it means possibly getting your research further." She slid a bit closer, placing a hand on his shoulder. "From what I heard through Nelson, the world needs your research, Charlie. It needs more people like you."

"Thank you." He bowed his head. "You know sometimes I wonder if it's too—"

"I know," she smiled sadly.

"Papa want Penny too?"

Charles looked at Penny. "Um..."

"Penny want help Papa."

He glanced at Julietta uneasily. "I don't know, Penny."

"If she wants to. It's her choice," she agreed. "I'm all right with it if she is."

Charles brow furrowed in though as Penny moved to stand in front of him.

"Papa?"

"Now, Penny." He bit his lip, nervously. "You are a smart girl. I want you to be fully aware of what you are offering. I am research-ing DNA. It's something that everyone has that explains a lot about why you are you. It is most easily found in the blood. If you are sure you want to, I would need to take a small blood sample from you. I would then put it on a slide like I have in the microscope and run some other tests on it."

"Penny see?"

He moved his chair, allowing Penny to approach the microscope and look in.

"That's my blood on the slide," he explained.

Penny gazed curiously into the microscope for about a minute before turning back to him. "Penny think interesting."

"Knowing all this, do you still want to give a sample?"

"Penny want help Papa make tings better." Penny placed her hand on her hips. "Penny brave."

"All right then, my little spark," Charles smiled. "Let me get the necessary things." Cleaning up his notebooks and grabbing the equip-ment, he stood beside the chair. "Who wants to go first?"

Penny immediately jumped in.

"All right, Penny, first I am going to clean a small spot on your inner elbow. Then I am going to draw the blood into this small tube. Okay?"

Penny nodded. "Penny brave."

He carefully drew a small vial. Setting it aside he cleaned up the small puncture, bandaging it. "You did very well, Penny. I order that you get an extra CCC tonight for being so good."

Charles put the girl's sample into cold storage and began to prep for Julietta.

"Momma next?" Penny beckoned Julietta over.

Trading places with Penny, Charles repeated the process on her. "Thank you." He sighed, as he placed Julietta's sample beside his and Penny's.

"No problem," Julietta assured. "It's for a good cause."

"Momma earn a kiss?" Penny teased, sticking out her tongue.

"Penny!" she chastised, though it held little in it.

"I believe Dr. Penny has determined your necessary recovery pre-scription." Charles laughed, shaking his head. "I'm inclined to agree with it."

"Well then, I will happily accept it," she teased as Charles bent down and kissed her lightly.

"Penny happy." Penny sighed, a bright smile on her face.

The moment was interrupted as Karrie appeared at the door.

"Good, you're all here. You're needed in the medical wing. Survivors from Johani have just arrived."

CHAPTER 42

"Auntie Marisa!" Penny shouted, racing towards the front of the medical wing.

Over the past couple of hours, Charles, along with Julietta and Penny, had been taking care of the various Johani members that trickled in. To their relief, most were unharmed save at most a few cuts and scrapes from travel. Turning toward the direction the child had run, Julietta and Charles breathed a sigh of relief seeing the Healeys.

"My, my, aren't you a sight for weary eyes." Marisa hugged Penny.

"Penny miss Auntie Marisa and Uncle Ollie." Penny smiled, turning to hug Oliver.

Tears sat in Marisa's eyes as Julietta and Charles approached. "We missed you too, Miss Penny."

"Thank the heavens you both are alive," Julietta greeted, hugging the woman.

"Alive, yes, and relatively intact," Oliver chuckled, hugging Penny back though holding his right arm away. "Mind taking a look at my arm, Charles?"

"Of course. I can check both of you over here. Aside from your arm, does anything else hurt?"

"I mean these old bones certainly ache having walked for many miles," Oliver chuckled. "But I think a good night's rest will do me just fine."

While Charles tended to Oliver, Julietta began to explain what had happened to them since they left Waterwealt.

"You had a rough journey to Matson," Marisa frowned. "Especially running into a Turner."

"Penny no like Turner man," Penny grimaced, having returned from grabbing her notebook. "Turner man bad."

"We had another run-in with a Turner in Matson." Julietta nodded toward Charles, explaining how they had joined the Constellation and her and Charles's work at Iota.

"Turner man hurt Papa," Penny pouted. "Penny defend friends."

"Sounds like you were very brave, Miss Penny." Oliver shook his head.

"She was. If it wasn't for her—" Charles stopped, letting the memory pass. "At least that Turner is gone."

Julietta continued to tell their story while he finished stabilizing Oliver's wrist. "Well, it is definitely sprained, based on the limited movement I'd also wager some hairline fractures. So long as we keep it stable it should heal up well enough. Once it does, I can show you some exercises to get strength back into it."

"Thank you," the older gentleman smiled.

"Penny, could you get me some more bandages?"

"Yes, Papa." Penny handed her journal to Marisa before racing off to get them.

"She speaks now." Marisa glanced down at the notebook. "Writes too…" She paused, raising an eyebrow. "Penny Milard-Hawthorne…"

"I was about to get to that," Julietta blushed. "The night before we left Matson…Charles and I were married by Lisle. We also asked Penny if…if she wanted to be officially adopted." She looked over to Charles who was grinning ear to ear. "She agreed wholeheartedly."

"Well, I'll be," Oliver smirked. "Guess you were right, Marisa. I owe you a date."

"Huh?" Charles looked confused. "Were you betting on something?"

Marisa started to laugh. "Oliver and I were betting on how long it would be before you two love birds made it official. I told him you'd marry before the cycle was over. He guessed this cycle."

"Seems like I missed by only a day though," Oliver teased, sticking his tongue out at his wife.

They were all laughing as Penny returned.

"What funny?" Penny asked, handing Charles the bandages.

"Oh, don't worry, Miss Penny. Just a silly bet between Oliver and me. We were wondering when your parents would get married."

"Penny happy Momma and Papa married," Penny smiled crookedly. "Asked to be officially Penny's. Penny said yes. Penny want both Momma and Papa name."

"Since we were to be officially Penny's..." Charles smirked. "We asked her to choose her last name. She wanted both so we all have both."

"You changed your name too, Charles?" Marisa quirked an eyebrow, smiling.

"Of course." Charles finished with Oliver's wrist, having him swap with Marisa so he could check her over next.

"Come here, Miss Penny," Oliver beckoned, helping her onto his lap. "Why don't you tell us about your trip to Apolis?"

Penny went on to explain, with some help from her parents, their trip to Apolis, showing Oliver her various journal entries.

"Penny write day in book to remember later. Penny want tell friends Nic and Mai in Matson next time."

"That's a very smart idea, Penny."

"Gov. Lisle gave Penny book."

"Everything looks good, Marisa," Charles assured as he finished checking her over. "Anything else I can do?"

"I am okay, thank you." Marisa's shoulders relaxed as she observed Penny excitedly showing Oliver some of the drawings she had made in her book. "You've done wonders for her, both of you."

"All she asked us is to be a normal kid," Charles shrugged. "We try our best."

"That's all you can do when it comes to children," Marisa chuckled. "Try your best."

"Thank you, Marisa," Julietta sighed, her shoulders slumping. "Not to change the subject but...um. We know bits and pieces from Byron when he spoke with Johani. What happened?"

"I had a feeling you'd ask that. No worries. As you know, Oliver and I set up a bakery in Johani to act as a front for the Constellation. After word got out about my delicious sweet bread it became quite the hot spot I must say. A perfect cover, and a perfect rumor mill. You'd be surprised how many folks are willing to talk when you sugar and butter them up with baked goods."

"Given how delicious your baked goods are, I have no doubt," Charles chuckled, finishing cleaning up his equipment and taking a seat.

"It was a couple of weeks ago, you all were already on your way to Apolis when we caught wind of a bomb test near Johani. One of the workers at Rho stopped in every morning for a muffin. They mentioned in passing to me about taking a vacation in the next few weeks about how I should do the same."

"Marisa had me run immediately to the Constellation," Oliver added. "Didn't take much for the agents to confirm the details. We were out of there within days."

Between Marisa and Oliver, they explained the trials and tribulations of travel, much of which was expected.

"Took us a while to find a town that was safe enough to supply at. By then many had deserted for other places." Marisa shook her head. "We passed through ol' Waterwealt on the way. Made a rather gruesome discovery."

"Turned out Harrison had gone back and done been murdered," Oliver frowned. "Found his body in the town hall. Most thought it was some bandits, but I found a 1950s-style hat nearby."

"Turner man." Penny shook her head.

"Yes, Miss Penny, Turner." Oliver patted her arm comfortingly. "We made sure to bury him proper but, needless to say, everyone was on edge."

Charles, Julietta, and Penny remained silent as they finished their story.

"All in all, not the worst journey here but taxing, nonetheless." Marisa sank slightly, exhaustion setting into her face.

"Penny, why don't you go and check with Ava? See if there is a room ready for Marisa and Oliver?" Julietta suggested.

Penny climbed off of Oliver's lap, giving him a sad smile before racing off once more.

"We do it for her." Oliver bowed his head. "We'd do it all again in a heartbeat."

"She called us Aunt and Uncle," Marisa chuckled. "Shall I take it she's adopted us?"

"Yes," Julietta confirmed. "If it makes you uncomfortable though—"

Marisa placed a hand on her arm. "Never. I am honored."

"I as well," Oliver echoed.

There was a silence that followed, the last obvious question lingering between them.

"My niece," Marisa's gaze fell to the floor. "When Iota was destroyed. Was she?"

"We don't know," Julietta swallowed a lump in her throat. "Many escaped that night. Likely as not, she escaped and is now at another facility. I know that is not a comfort, but—"

"It is, in some ways." Marisa looked over to Charles. "I know she is…not herself any longer, her mind taken. But…if she is alive, then there is a chance she can be saved?"

Charles leaned back in his seat, his brow furrowed. "Though my research is mainly in the genetics sector, I have been aiding in the search for a cure for the Bells. At the moment it comes down to what was used to wipe their memories in the first place. If we can pinpoint the chemicals there is potential to reverse the effects or at the very least counteract them so rehabilitation can take place."

"Rehabilitation?" Oliver looked nervous.

"Nothing invasive or harmful, I assure you. They are essentially, for lack of better terminology, psychologically brainwashed. Just as Penny needed time to process what happened to her and open up to us, so too will those turned into Bells." Charles's face fell. "I am not going to lie, it won't be easy given what Penny told us."

"Penny's told you her story?" Marisa asked, her voice quieter than usual.

"She did, in Matson," Julietta replied, her voice failing.

"I won't pry, but I trust it wasn't good." The woman shook her head. "All the more reason to continue our work."

At that moment Penny returned. "Room ready! Let's—" She stopped, seeing the sunken looks on all the adults' faces. "Oh, Penny too loud. Penny sorry."

"No, sweetie, you're all right." Charles beckoned her over. "You were a little loud but you're just excited to see your aunt and uncle. We were just talking about Marisa's niece."

Penny stood beside Charles, glancing over to Marisa and Oliver who gave her a sympathetic smile. "Told Auntie and Uncle Penny story?"

"No," Julietta took the girl's hand. "That is for you to tell them if you want. We told them only that you told us."

Penny nodded. "Penny tank…thank you. Penny tell Auntie Marisa and Uncle Oliver later. Room ready. Auntie and Uncle need rest."

"Well, you heard Dr. Penny's orders," Charles chuckled, standing. "Care to show them the way, Penny?"

"Penny show Auntie Marisa and Uncle Ollie to room." Penny held out her hands to Marisa and Oliver, both taking one as she happily, but slowly, led them to their room.

It had been a few days since Johani had arrived, an air of disquiet settling over the Constellation. With only Apolis left standing, everyone waited for Ola and Byron to decide what to do next. With nothing to do but keep working around the museum, Charles found himself spending hours in his private office analyzing the samples he had collected from Julietta, Penny, and himself.

Later in the evening, a bit after dinner, Charles had once more returned to his work. Head down in his notes, he did not hear the door open, or the footsteps cross the floor. It wasn't until gentle calloused hands came to rest on his shoulders that he realized he wasn't alone. Smiling he said nothing as the hands slowly began to massage his shoulders and neck, relieving the tension in them that he hadn't realized he had.

"And you say I have healing hands, Jul," he chuckled, leaning his head a bit further forward, allowing her better access to his neck.

"How did you know it was me?" Julietta laughed, her hands continuing to soothe.

"I'd know those hands anywhere," he smirked. "Plus, it's late. There is only one person I know who'd know to find me here at this hour."

She shook her head, reaching for the pen in his hand. "Speaking of the late hour…" He did not protest as she took the pen, tossing it on the desk. "You've been at it all day."

"You got me." His shoulders slumped. "Sorry, I'm just a bit nervous lately, as is everyone."

"I know." She pulled lightly on his shoulders, so he leaned back against her, her hands resting on his chest. "Apolis is the last satellite. Whatever Byron and Ola decide…"

"Exactly." Closing his eyes he relaxed into her. "At least we are safe for now. It's a shame we can't explore the city though. I'm sure there would be quite a lot of interesting sites to see."

"Yeah…Penny was saying how she missed being outside. Poor girl is cooped up just like the rest of us."

He rested one of his hands on Julietta's. "Our brave little girl."

"I heard you telling her earlier about the tests you ran on her sample. She looked so excited that it was helping you."

"I still feel a bit strange about it, but it did help me figure out a few things. I was just mapping her DNA in comparison to yours and mine."

"Oh?"

He shook his head, taking one of her hands and kissing it. "Later, I want to run a few more tests before I explain my theory."

"All right, Charlie," she sighed, running her thumb over his chest. "Why don't we head back to our room then? Penny is off with Karrie. Byron is with Ola. It's still early enough there won't be many, if anyone, around."

Charles opened his eyes, looking up at Julietta. "Is the good Dr. Julietta suggesting we tend to our itis?"

"Maybe," she chuckled, biting her lip. "I think the good Dr. Charlie could also use a bit of doctoring."

"Well, if you insis—"

Their conversation was interrupted as Ava appeared at the door. "There's been a development. You are needed in the atrium immediately. Bring your weapons, but keep them holstered just in case. I'll be down shortly."

CHAPTER 43

"Why would you think this is a good idea, Francis?" Byron scoffed. Julietta and Charles, having had their weapons already on them, made it to the atrium in record time to find Byron, Parker, Ola, and a strange man. Parker was standing between the man, whose hands were up, and his father who was pointing his gun at them both.

"Don't you trust my judgment?" Parker spat, annoyed. "This man says the government needs—"

"That statement alone should have been a red flag. Why would the government need our help? They haven't helped us in the 17 cycles we've existed."

The strange man winced. "Um, I can explain—"

"Quiet, you," Byron growled.

"What is going on here?" Charles asked, hand on his gun, Julietta mirroring him.

"It appears my son had compromised our position."

"What I've done is gotten us help."

Ola shook her head. "Now, Byron, we don't know that—"

"Everyone calm down." Ava appeared, along with Thomas. "We are not a shoot first ask questions later sort of organization, Sir Byron. I request you please lower your weapon."

Frustrated but understanding, he lowered his gun but kept it pointed toward the man. "All right, let's talk then, but I want him disarmed."

"I agree to it," the man stated, sounding a bit wary.

"Charles, Julietta, please have your guns out but not pointed at him. Thomas, relieve him of any weapons, then hold him," Ava instructed, stepping to stand beside Byron.

Julietta and Charles moved to flank the man, guns in hand but pointed at the ground while Thomas removed his weapons, two small knives. The man did not so much as flinch as Thomas took his arms, holding them behind his back.

"Anything else we should know about?" Thomas asked rather sternly but kindly.

"No, sir. I don't carry much," the man replied solemnly.

Ava shook her head. "Now, Parker, please step aside."

Parker eyed his father warily as he stepped out of the way. Byron remained unmoved.

"Now, let's start over, shall we?" Ava's eyes narrowed on the man. "Who are you?"

"My name is Vance Frederickson. Head of security for the current administration. I was sent here in lieu of the Head of Administration, Taylor Markham. Parker has a letter from her, certifying my identity and reasons for being here."

Parker handed Ava a folded-up piece of paper. Taking it, she did not open it.

"All right, before I read this, what is your reason for being here?"

"The administration is fully aware of the corrupt dealings happening with the Apolis Academy for the Future and the Constellation's more recent efforts to put an end to them. We—"

"If you were aware, why aren't the schools shut down?" Byron interrupted, adjusting his grip on his gun.

"Sir Byron, please," Ava frowned. "I will admit the timing is rather odd. The Constellation has been working for—"

"Don't tell this man anything!"

"Byron, I don't see the harm in it," Ola shrugged. "If we find him untrustworthy, you'll just kill him anyway."

Charles and Julietta glanced at each other nervously, their guns still pointed at the ground. A brief look at Parker gave them the acknowledgment and relief they needed. It would not come to that. He had used his powers on the man to determine his trust.

"Let's not get hasty, Madame Ola." Ava shook her head. "Mr. Frederickson, the Constellation, as you may know, has been in operation for over 17 cycles. Why now does the government take an interest?"

"Because we finally have proof." Vance sighed, bowing his head. "Up until about eight cycles ago, the administration was...oblivious. J.H.

333

did well using the academy to cover his tracks. That was until some of his goons made a target of the wrong family. As you know, the current administration has only been in power for about two cycles. Madame Taylor had an older sister named Miriam. She was married to Damian Bennet and had a child, who we later learned had powers. She and her husband were murdered, and the child never recovered. Madame Taylor was only about 16 at the time. Despite her protests, her parents refused to dig into the murders, too distraught and now plagued with questioning. They assumed it was a rogue bandit and left it at that, if only to calm the public. It wasn't until Taylor took office two cycles ago that a proper, albeit under the table, investigation began."

Byron seemed to shrink a bit, his gun lowering. "All right, so the current administration wants to put an end to this and bring justice for her sister. That's all well and good, but why now, and why do you need us?"

"Despite what it may seem like, the administration's power over the people is tentative at best. The world is still recovering from the Great War. Many places still lack clean water, electricity, and general survival necessities. The prior administration's focus was on the union of the cities to benefit all. The new focus is about recovery, both survival and knowledge-wise. There is distrust, in this idea among many. If the government all of a sudden went in and dismantled these schools that have provided work to many cities and hope, albeit false, to people that their children were safe and learning…it would be chaos."

"You said you have proof," Byron questioned. "Is that not enough?"

"Unfortunately, no. Our proof was enough to allow us to contact you. We need more if we are to convince the world at large of the issue. J.H. has done well to weave his web of lies. The bombs are terrifying people. They think we are the ones doing it. This has to end now, but we don't have the knowledge or the resources to do it. That's where you come in."

"How do we know you speak the truth?" Ola asked, sounding unfazed.

"I read him," Parker replied. "Everything he has said is the truth."

"Everything he's said is what he believes is the truth," Byron scoffed. "You can convince anyone of anything."

"My powers don't allow that," Parker growled.

"And how do we know that?" The older man shook his head. "For all we know your powers are fooled by self-taught lies."

"That's not how the powers work." Charles stepped forward, his gun still pointed at the ground by his side. "I've been deciphering Cone's notes and researching the genetics he studied. From what I've seen, I doubt Parker's powers would be so easily deceived."

Byron paused a moment, thinking. "You'd bet your life on it?"

Charles shook his head. "I'm taking a leap of faith. We have to. The way I see it, our back is against the wall. All satellites are down except Apolis, the last bastion of hope for these kids. If this man tells the truth, then this could be the silver bullet that brings everything to an end."

"And what if he lies?" Byron shouted. "Then we all die."

"Then we died trying to do something. If we just kill this man and forget about it, then what? There aren't enough of us left to go up against J.H. The bombs are getting more and more powerful from what we've seen."

"We can rebuild like before."

"There isn't time. It took nearly seven cycles to get the Constellation started to even stage one breakout. It took nearly another seven to get to where we were before we were again nearly wiped out."

Byron made to argue but Julietta stepped forward, stopping him. "We don't have another seven cycles, Byron. J.H. has gotten too far. He has some of the brightest minds working for him brainwashed into thinking what they do is important and thinking all that matters is what J.H. wants. I've seen firsthand how these people act. There isn't time anymore."

Byron's face fell, he knew they were right. "All right." He turned facing Vance. "What do you need?"

"You destroyed Iota. You had two agents in there." Vance looked at Julietta and Charles. "These two if our intel is correct. They are our ticket in."

Charles and Julietta looked deeply concerned. Ola, however, was the one to speak up. "What do you mean?"

"The school system is looking for you. Charles Hawthorne and Jessa Lynn. You are unaccounted for after the explosion. We, meaning my team, Madame Taylor, and I discussed a possible plan. We want to use you two to get into Omega."

"Absolutely not!" Byron shouted, his anger renewed. "You can't seriously think this is anything but a trap."

"Now Byron, let's hear the man out," Ola chastised.

"It's an easy in, Byron," Parker added. "Think about it. They can just waltz in the front door and—"

"You don't know what it was like at Iota, what I heard from them."

"Byron, we've argued this before..." Ola furrowed her brow. "As head of the Constellation, I think we should at least consider it."

"And as the co-head of the Constellation, I say no," he huffed. "I have that right."

"What do Charles and Julietta think?" Ava interrupted. "I mean, they are the ones who—"

"I don't want to hear more of this." Byron advanced toward Vance. "You need to leave."

"We wouldn't be sending them in alone. We'd send our chief security officer, George, and his team of agents with them for protection. It would only be for about three months after which we would go public with whatever they and the agents got," Vance explained, his voice shaking.

"They've done this once already, Byron," Ola shrugged. "And this time there is an end date. They can—"

"I still think we need to ask—"

Charles and Julietta stared at each other in stunned silence. The idea of having to go back to a school for any length of time terrified them, yet they both knew it was possibly the only way.

"Jul?" Charles whispered, holstering his gun and holding out a hand.

Julietta did the same, taking his. "I know." She swallowed a lump in her throat.

Before they could say anything, however, Karrie came running into the room, looking rather nervous.

Everyone stopped for a brief moment, the sudden appearance bringing them briefly out of the argument.

Ava raised an eyebrow. "Something wrong, Karrie?"

"I...uh...so I was watching Penny, right?"

"Where's Penny?" Julietta asked, her heart sinking.

Before anyone could answer, the soft sound of crying reached their ears. Letting go of Julietta's hand, Charles moved to the source of the sound, the atrium desk just behind them. Kneeling and opening the door he found Penny, curled up crying.

"Penny, how long have you been in there?"

Penny didn't reply, instead crawled out and wrapped her arms around Charles.

Julietta joined them a moment later. "Penny, were you spying on us? What did we tell you about—"

"Penny play hide seek with Karrie," Penny explained, tears running down her face. "Penny saw Parker with strange man. Penny thought Turner man. Penny got scared and hide."

Charles shook his head, hugging the poor girl. "It's all right, Penny. You did what we told you to do if you ever saw Turner and we weren't around. But how come you didn't come out once you realized it wasn't Turner?"

"Penny was, but Penny got scared hear shouting. Penny not want get in trouble for listening. Penny know not good to listen without permission."

"Oh, Penny," Julietta sighed. "I suppose you were in a bit of a strange situation. You should have just come out when you heard your father and I."

"Penny know. Penny sorry."

They looked at each other, hearts heavy.

"You heard everything, Penny?" Charles asked.

Penny nodded, standing up a bit so she could look at her parents' faces. "Momma and Papa need go back to school."

"Yes," Julietta frowned, tears in her eyes. "Momma and Papa need to go to Omega to try to stop all this."

"Dangerous."

"Yes, my little spark," Charles nodded, solemnly. "It is very dangerous."

Penny bowed her head. "Penny know why. Penny understand. Momma, Papa want protect Penny and kids like Penny."

Thomas let go of Vance as everyone else in the room glanced at one another, ashamed. In all their arguing they had forgotten who this all was for, and who this would affect the most.

"Exactly." Julietta could no longer hold it in, tears streaming down her face as she hugged Penny.

Charles wrapped them both into a hug, tears running down his face. "We love you, Penny. Love you so much."

"Penny know. Penny loves Momma and Papa too," Penny replied sadly. "Promise try best to come back to Penny safe?"

"Of course, Penny," Julietta sobbed, holding her a bit tighter.

"Forever and always," Charles added, his heart sinking. "We will come home safe to you. I promise."

It was Byron who finally spoke. "I suppose that settles it." He turned once more to Vance. "You can promise agents to protect them?"

"Yes, I can provide a few to go in with them. I can even grant the stipulation that your agents are our first priority to get out if things go south." He sighed. "It's all listed in that letter."

Ava opened the letter, scanning it. "He speaks the truth."

"All right then. Bring your agents tomorrow." Byron held out a hand. "We'll get all of the Constellation here together and discuss the next steps then."

Vance shook his hand. "Deal." He glanced over to see Charles had picked up Penny, carrying her over to the others. "I'm deeply sorry, Dr. Hawthorne and Miss Lynn. We didn't know—"

"It's Milard-Hawthorne." Julietta rested her head on Charles's shoulder. "We knew this may happen. If it means that someday soon our Penny will be safe and kids like her will be safe. It's a risk worth taking."

Charles nodded in agreement, holding their little girl a bit tighter.

"Very well," Vance cleared his throat, a pained look in his eyes realizing what Julietta had meant. "I shall see you all tomorrow."

CHAPTER 44

Doctor Charles Hawthorne and 'Jessa Lynn' were found by some government agents just outside of town sick and injured. Once they were more coherent, they explained how they escaped a horrible attack on Iota but were separated from the transports. They decided to head for Apolis hoping to find answers as to why their school was attacked. Now that they are back on their feet, they wish to return to work at a school.

Vance gave this story to the head of Omega-782. Almost immediately, they insisted Charles and Jessa be brought to them. After some discussion, mainly to buy Julietta and Charles a bit of time to prepare, they agreed to have them return to Omega in about a week.

In the days leading up to going to Omega, they spent as much time with Penny as possible, knowing very well there was a chance they would not be all together again. They had agreed that if it all failed and only one made it out, the survivor would run with Penny. If neither did, the Constellation was to send Penny back to Matson to live with Lisle in the hopes of buying her a chance at freedom. They had made the deal with Lisle, with Penny's blessing, when they first went into Iota and reaffirmed it with her and Penny before they left for Apolis. Though neither wanted to consider the first scenario, it was the second they dearly hoped would not have to be enacted.

Upon being welcomed to Omega they were taken to be questioned separately under the pretense of wanting to know what happened there so they could help them process. Thankfully, they had been prepped for this eventuality and easily sidestepped the various questions that attempted to tie them to the attack. Once their interrogations had concluded, they were brought back together and led to an office on the second floor.

Entering, they were greeted by an older man, with gray hair and green eyes, who gestured for them to sit.

"Welcome, Dr. Charles, Jessa. I am honored to meet your acquaintance." The man waited for them to settle in before taking a seat himself. "I have heard of your unfortunate departure from Iota. Rest assured the proper authorities have been contacted to investigate."

"I am happy to hear that," Julietta feigned relief. "That night in Iota was...I can only hope that our work can continue here."

"Agreed. I assure you, sir, if you would give me the chance I would very much like to continue my research at your earliest convenience," Charles added.

"I am humbled to hear that even after your great ordeal both of you are willing to step back into work." The man smiled, his grin unsettling. "It is, therefore, my pleasure to inform you I have reinstated you into the institute employee system and have issued you both promotions. Dr. Charles will be given his own laboratory with an assistant to continue his genetic research and Miss Jessa will be trained up on the machines here and allowed full access to the maintenance workshop."

Charles and Julietta glanced at each other, a brief flash of concern in their eyes, though their faces maintained the facade of joyful brainwashed workers.

"Thank you, sir," Julietta nodded.

"Indeed, thank you." Charles raised an eyebrow. "Um...pardon me, but I don't believe you gave your name."

"Oh, how unprofessional of me. I do apologize. I am J.H., head of the Engineering sector of the Apolis Academy for the future."

Julietta and Charles had met J.H. and somehow managed to keep a straight face. It would be one of many encounters with the man as they began their jobs at Omega. Every workday from about an hour after sunrise to an hour before sunset they worked. Julietta was quick to learn the machines, and within a week was allowed out into the facility proper. Her victory was rather short-lived, however, when she learned they tracked who worked on what machine, thwarting most of her ability to sabotage as she went. Undeterred, she found other means of helping the Constellation.

First and foremost, she discovered quite early that the students here were all of the age 16 to 21, the age of Bell training. She witnessed firsthand in passing and during hotfixes just how well they brainwashed the poor young adults. Most of the teens resisted, but by the time they reached their twenties, they were nearly broken. It also came to her attention that the majority of the staff in Omega lived there, only those with families being sent home at the end of the day. She and Charles had been offered rooms but they declined, citing the stress from their daring escape at Iota would not allow for them to be comfortable just yet. Regardless of whether they lived or left, there was one thing in common, they all seemed to firmly believe in J.H.'s mission of 'understanding' and controlling the Curied. It was as if they were of one mind, brainwashed. A possibility, Julietta thought, that was more likely than not true.

Charles, for his part, did his best to drag his feet on his research. Given he was the only researcher to have any prior knowledge of Dr. Cone's work, they were at his mercy. However, he was watched like a hawk by his assigned assistant, Eveline Kelton. Many days he found himself unable to do anything but drag his feet, leaving the Constellation with no new information.

It was almost what should have been the end of Damp. Having worked at Omega for nearly a month and a half, Charles was struggling to maintain his slow pace. The other researchers, who initially had welcomed him with seemingly open arms, had started to question him more and more. His assistant would ask daily if he needed anything specific to hurry progress along. Every day he made up some excuse or another, asking for a certain journal or book or test to be run in an effort to grind things to a halt. Unfortunately, his run of this was getting old. He had to produce results soon or risk being found out. After a brief discussion with the Constellation, they agreed he could at the very least release Dr. Cone's notes to them with minimal notes from him. A small price to pay to keep his real research hidden.

"Dr. Hawthorne, is there anything I can do for you today?" Eveline asked.

Charles had become accustomed to Eveline's grating voice and her near-constant questions about his work. Sitting at his desk, he turned to greet her. "Good afternoon, Dr. Kelton. No, nothing at the moment."

"Dr. Hawthorne." She approached, standing beside him. "With all due respect, sir. Your work, as I understand it, is highly important and vital to J.H.'s mission. Therefore, I ask again, what can I do to help expedite this process?"

He had expected this question and had his answer ready. "Well, I am on the precipice of an interesting breakthrough," he sighed, shaking his head. "The only thing I can think that may help speed this process is a fresh DNA sample. The ones that I have are a couple of weeks old now, deteriorating."

He did not expect her answer. "That can be arranged, immediately in fact." She smiled, her grin bearing no real emotion behind it. "If you would come with me?"

Unable to quickly come up with an excuse, Charles found himself being led from his second-floor laboratory towards a far back hallway, not unlike the one Julietta described in Iota as where they took Joyce. The door to it was digitally locked, his keycard able to unlock it, to his relief.

"You need a fresh sample; this is the best place for that. I heard that only yesterday a specimen was being added to the collection."

His heart sank as they made their way past various rooms, their doors locked and windows darkened. Finally, at the end of the hallway, they came to a door marked 'Specimen holding.'

Once more his keycard worked, though after entering he wished it hadn't. It did not take much to understand the nature of the room he had been brought to as the icy cold air hit him. This was a morgue.

Allowing Eveline to take the lead he was led through another set of doors to a room lined with metal drawers. Though as a doctor, death and bodies did not typically phase him, there was something about this place that sent an awful shiver down his spine, one he hoped he could play off as a reaction to the cold.

"Dr. Markson," his assistant greeted a man who was seated at a table at the back of the morgue working on some paperwork, a sandwich from the cafeteria beside him. "This is Dr. Hawthorne."

"Ah, Dr. Hawthorne. I've heard a great deal about you from J.H. If there is any way I can be of assistance—"

"That is why we are here, actually," Eveline smiled. "Dr. Hawthorne is in need of a specimen sample that is fresh."

Dr. Markson's eyes lit up, though behind them Charles could see no real emotion. "You are in luck, doctor. We had a specimen come in just last night. If you would follow me, though, please don't mind the mess. My assistants are on lunch break and haven't cleaned up since this morning."

Charles nodded, hoping the expression he held of indifference hid well his racing heart. The smell of blood and bodily fluids hit his nose as he was led through a large room with various surgical tables cordoned off by white dividers. Some were empty, though most held a stained sheet concealing a form beneath. Beside each of these were small rolling tables with various instruments, vials, and the like. From what he could tell this place was anything but what a morgue should be.

"Fresh specimens are coming in slower nowadays. The ones out there are on their last procedures before they are to be disposed of. With Iota being destroyed, there has been a delay, of course."

He did not reply, a pit settling into his stomach as he was led through one final door. This room was somehow colder, the feeling only amplified by the stark white walls and floors of the room. Along the back wall was a table with various surgical tools with a sink beside it. What lay on the surgical table in the center, covered in a sheet, threatened to break him.

"This specimen was released and brought in last night," Dr. Markson explained, grabbing a clipboard from the table.

As he did, Eveline pulled back the sheet to reveal the head and shoulders of the body, a woman, around her neck a penny etched with the alchemy symbol for earth.

"Experimental ID E-51351291, Curied, 21 Cycles, power classification 5." Dr. Markson read out sounding rather pleased. "A shame really to release such a specimen. From what I saw before I completed the procedure, this experiment was fully indoctrinated. It would have made a fine Bell, but when Curied are this rare and strong they must be taken to ensure J.H.'s vision."

Charles could not bring himself to reply, his heart shattering as he gazed at the dead woman before him. She had been given some chemicals, given the blue shade of her lips and eyelids. That was not what shook him, however. It was the relaxed and calm expression that rested on her face in death, as though she were happy to be free of her torment.

"Dr. Hawthorne is in need of a DNA sample to finish up his latest breakthrough," Eveline chirped, her voice tearing at Charles's ears.

"I see. A blood sample would do nicely for your work, yes?" Dr. Markson turned, grabbing a needle from the table before removing an arm from beneath the sheet.

Charles's eyes flitted to the blood-ringed injection holes in the arm, a gesture noticed by Dr. Markson as he began to draw the blood.

"I can assure you the chemicals used have been flushed out of the specimen. I did the flush injection myself this morning in preparation for the exploratory autopsy this afternoon. That was the paperwork I was filling out before you both showed up."

"I see," Charles replied, his voice a bit quieter than he expected.

Taking the now-filled tube, the man labeled it before handing it over to Charles. "That should do it. Please let me know if there is anything else I can do for you. If you need more blood or maybe a tissue sample just come find me, but do so quickly. You'd be surprised how many other researchers are vying for fresh samples. Of course, your work is to take precedence given its context. If all goes well, I should be completed with this specimen by the end of the day. Then my assistants will take over collecting the requested samples. Hopefully, by then they would have released the other two currently in holding."

"Thank you, this should be enough for now," Charles replied, using every ounce of willpower to keep his hand steady as he took the bottle. "I really should get this back to the lab and into cold storage as soon as possible. I will let you know if anything further is needed."

"Very well." The doctor grinned, turning back to his tools, and grabbing a rather sharp-looking scalpel.

Charles did not wait to see what was about to happen, instead walking back to the lab as fast as he reasonably could without drawing suspicion. Hand gripping the blood bottle he placed it in the cold storage before sending Eveline to get some new beakers and then to lunch. Only once he was sure he was alone he found himself emptying the contents of his stomach in the restroom. Willing himself to maintain cool indifference, he managed to return in time for his assistant to arrive to continue their work for the rest of the day.

CHAPTER 45

Julietta sighed, leaning back in her armchair. It was late, past midnight. Upon returning to the museum after work, she and Charles had dinner with Penny, playing hide and seek for a bit with her before sending her off to bed. Julietta was worried about Charles, seeing how distant he acted. She had asked him on the walk home about his day, but he'd given non-specific answers. She had a feeling something had happened, but did not pry knowing he'd tell her when he was ready.

Taking a long look at the painting before her, she frowned. Working at Omega was not easy on the mind or heart. That's why she found herself many evenings in the museum's art gallery. She had asked Ava about it when they first arrived and was given it as a private space to restore, both the paintings and her sanity.

Setting down her paintbrush on the small stool beside the armchair, she stood, stretching. This was the fourth painting she'd attempted to restore. It was hard, messy work, but necessary if she was to cope with the horrors of Omega.

Coping, that was what they were doing. It was why Charles spent many hours after dark in his office in the museum, why she would come here, and why they would talk many nights before passing out exhausted beside each other. It was this extra work, however, that kept the edge off on the worst days.

Feeling tired, she resigned herself to heading back to their room. As she started to clean up, a thought crossed her mind. Charles had gone to his office after putting Penny to bed. She had suggested he join her in the gallery, given he had not had the chance to visit, but he declined needing to work on something with his research. She had not pushed him then, knowing it would do no good, but if he was in as bad a mood as she thought, he likely was still there. Leaving her paints, she instead headed for Charles's office.

As she expected the only light in the medical wing came from beneath the door to Charles's office.

Shaking her head, she knocked. "Charlie?"

There was no reply.

Nervous, she tested the door, to her slight relief, unlocked. Entering she found him at his desk, asleep, papers scattered about him. Gently placing one hand on his shoulder, she brushed some hair from his face with the other. "Charlie." She spoke softly.

He began to stir, his eyes fluttering open. "Jul…" He slowly sat up.

She frowned, seeing the pain in his eyes. "You fell asleep working again."

"Sorry, Jul. I just needed…"

"Come with me."

He did not argue as she took his hand, leading him out of the room toward the gallery.

"I did another hotfix today," Julietta started as they walked. "It was… difficult to say the least."

"No sabotage this time?"

"Couldn't with the Miss Bell watching my every move." Her shoulders slumped. "I haven't been able to sabotage anything for the past two weeks."

He did not reply, his head bowing as he gave her hand a small squeeze. They walked the remainder of the way in silence. Stopping before the gallery door, she turned to him. "Something happened today, didn't it?"

"Yes."

"Do you want to talk about it?"

He paused for a moment, his mind turning. "I…I asked Eveline for a fresh sample and…she took me down to the morgue."

Her face fell. "What…what did you see?"

"Many bodies, covered, but there was one specifically, a woman, released the night before. I saw her face. She had a penny around her neck marked with earth. There was a doctor, Markson, who was prepping her for an autopsy and…sample collection." His voice shook as he explained in detail what exactly he had seen.

"I'm so sorry, Charlie." She embraced him.

"It was sickening." He embraced her back, his arms scarily light around her. "I ended up sick in the bathroom for most of lunch trying to pull myself back together."

"I know how you feel," she sighed. "Some days I can barely keep it together. It's why I've been working so late in the gallery."

"That's why you found me in my office."

"You always show me your work." She stepped back, unlocking the gallery door. "Let me show you what I've done."

He followed her in, his mind still heavy, as she led him across the fabric-covered floor to her first art piece.

"Persistence of Memory," she smiled. "The clocks were difficult yet satisfying to paint."

Charles inspected the painting, a slight glimmer of light coming to his stormy eyes. "You never fail to impress me." Moving to the next, he read the placard beneath it. "'Starry Night Over the Rhone.'"

"Reminded me of the ocean painting in Waterwealt I never got to finish."

"I remember that," he frowned, his voice tone dropping.

Seeing his mood darkening again she placed a comforting hand on his shoulder. "It's all right, Charlie. I'm getting to paint here."

He nodded, walking over to the third painting, 'Madame Monet and Her Son.'

"Can you imagine a field so green? And a sky so blue?" Julietta asked, her voice light.

"It would be beautiful," he smiled, sadly. "Maybe someday the world will be like that again."

"Maybe…" Julietta took his hand, leading him over to her workstation where the last painting sat, unfinished. "I've been working on this one the past couple of weeks."

His hand fell from hers limply as he stepped in front of the makeshift easel. Before him was the image of a young woman, her hair wrapped in cloth, a single pearl earring dangling from her left ear.

"Charlie?" Julietta looked worried, seeing the color drain from his face.

He did not respond, remaining rooted in place, his arms hanging loosely at his side.

"Charlie, are you—" She reacted immediately, as he swayed slightly. Placing an arm around him she guided him quickly back into the armchair behind him. In her haste, she knocked into her paints, coating her left hand in blue and sending the rest to the floor in the process. "Charlie, you're shaking."

Charles bowed his head, unable to answer.

Checking his pulse at his wrist, she furrowed her brow. "I'm going to get some—" She stopped as Charles's hand grasped hers tightly.

"Jul…" His voice shook as he lifted his head to meet her gaze.

Julietta's heart broke, seeing how red his eyes had become, the deep pain within them on the verge of tears. She realized quickly this was not an illness, but an all too familiar pain. "Charlie."

He pulled on her hand weakly, a silent request. Without hesitation, she moved to sit in his lap. Wrapping her right arm around him, she pulled him to her, gently resting his head against her shoulder. "I'm here, Charlie. I'm not going anywhere."

"It could have been you." The hold he had kept on his emotions broke, tears streaming down his face. "That could have been Penny someday…"

She said nothing, instead running her paint-stained hand soothingly through his hair and down the side of his face, ignoring the blue streaks she left behind.

"She was someone's daughter, someone's friend… She was someone. Yet, they treated her like she was nothing more than cattle for the slaughter. No name was given, no respect for the body. She was just lying there in a cold room covered in a sheet, a number, a specimen for harvest."

She held him a bit tighter, tears forming in her eyes.

"I wanted to scream. I wanted to run. I wanted to fight. I wanted them to understand. But I just stood there and…and acted like nothing was wrong." He shook, closing his eyes. "I felt like a monster…I'm a monster."

Julietta shook her head, "You didn't think when you asked for a specimen that they'd give you one, did you?"

"I—I thought it would buy me time, an excuse to delay giving them Cone's work. Everything else I've asked for has taken time and paperwork." He shook his head. "I've seen death enough times before. It comes with being a doctor. But seeing that poor young woman lying there…" His voice broke, his body tensing as he struggled to speak, finding it hard to take more than a shallow breath. "Her murderer was right there and I couldn't do a damn thing but pretend it was fine. I was helpless, useless."

"You are not a monster, Charlie," she soothed, her voice calm, steady, and gentle. "A monster wouldn't be risking his life to get the

Constellation and the government information to save all those kids. Wouldn't have done everything in his power to stop Cone from continuing his work. A monster wouldn't have had to spend time sick in the bathroom at what they've seen. Wouldn't be here right now, vulnerable and honest."

He did not respond, instead, willing himself to take a few deep breaths.

"You have a good heart Charlie, a beautiful one. You want to help people, and save people as a doctor and as a Constellation member. Despite everything, you've maintained your humanity. It's the one thing that we cling to every day. That's why you'll never become like the monsters you long to slay."

He could not bring himself to speak, instead letting Julietta's words wash over him, letting her presence still him.

"I know how you are feeling, Charlie. Every time I send a machine back with no sabotage a small part of me feels like I am breaking, bending to their will. But I remind myself why I am doing this. I remind myself that for every forsaken machine, I have clawed my way toward ending this by other means."

Though silent tears still ran down his face, his body stopped shaking.

"Sometimes you have to lose a little to gain a lot. It's not perfect or right, but it's what we have to take solace in."

Julietta held Charles quietly for a time, letting him process as he slowly relaxed more and more into her arms.

"I'm…I'm sorry, Jul," he finally whispered, his eyes opening.

"What do you have to be sorry for?"

"I should have just told you what happened today. I should have—"

"Ssh," she chided, feeling his body tense once more. "Your mind wasn't ready and your heart was hurting." She shook her head, resting her hand on his neck. "How many nights have you let me do the same? Let me come here to sort out my brain before telling you and working through it with you. How many times have you held me like this while I cried?"

He did not answer, once more focusing on breathing.

"You've done it many times for me, Charlie. There is nothing to be sorry for."

After a few more minutes, he settled as she wiped away a few stray tears from his face.

"Your art is beautiful, Jul...I didn't expect it to—"

"Charlie..."

Gazing up at her, he smiled. "They are beautiful. Everything you make and paint is beautiful."

Taking her still lightly paint-stained hand, she carefully undid the top few buttons on his shirt, using it to draw a blue heart on his chest, over his heart.

Taking some paint from her hand he repeated the same on hers. "What on this earth could I have done to deserve someone like you?"

"I ask myself every day, since we met, the same about you."

Charles frowned, his expression dropping as a thought crossed his mind. "Some husband I'm turning out to be."

"What do you mean?" She quirked an eyebrow, his tone concerning her.

"It's about Damp's end, Jul. Your 25th cycle. And here I am making you cry and with nothing worthy to give you."

"I've made myself cry, Charlie, not you." Resting her hand over the heart on his chest, she leaned in and kissed his forehead. "And you are mistaken. You've already given me the most amazing gift I could ask for."

"What do you mean?" He quirked an eyebrow, confused.

"It's the gift you give me when you get up early to make breakfast or stay up late waiting for me. It's how every time you argue with me and then you hold me a bit closer later that night despite who was right or wrong." She brushed the back of his ear with her right hand, giving him a crooked smile. "It's you being there, both when I am happy and when my world seems to be falling apart. And you becoming a father to our daughter." She relaxed looking into Charles's eyes, a lightness coming to them. "It's the gift you've given me hundreds, even thousands of times over every day since we've met. Even now, crying in my arms you've given it. You've given me your heart, Charlie, your love. That is the only gift I ever truly want from you, and you have already given it to me."

"You deserve more, Jul. I should give you the world for what you—"

"You've given me the world," she hushed. "You and Penny are my world."

Charles stayed quiet for a moment, his heart mending. "You and Penny are my world too."

Leaning in she kissed him once, twice, the third finding herself wrapped in his arms as he deepened it.

"You have my heart always," he sighed into her lips before pulling away.

"And you have mine, always," she echoed, resting her forehead against his.

"When this is all over, we'll go back to Matson, restore that museum so the world can see your beautiful mind at work."

"And so you can continue your medical work in peace, and help the world how you've always wanted."

"Where Penny can grow up and learn with her friends, safe and loved."

Julietta looked deeply into his eyes, relieved to see the mischievous spark in them that she loved returning. "Where we will grow our family."

"Where we will grow our family," he affirmed, his body finally completely relaxing into her arms, exhausted.

"Close your eyes, Charlie. I'll wake you when I am ready to go to bed."

He did not argue as she rested his head against her chest. Tracing the painted heart on his, she quietly lulled him into sleep. Sitting there in the quiet gallery, holding Charles as he held her, Julietta felt peace for the first time in a while. She stayed there for about an hour, just letting her mind wander to thoughts of the beautiful future.

"Charlie?" she whispered.

He was sound asleep.

"I promise Charlie, we'll get through this." She rested her hand on his chest, feeling his now calm heartbeat. "Just as you promised, we will come home to Penny. We will have our future together. I promise."

The Damp season wanted to cling on despite the intense heat of Hot rolling in. Within only its first week, Apolis was plagued by a near-constant rainstorm that only seemed to stop long enough to dry everything out before soaking it once more. The heat, of course, made this quick work but also left the air feeling like you were walking through a thick soup.

It was later in the evening, towards the end of the first week of Hot. Byron, Ola, Penny, and the rest of the Constellation had spent most of the day plugging the seemingly endless leaks in the museum that had sprung over the past few days.

Penny had gone to her room an hour before to start getting ready for bed, only to be soaked as the ceiling began raining down upon her, sending her running for Byron. Changing into dry clothes and now unable to sleep, she found herself hanging around the museum's first floor, replacing some of the buckets that had begun to overflow.

Life in the museum had been reasonable for Penny, albeit stuffy sometimes. Most of the time she found herself in Ava's office working on the various electronics brought to her. Occasionally, she would hang out in the medical wing learning basic first aid. In the evenings, while she waited for Julietta and Charles to come home, she'd work on her writing and numbers or tinker with Nelson. Those times were the hardest, waiting for her parents, only second to having to watch them leave each morning.

It was about an hour past the time her parents should have been home, hence why Penny decided to maintain the first-floor buckets. She had just finished swapping out another in one of the frontmost exhibits, pouring the full one out the nearby window, when she heard the door to the museum creak open.

"Momma! Papa!" she cried, spotting Julietta and Charles standing at the atrium desk, removing their dusters.

Seeing Penny, their faces lit up as she embraced them.

"How's our little spark?" Charles asked, tossing his and Julietta's rather water-ladened dusters onto the desk.

"Penny help change buckets." The child smiled, hugging them a bit tighter.

Julietta chuckled, adjusting the red bandana someone had given Penny to wear. "You look just like one of those riveters of history."

Penny stepped back, posing like the posters she'd seen on the museum walls, holding a flexed arm. "Penny brave! Penny strong!"

"Yes, you are," Charles sighed. "But even strong and brave Pennys need sleep."

"Penny tried. Penny bed now water bed."

"She's not wrong," Byron said, coming down the stairs. "There was a bit of a leak in her room. I spent the better half of the last hour trying to dry it out."

"This rain is doing no one any favors." Julietta rolled her eyes. "I've spent the better half of this week drying out machines. Though I must admit it's slowed things down."

"That's good news, at least." The older man smiled. "About time Mother Nature helped us instead of hurt us. Though it seems to have also delayed your coming home tonight."

Penny looked up at her parents, noting the concern in their eyes. "Rain not make Papa, Momma late?"

"No," Julietta frowned, shaking her head. "That obvious?"

Penny nodded.

"There's been a development," Charles grimaced. "Something we'll need Ola, Ava, and Vance to discuss."

Byron's shoulders slumped. "I'll have Ava radio Vance to come by in the morning. You two better go get some food. Penny will have to stay with you while her room dries out."

"Penny stay with Momma and Papa?"

"Of course," Julietta agreed, glancing over to Charles who nodded. "How does a pillow fort sound?"

"We'll even help you make a bed for Nelson and Margie," Charles offered, grabbing his and Julietta's dusters.

"Penny happy." Penny gave a crooked smile, taking their hands as they headed for the cafeteria for some CCCs before bed.

CHAPTER 46

"A party?" Vance looked incredulous. "Why on earth would they throw a party?"

Charles and Jessa had been invited to a party at Omega, to be hosted in a couple weeks.

"Rumor has it J.H. is going to make some big announcement." Julietta leaned up against Ava's desk, shaking her head. "It's all everyone is talking about."

"That doesn't bode well for us," Ola frowned. "An announcement means progress, which I thought you were holding back."

"We tried, but it's Jul, me, and five agents against a whole facility. We're hardly an army." Charles shrugged, sinking back in his chair.

"Penny fight J.H. if Penny was not small," Penny pouted, crossing her arms. "Penny want save friends like Momma and Papa."

"I know, Penny," Julietta sighed. "We are doing our best."

Penny, who was sitting on Ava's desk, moved closer to her, a sad look in her eyes. "Penny not mean Momma and Papa no do good. Penny proud of Momma and Papa."

She wrapped an arm around the girl's shoulders, smiling. "We know."

"Well, the way I see it you two are going to have to get all dolled up and go." Byron's brow furrowed. "I am guessing this invitation is more of a requirement?"

"Can't we just send the government agents? Would it seem suspicious if you didn't go?" Ava asked, sounding worried. "It seems rather odd a place so focused on progress would be willing to stop even for half a day for a party."

"Attendance is highly encouraged." Charles rolled his eyes. "As much as I'd rather not wine and dine with the likes of J.H., we need to know what the announcement is."

"The employees are all but brainwashed. It would be obvious if we didn't attend for any reason," Julietta explained. "It's a test."

"Well, I guess it's settled, you two will go and all we can do is wait and see," Ola stated. "You said formal wear is encouraged?"

"Highly encouraged. J.H. seems to want this to be a spectacle." Charles raised an eyebrow. "We'll need to think of—"

"I think I can help with that," Ava interjected. "We are in a museum after all."

The evening of the party quickly approached. Julietta and Charles, along with all personnel not living on site, had been given leave after lunch to go home to get ready for the evening's festivities. In her and Charles's bedroom, Julietta sat nervously on a chair while Marisa set her hair with a feathered headpiece.

"My, my, Julie you look lovely," Marisa complimented, tucking in a few more pieces of hair. "Just like them flapping women from the 20s."

"Yeah," she chuckled slightly, her hand coming to her stomach.

"Nervous?"

"Very." She sighed, turning to look at her friend. "Tonight is dangerous."

"No more dangerous than any other night." Marisa shrugged, reaching for the make-up she had brought earlier for Julietta, helping her touch up.

"I suppose not."

The woman frowned, seeing Julietta's expression. "Yes?"

"Yes."

She shook her head. "The universe has a strange sense of timing."

"You're telling me." Julietta stood, smoothing out the dress she had borrowed from the museum. "Thank you, Marisa, for everything."

"Of course, dear. Whatever you need. I'm here."

The sound of a guitar being played in the other room brought them back to attention.

"Sounds like Oliver found himself a guitar," Marisa smirked. "Guessin' your dancing man awaits you."

Stepping into the common space, they couldn't help but smile. Oliver was sitting on one of the couches, playing a waltz on the guitar while Charles, dressed in a rather nice 1920s-style navy blue suit, complete with dress shoes and hat from the era, was teaching Penny how to dance.

"One, two, three; one, two, three; one, two, three. You are a natural, my little spark," Charles chuckled.

"Penny like dance." Penny smiled up at her Papa.

"Looks like Miss Penny could show you a thing or two, Julie," Marisa teased, drawing Penny's attention.

The girl stopped dancing, eyes wide with joy seeing her Momma dressed up. "Momma pretty!"

Julietta was dressed in a dark blue fringe dress that came to her knees with black nylon tights beneath, and black short heels. Marisa had done her hair up in a style from the era, complete with a feathered headband, and bought her some make-up from a small nearby shop. Ava had even found some pearl jewelry.

Julietta blushed, catching Charles's eyes on her. "Well?"

He approached, taking her hands. "You look beautiful." He kissed her cheek.

Penny tugged on Julietta's sleeve lightly. "Momma dance with Penny?"

"Of course," she answered. "I could use a bit of practice in these heels. They are nothing like my boots."

Oliver continued to play while Julietta waltzed with little Penny, taking to the heels and steps like a duck to water. Charles stood beside Marisa, an ache in his heart seeing his girls dancing. Tonight, despite its seemingly innocent nature, would be dangerous. There was no doubt in his mind that the party would be anything but what it seemed. They had a plan.

They would travel together to the facility, just two co-workers arriving on the same transport. Once in, however, they would need to remain relatively apart as expected. Even after being 'found together' by the government, to Omega, Charles and Jessa were just two workers from Iota who happened to be stuck together after its destruction. They would remain at the party until after the announcement, at which point they would wait until at least two of the government agents departed before taking their leave. It was not a foolproof plan by any means, but they had little choice.

Letting them dance a bit longer, Charles signaled it was time to leave. Thanking Oliver and Marisa, then kissing Penny goodbye, they headed for the transport station.

The evening was muggy but tolerable. The rain had finally stopped. Walking along the streets of Apolis, Charles could not help but notice the discomfort in Julietta's eyes.

"You okay?"

"Yeah, I'm fine," Julietta smiled, her expression slightly pained.

"Is it the shoes?" He quirked an eyebrow, not quite believing the question himself.

"No, they're fine. I'm getting used to them."

"Nerves then?"

"A bit."

He remained silent for a while, keeping an eye on her. "You really do look beautiful."

She turned, giving him a genuine smile. "You know I always wanted to see what it was like wearing a dress. Just wish it was under better circumstances."

He took her hand. "When this is over, we'll have to have our own party where you can dress up and feel good about it."

He became concerned looking into her eyes. In them reflected something dancing on the tip of her tongue. She shook her head, thinking better of saying it as she replied. "We are near the station. Best act natural."

The party itself was rather lively and crowded. The main atrium of the facility had been transformed into a reception area, while one of the warehouses had been cleared out and set up to be a huge dance space with tables and chairs surrounding it. After arriving, Julietta and Charles separated, heading for their respective co-workers so as not to arouse suspicion.

It was hard for Charles to keep up the facade of a happy brainwashed employee, particularly with Eveline and the other researchers nonchalantly turning the discussion from small talk to guesses of the announcement.

"I think J.H. is going to announce a new school opening," Eveline suggested while sipping her champagne.

"To replace Iota? I hardly think it's been long enough," chirped another researcher named Carlotta.

"Personally, I think it's better to not open another school and divert the resources to the ones already opened," commented a doctor named Percival. "I honestly could use some more specimens."

"I second that," added Dr. Markson, taking a long drink of his wine. "Not enough releases to keep up with demand."

"What about you, Hawthorne? What do you think?" Carlotta asked.

Charles shook his head. He hadn't been paying much attention. "Sorry, I was thinking."

"You are at a party. Thinking is for the work day," Eveline laughed, grabbing his arm. "Come, why don't we get you a drink? Some wine or champagne…"

He pulled away. "No, thank you. I…I am quite all right with water for now."

"Oh, Hawthorne, lighten up." Dr. Markson downed the rest of his wine. "I am sure whatever it is J.H. is announcing will be wonderful, just wonderful."

"I assure you, I am in agreement." Glancing around the room he spotted Julietta slipping out one of the open warehouse doors. "If you would excuse me, the heat is rather stifling me. I think I need a bit of air, then I shall join you for a drink, Eveline."

"Suits me just fine," the woman smirked, a sparkle in her eyes. "Come then, Markson, you look like a man in need of a refill."

Taking his leave, Charles made his way over to the open door, hoping no one would notice as he slipped out into the night air.

Outside of the warehouse, the loading dock had been left fairly untouched, a few decorative flowers and bushes covering the chain link fence that kept them in the facility and the wasteland out. It wasn't hard to find Julietta sitting on one of the benches that had been placed outside.

"Jessa?" He looked around, making sure no one had followed before taking a seat beside her. "Jul?" he whispered.

Julietta glanced over to the door, before taking his hand. "Charlie…"

He frowned, despite the hot night her hands were cold and clammy. Setting down his glass of water beside him, he used his other hand to check her temperature. "You're overheating." He handed her his drink. "It's awfully stuffy in there."

She drank the water gratefully, setting the empty cup beside her. "Charlie…there's…there is something I—"

They both paused, catching Eveline and Dr. Markson's voices near the door. Thankfully, they did not have to wait long for them to vanish into the crowd once more.

"I can't stay long. I told Eveline I'd get a drink with her," he huffed. "I'd rather be tased by one of those wands than socialize with them."

"Charlie…" She chuckled slightly, a bit of lightness coming to her sad eyes. "I know what you mean. The maintenance staff are an incredible bore. I've spent the last two hours listening to them drone on about the lack of Allen wrenches in the workshop and the great debate between metric and standard measurements."

"I am sure that was very riveting," he laughed, checking her temperature once more before checking her pulse at her wrist. "You feeling a bit better?"

"I'd feel better if I could spend the evening with you."

"I know Jul, but we have to keep up appearances," he sighed, shaking his head. "Speaking of, I probably shouldn't be caught sitting so close to you."

He made to stand, but she stopped him, gripping his hand tightly. "Charlie, there is something I need to tell you."

He looked nervously over at the door. "Let's go to the far end then."

They slipped around the side of one of the shipping containers. Remaining silent, they waited a few moments to ensure they hadn't been seen.

"What's wrong?" Charles asked, concerned.

Taking both of his hands in hers, she bowed her head. "You…you know how…how we talked about the museum in Matson?"

"Yes?"

"How we…we said we'd go there after all this so Penny can grow up with her friends and we can be a family?"

"Yes…what's wrong? Did something happen to Matson? What did—"

"We talked about growing our family."

Charles felt as though his heart skipped a beat. "Yes, and we will."

She shook her head, tears running down her face as she looked up at him. "We are."

His eyes went wide. "How…how many—"

"I've missed three. I didn't think about it until recently with everything going on."

"How long?"

"Marisa got me a test this morning." She averted her gaze, upset. "I'm sorry, Charlie, I've wanted to tell you all day, but—"

She stopped as Charles gently placed a hand on the side of her face, lifting it to look at his. He had tears in his eyes but was smiling.

"They'll have your beautiful eyes."

"You—you aren't scared?"

"Terrified, but also overjoyed. How couldn't I be?"

Taking his other hand, she placed it on her stomach. "And your crooked smile."

"We're having a baby," he chuckled, kissing her gently. "Guess my swimmers were stronger than we anticipated."

She burst out laughing, the nerves finally relaxing. "Oh, Charlie…" She breathed, resting her forehead against his chest. "I am so happy but so, so terrified. Coming here tonight…having to work for another three weeks…"

"I know." He moved to wrap his arms around her. "Whether you told me earlier or not, we still had to come. We'll have to let everyone know so we can adjust our plans in case…"

"First we tell Penny, then everyone else."

"Agreed."

The sound of a microphone calling everyone back into the warehouse shook them from their moment. They were at Omega, still not safe. Not wanting to leave each other's side they placed themselves just outside the door as J.H. took to a small stage that had been set up at the front of the place.

"Thank you all for joining me on this fine evening. As I am sure many of you are aware, a great deal of progress has been made since the first expansion of the Apolis Academy for the Future opened nearly 20 cycles ago."

There were cheers from the crowd, Charles and Julietta feigning agreement as J.H. rambled on about the various achievements and discoveries of the last 20 cycles. Most of the things mentioned, they had figured out or conjectured, nothing surprising them fully.

"After all this, there is one last achievement I would like to announce. As of a few weeks ago, I am delighted to report the final version of the Polonium Neutralization Device is ready for testing! We have already sent off for the necessary components from our facilities. Within the next month, all should arrive for the final test on Apolis itself!"

Cheers and shouts of excitement filled the air. Charles and Julietta lost any sense of face as they looked at each other horrified.

"Char—" Rough hands grabbed Julietta before she could say another word. She didn't have time to shout as a strange-smelling cloth came to her face, stifling any chance of crying out. The last thing she saw was Charles being dragged out back to the loading docks, struggling, before her world went dark.

CHAPTER 47

Penny had been asleep for several hours when she was awoken by the sound of voices in the common space. Glancing out her window, she frowned. Looking at the night sky, she knew it was very late. Her parents should have been home by now.

"Right now, they are being treated," Sir Byron said in the other room.

"How many?" Auntie Marisa asked.

Not comfortable with what she was hearing, she sat up in bed. Reaching for her compass that she kept on her bedside table at night, she let her sparks dance along its sides. Pressing her pointer finger on the engraving, she touched the first star with another. The compass swung, facing the direction she feared. Moving her finger to the second star, the needle did not move. Letting her power fade, her heart sank as the needle fell directly north once more.

"She needs to know." Sir Byron's voice was heard again as there was a knock at the door. "Penny?"

Byron entered the room, Penny staring right at him, compass still in hand.

"How much did you—"

She shook her head, tears in her eyes. "What happen?"

"Get dressed. We need to talk."

She followed him to the medical wing where Ava, Ola, and Vance were waiting.

"Why did you bring her?" Vance quirked an eyebrow.

"She deserves to know," Byron spat. "Has he said anything?"

"June is taking care of him right now. He's hurt pretty bad." Ava sighed, shaking her head. "Before he passed out, he gave us this." She reached over, taking an opened envelope from the nearby table. "We already checked it for anything nefarious, but haven't read it."

Byron took the letter. "To the Constellation, it seems our little game of chess has neared its end, your remaining pawns in my custody. Rest assured they are being taken care of. They are alive, for now. If you'd like to keep it that way, then I ask just one thing. I believe the time has come for a family reunion. Bring my sister, your Queen, to me within 24 hours and maybe your pawns will see another day. - Jasper H."

"Sister? Queen? Who?" Vance looked confused, while everyone else's eyes came to rest on Ola.

The woman's face paled. "No...no, I...I—"

"J.H. is your brother?" Byron asked, sounding in disbelief.

"J.H. take Momma and Papa..." Penny sat on the ground, tears running down her face.

"Yes, Jasper is my brother," Ola replied, her voice barely above a whisper. "I'm...sorry."

"Sorry? Sorry is not going to bring those agents back...not going to bring Charles and Julietta back!" Byron shouted, throwing the letter to the ground. "How could you lie about this?"

"You think I am proud of this?" Ola spat back. "Proud of the monster my brother became?!"

Ava moved over to Penny, placing a comforting arm around her while Ola and Byron continued to argue. "It'll be all right, Penny. I am sure we'll think of something."

The little girl wiped her tears, standing. "Stop."

Byron and Ola continued.

"STOP!"

Everyone froze, Penny had never shouted before.

"Miss Ola lie, but Miss Ola also try stop brother. Now problem. Momma and Papa danger. Need save Momma, Papa, and others."

"Penny is right," Byron sighed, his anger abating. "There is no time to argue now. We need a plan."

"Well, the answer to that is simple, he wants me." Ola sank back into her chair. "Use me to bargain for the others."

"You're joking, right?" Vance interjected. "We can't just assume he'll let them go. You've seen the reports. These people are insane."

"Then what do you suggest?" Ola replied, her frustration clear. "Those people are trapped there because of me. I should have never put the idea in his head to—"

Everyone went silent.

She paused, taking a deep breath. "It's a long story that we don't have time for."

"Then make it quick," Byron growled. "We need the truth, the whole truth, if we are going to figure this out."

"I was five cycles when Jasper accidentally discovered his powers. He was only three. During a tantrum, he sparked, electrically, setting fire to some crops. Thankfully no one was injured, but people became rather wary of our family. We ended up moving to Akacaster about a month later. From that moment, our parents became very strict with us both. We couldn't go out alone; were restricted in our socialization with people. Instead, we worked around the house and later in our parents' shop. They feared my brother's power and were worried some-thing would set me off to reveal some unknown ability. Eventually, they relaxed with me given I never manifested anything, but with Jasper... they...they told him he was dangerous, and that everything they did was for his safety. It nearly broke him."

"At 16 I convinced him to run with me. We ended up in Apolis; got jobs at the archives. I worked my way up, eventually gaining access to books. Jasper, on the other hand, was more of a talker, despite his sheltered upbringing. He took on more of an admin role and convinced the archives to give me a shot as a researcher so I could try to understand why he has powers. It wasn't enough. Despite hours of digging and following leads, I just couldn't figure it out. I needed help. We talked about bringing my research to the Apolis Academy for further study. They agreed. At the time, I hadn't realized just how twisted my brother's sense of his powers had become. I was up to my eyeballs in psychological research when he told me about the branch of the school he planned to head. I was blind."

"So, you set him on the path..." Ava's shoulders slumped. "And he took it too far."

"I never wanted this to happen. I just wanted to understand where his powers came from. I—I couldn't figure it out so he took matters into his own hands."

"What now, then?" Byron questioned, shaking his head. "How do we stop him?"

"I...I...wait. I might have something." She turned, wheeling toward the door. "I'll be right back."

"I hope whatever she's gone to grab is useful," Vance frowned. "We can't afford for this to—"

"He's awake," June beckoned.

Vance was immediately to the man's side. "George, what happened, what—"

"It's a bomb. The announcement was for the final bomb on Apolis. In about a month..." The injured man winced. "It...it was a trap. They... they knew. They took Charles, Julietta, and our other agents Heidi, Mel, Connor, and Sal. They...they let me go as a...as a warning."

Everyone's faces fell.

"Rest, George. We'll figure this out," he shook his head, moving so June could continue to tend to him.

"We have to go in," Ava's voice broke. "What choice do we have?"

"We are out of time. We need to get what information we can get and rescue our agents." Byron crossed his arms, deep in thought. "Vance, can you get us some help?"

"I'll see what I can do," the man replied, heading for the door. "I'll be back within the next couple of hours."

"Penny go to."

"Ava, could you go check on Ola?" Byron asked, waiting for her to leave before addressing the girl. "Now Penny, you know that's not possible."

"Penny go save Momma and Papa." She placed her hands on her hips, staring directly at Byron. "Penny can go. Sir Byron need Penny help."

"It's too dangerous. We can't risk you being sent back into the school system. You are going to stay here and get ready to go back to Matson to live with—"

"Penny not go Matson. Penny go to Omega."

"No, you will not."

"Penny has compass." She held out her compass letting her sparks dance along it. "Penny find Momma and Papa fast."

"Be that as it may, it's too—"

"Penny know dangerous. Penny know if caught Penny return to school." She sighed, shaking her head. "Penny also know if Constellation fail, Penny go back to school anyway. Penny know this last chance." She let her compass fall to her chest. "Penny want help. Penny can help. Penny small, but Penny brave. Penny not scare anymore. Penny be careful. Penny do what Sir Byron say if let come."

Byron remained silent. Gone was the scared and weak little girl he met in Rho. He knew she was right. If they failed tonight, it would not matter. She would be caught and taken.

"You won't stay here, will you?"

She shook her head. "Penny don't care if trouble. Penny help now."

Before he could answer, Ava appeared looking frantic. "Ola's gone."

"What?" His eyes went wide.

"Ola went see brother," Penny sighed. "Ola know, like Penny, no time."

Charles ached everywhere. The last thing he remembered was listening to the announcement from J.H. before he and Julietta had been grabbed. He had fought against their captors before being knocked out, likely the reason for the various pains that now riddled him. Thinking about Julietta, and wondering where she was, drove him to consciousness a few seconds later.

Blinking, it took him a minute to come to an awareness of his surroundings. He was lying on some sort of cushioned table, not unlike the surgical ones on display in the museum. His jacket and hat were gone, his white dress shirt torn with some blood, and his hands bound in front of him with a thick rope. Whoever had brought him here had not been gentle. Forcing himself to sit up, he did a quick inventory of the rest of the room. Much to his disappointment, it was rather empty, clinical with white floors and walls. The only furniture in the room was a set of cabinets on the right wall and an empty table with a sink behind him.

The wall on his left brought him to his feet. Inset into it was a door to another room and beside it an observation window. Stepping up to the glass, he pressed his forehead against it, letting his eyes adjust to its tint. His heart sank. In the other room was Julietta, strapped to some sort of chair, much like the one Joyce had been killed in. She was still in her dress from the party, her hair in disarray, her shoes gone, and her eyes closed.

"Jul!" he shouted. There was no reaction. "JUL!" He tried again, this time pounding on the window with his bound hands.

To his relief, her eyes fluttered open. "Charlie!" She replied, sounding relieved. "You're alive."

Adrenaline now rushing, he checked the door out of desperation. Locked. "Hang on, I'm going to see if I can find a way to you."

A quick search of the room yielded no immediate solution. With everything locked, his hands bound, and strength waning, there was little chance of finding more. After about 15 minutes he was forced to give up, finding himself once more at the glass, thoroughly frustrated.

"I'm...I'm sorry—"

"It's all right, Charlie," she soothed, giving him a sad smile. "It's going to be all right."

He closed his eyes, taking a few deep breaths. They were trapped, with no way out. He couldn't protect Julietta from whatever was coming; couldn't protect his unborn child.

His thoughts were interrupted as a door in Julietta's room opened. J.H. stepped in.

"Good, you are awake." The man grinned. "I was just coming to check up on you."

Julietta and Charles stared daggers but remained silent.

"Oh, come now, is that any way to repay my hospitality?"

"Knocking us out with chloroform wasn't very hospitable," Julietta spat.

"Now, now, Jessa. Did you really think I would not figure out my dear sister's little ploy? That I didn't know Jessa and Charles from Iota were pawns of hers?"

Julietta glanced over to Charles, exchanging a look of confusion.

"Wait, did my sister not tell you?" J.H. chuckled, walking to stand an equal distance between Julietta's chair and the window. "Then again, why would she?"

"What do you want?" Charles spat, angrily.

"What do I want? Well since you asked, I'd like to have a little demonstration for my sister of what I've been working on."

"We don't know what you are talking about," Julietta grunted, struggling against her restraints. "We are just—"

"Come now, Jessa. Or should I call you by your real name, Julietta?" The man shook his head. "I know you work for my sister, Ola, and her little star group. I know you helped to destroy Iota and have been spying on me for the last two months."

They froze.

"Allow me to finally properly introduce myself." He bowed with a flourish. "My name is Jasper Hampton, head administrator of the Apolis Academy for the Future: Engineering branch. Though we all know that is not my primary focus." Jasper reached for a button on the wall by the door. "Bring her in."

There was a pause as the door to the room Julietta was in slid open. A moment later Ola appeared, bound and gagged in her chair, being pushed by a familiar face, a Mr. Turner.

Seeing Julietta and Charles, Ola's eyes went wide, a deep sorrow within them.

"Well now, sister, shall I tell them why you are here; why we are all here?"

She could not reply, instead resigning herself to bowing her head.

"My dear sister, here is the reason I started this place. Over 20 cycles ago she gave me the idea, the motivation." Jasper began to pace. "You see, much like E-165141425, or Penny, as you call it, I am a Curied with an electric personality." Sparks danced on his fingers. "I discovered my powers young and was taught a harsh lesson about what happens when powers go unchecked. Ola helped me escape that, promised me if I'd come to Apolis with her she'd find a way to help me. Instead, she got lost in her psychological studies, unable to figure out what ailed me. So, I took it upon myself to find an answer. Unfortunately, I am not adept in the scientific arts. My talents lie in more business-based pursuits of the mind. I came up with a strategic plan, proposed it to Apolis Academy, and within a few months had a team of researchers diving into what I deemed to be a noble endeavor, not only the understanding of what we dubbed 'Curied,' but a cure!"

"The powers you have are not a disease," Charles spat. "They are a natural progre—"

"They are a menace to the wielder and society at large. That's where the polonium bomb comes in. The first component of my three-step cure."

"You are mad," Julietta grunted, pulling again on her restraints. "Bombs are what got us into this mess in the first place."

"And they will get us out of it. As will my second creation, the one I wish my sister to see. Mr. Turner, if you would kindly step up to the glass?"

Mr. Turner made sure Ola was locked in place before swiftly striding to the window. Charles did not move an inch, instead staring angrily at the pale man's face.

"Turner is the perfect Curied. They are strong, fast, and obedient. Their current objective is to find me the other Curied out in the wastes and bring them to be handled properly, the last part of my three-step cure."

Julietta glanced over to Charles, a look of fear in her eyes.

"Once I've collected all of the Curied and neutralized the chance of more being born, only my Turners shall have powers. Just think of the possibilities! Custom soldiers, workers, and researchers! All dedicated, powerful, and obedient to their creator!"

"It will never work," Charles growled. "You can't play with genetics like that."

"Oh, but I have," Jasper grinned, snapping his fingers. "Mr. Turner, show him."

Almost immediately Charles felt an intense pressure in his mind, like thorny vines wrapping about it, strangling any thought he dared. He had felt similar pain to this in Matson, similar but not nearly as intense. It took every ounce of willpower not to fall to his knees instantly.

"Now Mr. Turner, command him."

"Stay."

Charles's eyes went wide, seemingly frozen in place.

"Fetch him."

Julietta and Ola watched in horror as Charles stood like a statue, allowing Mr. Turner to open the door and all but drag him into the room.

"See, dear sister, how easy it is to keep people in line with this power. I learned that from you. You always told me to listen to you, didn't you?"

Tears were now streaming down Ola's face.

"Make him talk, Mr. Turner."

Mr. Turner grinned menacingly as he asked. "Where is the Constellation?"

Charles remained silent, staring straight ahead.

"Did you not hear me, boy?" The man glanced at Jasper nervously. "Where is the Constellation?"

Charles turned his head to face Mr. Turner, his expression blank. "Bite me." Without warning he attempted to swing at Mr. Turner, however, the false Curied was quicker, redoubling his mind attack as he shoved him hard into the table in front of the window.

The sound made Julietta cringe as Charles crumbled to the ground with a cry of pain.

"I said, tell me where the Constellation is," Mr. Turner growled, kicking Charles.

"Never," he hissed through clenched teeth, sweat now forming on his forehead from the effort.

"If he won't talk," Jasper smiled wider, his teeth glistening. "Then maybe his friend Julietta here will."

"No!" Charles shouted, but his plea fell on deaf ears as the pain around his mind intensified once more, a gasp of pain from Julietta reaching his ears.

"Talk, Julietta," boomed Mr. Turner, a strained expression on his face as he maintained his hold on them both.

"Don't, Jul..." Charles gasped, unable to take more shallow breaths.

She remained silent, her eyes focused on Jasper, defiant.

"TELL ME!" growled Mr. Turner, sounding desperate.

"I'd rather die," she spat at Jasper, her nose beginning to bleed as tears rolled down her face.

Jasper's face fell for a moment, before stealing into an expression of stone. "Very well then. Keep hold of them, Mr. Turner." He turned to the wall behind him, removing what looked to be a metal rod with a cage at the top. "If my creation's power alone isn't enough, maybe a bit of my own power can persuade you."

The sound of an electric charge building filled the air as the rod in his hand began to glow a sickly blue, sparks dancing around the cage at the top. "You recognize this, this device, my power. I had made a similar in effort to keep people in line in the institute. Those, however, were tame compared to what I can do...what your precious Penny is capable of doing. Maybe if I show you, you'll see my point of view."

Jasper raised the rod, preparing to strike Julietta.

"I'll talk!" Charles's voice stopped him. "Don't...don't hurt her." He breathed heavily, struggling to maintain control of his mind. "I'll talk, just...don't hurt her."

Jasper stalked over to him, his Cheshire grin threatening. "Well, at least someone has seen reason. Bring him up."

Mr. Turner, still maintaining his control, grabbed Charles roughly, forcing him to kneel before Jasper.

"Now, Charles." The man chuckled. "Tell me...Where is the Constellation?"

"The…the Constellation is…is here." Charles looked at Julietta, a pained but mischievous smile forming on his face. "It's out there too, where people…people want good in this world." He turned to look Jasper in the eye. "It's where everyone who wants to defy you is."

Jasper cried out in anger. Julietta closed her eyes as the rod hit, unable to bear witness as Charles cried out in pain. When she opened them again her heart sank seeing him curled up on the floor twitching slightly.

"Fool, stupid fool."

"The only…fool I see…is you," Charles spat.

Jasper powered the rod, shocking him again. "I'll give you one more chance, Charles."

Charles breathed heavily, turning towards Julietta and mouthing 'I'm sorry.' He willed himself to focus, turning back to J.H. "No one will bow to you."

"Then you shall be terminated," the deranged man's voice dropped as he raised the rod, a lethal crackle emanating from it.

Charles looked to Julietta one last time, mouthing 'I love you' as he braced for the hit.

It never came as a loud bang, broke the air, the sound of the rod, no longer charged, clattering to the floor as Jasper, clutching his right shoulder, turned and shouted, "YOU!"

CHAPTER 48

"That announcement sure was something, don't you think?"
"It's about time J.H. said something," Leona scoffed, leaning
against the cabinet in the break room. "Kinda sucked we couldn't go
to the party though."

"You know why."

"Of course I know why, but I think the number of guards for two
unconscious troublemakers is a bit excessive."

"What about the other four we captured?" John argued. "They were
quite a handful."

"Won't be after tomorrow. Termination, the lot of them."

"Fitting, I suppose."

Leona and John's conversation was interrupted by the sound of
metal clicking on the tile floor.

"What the heck?" John shouted as a small metal robot appeared
before them from nowhere.

"Hello," greeted the mechanical man.

Leona went to move closer but stopped as her key ring caught on
the cabinet door. Turning to unhook it she heard a grunt followed by
a thud. "What the—"

Before she could react, something hard hit her in the back of the
head. She crumpled to the floor unconscious.

"Did I do well, Sir Byron?" asked Nelson.

"Very," Byron chuckled. "You can come out now, Penny."

The door to the cabinet opened, the girl crawling out.

"Did you get the keys, Miss Penny?" Nelson asked.

Penny smiled, holding up her pocketknife, screwdriver in hand, and
a set of keys she had removed from Leona's waist.

"That should do it then," Byron sighed, looking down at the gun in his hand. "We better keep moving, don't know how long these two will be out."

Penny nodded, closing her knife before checking her compass. Applying her powers she checked the first two stars again, both still pointing in the same direction.

"Penny coming Momma and Papa."

The Constellation had breached Omega just before dawn. While the others worked to free students and gather intel, Byron's sole goal was to find Julietta and Charles, with Penny's help, and then get them all out. Using her compass, Penny had found a locked door that required manual keys rather than the digital ones she had been able to override up to this point. It was Byron's idea to get them off a guard, and Penny's to trick them with Nelson.

Sneaking back along the hallways toward the locked door, Byron made quick work of any guards they came across, earning himself only a few bumps and bruises. Penny stuck to the shadows as directed, short-circuiting doors and ducking behind corners as needed, her cycles of playing hide and seek coming in handy.

They reach the locked door in record time, the sound of someone crying out in pain reaching their ears.

"Papa!" Penny cried as she fumbled to unlock the door.

"Steady," Byron whispered, his voice sounding heavy.

Pushing the door open they found themselves in a small office that had another door leading off it.

"Stay behind me," he instructed, taking the lead to the next door. Reaching for the handle, he pressed on it lightly. Unlocked. Before he could decide what to do, he heard Charles's pained voice. "No one will bow to you."

Another male voice followed, the sound of electricity charging. "Then you shall be terminated."

Byron didn't think, he acted. Bursting into the room he glanced around. Clocking the man with an electric rod posing to strike someone on the ground, he fired his gun. The moment seemed in slow motion as the man dropped the rod, the man beside him, a Turner, fixing his gaze on Byron. His victory was short-lived as an instant later his mind felt entrapped, his faculties not his own as he held the gun straight out, unable to move, his other hand gripping Penny behind him.

"YOU!" Jasper shouted, turning toward Byron.

"I have him, sir," Mr. Turner grunted, his powers clearly stretching thin.

"Bring me my sister and the girl. Kill the others," Jasper growled, holding his shoulder tightly as he pressed a hidden button on the wall, disappearing down a secret door that shut immediately behind him.

Mr. Turner waited, ensuring his boss was well gone before returning his focus to Byron. "Maybe you will be more…compliant," he spat, his voice shaking. "Give me the girl."

Byron tried to resist but couldn't as the hand gripping Penny began to push her forward. The child tried to pull away, but Mr. Turner's power over Byron was stronger.

"That's right, hand her over."

Penny resisted a bit more, one thought in her mind as Mr. Turner reached out towards her.

"Penny brave," she whispered as she unleashed her sparks into the man and, unfortunately, Byron, who received a slightly less potent jolt.

There was a moment of pause before Byron and Mr. Turner hit the floor gasping in pain. Immediately, Penny dove out of the way, hiding on the opposite side of Julietta. "Sir Byron!"

BANG!

Mr. Turner didn't have a chance as Byron, whose mind was once more his own, recovered quickly from the shock, took aim, and fired, killing him.

"Penny…" Julietta gasped, her mind freed.

"Momma!" Penny stood, shaking.

"I'm…all right. Help Papa."

Penny nodded immediately, running to her father's prone form. "Papa…" She took out her pocketknife, cutting the bindings from his wrists. "Papa?"

Charles groaned slightly but his eyes did not open as Penny gently shifted him onto his back. Resting her head against his chest she frowned. "Papa heart fast. Papa hurt."

"I'm…all right, Penny," Charles coughed, taking a few shallow breaths. "I'll be all right."

The girl shook her head looking over to Byron who had unbound Ola and was now checking working to free Julietta.

"I got her Penny."

"I'm going after him," Ola asserted, rolling towards the hidden door. She paused only a moment, waiting to see if Byron would stop her. He nodded. It was all the confirmation she needed as she turned, disappearing behind the hidden door.

Turning her attention back to Charles, Penny pulled on the sleeve of her black jacket, using it to wipe the sweat from his brow. "Papa be okay. Penny here."

After a minute, Charles's breathing calmed, his eyes fluttering open. "My little spark," he smiled sadly.

Penny once more put her head on his chest, relieved to hear his heartbeat calming. "Papa still hurt, but okay?"

"Papa okay."

At this point, Byron had gotten Julietta's restraints off. She stumbled off the chair, kneeling beside her husband and child. Taking Charles's wrist, she checked his pulse, strong and steady. "Charlie…"

"I'm all right," he sighed, "Just need a minute."

"We need to get you both out of here," Byron urged. "Do you think you can stand?"

"He shocked him, Byron. He almost—" Before Julietta could finish, Charles attempted to sit up.

"Penny help Papa." Penny frowned as she helped steady him.

Byron shook his head. "Penny, you help your mother. I'll take care of your Papa. Let's get out of here."

Rolling down the darkened hallway, Ola's heart raced. Her brother had lost his mind. He created a bomb to alter people's genetics to prevent powers from being born. He created the Mr. Turners to destroy the Curied. He planned to capture every Curied and harvest them like cattle. He was deranged. He was unhinged. He was her problem.

Reaching the end of the hall, she came upon a lift already down. Flipping the lever to recall it, her mind raced with what-ifs. She had to face him and convince him to end this. And if she couldn't, she had to destroy him.

The lift came to a stop at the top, opening to her. There was no turning back. Rolling onto the platform she flipped the internal lever and began the descent. A part of her wondered if she would be back here; another part knowing she was being lowered into her own grave.

Reaching the bottom, she took a deep breath before rolling out into the space. Before her was a laboratory in disarray. Unlike the pristine labs in Rho, Iota, and Omega above, this lab was dark and dingy. Its walls were of dark gray concrete, nearly every inch of it covered in blueprints, diagrams, and chalkboards covered in chemical equations and the like. Around the room were scattered cabinets, shelves, and tables, each laden with chemical tubes, microscopes, and strange equipment that Ola did not dare guess what they did.

It was what lay in the center of this room however that made her heart sink. At its center was a surgical table, bloodied and stained, with various restraints and electronic devices lying across it. If she had to guess, this was where the Mr. Turners were researched and made.

"So...my creation is dead," Jasper's voice shook as he appeared from the shadows, still clutching his right shoulder. "Your man killed him."

"You're bleeding badly. Let me—"

"No, stay back," he growled, backing against one of the tables by the far wall.

"I just want to help you, Jasper. I didn't intend for you to be—"

"Of course, of course," he began to laugh, silencing her. "You didn't intend for me to be shot. You never intended us to be here, just like you never intended to help me."

"That's not true. I spent countless cycles trying to help you, trying to protect you!"

"Protect me?" He shook his head, laughing harder. "I'm not the one who needed protection. People need protection from me, from people like me, from Curied powers." He stumbled forward, leaning against the bloodied table at the room's center.

Moving forward she stopped on the other side of the table. "Please, Jasper...let me help you. After I bandage your wound...then you may do what you wish."

Jasper waited a moment, his green eyes locking with his sister's. "Very well," he grunted, grabbing a chair from beside one of the tables and sitting.

Keeping an eye on her brother, she quickly grabbed what medical supplies she could find in the cabinets. While searching, she spotted something lying in a tray near the back of one of the tables, a syringe labeled 'termination injection.' Thinking fast, she slipped the syringe under her leg, ensuring the cap was loose, but not so loose as to impale her. If this went well, she wouldn't need it.

Wheeling over to her brother, she carefully helped him remove his lab coat and lifted his shirt on the right side. Byron's aim had been true, the bullet lodged in his back right shoulder.

"I can't pull the bullet out now, but I can at least stop the bleeding."

"Do what you can," he grunted, sounding pained.

She remained quiet at first as she cleaned the wound, prepared at any moment for him to pull away. When he didn't after a time, she began to talk.

"I missed you, brother. More than you can ever imagine."

"You missed me...pfft. Then why didn't you help me? Why did you try to stop me?"

"Because Jasper, I could not agree with what you've done. Your powers are a gift, yet you—"

"My powers are a disease, one you told me you'd cure."

"I said I'd look into how they came to be. I never said I'd find a way to remove them."

"Then what good was your research? You know how this plagued me, how it plagues so many."

"I know that you were taught your gift was a curse, but believe me it is not."

"That's not what Mother and Father taught us, not what the people of Linton said when I burned their crops."

"That was an accident. You were only three cycles."

"It was a sign, Ola. It was a sign of my future, the world's future if we don't rid it of people like me."

"That's the kind of logic that caused the rain of bombs."

"What do you know?"

"Too much. I've read enough about psychology to know—"

"Pfft, you should have been looking at genetics, sister. Then maybe things would have gone differently."

She remained quiet as she finished bandaging his shoulder. "You truly think this cure of yours is the answer?"

"Yes." He swallowed. "Yes, I do."

"Then show me what you intend to do."

Jasper looked at Ola for a moment, warily. "You...you really want to see?"

"As a scientist, it is my duty to look at every possible solution, even the ones I think are rather far-fetched."

"Then follow me."

Wheeling behind her brother through a maze of other corridors her heart quickened. After what seemed like an eternity, they finally came to a set of metal doors.

"This…is the final solution, Ola."

She gasped as her brother pushed her chair into the machine room, its walls lined with metal boxes and tools of all kinds. It was however what sat at the center of the room that froze her into stunned silence. Mostly built, sitting on a pedestal, was a large bomb.

He brought her to a stop beside it, nearest what looked to be a control panel. "This is my final cure. It is nearly complete, save the payload components from each of my institutes. I purposely had each develop a separate concoction to speed things along. Once they all arrive it is a matter of using the most stable."

"This is…is…" She shook her head, unable to come up with anything that would not offend.

"You hate it."

"I didn't say that."

"You didn't have to." Jasper's expression darkened. "You've lied to me, sister."

"I didn't lie to you. I never lied to you. I wanted to see your creation. Wanted to see your point of view, but you have to understand—"

"You're a liar!" He shouted, taking hold of her chair, his face barely an inch from hers. "You are a liar like the rest of them. Lying to me about progress, lying to me about their loyalty, lying to me that I am anything but a monster," he spat, his eyes tearing. "I'm a monster, Ola. Powers turn people into monsters. You are lying to yourself if you think otherwise. Lying to me. You are nothing but a—ARGH!"

He stumbled back, holding his neck, a syringe jammed into it. "What, what have you done?"

"I never lied to you, Jasper…" She sighed, tears sitting on the surface of her eyes. "I never thought you were a monster."

He fell to his knees feeling weak. "How…how could—"

"I'm sorry."

Jasper fell to the ground, taking a few more ragged breaths before going still, dead.

Ola slumped in her chair. She had to do it. She had to stop him, yet her heart was broken. Taking but a moment to steel herself, she moved towards the panel on the bomb. Pressing a button, the screen lit up before her, a timer upon it. Pressing a few keys she adjusted the time to its maximum, 30 minutes. It was all she could afford. 30 minutes would have to be enough for Byron to get out with Penny, Charles, and Julietta, enough for him to have hopefully signaled the other Constellation members to get out. Anyone else she didn't care about. This had to end now.

Pressing the last button to confirm, she watched as the timer began to tick down, second by second. She would not be getting out; there wouldn't be enough time. Turning, she looked over at the corpse of her brother on the floor, dead at her own hands.

"I'm sorry, Jasper," she whispered, tears running down her face. "I couldn't save you…I couldn't save us."

CHAPTER 49

Hailing the other Constellation members via talker, Byron and Penny made their way with Julietta and Charles through Omega and eventually out to the wastes with little delay. When they had entered, someone had hit an alarm sending many of the scientists and students scrambling for the exits, leaving only a few guards who were not hung over from the party to defend. The guards had not stood a chance.

The sun had just crested the horizon. Having made it a reasonable distance away and with Charles's and Julietta's strength waning, Byron led them over to a small rocky outcropping, finding a sheltered area out of the steadily increasing heat of the morning.

"You can rest here." Byron sighed, helping Charles sit up against the wall of the stone hovel while Penny did the same for Julietta.

"Charlie?" Julietta frowned, taking his hand.

"I'm all right," he smiled, turning to rest a hand on her stomach. "Are you okay?"

Byron stepped away for a moment, sending a call out on his talker. "Sounds like there are some folks still trapped," he frowned, turning back to the others.

"We are lucky we got out." Charles sighed, taking Penny's flashlight he wore around his neck in hand. "When we made you that compass, Penny, I'd hoped you'd never have to use it."

Julietta took her flashlight in hand as well. "These have proven their weight in gold."

Byron sent out another call. "Still a few more and no sign of Ola." Reaching into his pocket he produced a small flare.

"What that?" Penny asked.

Byron looked down at the child, smiling sadly. "You know how to use a flare, Penny?"

"Yes. Papa taught Penny back in Watwealt."

"I'm going to need you to be brave, Penny."

"Penny brave."

"Byron…" Charles shook his head. "You aren't…"

"I have to." He bowed his head. "I'm not letting anyone else—"

The ground shook, hard. Byron's eyes went wide as he instinctively pushed Penny towards the hovel and into Charles and Julietta's awaiting arms as the sky above once more turned black and the world around them filled with dust.

Huddled in the dark, Charles waited about a minute to ensure the world beneath him had stopped moving before daring to open his eyes. "Is…is everyone okay?" He coughed.

"Shaken, but not stirred," Julietta assured.

"Penny okay," Penny coughed. "Penny hurt Momma and Papa?"

"No Penny," Charles grunted, as they slowly untangled themselves. "Where's Byron?"

Turning on her flashlight around her neck, Penny pointed it towards the entrance of the hovel. "Sir Byron not here."

Taking a moment more to steel themselves, the three climbed out of the hovel, in shock. Omega had been leveled.

"Sir Byron!" Penny cried, spotting him about 20 feet away from where she had last seen him. He was lying on the ground, motionless.

Despite their injuries, Charles and Julietta raced to his side.

"Byron!" Charles shouted, kneeling beside him. Julietta joined him, helping turn him onto his back.

"He's bleeding badly," Julietta frowned, accessing the wound around a large piece of metal jammed into the front of his left shoulder.

Charles's face paled as he checked the man's vitals. He couldn't find a pulse. "Shit," he cursed, his hands coming to Byron's chest starting compressions. "You'll need to get the bleeding to stop."

Julietta turned to Penny. "Give me your jacket."

The girl obeyed, emptying her pockets quickly, before handing it over.

Thinking back to the first aid Charles had taught her, Julietta shook her head as she in vain attempted to staunch the bleeding. "I can't remove it, not without risking him bleeding out."

Penny thought for a moment, a word she'd heard her Papa and other doctors mention coming to mind. "Catzation." She flicked open her knife before sparking her fingers.

Julietta glanced over to Charles who had paused a moment to give Byron air. "How hot does it have to be?"

"As hot as she can make it," he grunted, checking the man's pulse again. Nothing.

Penny worked quickly, the blade turning red hot in less than a minute. "Catzation ready!"

Julietta didn't hesitate to take the knife. "Penny, go find the flare," she instructed as she pulled the shrapnel from Byron's arm, immediately applying the hot blade to it. It took less than 30 seconds to seal the wound. "What else can I do?"

"Give him some air."

She nodded, moving towards Byron's head. Charles had taught her about this one evening back in Waterwealt. Had explained the technique used to try to save someone when they stopped breathing. Tilting Byron's head back she gave him a breath, two breaths.

Charles checked his pulse. Nothing. "Come on, Byron," he pleaded, starting compressions again while Julietta continued to give rescue breaths.

They had been at it for nearly five minutes now with no success. Exhaustion starting to take hold, Charles struggled to keep going. Just as he was about to ask Julietta what she thought they should do, Byron suddenly gasped for breath.

"Byron?" Charles panted, checking his pulse. It was a bit slow, but it was there.

"It's all right, Byron, we got you," Julietta soothed, tears running down her face.

The man's eyes fluttered open with a groan. "Char—Charlie... Ju—Julie..."

"It's all right Byron," Charles sighed, sitting back exhausted, tears now streaming down his face. "We're all right. You're all right."

"Guess...you borrowed me...a little more...time," he chuckled, taking a few deeper breaths.

Penny returned to Julietta's side a minute later having found the flare. Seeing Byron awake she smiled. Sparking her fingers with what little of her power she could muster she lit the flare, jamming it into the dust beside them. J.H. was gone. Momma and Papa were safe. They had made it out of Omega. They were alive. It was this thought that she held onto as the government rovers pulled up, Ava and Vance rushing towards them to take them away from the destruction of Omega to safety, to home.

In the weeks following the destruction of Omega and the death of Jasper Hampton, government agents were sent out to the 22 remaining facilities to shut them down as the truth of Apolis's Academy for the Future was revealed to the public.

Jasper had done great harm in his pursuit of a 'cure' as files regarding terminations, releases, and experimental treatments came to light. The governments of the various cities took it upon themselves to sort through the various documents, working together to notify families of the status of their children.

Each child recovered from the facilities was taken to local medical centers to be assessed and treated as needed. It would be likely cycles before many of them would recover mentally from their experience, but with the patience and care of the doctors and others, they would.

For each happy reunion, however, there were also sad stories. Some families, of course, had lost children many cycles ago who had unfortunately been released at 21, while some children found they no longer had anyone to be returned to. Thankfully it seemed the public at large, horrified by the revelations, was coming together to provide comfort to those who lost, and caring, safe, and loving homes for the orphaned. Of the orphaned found was Nicole, Dimetre's sister, who, after clearing a medical assessment, was sent to Matson and adopted by Henrietta.

As for the various employees, once they were brought out of the facility and given medical care, most returned to their former selves, with the unfortunate realization of their horrible deeds. The brainwashing effect J.H. had laid over them was due to a mixture of deceit, heavy persuasion, and chemical influence.

Upon searching the living quarters within the facilities, many of the rooms were found to contain what looked to be bottles of vitamins laced with chemicals that were known to addle the mind allowing it to become susceptible to suggestion. This same chemical could be found in the systems of those who commuted each day, likely dosed by other means.

The Bells were a bit harder to aid, most having completely lost any form of identity of self. However, as Charles and the other researchers of the Constellation had theorized, with enough time and patience they too were slowly brought back to some semblance of normality, returned to the care of family members, or set up in community homes in the various cities for the time being.

It was a long process, one that would take cycles for the world to recover from.

Having been rescued by Ava and Vance after Omega was destroyed, Charles, Julietta, Byron, and Penny were immediately taken to a medical facility for treatment and observation.

Penny had been relatively unscathed save a few bumps and scrapes from when she fell into the hovel before the bomb exploded. In Charles's and Julietta's case, aside from a massive migraine that lasted for a few days, exhaustion, and, in Charles's case, some burns where the taser rod had struck him and rather bruised ribs from Mr. Turner kicking him, they were okay. After about two weeks of care and observation, they were discharged with no lasting effects from their ill-fated time in Jasper's captivity.

Byron, having nearly died, took a bit longer to recover, discharged after a month of care. In that time, his son visited him nearly every day, thanking Julietta and Charles profusely, a sentiment Byron echoed each time he saw them.

About three months had passed since Omega was destroyed. Dust season was rolling in, burying what was left of Omega beneath several layers of dirt and sand. With recovery well on its way, Julietta, Charles, and Penny were getting ready to leave for Matson.

"Do you hear it, Penny? That's your little brother or sister in there," Charles explained, holding the end of the stethoscope to Julietta's now visibly pregnant stomach.

"Penny hear sibling." Penny's eyes went wide, a bright smile on her face. "Penny can't wait see sibling."

"In about three more months," Julietta sighed, relaxing into the pillow. "We are all excited to see your sibling."

There was a knock at the bedroom door. "How's it going in here?" Marisa asked.

"Penny hear sibling!"

"I'm glad to hear that," Marisa smiled. "You almost done, Charles?"

"Nearly, just a couple more checks."

"Penny, why don't you leave your Papa to finish your Momma's check-up and come help me finish packing?"

"Okay!" Penny turned back to her Momma. "Bye sibling, see soon!" She hugged Julietta's stomach a moment before handing Charles the stethoscope and racing out of the room.

"She's going to be a wonderful big sister," Julietta chuckled, placing a hand on her stomach.

"Ready to listen?"

She nodded as he placed the stethoscope in her ears, helping her find the right spot to listen.

"It's beautiful." Tears came to her eyes as she listened.

"It is," he agreed, taking the stethoscope from her and continuing his examination. "Does anything hurt?"

"Not really. I mean my back is sore but nothing out of the ordinary at this point."

He moved the stethoscope to different parts of her abdomen, listening intently. "Everything sounds good." He kissed her baby bump before pulling down her shirt. "Now for Momma."

"Well, doctor, how am I sounding?"

"Beautiful as always," he smirked. "Heart and lungs sound good. I can help you with the back pain later if needed. All in all, you are both ready for travel."

"And you?"

Charles took off the stethoscope, and placed it in Julietta's ears once more before placing the other end over his heart.

Listening to Charles's strong calm heartbeat, she relaxed. "I was so scared, Charlie, when J.H. shocked you, I was…He could have…You protected me."

Since their recovery, they had spent a good deal of time discussing what they'd been through both with each other and Penny. They helped each other work through the lingering fears and accepted it all. But that did not mean the nightmares didn't occasionally come back.

Charles rested a hand over his heart, the other taking Julietta's, resting it on her belly. "I had to, for both of you and Penny."

"You fought against Turner."

"So did you."

"It was like my mind was in a vice."

He let go, taking the stethoscope from her and placing it in his bag. "Jul…how would you feel if—if our child was like Penny?"

"What do you mean?"

"I mean if our child has powers?"

Julietta sat up. "To be honest, I hadn't really thought about it. With everything that was happening the idea of our child having powers didn't cross my mind."

"They likely will."

She quirked an eyebrow. "How do you know?"

"Did you find it strange that you and I were able to fight Turner, but Byron wasn't?"

Her brow furrowed, thinking. "He…he was able to be controlled and we weren't."

"Remember how you and Penny gave me your blood samples?"

"You've seen something in them?"

He nodded. "During my research, I was able to isolate the gene that determines whether or not a person has powers from both someone with powers and someone without. I didn't get a chance to tell you, but you and I both have that gene."

"How? We don't have powers as far as—"

"It's inactive. We carry the potential, but it never activates within us. It's why Turner's powers never worked on us, why we never were affected by the brainwashing chemicals like most. Based on genetics, that means our child will either be a carrier or have powers."

She took his hand, squeezing it. "So long as they are happy and healthy. I'm happy."

He smiled, gazing into Julietta's eyes. "So long as you all are happy and healthy, I'm happy." He leaned in, kissing her.

"I was wondering if you'd say anything about my usual prescription." She chuckled.

He laughed a mischievous twinkle in his eyes. "Always, Jul."

There was another knock at the door, this time Byron, who now walked with a cane, limping in. "Ready?"

Ava had arranged for a rover to take Charles, Julietta, and Penny back to Matson. The Healeys would be traveling with them to set up shop while their niece, who had been found alive, was undergoing Bell rehabilitation at the medical center with Victor. Byron, however, was going to stay in Apolis with his son for a few more months to help Vance with the ongoing recovery efforts before both would return to Matson. Before they could leave, however, there was one last person who wished to see them, the Head of the Administration Taylor Markham.

Entering Markham's office, the group was greeted by Vance standing beside a large desk where a young woman with black hair and piercing blue eyes stood, smiling.

"Sir Galigar, Dr. Milard-Hawthorne, Mrs. Milard-Hawthorne, and Miss Penny, welcome. Please sit," the woman gestured, waiting for them to be seated before sitting herself. "It is an honor to meet you all. I am Taylor Markham, head of the administration. I am forever in your debt for what you've done."

"It was nothing, Madame Markham," Byron smiled. "We are just happy to finally put an end to this horror and reunite the families."

"I can assure you all efforts are being made to have families reunited or, in the case where this is not possible, find loving and caring parents for those affected."

"Like me!" smiled Penny, who was sitting on Charles's lap. "Penny love Momma and Papa."

"Yes, Penny. Just like you." Markham sighed, a tinge of sorrow in her voice. "I also confirmed with Vance any research found in the facilities is currently being scrutinized and archived in a safe location. Though we don't approve of most of it, there was some, like your work, Dr. Milard-Hawthorne, that would be of great benefit to society if handled correctly. I am assuming you will continue your medical endeavors in Matson?"

"Please, just Charles, and yes. I intend to continue cataloging all medical knowledge I come across. We have a museum waiting for us in Matson." He smiled at Julietta. "As for genetics specifically, I intend to only refine what I have researched for understanding. The human genome will be mapped but nothing more. I do not wish to push it much further unless deemed necessary by the medical community at large."

"A wise and noble answer," Markham agreed. "Speaking of research and documentation, I have some news I wish to share with you. Thanks to your efforts, I have discovered the fate of my niece, Kira Bennet. It appears she is alive and well."

"That is wonderful news," Byron replied, similar agreements echoed by all.

"Yes, it is. However, there is something more to it. You see, like all the other children, she doesn't know that she is Kira Bennet."

"An unfortunate lasting scar from Jasper." Vance shook his head.

Charles looked at Penny, his brow furrowing. He and Julietta hadn't thought to look for her file, to discover her true identity. "Why…why are you telling us this?"

"Charlie?" Julietta quirked an eyebrow.

"It's all right Mrs. Mi—"

"Julietta."

Markham smiled. "I can assure you, Julietta. Your husband has every right to ask."

She thought for a moment, her eyes landing on Penny.

"I can assure you both, I don't intend to take her away. I simply wish to let her know the truth."

Penny hopped off of her Papa's lap and approached Markham. "Madame have Penny file?"

"Yes, Miss Penny. I do have your file."

"What say?"

Markham reached for the folder on her desk. "Experimental ID #: E-165141425, Name: Kira Bennet, Age: 10 Dust, Parents: Damian and Miriam Bennet (Terminated), Power Classification: 10, Category: Fire, Specificity: Electrical, Status: Alive. Last Known Location: Apolis… There is also some health data in here that I will give to your parents."

"Penny name Kira?"

"Yes, Penny. Your name was originally Kira."

"Madame Markham, Auntie Markham?"

"Yes, I would be considered your aunt. I am your biological mother's sister."

"Penny first Momma and Papa gone?"

"Yes, they are, unfortunately."

"Penny understand." The child bowed her head. "Penny forgot real name long time ago."

Charles and Julietta got up, moving to stand beside her.

"You all right, my little spark?" Charles asked, bending to be at eye level with her.

Penny nodded, hugging him. "Penny okay. Penny have Papa Charlie and Momma Julie now. Penny love her Papa and Momma."

He hugged her tight. "Papa and Momma love Penny too."

Julietta embraced them both. "Papa and Momma love their Penny."

"I couldn't ask for better parents for my niece." Markham stood, a tear in her eye. "My sister and brother-in-law would be proud of who you chose Penny. If you ever need anything, know I am in your debt."

"Thank you, Madame." Charles sighed, picking up Penny who snuggled into his arms.

"Please call me Taylor."

"Thank you, Taylor." Julietta had a hand on Penny, the other on her stomach. "We promise to take good care of her."

"From what I've seen and heard, you already do."

"Penny still Penny?" Penny asked, sounding nervous.

Taylor, Charles, and Julietta looked at each other, a silent understanding passing between them.

"Well Penny, I think only you can decide that." Charles smiled. "What do you want your name to be, little spark?"

Penny sat up slightly, looking around the room at all the people she had come to call her family. "Penny think...Penny now 10 cycles. Penny little before, but not now. Penny was lost. Penny then found by new family. Penny have found family and aunt now. Penny lucky. Penny then...Penny is...I...I am Penny. Penny Milard-Hawthorne," the girl smiled, for the first time truly feeling to know herself. "I am a lucky Penny."

EPILOGUE

"R eady or not, here I come, Adam." Penny chuckled, opening her eyes and turning to face the room.

It was the end of Dust, about two and a half cycles since the fall of J.H. The world found itself recovering, the institutes slowly becoming nothing more than a distant memory. Upon returning to Matson, Lisle, as promised, had a museum waiting for them. Around mid-Cold, Julietta gave birth to a son, Adam, who immediately took to Penny as his sister. About a season later, Penny began attending normal school in Matson, along with Nicolas, Dimetre, Nicole, and Maya.

To help other kids like them, Henrietta had set up an after-school program where she and well-vetted others would work with the children one-on-one. Once a week, they would work with them to understand their gift, as they called it, and the good they could do with it if they so chose. After a cycle of success, others began to crop up in other cities, slowly spreading to places as far as the Capital. By doing so, they started to establish the notion that these powers were indeed normal and that those who wielded them had the same freedoms as everyone else, which is what the Constellation had always wanted.

"Hmm...now where could my little brother gone?" Penny teased, feigning ignorance to the fact that Adam had cloaked himself beneath the couch in the living room, his shadow giving him away. "Is here?" she asked, opening a cabinet. "No? How about here?" She looked behind one of the two large chairs in front of the fireplace. "No..."

She could hear giggling coming from the couch as she looked in more obviously wrong places.

"Just where, oh where, can brother be?" The girl laughed, no longer able to keep a straight face. "Oh, I know." She flipped on her flashlight around her neck. "Here!"

Flashing the light under the couch, Adam's shadow became more pronounced, a moment later Adam himself appeared. "How sis know?"

"Lucky," Penny chuckled, helping her nearly two-cycle-old brother from beneath the couch. "You getting better, but I had cycles of practice."

Adam crossed his arms, pouting. "I want be good as sis Penny."

"You will. It just takes practice. You have advantage with blending gift. You'll be as good as me in no time."

"Promise?"

"Promise."

The boy smiled, hugging his sister. "Otay, sis Penny. Love you."

"Love you too." She hugged him back.

"What are my two little ninjas up to?" Charles smirked, leaning on the entryway. "Should I be worried?"

"No, Papa." Penny smiled mischievously. "Just teaching Adam how play hide and seek."

"Penny teach me how hide better with power!" The boy shouted, running to his Papa who picked him up.

"My spark teaching my little chameleon," Charles teased, tickling Adam and eliciting a fit of laughter. "I guess I'll have to ramp up my seeking skills huh?"

"He's learning from the best." Penny stood proud, hands on her hips.

"No doubt about it. Your mother sent me to get you both. Guests will be arriving shortly."

"Penny party time! 'Appy Tirteen Dusty Sis Penny!" Little Adam cheered.

"Thank you," she beamed. "Let's go then!"

Charles and Julietta, with Marisa, Oliver, and their niece Kayla had turned the front lawn of the museum into a fun party space. Decorated and filled with tables of food, presents, and games it was perfect for the celebration of Penny's 13th cycle.

"There's the birthday girl," Julietta smiled, brushing a stray piece of hair from Penny's face. "How does it feel to be a teenager?"

"So far good."

"I've made you some of your favorite sweet bread," Marisa winked, a twinkle in her eye. "And some extra so your Papa can make you breakfast tomorrow."

"I also threw in some cookies," Oliver added. "Can never have enough CCCs, right, Penny?"

Penny hugged them. "Thank you, Auntie Marisa, Uncle Oliver."

"Happy 13 Dust, Penny," Kayla approached, a bit shy.

"Thank you. It's nice to see you, Miss Kayla."

"Kayla has been wondering if you plan to spend Cold break working at the bakery again?" Marisa inquired. "You two had fun last Cold."

"I plan on it if Momma and Papa okay with it."

"Of course," Charles chuckled. "Though I'll have to start doing extra work to keep off the weight from all the delicious baked goods you bring home. Then again, your brother keeps me plenty busy playing hide and seek."

Julietta playfully hit Charles's arm. "Says the one who carried half of these tables by himself."

"Speaking of tables, better go get that extra one." Charles set down Adam, watching him toddle over to his sister. "Most of Penny's school friends should be arriving any minute."

Henrietta was next to appear with Dimetre and Nicole in tow. Both were thrilled to be celebrating Penny's 13th, even more so when they saw the number of sweets on the table.

"After dinner, you two," Henrietta chastised, as her children ran off to play with Adam and Penny.

Slowly but surely more folks trickled in, the sound of laughter and chatter filling the air. Byron, his son Parker, and Parker's wife Nia appeared after about 20 minutes, greeting Penny as she ran past playing a game of tag.

"I see our little spark is enjoying herself." Byron gratefully took the chair Julietta brought for him to sit on.

"Very much so," Charles sighed, placing a hand on Byron's shoulder. "She isn't a kid anymore."

"No, no she isn't. You, sir, have a teenager on your hands."

Lisle and her family were the last to arrive. "I'm so sorry we are late. Had a bit of morning sickness." Lisle blushed, her hand on her very pregnant stomach.

Penny ran up to Nicolas and Maya. "Hi!"

"Happy 13 Dust, Penny!" Maya shouted, hugging her before running off to play with the other kids.

Nicolas approached, holding out a light purple lilac. "Happy 13 Dust, Penny." Nicolas smiled shyly.

"Thank you, Nicolas," Penny blushed, taking the flower. "Want to come play?" She held out a hand to him, the boy taking it as they ran off towards the other kids.

Charles and Victor glanced over at each other, eyebrows raised.

"Did I just see what I think I saw?" Julietta asked.

"Like I said, you have a teenager now," Byron chuckled with a wink. "Good luck."

"Nicolas spent all morning picking that flower," Lisle explained, finding it hard not to laugh. "I think he has a little thing for your Penny."

"Oh, dear…" Charles shook his head, a hand coming to it. "I don't know if I am ready for that."

"Can a parent ever really be ready?" Julietta wrapped an arm around her husband. "It will be fine, Charlie."

"And, hey, if it works out, then you and I will be in-laws," Lisle teased, eliciting an eye roll from Victor and Julietta.

"Let's just stick with her turning 13 for now, okay?" Julietta kissed Charles on the cheek. "Come on, it's time to wrangle the kids for food."

The party was a blast, with everyone enjoying themselves. Near sunset, people began heading home, leaving Charles, Julietta, Lisle, Victor, Byron, Parker, and Nia as the last guests.

Sitting around a small bonfire set up while Maya, Nicolas, and Penny played nearby, the adults sat chatting.

"They grow up so fast," Julietta sighed, holding a sleeping Adam in her arms. "Penny's come a long way since she first appeared in Waterwealt."

"You're telling me." Lisle's hand came to rest on her own belly. "Maya's nearly seven already, Nicolas will be 13 next season, and before you know it the one on the way will be toddling around."

"Nia and I've been talking about having kids soon," Parker noted. "How do you feel about becoming a grandpa, Byron?"

"I'm old enough for it," Byron chuckled, sipping a glass of whiskey. "My adventuring days are over. I am well ready to be Grandpa Byron."

"What about you, Julie? Thinking of having another one?" Victor asked, leaning back in his chair.

Julietta looked over to Charles who smiled. "Charlie and I talked about wanting more kids, just want to wait until Adam is a bit older."

"Fair enough," Lisle yawned with a chuckle. "Kids are a handful, but a wonderful handful."

"I think it's time we head out." Victor called Nicolas and Maya over.

"Bye Penny, happy 13th!" Maya cheered, as Victor picked her up.

"Bye, Penny. I'll see you at school." Nicolas hugged her.

"I'm going to put Adam to bed. You should start getting ready too, Penny. It's way past your bedtime."

"Awe...but Momma..." Penny yawned, not helping her case.

"No buts. Even teenagers need their rest."

Penny thanked everyone for coming, wishing them good night as she took Charles's hand, following her mother up to their apartment.

"Love you, Papa."

"Love you too, my little ninja," Charles smiled, kissing Adam on the forehead before turning back to Julietta.

"I got my talker tuned to the sound monitor Penny fixed. Should be all right while we chat," she whispered as they left the room, heading for Penny's next door.

Penny had changed into her pajamas and was now seated at her desk, drawing in a notebook.

"Did you enjoy your day?" Her Papa asked, leaning on the desk beside her.

"Yes, Papa. Thank you," she smiled, turning to hug him. "Thank you and Momma for everything."

"No problem, my spark."

Her momma approached, embracing them both. "We love you, Penny."

"I love you too," the girl sighed, tired. "I'm going write a bit before bed, okay?"

"Okay, but not too late," Charles chastised as Julietta took his hand, pulling him away.

Opening the window above her desk, Penny looked out to the front yard where Byron, Parker, and Nia were waiting for Julietta and Charles. Smiling, she reached for Nelson who was sitting on her desk beside Margie, and now two other small stuffed robots.

Flipping the switch on him she frowned. His battery was not charged. Taking it out, she placed it between her fingers. Since Omega, she had learned more about her power, about how the electrical charge within her acted like a battery. She had used up a good deal of charge that day, restricting her to only basic sparks for nearly a month until she was back to her normal level. Her power cap had grown since, as did her control of the charge.

She had taken to helping Julietta and Charles with their restorations, lending her power to various machines and electronics if only to power them long enough for study. It was fun for her to make things come to life, to bring back the history of the past even for a short time. After about two minutes the battery was charged. Placing it back into Nelson, she flipped the switch again.

"Hello, Miss Penny, and happy 13th cycle."

"Thank you, Nelson," the girl smiled, setting him back on the desk. "How are you? New upgrades sitting well?"

Nelson nodded. "Yes, Miss Penny. I was able to fully download the next set of data from the computation machine in your workshop last night before I had to come back here to await recharging. I plan on working with Nia this week to get the information written up and distributed in due time."

"Good." Leaning back in her chair, she closed the notebook in front of her, moving it off to the side.

It had taken her most of Hot to get the computation machine in working order, a good deal of energy to get it to stay powered long enough for Nelson to download a batch of data. Thankfully, Nicolas had started helping her. He was rather adept with his hands, though his telekinesis sure came in handy when it came to adjusting the smaller parts. This was the current use she had found for her power, a good use, a satisfying use.

Reaching over to the stack of cards on her desk she pulled out the one from her Aunt Taylor. She had written an apology for not being there, promising that she'd visit during Cold. She also wrote how proud she was of Penny's work with pulling the information from the computation machines.

She understood why her aunt could not come today. Things were still shaky in the administration and the world at large despite the great strides since Omega's fall. She'd be happy to see her aunt but was also happy to hear she was hard at work righting the wrongs of J.H.

Penny glanced over to the box of presents she'd received from her friends and family with a smile. Had it really been only five cycles since she escaped Rho and found herself at Momma Julie's doorstep? Walking over to the box, she pulled out the gift from her parents: a beautiful leather-bound notebook with a set of pens and drawing pencils. She had talked with them about writing, and how much she'd enjoyed journaling during their trip to Apolis. It had helped her work through a good deal and helped a lot of others do the same.

Sitting back at her desk, she set down the notebook and writing utensils.

"What will you write in this one?" Nelson asked, sitting at the top of the notebook.

Looking up at the stack of notebooks on the shelf above her desk beside her electronics books her brow furrowed in thought. Some contained schoolwork, one for each cycle she'd studied so far. Another contained sketches of circuit boards and notes on the various restorations she was working on with Nicolas. The smallest one was the journal she'd kept from Matson to Apolis. Then there were the two she used to keep the knowledge she learned from her parents, one mechanical and one medical. The last, which was sitting beside her, was filled with random drawings, a skill she was slowly learning to master.

"I'm going to need your help for this one, Nelson."

"Of course, Miss Penny. What do you need?"

"I...I want to write my story. I want to write down everything that happened from when I was taken, to escaping Rho, to living with Momma, to Papa saving me from Turner... everything."

"That sounds like an interesting idea, Miss Penny. May I ask why?"

"I want to remember; I want the world to remember what happened. If I learned anything from Momma and Papa, it's that the world can learn a lot from the past. It can learn a lot so the future can be better."

"A wise thought, Miss Penny," the little robot replied, his eyes lighting up a bit brighter. "I'll be glad to assist."

It was nearly midnight when Julietta and Charles returned to the loft, Byron, Parker, and Nia having left for home. Entering Penny's room, they chuckled quietly. The girl was sound asleep at her desk, the notebook they brought her open in front of her.

"She fell asleep about an hour ago," Nelson whispered as Charles carefully picked her up, laying her on her bed.

"Surprised she stayed up that long," Charles sighed, placing a blanket over her.

"I'm not. She had enough CCCs to power a whole drill pump," Julietta chuckled as she peeked at the notebook.

Reading the first couple of lines, a sad smile appeared on her face. She said nothing as Charles joined her, his eyes too skimming the open page briefly.

"She's growing up to be like you," Charles wrapped an arm around Julietta's waist. "She has your beautiful mind."

Julietta nodded, taking his hand. "And your beautiful heart."

Turning to her, he kissed her lightly. "Let's get some sleep... and maybe talk about giving our Adam and Penny another sibling soon, hmm?"

"Sounds like a wonderful idea, Dr. Charlie," she teased as they left the room.

"I'd like that Momma and Papa," Penny whispered, relaxing into her pillow. "And I love you too."